THE BONES

A NOVEL

Laura Wythe

THE BONES

ISBN 978-1-7750807-0-1

Cover and interior design: Charlotte Fleming

Cover photo: Laura Wythe

Author photo: Charlotte Fleming

For my daughter,
whose presence in this world
gives me hope, always.

Lovers

☙❧

~ 1 ~

THERE IS NO THUNDER TO ANNOUNCE the coming of rain, which falls without fanfare, trickling tenderness, pouring down love, pressing into the earth. Rain is a wondrous lover, teasing the vast surfaces, and smallest orifices, of the planet. For her part, Earth trembles with pleasure, molten rumblings that seldom reach the surface.

Since dawn, rain has flowed over the curved breast of Earth, rushed down her peaks with building momentum, pounded her shores until the waters break and rain rises again. In long licks of tide, they incubate life, hatch it, grow it, then collect the bones. Earth knows each bone, gathers them to her like a mother would her children—into coral reefs, octopus dens, elephant graveyards, rifted valleys, chalked shorelines. Most of the life forms drop their hollow remains without attachment, making it easy to press the bones into her service. Her weighty mass shifts and thrusts the ossifications into cliffs, and into the linings of aquifers where rain runs like a tongue over the porous masses, carving whorls of pleasure into this deliciously soft side of Earth.

Such pleasure.

However, the current bloom of bipeds, humans, whose masses of bones used to be found on famine-sown and blood-soaked plains wrapped in delicious shrouds and lain under the dirt; or lost in marshlands bodies covered in felted woolens; or set adrift on the waters on pyres of fragrant wood to burn or sink; or hidden in the cliffs where birds pick them clean—now the humans dispose of the spent blooms without returning to the Earth. They hide a stone's weight of ashes inside clay or bronze jars; they hoard bones inside crypts, and in silica cases, in museums, temples, cathedrals. Even when they inter their dead beneath her soil, they hide the bones from her in boxes lined with lead. Worse, they steal the very materials that she manufactures, and use these to hoard the bones. They unearth old sea beds and grind calcified collections of past blooms into something called concrete. They withhold even their footsteps from her, pouring this aggregate over the tangled garden Earth loves, the garden she grows to lure rain from the sky, to caress her contours, to flow from peaks into the valleys of her love. She could weep in frustration as rain beats at the unnatural surfaces, and she is left to take the violence of the runoff, the mudslides and flooded gardens.

The bipeds are a problem.

In the moment it takes for Earth to circle the star, rain falls, placating and searching for a way to return to pleasure.

~

In this same moment, rain lives in human time, dropping doubt and slicking fear across the glass-faced buildings sheltering millions gathered along the north shore of a huge continental lake. Rain will continue the assault for as long as it takes, constantly dripping reminders of human inadequacy, to satisfy the desire of a planet with one set of beloved bones.

Exact and cunning, rain isolates—among the human habitats—one building, and falls across its crystalline face, watching, and then infiltrates the very biology of one human organism. Rain mingles with her blood and lymph, courses through the soft *pia mater* inside her skull to know her thoughts and actions. Rain discovers that it's true.

This one desires the same bones as the Earth, as much as Earth.

She shall have them.

~ 2 ~

THE CITY OF TORONTO SAT AT THE EDGE OF LAKE ONTARIO, the harbour front at an elevation of 76.5 metres above sea level. A tilted plain gouged by small rivers, the city was unremarkable except for its flatness and sloping gain of approximately 130 metres in elevation. People could stand at the harbour, look up at Toronto and see the progress of over 200 years rising like a wall, the horizon filled with the accomplishments of settlers from every corner of the globe.

For over a year, rain seemed to select one neighbourhood, then another, and drown them. On Christmas Eve, the Gardiner Expressway swayed and fell into the rising lake. Still, everyone carried on, raincoats buttoned and umbrellas up. Condominiums were bridged, and commuters clogged the 401, well north of the lakeshore. "North" they'd say, but it wasn't true north. Higher, that was a better word. All movement was to a higher elevation as the run off destroyed the shoreline of the sloping city.

On New Year's Eve, a deluge dropped into the subway line at Union Station, rupturing it along the waterfront. The electric power surged and the deaths were swift. Party goers floated to the surface. Lake Ontario had breached the base of Toronto and muscled its way into the business district, into the underground maze of concourses that linked high rising towers. Engineers tried to pump the water out but the lakeshore, formerly at 76.5 metres above sea level rose by 15 metres and lapped along the length of Queen Street West. The city's core stability was lost. Towers rocked like old frigates abandoned at sea. They crumbled. The city was disrupted beyond repair; the true exodus of power began. Bay Street would rebuild in Winnipeg, of all places, leaving the lower concourses to run like sewers. The Mayor's office shifted north and west to higher ground in North York, situated at a mean elevation of 209 metres above sea level, taking over the Student Centre at a university. The President refused to give up her offices.

There was no thunder or lightning to celebrate, just rain springing from every orifice of the stricken city, and regrouping to fall again. The result was complete misery. The creeping rain rose against foundations and scuttled across thresholds, unsettling everyone and everything. The collapse of infrastructure was inevitable.

Sitting at only 119 metres above sea level on trendy Bloor Street, the Royal Ontario Museum decided to pack it in before disaster undermined its foundations. Along with the seat of the provincial government, it would resettle hundreds of kilometres to the north of Toronto in Sudbury, Ontario, an outpost beyond the reach of the current rain.

～

The Blackwood family had survived the long and dangerous winter. The spring rain was seasonally warm, not really a change from the winter. Snow, some said, would be rare. The globe was warming after all. Others claimed the cold weather would return with a vengeance, and plunge them into an ice age. Regardless, this spring was not marked by the return to the city of grey-headed snowbirds, cheeky robins or perky daffodils. Gardens were under water, the earthworms drowned. The snowbirds travelled farther north, or west. The ROM was moving beyond the reach of the stalled rain system, and Catherine Blackwood must move with it.

At the end of her last working day, she slowly closed the long slim drawer of a cabinet, appreciating the whisper of the nylon runners against the metal guide, feeling for friction that would indicate dampness in the cabinet. All was good. She removed the cotton gloves from her immaculately kept hands and stepped back, gesturing to her husband, Thomas, to heave the cabinet into the last empty crate. Humidity had always been their worst enemy. Even she had to concede it was beyond the control of the museum's environmental system. The air was saturated. There was simply nowhere for the moisture to go. Dumping it in the street was illegal. Her irreplaceable collection of textiles was in grave danger of rotting away.

"Let's go."

"The scurry of rats." The Blackwood's adult daughter, the ever-awkwardly tall and slight Clementyne, made the old joke. She'd come from Waterloo to help her parents pack up and get out. Unfortunately, Catherine knew Clementyne's husband considered them the "problem parents" for remaining in the city while everyone else fled. His own parents had returned to the Middle East. She'd told Clementyne that one simply assessed the dangers and lived accordingly. She accused her colleagues of panicking, and went further, explaining calmly, "The way to survive is to let the water run like madness. It will pass. Avoid direct confrontation. Pluck out your eyes if necessary: the sights can be horrible."

"And so Gloucester wandered blindly."

"He was cared for, and so are we. Thank you for coming."

Catherine saw the fabric of the city had been rent to pieces, but also saw the surviving patches were islands made of stronger cloth. The novelty stuff and glitter of greater and lesser lives were bound to unravel, wash away, and sink. Such was the way of this rain. Clementyne's husband, a brilliant wave-particle theorist, had said, "Enough with the poetry!" and told Catherine and Thomas that rain in varying degrees was predicted for the foreseeable future and beyond. They must leave for their own safety.

Catherine chuckled at the memory, then bent over to remove her vintage heels. Her deep gold hair remained in place, a miracle of spray lacquers she'd begged from the furniture restorers.

"I'll miss the Shoe Museum."

"You'll see it again," Clementyne said. "Everything is moving to Sudbury."

"A bit funny, how we were going to ship our garbage up there. Now it's our culture." She pulled on sturdy rubber boots that came to her knees, farm boots with lug soles, and stood up, slipping into the coat Thomas held out and taking up her handbag and umbrella from Clementyne.

"Garbage would be a more accurate indicator of cultural habits." Thomas let his hands fall on her shoulders.

Catherine smiled wanly and reached up to stroke the dark stubble on his chin, and pressed a soft fingertip against his lips. "Not another word." She tugged the belt of her coat tighter and grimaced at the harsh feel. The oiled canvas never softened. Her wardrobe was difficult to maintain these days. Cashmere gathered moisture like a sponge. Linen hung shapeless. Cotton was cold and bunched, and rubbed until welts formed on her tender skin. She knew textiles inside and out, had grown and conserved the ROM's collection into a world-class offering. Now it was boxed into crates. Without the displays, who would care?

She remembered last year, when the rain first fell, how she'd risked her life to return to the farm community where she grew up in Southwestern Ontario. Struggling through flood waters, she gathered up clothes and fabric stored in attics and closets, in chests, in kitchens or folded at the foot of a bed still in use, hanging on walls, or over windows, gathering dirt on the floors. Faster than the rain fell, she'd stripped a whole county of its delicate treasures, and got out just before the watershed peaked. So much damage done. Yet the one thing she really wanted wasn't there, still missing, and she desperately wanted to find it, to wrap it in a fine scented cloth, and honour its meaning to her life

Right now, all she could do was follow Clementyne and Thomas out, swing the door shut behind her and set the security code. Dehumidifiers roared in the hallway, tumbling the damp air of the building, rolling it into drops that fed clear tubes and hoses which ran into distilleries that made fresh water for coffee and toilet flushing. The water cycle was diverted, but it simply wasn't enough. In any case, no one was left to use it.

The lone security guard waved at them to stop while he glanced at the outdoor cameras, looking for downed wires. He walked them to the door, opened it a crack, listened for running water before letting them go. Flash floods could happen.

The Blackwoods joined a small five o'clock queue of disaster-hardened citizens at the bus stop. Behind them, the museum shone like a beacon, its crystal face piercing Bloor Street. A lighthouse shrouded in fog. The city fought to keep as much transit running as possible. The east-west subway hub at the ROM on Bloor Street, 119 metres above sea level, was said to be safe, but no one would go down into the tunnels. It made people nervous after the collapse at Union Station. So, the subway tracks rusted and buses took to the streets again. Traveling east, as the Blackwoods would, the Bloor Viaduct was the next hurdle for commuters. It held, but for how long? The Don River rose, peaked, fell, and rose on a daily basis. The Parkway that ran alongside it had disappeared. One day, the Viaduct would fall too. Their house was two stops before it.

～

The Blackwoods' home in Rosedale overlooked the Don River Valley. It was intact, but unfit to live in. Untrustworthy. Two of the neighbours' houses had already slid into the ravine. There was no warning to say the water-stressed timbers had such a journey in mind. The stone foundations had been sworn to silence. The rest of the neighbours, spineless rats, had left in such a hurry, they hadn't even cleared out their homes, just posted security, which the Blackwoods had to pass through each time they returned. Each time, it was a different house minder, and each time they followed the same routine—producing ID and placing a mark next to their names. Who else would come here but her stubborn family? Thomas' car was the only one parked on the street.

"Come inside, Mom."

They wandered after Thomas as he walked through the rooms, his large work-bitten hands touching crates like they were an extension of his love—his wife, his child. Clementyne had inherited her father's practical understanding of spaces and ability for arranging objects in them—and more. While he built displays and dioramas for museums across the world, while his hands felt artifacts for their soundness, for the truth of their making, puzzling out their secrets for the sake of reproduction, she never cared for duplication. She wanted to make the unseen visible, just as Catherine had with her textile collections, bringing the hidden world of women into public galleries.

Before the rain, the Blackwoods' home was filled with history and a fine taste for comfort without specifying any particular era. Carved wood, polished with beeswax and turpentine, glowed among rough silks; wool tapestries and painted textures covered walls and floors. Their living space had often been written up in magazines, likened to a garden blooming in May with colours and textures arising from the dark hardwood floors, gathering and filling an airy space with joyful colour. Their home was boxed, ready for transplant. The house looked naked. The roads to the north were open to truck traffic once again.

Catherine ran her finger along the moist lattice of the French doors that overlooked the garden. The water felt cool, her skin a warm sponge soaking it up until there was no difference between her and the bead of water that dripped onto the threshold and pooled by her boots. Saturated. The roar of portable hydro generators outside, the sound clear, even over the noise of the river, gave her headaches. The regular power infrastructure was shot to hell. Entrepreneurs drowned almost daily as they gathered and sold the electricity to run lights and dehumidifiers. Why, Catherine wondered, didn't someone invent a water compressor? She turned to Clementyne and asked the question out loud, adding, "And make it into icebergs or something?"

"You're thinking diamonds, Mom. Water expands when it's ice."

"You'll ask Hiram about it when you go back to Waterloo, won't you?"

"Yes, but you could ask him yourself."

"I expect everyone asks how he's getting on with the water problem, don't they? Or they wouldn't call him TinTin."

"He wouldn't mind if you asked."

In reality, Catherine was afraid that she understood perfectly. As much as she'd stood her ground against it, there was no solution for the rain.

Blame the SUVs that ruled the roads—and the oil producers. Blame the politicians who knew that pollution was bad and silenced the scientists; blame the spike in population that came with industrialization. Blame the bloody cotton Ginny!

Blame was worse than the weather, a type of root canal pain. She'd had enough of it. Now if everyone would just agree: it was the fault of global warming, and what could they do about that?

Thomas called them over to the focal point of the living room, a huge stone fireplace. The wall above had the look of a blue-black bruise, and water struck the oak mantel as regularly as a clock. With one swift pull, he uncorked a bottle of champagne. Clementyne drank hers quickly, not waiting for the last glass to be poured, and Thomas threw his back as well.

Catherine sipped from her crystal flute, trembling with anger that no one had thought of a toast, that they were forced out by the simple fact of too much rain. She smiled brightly and turned to propose one. Her family was already at the door, motioning for her to drink up. In a moment, her glass was drained. Then she dashed the flute against the hearth.

"Fuck it!" she swore as it shattered. Then she said it louder, daring the others to contradict her.

~

They drove north to a Flood Safety Centre in Richmond Hill, 233 metres above sea level, and a suite of rooms where they kept their transition luggage, and Clementyne's gear while she was helping them to pack the house in Rosedale.

"Clemmie, do you know where they're shipping Hiram yet?"

"I hate when you call me that."

"But have they decided?"

"The university is scattering programs across the globe, in a random pattern. As TinTin says, 'It's the most scientific measure for surviving the equally random patterns of climate disruption.'"

"For Pete's sake, how will they stay a university if they do that?" asked Catherine. A culture dispersed never returned to the same form. There were limits to how far a fabric could stretch.

"TinTin's program is small. Everything is backed up and we're ready to leave with a day's notice. Waterloo isn't as bad as Toronto. You could stay with us. Mom?"

"Thank you, Clementyne, but Flood Zone Four is calling out to me."

"You're hopeless."

"You know how the media overplays the flooding."

"Uh, no, I actually found the opposite was true in Toronto."

"Did you really find it changed?" Thomas asked.

"Of course I did. You guys don't see it because you've been living there."

"And now we're moving on."

Clementyne settled deeper into the back seat.

Catherine struggled under the seat belt to open her coat to admit the warmth of the car's heating system. Thomas spared her a quick glance.

"Just getting comfortable," she murmured.

Thomas exhaled deeply, and Catherine stirred enough from her reverie to briefly pat his thigh. He didn't explain the source but kept his hands on the steering wheel. The drive could be nerve-wracking. He preferred to travel this stretch of highway at night when the watery voids and collapsed buildings were less visible. She glanced over her shoulder. Clementyne had her eyes closed listening to her music, or perhaps she was sleeping.

In the morning, she would leave Thomas at the Richmond Hill base, 233 metres above sea level, and drive Clementyne back to Waterloo, another 30 metres higher. Then for a second time, she would take her safety into her own hands and drive south to what remained of the farm, only 188 metres above sea level. The rain had ruined her family farm, the fields soaked for a second season. But what was a year or two in the larger scheme of things? The house still stood and the road was open again. It would be like going back in time, to when her family had settled two hundred years ago, and the river valley had been filled with sour-gas oil springs. They'd come for the rich muck from alluvial flooding. Despite rumours, they'd found no cannibalistic tribes, only the land thick with vegetation and damp, rotting weather which consumed the weakest of heart and body. The land had been drained and dried out. Now two hundred years later, the water had returned. It was just a cycle come around again.

She could let the rain take the farm, the land. In fifty or one hundred years it might dry out again. Someone else might find a lost button, and match it to an outfit she wore in a photograph shaking hands with the Prime Minister, and find more artifacts on her parents' farm, and then catalogue a collection based on her life and work. At least, she hoped she'd be admired that way and that her life would be worth the effort. But Catherine couldn't let that someone else find her Holy Grail. It was her life's dream to uncover the bones of Tecumseh—Indian politician and fighter, legendary friend to hardworking settlers.

Let all the land be flooded, let everything be drowned, but not this one hope that in her lifetime she would find the hero who'd died in the field beside her farm. Ever since she could remember, the rumours of the whereabouts of his bones floated up and down the settlements along the Thames watershed. She had to be the one to find them.

~ 3 ~

RAIN KNOWS HIM from filling his footprints, from tracking his travels through the great Mississippi's watershed, and rain knows where he fell, and afterwards remembers washing his bones clean in a tree-top bier, as the bones of his older brother had been washed after another battle. This younger brother's were not left in the field to sink into the Earth, but were gathered from the tree and traveled. Where?

Rain rises and falls in the central watershed of the continent, retracing his footsteps, sleuthing to discover those who hide him, seeking a lover's desire, the bones of this man. He had a vision, a wonderful vision. It did not bloom after he fell, yet his dream is of the Earth and it lives like all good dreams do until someone else sings it into being.

Rain gathers along the rivers that drain the continent north to south between the crests of mountains, east and west; Rain spreads the rivers ever wider, filling the soft belly of the plains, taking in whatever is there with sucking motions, the rivers breathing out and out. At the same time, rain congregates to the north by the Great Lakes, covering the vast geography where his bones had travelled. When Rain finds the skeleton, the Earth will heave, and the waters ride high, and the clouds will touch the Earth in places that have never been exposed before.

~ 4 ~

SOME OF THE HEAVIER CLOUDS had lifted in the night. The vague shape of the sun could be made out if she squinted really hard. It was a good omen, if the diffuse light didn't reflect off the car's finish and make a tiresome glare. Catherine's car was packed for her journey south. Clementyne sat in the passenger seat, waiting for her parents to say goodbye.

"You might need your sunglasses today."

"They're tucked in the visor." Catherine smiled, her expression growing sterner as she curled herself into Thomas' embrace. "While you're in Toronto, I don't want you taking any chances. I don't want you touching anything electrical, or crossing the street against the current." She pulled his face closer to hers. "Do you promise?"

He laughed. "Do you promise me to turn around and come back if the roads are even a tiny bit more dangerous than Hiram says they are? Do you promise to get the sorting done quickly so that we can ship the farm contents on the weekend? And will you please drink the bottled water. The well must be contaminated, no matter how deeply you say it's drilled."

Her back stiffened. "The flood waters have subsided. People still live there."

Thomas made sounds in the back of his throat.

The rain had eased. The river had peaked in Muncie at 203 meters. The runoff poured all the way down the watershed into Lake St. Clair. From there, it roared past Detroit and Windsor into Lake Erie where it gathered with more run-offs and tumbled *en masse* over Niagara Falls. They had seen the floodwaters bully along Toronto's waterfront, now at 92 meters above sea level which happened to be the lower side of Queen's Avenue West. The rain that fell on

Toronto had scurried downhill, eager to run wild with the lake, and meet up with the St. Lawrence River, and smash against the rocky islands at Kingston. The surging forces continued to undermine Montreal's islands but without spectacular success before they gave up and merged with the Atlantic Ocean. There, in its exuberance, the rain would overcome the Gulf Stream, pushing the warm current miles out into the Atlantic. That was the way it damn well worked in this part of the world.

"At the moment," Thomas said softly, "the roads to the farm are dry. Just passably dry." His voice rose. "But if anything changes ..."

Catherine opened her mouth, then clamped it shut, a migratory bird programmed to return to her birthplace. She had no choice but to follow that instinct and face the consequences once there. She pulled Thomas down to her level, kissed him until her spine softened and she flowed with him to a peaceful island. He broke away first.

"I got it."

"What?"

"The crate," whispered Thomas, "is on the back seat. The object within is well padded, but don't slam on the brakes."

"You think they will like it?"

"I'm sure they will. Now listen carefully so you'll have the spiel."

Hiram was rigidly ethical about which gifts he would accept from them, drawing the line at the grey areas of the artifact trade she and Thomas strayed into from time to time. Not only must the paperwork for the artifact be solid, its historic background must be as innocent as possible. No murdering hands, no power struggles. Thomas had found what he thought was the perfect gift.

"I'll call you when we get to Waterloo," she said, pushing him away. "Clementyne has that dreamy look on her face, a project coming on, so I may not stay for long."

"You're to stick to the plan," said Thomas. "No driving at night, no short cuts, no—"

Catherine was in the car, had the window rolled down.

"You're a hypocrite, Thomas Blackwood!"

～

Clem soaked up the passing landscape as only a passenger could. Her fingers swept graphite across her sketchbook pages, catching at veils of chiaroscuro as blurry vistas brightened or darkened, came into focus and then passed. The smudges on the page developed sudden flurries of line, a focus; then she turned to the next page. She didn't think about what she drew, only to capture her impressions of the haze. It might mean something later.

The trip to Toronto had pulled her outside the cocoon she had lived in with TinTin. The rain, aka The Enemy, was shifting in her imagination. It had become a character with more depth than she thought possible. The practical concerns that had immediately shot up with the umbrellas when the rain started now seemed parochial. In fact, the open umbrella and its nylon shell seemed to be in the way, a barrier against the true experience of *Rain*. Packing up the house where she'd grown up had generated a gust of wind, had caught her umbrella and turned it inside out, leaving her wet and shivering, but excited. Her world was changed; no matter how she walked through it, it would never match with her memories. Her Toronto was fundamentally gone and in its place, not ruins, but a new city. The inhabitants had mutated, had adjusted in ways that, thankfully, Waterloo hadn't been asked to yet.

So, what was true about the rain? She turned the inquiry like a kaleidoscope. *We think we know what the rain is,* she wrote in a corner of a page, *but what if we are wrong? What if we don't know rain at all?*

Clem cracked the car window open and settled into her seat so that a spray pelted the side of her face, dampened her hair. The smell of speeding through the mist clung inside her nose and at the back of her throat. She thought with surprise, I like it. The sketchbook, open on her lap, dimpled and wrinkled.

"Clementyne, please close the window. You're letting the rain in."

The car wove through Waterloo's expressway traffic, then negotiated the side streets. They pulled up to a tiny wartime house within easy walking distance of the university, a white frame with black trim and decorative shutters, with a detached garage for bicycles and TinTin's yard tools. The yard was large, or so it seemed, because the house was so small. The backyard was enclosed by a hedge and the patio shaded by an arbour of wisteria. From above, from the bedroom window on the second storey, the wisteria looked like a magical bower. When they first moved in, Clem had said to TinTin, "We should sleep out there."

"You'd fall through," he'd replied.

"Damn physics."

"Damn poetry."

Clem brought the magic inside. She painted the bedroom with a low border of wisteria leaves, carrying the leaves over the carpet with careful stencilling. The rest was just sky, an uneven blue that floated above the green bower. A modern birch bed frame hugged the floor. The only light was a lamp with a wrought iron Art Deco base. The glass shade had a wisteria pattern. The bulb was red so that the light it cast made the blue wall look soft and black.

There were rules about what was or was not allowed in this room. A window must be cracked open no matter what the weather. One book at a time, each, was allowed in bed, and it must fit under the pillow. Their tiny book reading lights could illuminate open pages, or the hand shadows of birds they might invent. The cat was not allowed. Shoes and clothes—gowns, pyjamas and robes—were not allowed. That's what the spare room was for. Chocolate and other lovers' fruits were welcomed if carried in on beautiful leaf-shaped glass plates. Sighs and kisses, rolling hugs and fluttering hearts were allowed, as were flights of fancy.

The rest of the house was adequate, with the kitchen at the front, and across the hall, enough space for a dining table. A comfortable grouping of couch and chairs filled the living room that faced the back yard. The basement was still dry and good for storage. It was divided by a line on the floor, fairly measured and drawn, into his side and her side. She was proud to say that a casual visitor would find it hard to tell which side belonged to the artist and which to the physicist.

Clem hauled her luggage out of the car and past the raspberry canes that crowded against the driveway, prickly repellents to short-cutters like the postie or paper kid. Every summer, TinTin threw a shocking pink net over them to keep the birds away. In July, he dressed in a long sleeve turtleneck sweater, in long pants that he tucked into socks, and shoes. Then he'd climb under the net to pick the fruit.

"We'll conceive one July. We shall name the child Raspberry."

"Like a wet kiss?"

"Like a cat's pink tongue."

~

Since he'd married Clem, he'd come home for breakfast every day, the only regularity in their lives. On this day, in order to meet his mother-in-law at the house at 11:30 a.m., TinTin decided it was easier to change time than adjust his routine. The clocks in his anticipated working environments at the university were turned back by four hours so it would seem like he was leaving as usual at 7:00 a.m. A memo went out, nicely asking his co-workers to adjust to "TinTin Time." Most responded by saying that they wouldn't notice the difference. Others appreciated the illusion of a twenty-eight hour day.

By the time Clem walked into the house, TinTin was dancing on his toes. "I made sandwiches, and we have an array of antipasto on our Renaissance-dated majolica platter, the one that Catherine gave us. The figs and peaches among the blue vines seem perfect for this day. Last night I heard that Florence had rain—at last!"

"Mom will like this so much."

TinTin nodded his pleasure.

He met Catherine in the front hall, carrying in another of her mystery boxes from the car, and a second box balanced on top with a label from a Middle Eastern bakery that he knew well from his youth in Toronto. He rushed to help, taking the pastry before it slipped. Fresh pastry was such a fragile commodity in this humid environment.

"Would you put the pastry in the fridge?"

TinTin hesitated. "Or we could eat it now."

"Clementyne said you made sandwiches."

TinTin nodded but didn't say that the sandwiches could wait. He had filled a tin with silica gel chips to absorb the humidity, and put down a layer of wax paper before packing them inside. The pastries were a rare treat. He knew he must not argue, and put the box in the refrigerator.

Clem had dug her sketchbook out from her bag and was sitting at the tiny kitchen table flipping through the pages. "I have some new ideas."

He eyed the drawings with regret. "I think that Catherine is waiting for us in the dining room. The table is set."

She closed her book. "You're a good man, TinTin."

He picked up the beautiful platter, leaving the sandwiches for Clem.

～

The packing crate remained on the coffee table throughout lunch. Catherine checked her watch discretely. She needed to allow five hours, to be on the safe side, to drive to the farm. As soon as the pastries hit the plates, she glanced at the box and began the sell.

"Thomas has a friend from England who deals worldwide in weather instruments." She had their attention. "This friend had a number of articles he was storing down at a warehouse at the harbour until it flooded, and he asked Thomas to move them. To repay the favour, he let Thomas pick out a piece that was redundant in the collection. Thomas thought you might find this one interesting. See if you can guess what it is."

Hiram gently prised the case open and cleared the packing materials away. He lifted out a glass box with an oak base. Inside was a cylinder, something like the mechanism of a music box. Hiram smiled. "It's a barograph. We use the meteorological digital service all the time."

"This one is mechanical. A Short and Mason, circa 1879," Catherine said. "The inventor was Lucien Vidie."

"Yes," said Hiram. "I know about Vidie cans. Does it work?"

"Thomas thought you might have to tinker with it a little because it's been in storage. See this cylinder? The little arm rests on it. It has a nib to record the rise or fall of the barometric pressure. What do you think?"

"I'd like to take it into the lab, if that's okay with Thomas. The mechanical aspect is rather interesting."

"The lab?" said Clementyne. "The case reminds me of Snow White's glass sarcophagus, when she's laid out after choking on the apple. I think I might find a better use for it."

"Be serious."

Catherine smiled. Hiram had crouched down to look into the glass case at eye level, his head cocked. They would have it in pieces in no time. She had the discipline, now, not to cringe at the results of their appreciation. Thomas told her that Sir Francis Bacon did the same with artifacts from the Antiquities. This was why so few textiles survived. Unlike a barograph, once fabric was cannibalized by copyists and competitors, it couldn't be put back together.

Catherine's farewells, though brief, usually caused discomfort. Hiram suffered the most from the long hugs she gave them. She needed to hug, to know them physically—the texture of their clothes, their hair, the feel of flesh and bones beneath. This was the way she passed her love on, directly into their personal space. This time when she kissed Hiram on the cheek, he surprised her by holding onto her arm for a moment.

"Thank you, Catherine. Please be safe on your journey."

~ 5 ~

THE BAROGRAPH SAT ON A TABLE in TinTin's lab, in its weathered glass case, steadily pumping out straight lines. Steady lines which indicated the barometric pressure was unchanging. To his delight, his colleagues watched it for thirty minutes, then for an hour. Then they trickled away.

"Can I take it home now?" asked Clem.

"No," he said. "I'm sure that once everyone is gone, it will do something more. These things can be quite perverse."

"Then I guess I better get back to my studio."

He hadn't meant it that way. He thought she would be interested. But she was gone.

~

TinTin's fellows at the university were still hopeful that he could find a way to help with the rain. A Weather Net. Before they had dispersed across the globe, they drank cappuccinos, played Ping-Pong and rubbed TinTin like he was a lucky charm for any new ideas. TinTin, in turn, got the old guys talking about quarks and quantum theory, about how those ideas arose in the first place. His favourite fossil was a former Soviet theorist specializing in the history of paranormal thought and cogent applications relating to intuition.

"We're just another layer in the universe," he'd said, "like the fish that swim and breathe in water. We look down on them, capture them, pollute and change their environment, so it's probable that there are life forms in a medium above us, doing the same."

TinTin wondered if there was a kernel of truth to this, if the human-made climate change was a response to a need or event happening somewhere else.

"Blame Theory," Clem called it. She favoured Chaos Theory—the idea that a tiny random spark could initiate change. According to her, life could turn on a dime, a whim.

"What would be the anomaly this time?" asked TinTin.

"We wouldn't know. You're into Blame again. The point is to watch carefully. Ride the wave. Trust in the future."

TinTin preferred the path of interference. He needed to have some control over his environment. As a child, he'd experienced the removals on the West Bank. When the Twin Towers were destroyed, he was a new immigrant to Canada, had just started grade nine at the Toronto University School. His high school years were filled with pressure from faculty to find solutions to terrorism. All his classmates were expected to, but he took it more seriously, and the other students started to call him TinTin, even though his hair was dark; his need to save the world was that clear. Pressure also came from his father, an Arab, and his mother, a Jew. Every day they reminded him that it was his destiny to bring peace to the world. How could anyone fail with that kind of support?

Throughout high school, he worked with his best friend, James, on the Theory of Everything. James suggested it might be good to get the theory of one thing right, and it may as well be the Theory of Everything, and so James' nickname was born: Simple Pi.

They were seventeen and it was summer. They were lying on their bellies at the top of a ravine by the old Toronto brick works. The light around them was dappled, broken by the lush deciduous trees overhead. Sunlight. Below, another kind of light danced, rising from the dust and heat of the clay pit. They discussed the Theory of Everything. TinTin wanted to test the theory with a practical application. "What if we could keep bombs from falling in our neighbourhood?"

"The Annex is not going to be bombed," Pi said.

"Anywhere can be bombed. They're not called terrorist attacks for nothing."

"Okay. Tell me about bombs."

"They blow people and homes to pieces," TinTin said. "I've only seen them fall from rockets, not close up. Just the mention makes my parents cry. Not all the time. Bombs make them angry too."

Simple Pi picked up a stone, lobbed it in the air and whistled as it fell with a thud among the brush below them. "I'd want my own rocket launcher to strike back."

"Then I'd need one to stop you. And so it goes on and on. How do we simply keep them out?"

"I have the answer!" Simple Pi clapped his head.

"What?"

"Apply the Theory of Everything."

And they laughed until overhead an urban squirrel scolded them.

TinTin had a thing for light waves and that kind of energy. He knew energy radiated from the earth. The problem was humans couldn't see it, not all the wave lengths. Still, a Theory of Everything had to include the unknown, they told each other, the kind of magic needed to keep out bombs and rocks.

TinTin believed the earth emitted an unknown wave-a fifth wave, they decided to call it. He'd seen it when he lived in Jericho after one particularly close concussion from a rocket. The city was made from rock and sand. Spring water came up from the dry ground like a miracle. It was the oldest continuously settled city in the world, and people came in droves to dig it up, saying the land kept a record. When the bomb exploded, before he heard a sound, just for a millisecond, he thought he saw a shimmering wave of light rise from the ground. Not sunlight. A huge wave like a whiplash that had no end.

He hadn't the maths to explain what he saw, and kept drawing it over and over, one wave to circle the earth. A girl in his class, an art student, became interested in his rough sketches and started hanging out with them. Clem didn't have physics or a theory of anything to hold her back.

"They're G-waves," she'd told them. "I've read about them. They circle the earth, are generated by lightning."

"G?"

"G for the earth, silly, for Gaia."

~

That was Clem, and he wished she would come back to the laB It was quiet without her. The only sound was the infinitesimal scratching of the series of nibs across the card inside the barograph. TinTin, now the Quaker Chair of Peace and Technology, sat across from his still best friend, the blond and cool, still single, Dr. Pi who wore the concentrated look of a chess master working out his next move. Together they watched the old technology record the air pressure: steady, consistent.

The Safety Net had been easy to construct, thought TinTin, as natural as riding a bike. On another summer day, TinTin and Pi weren't even thinking about theories. They were competing to impress Clem. Scrambling down into the hot valley of the old brick works, Pi threw stones and TinTin pointed his cell phone at the rising shimmers of light and hit SEND. It was funny, then an arc of light, a barely visible shimmer of light or heat or g-source wave, shot over the ridge like a rainbow.

"Nice move," Clem said.

"Right, but let's see if he can do it again." Pi was just jealous.

By the end of that summer, TinTin could collect and arc random waves over an earth wave (which he never saw again) using cellphone technology. He put together an invisible bubble in his backyard to keep out the neighbour's dog and its habit of peeing the grass yellow. To be fair, his cat could no longer access the neighbour's garden and use it as a litter box. With that success, he expanded the bubble to include the house and driveway. Then there was the problem of having to open up the bubble every time someone wanted in. He thought perhaps something like a remote for a garage door would work. Simple Pi suggested using recent research which had developed universal codes for all objects and elements. Eureka!

The bubble was a permeable net for selected items. They spent months codifying the components of their immediate world into frequencies. These were tested and refined and assigned barcodes until only the desired objects could pass. Mercury amalgams, the plastic of contact lenses, Egyptian cotton, and commercial dyes. His mother could carry groceries across but not a handgun. His father could drive his Toyota through the net but the neighbour's Volvo would not pass. They watched with delight as the net caught random objects and literally left them at the curB The problem of banning cheap ice cream made with glycol was tough to solve, as glycol was also in the car's antifreeze; then they discovered a simpler system of barcodes which could be combined into an infinite number of variations. All they needed were microwaves, those from the sun and the increasing number produced by wireless communication.

The net could have been made useless by the rain if it weren't for the popularity of wireless technology. Rain wasn't as easy to bend as microwaves. It was slippery in character. It moved erratically across the global chessboard, its feints and routs worth lifetimes of study.

While he waited for the barograph to change and for Pi to say something—anything— about weather that he hadn't heard before, TinTin rolled wave properties around in his head. He'd been focused on putting soft, vertical nets between microwave towers to anticipate and mimic weather fronts, but the shape was always umbrella-like, spider-like. Like the Safety Net. The problem was anything that caught the rain proved disastrous. When the flooding first started, Net technology had been applied to Manhattan, and it created a fiercer runoff in the neighbouring boroughs. The subway and sewer systems became conduits for a back flow. The differential in the ground-based water pressure set the pilings of skyscrapers rocking. Old fashioned dykes and dams, levees and sandbags, were still the best defence for property. Until someone came up with a way to turn the rain off, letting it fall unimpeded was the safest strategy.

He looked across the barograph at Pi. They might have to cede this game.

They almost had given up with the Safety Net. In a four-by-four booth at the school science fair, TinTin and Pi had presented their experiment to the world with the showmanship of great magicians. Yet the head hunters for colleges were baffled and sceptical whether the application would work *in the real world*. The presentation looked *too futuristic. A force-field is decades away.* The boys didn't even get invited to the city-wides. A student from nearby Bishop Strachan School won by delivering a new advance in cancer research.

"Much more appreciated by the pharmaceutical industry," was the way Simple Pi explained the win.

By his graduating year, TinTin knew he needed more than theory, more than a backyard experiment to convince people that he had a solution for peace. He set up an impressive demonstration. NASA and NORAD were the first agencies to notice the net around his neighbourhood, Toronto's Annex. Only North American-made cars could pass through. The traffic tie-up was comical. Cars and trucks literally either passed through or stopped in their tracks. At high speeds, it could have been dangerous, but TinTin anticipated the problem, adding a thickness to the net, making it viscous so that vehicles slowed gradually and came to a standstill. Inertia and drag. The whole thing lasted only for a minute, then he pulled the net.

He was bending waves like a kung fu master, or so Pi bragged. Best of all, it was the perfect solution for pleasing his parents. Peace and technology. At eighteen, he and Simple Pi were equal parts thrilled and terrified when the experiment worked. The media and hacker buzz was incredible. Everyone searched for the source. UFOs were suspected by the hippies and left-wingers. The Right believed it was the work of terrorists. NORAD solved it in eight days, but still didn't know how, or by whom. The terror of discovery soon took over their lives. He spent long hours with his parents discussing the best way to come clean. Pi hadn't even told his parents. They both worked like crazy to write up the applications, and in the end, they decided to publish everything online through an opensource network. Clem, his girlfriend by then, had christened it the Safety Net. It would be available to everyone. Screw the money, he told Pi, every neighbourhood deserved safe borders.

Clem took charge of the press releases. His picture, and Pi's, was sent to media outlines and social networking pages. They were afraid of being disappeared. By the time the secret service came for them, it was too late. Everything to know was out there and everyone knew who they were.

People were free to come and go across borders now. Everything else was controlled through bar codes. Guns and munitions piled up outside customs' offices. Illegal drugs remained inside the panels of vans captured by the Net. Drug mules no longer packed their bodies with heroin or cocaine; DDT stopped drifting from countries where corporations had no ethics. This new security had made his father-in-law cry. Artifact smuggling, in even the poorest nations, had come to a standstill.

Ingenious ways had been developed to use the Safety Net's coding system, but no new applications had been found for the waves themselves, nothing that could take care of carbon dioxide emissions, ozone, methane, general particulate matter, the radiation from solar flares. And now the rain.

Not even ten years had passed and TinTin felt old. He'd already made the discovery of a lifetime. He'd lost touch with the G-wave and the Theory of Everything. Only Clem kept pushing at the theories with her artwork, willing to turn the world on its head again.

~ 6 ~

THE LIGHT RAIN HAD A STEADY CONSISTENCY that matched the regularity of the car's windshield wipers on low. Wipers were second nature, a constant presence. However, the sound of rubber on the road varied. On the stretches of new asphalt, they whispered almost high-pitched enough to be inaudible. Annoying. Smooth. Hypnotic. The rough sections of broken tarmac shot pockets of water thudding up into the wheel wells and chassis. Rhythmic. Low and grumbling. Cleansing. Water in the roughest sections tore across the car as though to possess it, ripping screeches that jolted her attention away from her audio book as she wrestled for control of the car. This rain was no one's friend. Discordant. Taut and strong. Controlling.

Like most drivers, Catherine straddled the centre lanes to avoid the crumbling shoulders. She was halfway home. Go with the river. Stay with the highest points.

Poised at the north end of London at 281 metres above sea level, she looked down at the city, at the 30 metre drop in elevation. She could see the Thames River and its tributaries, how they gathered in the centre of the city and spread ever-wider southward to roll into the bed of the old sea that was rising again. She crossed the ancient shoreline and sped through the city.

The road home shot straight before her. There would be no more hills or twists. She noticed a change in the quality of green. Here, where flat expanses of water and wood lots dominated, the green was good and right. Trees were heavily burdened, in full leaf already. The fields were verdant with grasses, so densely lush that you wanted to drink from them and be refreshed, and perhaps you would live forever. The colour could have been overwhelming but for the contrast of brown water-soaked fields with their milky reflections of cloudy sky. Some of the ditches along the roadside were thick with last year's bursting cattails. Birds nested in the beige down. Redwing blackbirds. Ducks and geese paddled in the fields. A glimpse of a patient heron stalking fish.

There was a bridge to cross at Lambeth, 248 metres above sea level. She dared not look at the creek that swelled on either side. Then another at Mount Brydges, this one reconstructed by army engineers, and barely clearing the span of the flooded river. Tiny baby frogs massed on the road there, likely hatching from the mud that had collected along the abutments. The crossing was hideous, as was the greasy feel to the car's tires on the road for the next few kilometres.

The land settled out into the flat seabed, about 200 metres above sea level and gradually dropping. The highway sat just enough above the water to make it seem like she was floating. Hoses and barns looked like islands in the distance. A thin umbilical line to follow home, a lifeline between water and sky. The grey orb of the sun, pale and far to the west, was searching for an opening in the clouds, electrifying the edges with light. Would the sun touch the earth again?

It did break through. Catherine gasped at the beauty, and as though embarrassed by her reaction, the sun quickly pulled back. It had not been expecting a witness to such purity. She was the only traveller on the road.

Catherine fought back yawns and turned on the air conditioner to wake up. Dark shadows filled the underbellies of the thick clouds and cast more shadows across the flooded land. Here you could see how rain gathered, she thought, and you could see the water cycle, the warmed shallow lake that released vapours, gathered up into the sky as though by a sponge, and held. Thank goodness the clouds absorbed so much rain, an extra seven percent for every degree it got warmer, she'd been told. There would be a downpour eventually, but not yet, she prayed.

By the time she drove into Chatham County, at a mean elevation of 181 metres, the sun had set. The clouds flopped belly-first onto the fields and road, so thickly that she wanted to open the sunroof and stand, to see above the fog, to see her way from a higher vantage point, but there was none in this flat land. The feeling of being pressed in, of needing air, but not that swampy air. Concentrate. Into the thick air, she sang a childish, wordless tune, following that thread of comfort through the fog.

At last her headlights caught the reflective strip of her mail box. *Lennon*, her family's name. The lane to the house was clear. A robin, startled by the headlights, flew away from the nest it was building in the rafters beneath the broad front porch. She would set out some coloured thread for that enterprise and see whether the bird preferred cotton or silk.

She called Thomas from her mobile, afraid to leave the car. When he answered, his voice sounded shockingly clear, as though he sat in the car beside her. It took her breath away.

"Thank heavens you're alright!"

She let him berate her for calling so late, for driving in the dark, for being so far away and leaving him helpless to save her. She needed the time to catch her breath and think. She pulled a large battery-operated lantern from her travel bag and shone it on the house. Thomas was questioning her. "How is the house?"

"I'm just going in now."

She looked around the front entranceway, so familiar, then wandered down the hall with the feeling of looking for her parents even though they had been gone for years. The sense of their presence was a comfort just the same, as much as Thomas' voice.

"It's remarkably intact," she told him. "Frank Dolsen and his boys took care of it just fine. I don't see the mould we had in Toronto. We did the right thing, running dehumidifiers all winter. It helped that we kept the basement dry from the beginning."

Catherine walked from room to room, shining the light into corners, looking for signs of water in the ceilings of the bedrooms, for bubbles under the wallpaper. Methodically she searched for runs of mould on the painted walls and tested the carpets with a broom handle for hidden pools. She reassured Thomas that she wouldn't turn the power on until she had an electrician check the wiring. Oil generators were supplying electricity to the dehumidifiers even though the hydro lines were working again.

In the good parlour, she listened as Thomas described his day. She found an oil lamp and trimmed it with a fresh wick she had brought. Soon she had a small fire lit in the wood stove. A can of curried chick peas warmed on top. She thought how her mother would disapprove of cooking in here.

Then she saw that Clementyne was trying to get through. It was uncharacteristic of her, and she said her goodbye to Thomas quickly.

"We just wanted to make sure you got there safely," said Clementyne. "We're monitoring the weather and if this old barograph is reliable, there isn't going to be a change in the pressure any time soon. That's good news, Pi says."

"Tell him that the route he suggested was perfect. Hardly any traffic and not one detour."

"I'll tell him now. And TinTin sends his love too."

"He's a good man, just like your father. Both of them."

"I know, Mom. I know."

Catherine wrapped herself into the knitted afghan that she'd warmed by the fire and settled into the well-used rocking chair beside it. She turned the lamp down; firelight from the cracks of the cast iron stove flickered over her. She rocked in the chair until tears flowed and her body stopped shaking. She had made it home, by herself. Alone.

As though to be sure, she lifted her eyes. Rain streaked across the eight section window panes, pressing darkly against the house, stalking her, the one presence that could be counted on these days. She had made it home but nothing felt solid beneath her.

"When I find those bones," she bargained, wiping the tears from her face, "you can have the farm. But be warned, I'll fight you with everything I have until they're in hand."

The rain didn't skip a beat, the windows didn't blink. So, thought Catherine, she may as well eat a bit of the curry heating on the stove. Once she did, she would feel better. Like a child, she would feel better with something in her stomach.

~ 7 ~

BEFORE HE GAVE UP ON A WEATHER NET, perhaps he should look at Clem's recent ideas, at ways to flow the water to where it was needed. He'd give up on the idea of control, but not the game. On the way to the university after lunch, he'd asked Clem how he might do it. She'd pulled her cellphone from her pocket and waved it in the air.

"Like before: magic!"

"Funny girl."

The barograph churned steadily. He grabbed his jacket and said to Simple Pi, "I'll be back soon."

"I'll call you the minute anything changes," Pi said, "if I don't fall asleep first."

TinTin shrugged into his coat.

He chased through the halls of the university looking for Clem. Besides him, only ennui floated through the corridors where rumours once had, through the keyholes and the cracks of securely locked lab doors, circulating on the air currents, either hot and stuffy, or cool enough to chill the ankles. Which research facility had stayed, which had moved in the night? Only a few were left to care.

He found Clem alone in front of the glass walls of the great common room, her sketchbook opened on a table, the page covered with spiralling doodles. On the outside surface of the windows, huge wipers swept rain from side to side, like a pair of giant metronomes. Perversely, they didn't help the visibility, as the mechanical engineers had hoped, but seemed to smear the rain. With her umbrella in hand, Clem stood at the pivot point of one of the blades and moved her arm in sync with the arc of the wiper. The edge of her hand squeaked like rubber across the glass. At the end of each arc, she stopped and swung her arm the other way. Rain ran down the edge of the blade outside the window, but she'd created an illusion that it ran down her arm. Her video camera was set up on a table, pointing at her, catching the action.

"Look at the pattern. It's like I'm twisting the rain into yarn."

"I'm worried about you." He was teasing and curious at the same time. Gently he took her hand away from the window. Tall and slender, she was a fairy child. Her fingers could wind around his, the way a tree roots itself in the soil.

Clem shrugged but let him hold her hand. "Come say goodbye to the boats. Dissolution has served its purpose. It's time to try another tack."

Months ago, she had given up painting on canvas, tossing out the fungicides her father gave her to keep the canvas from rotting, and began work on a series of boats, sculpting them from a high-grog clay body, putting them, unfired, into waterways where she documented their dissolution.

"To hell with preservation!" she'd said, then covered her mouth with her free hand. "Don't tell my parents I said that."

"I won't, not ever."

Clem pulled him along to the strange and wonderful places where the clay boats were hidden—under downspouts, beneath a variety of trees and benches, out in the open on the lawns, on the rarely used patio tables dotting the research institute's penthouse deck, in the parking lots. She shot a minute of video at each location. As they stood under the eaves of the cafeteria window, Clem moved in for a close-up of a series of fine, steady drips perforating a rather delicate vessel.

"Water torture," whispered TinTin.

"It's beautiful."

The spring rain had thickened into a C-grade syrup. He was shivering despite his jacket. Storm clouds that used to build up over the lakes and travel inland with a vengeance—striking, illuminating, destroying, cleansing—couldn't find enough differential pressure to produce a breeze, let alone a clap of thunder. Nothing broke the cloying, chilling humidity.

His teeth chattered. "I'm too cold to stay out any longer."

"You were born in the warmth of the Middle Eastern sun, poor thing." She stopped filming. "I will leave the boats to the elements for good, and take you back inside."

Back down the long hallways, he talked out the Weather Net problems with Clem, his words tripping over theories. A week without Clem had taken its toll.

"With all the information that the Safety Net has yielded, with the ability to categorize and rank, it has become so easy to create a hierarchy of things that belong and things that don't."

"Water is another story. We calculate content percentages roughly: eighty-eight percent for human bodies; fifty-five percent for a comfortable ambiance; tree transpiration varying throughout a daily cycle; a dog panting. All these and more create their own microclimates. Anything organic has water content. Humidity is omnipresent but constantly variable and on the move. It's a system rather than a material."

"A good one," Clem said. "Mom has virtually no wrinkles."

"And my mom looks twenty years older since she moved back to Jericho. The dry air is sucking her youth away."

"Don't ever, ever, say that to her."

"I wouldn't. But I noticed."

He paused, then the tape in his head started up again.

"Preventing water damage is equally hard. The Net hasn't been successful as a barrier because the pressure becomes too great. Water accumulates and needs to find its lowest point, to return to the earth. Water thwarted builds up pressure. The pressure will take out anything in its path. As a system, rain water prefers to disappear. The absence of rain, the absorption into the earth seems to be the system's ultimate goal. We're on tiptoes here and still the rain falls. We need to provide the rain with another way to disappear."

"Yeah, like Stealth Rain. Or Runny Nose Booger Rain."

"I need a tissue, I know. Clem, would you just give me one?"

When they got back to the lab, Clem gave Pi a friendly peck on the cheek, which always made him blush. Then she ran her fingers over the shapes TinTin had drawn earlier on the electronic white board. She wiped the board clean and made her pronouncement.

"You've developed a Moses complex."

TinTin and Pi groaned. Pi said, "I thought we banned biblical comparisons."

"It's like when Moses thought *he* could part the Red Sea. It didn't work for him. It's God's will, dear boys. We can count things, group things, build from what's here, but we don't create. You can't change the weather. You go with it. This stuff—it isn't rain-like.

Go back to Noah."

"Just this afternoon, you said that boats were *passé*."

"For Noah," Clem said, "it was a boat. What does the rain want of us?"

TinTin corrected her. "*God* told him it was a boat."

"Listen. If God were thinking like this rain, what would the solution be?"

She opened a new page on the electronic board and swept the edge of her hand across it like she had on the windows of the Great Hall. TinTin watched the board register the action, a series of tiny stutters of skin pressed against the hard polyester sheet. He held up her video camera, asking permission to download the day's footage. Clem nodded as she changed the colour of the ink layer. She resumed sweeping. It looked like she could do it for hours.

Simple Pi stared and she stared back at him. Another flush came up on his fair skin, like she was really bugging him.

"Now you're suggesting windshield wipers?" he said.

"Not you too!" Clem said. "Don't look at the thing, look at the action."

"Nothing is holding the rain back," Pi said. "It's falling from the sky as it always does, making everything stagnant. Every day is grey. The weather cell around us is dead. Death star stability reigns while I long for the days of quasars." Pi sat down next to TinTin at the computer, ran his hand through his pale spiked hair. "Maybe Clem is on to something. Maybe we'll just set up a stand to sell beanies with wipers. Personally, I hope God comes back and tells us a boat is better."

"Something about this is right, man," TinTin said. "Her boats are sunk. It's not the way to go."

"I bet that wooden boats would float."

"Funny." Clem joined them. She scrolled through the wiper images, selected one and jabbed a finger at the monitor. "If there was a God, She'd want us to look closely. The weather cell isn't dead. Little tiny jumps up and down."

"Oscillating," said TinTin.

"Look carefully and you'll see the same action on the barograph. The edges aren't smooth."

"There is no true stasis," whispered Pi.

They magnified the image.

"A wave."

"Just enough movement to create a permeable barrier."

"Just enough pressure to move and contain the water."

"Not a net at all."

"A muscle contracting."

"A tube."
"A sprinkler system."

Wooing

෨ဢ

~ 1 ~

RAIN FINDS THE SKELETON, hidden, picked clean and wrapped at the cusp of a central watershed. It will take some finesse to set the bones free, to float them to the point of climax where Earth will best receive them.

When flesh and sinew covered his bones, they travelled the continent widely with the urgency of love. Within those bones is a memory of a virgin continent. They are made of the stuff of Earth, of plains and forests, bodies of water, the sky and all that relates to the universe and her sibling planets. They contain a life that reverberates between the human constructions and her skin.

Earth remembers his heart pounding across her grasslands, his breath in her forests. She trembles with delight.

~ 2 ~

HUMANS WANDERED THE EARTH, and then they settled.

In the late 1790s, the first wave of European settlers breached the Northwest Frontier of America and poured over the Appalachian Mountains into the Ohio Valley. Spilling up and down the Mississippi and Missouri watersheds, they flooded the continent, breaking with each of the peoples they found. Settlers pushed and shoved and fought, built stories of how they won over a harsh land, and made it good.

Over two hundred years later, pockets of the past remained, hold-outs from the modern era, native communities, religious orders—and oddballs including living anachronisms like Rebecca Galloway. She practiced a way of life in Greene County, Ohio, as though time stood still and the Northwest Frontier had just opened. However, through no fault of the young Miss Galloway's, the present age brought changes in climate, and another wave of resettlement was about to occur. Rebecca's legacy was literally drowning, just as her parents had been recently drowned in the high waters.

Only newly come of age, Rebecca spent the rain-soaked winter wandering the Little Miami River and its swollen tributaries. Its banks had washed over, flooding fields and woods. The river was everywhere and only an expert like her could keep the landmarks straight. The canoe she paddled was as well cared for as it was on the day it launched onto the Little Miami in 1804. The birch bow was peaked high enough to carve through the coursing waters of the spring runoff, yet she could not keep her feet dry, no matter how skillfully she navigated. Her hands were dirty, her legs hairy and her bum smelled like pee and musk. Under her breasts, she found mould. The rain had her down, but the loss of her parents late last summer had turned her wild.

On this day, she'd been paddling against the current of Massie Creek for some time, the effort getting harder, the water chopping across the bow as though to turn it, and her, back.

Paddle easy, keep the rhythm, her daddy used to say. To control the craft with just one person in these rushing waters was a challenge. She'd set stones in the bottom near the bow to balance the weight. Not the same as another pair of arms, but it would do.

It'll do just fine. Her daddy's voice seemed to ripple over her, gentle and friendly so she let go of her anger for a moment. Just for a moment.

She reached the sloping bank of the old grave yard where her ancestor and namesake, Rebekah Galloway, was laid to rest beneath a pitted tombstone that looked down the hillside at a wry angle. *Until we rise again,* it was inscribed. Like all Greene County children, Rebecca knew her genealogy from the countless recitations by her elders, and could read the gravestones as if they were a lesson in history. Her life was rooted here. She nudged the canoe up onto the slick grass.

Towering over old Rebekah's stone was Colonel James Galloway's monument to his life. He settled his family in the most beauteous land he'd seen in the new United States. In the year 1797 the Colonel knew exactly which five hundred acres he would claim, a place not far from where the Shawnee government had settled, an area he knew from working the backwoods with Daniel Boone and from fighting three Indian wars. The tract was opened to settlers, traded in the Treaty of Greeneville for twenty thousand dollars in goods. The Indians were promised more goods should the day come when they learned to co-exist peaceably. When they put aside their savage ways and lived as true Christians. A fair trade, the new settlers maintained. They just wanted to live in peace.

The names of Rebecca's relations rose from the slippery hillside, leaning into the rain as though to shelter the earth. On the other side of the Colonel was his son, James Junior, the state's first governor. Rebecca didn't climb that high. She sank to her knees in front of the newest tombstone, upright and black as midnight in the grey afternoon. With fingers as warm as the stone was cold, she explored the names etched into the mirror-like surface.

Samuel George — Sarah Zane
GALLOWAY
Form'd from this soil, this air,
Born here of parents born here from parents the same,
and their parents the same,
I, hoping to cease not till death.
~Whitman~

Her parents. And now, only her. The last of her line.

"I'll do you proud. I promise," whispered Rebecca. From her rucksack, she pulled out bread and soft cheese, and watched a white-faced girl eating in the reflection of the granite. Nodding to her, Rebecca broke off a piece of the soft, squished bread and put it at the base of the grave, the somber girls briefly touching foreheads. "That ye shall live," she said, the sweat of her exertions coursing down her face, blinding her, and she wiped the rivulets away with her handkerchief.

Her legs were cramped from the trip up river, aching to the bone, as was her heart. To ease the cramps, she walked among the stones. For her heart, she drank from a skin slung over her shoulder, water laced with whiskey from the distillery that had continued from the time of the Colonel, two centuries ago. A necessity then, whiskey offered the first settlers some relief from the misery of their lives in the thick woods, the physical labour, their women's labours and deaths, the loss of babe and child. The utter loneliness. She drank this medicine and pushed the canoe back into the swift flowing creek, letting the current carry her home. Her back would ache from holding the oar steady as a rudder in the rough waters. Tears streamed down her face and she did not care to wipe them. With her shoulders thrown back, Rebecca opened her soul to the river, shouting out the song that had rolled over her all the long winter.

Over the tree-tops I float thee a song!
Over the rising and sinking waves -- over the myriad fields, and
the prairies wide;
Over the dense-pack'd cities all, and the teeming wharves
and ways,
I float this carol with joy, with joy to thee, O Death!

She was the last one living the Frontier life, and it was her duty to carry the past forward as her parents, and theirs, and theirs had.

~ 3 ~

ON WEDNESDAY AFTERNOON, Catherine removed the last batch of quick breads from the electric oven. Her phone was ringing. It would be Thomas. She sat down at the worn pine table, its old varnish sticky from the humidity, to print labels by hand, the phone cradled to her ear. Lemon. Apple-Cranberry. Banana-Walnut.

"I've made arrangements for Saturday. Are you ready?" he asked.

"There hasn't been enough time to get through everything."

Catherine looked around the kitchen, the cupboards stuffed with the day-to-day wares she'd left behind, had mildewed. The doors were open to air them out, dishes of white vinegar set inside. The air must circulate, even if it was damp, even if it felt she was living inside a fog, there had to be some movement. She hoped her baking frenzy would help dry the place out, evaporate the excess. But the air only grew thicker. Her last trip had been more about Chatham County and its rich textile heritage than her family's farm. The gingham curtains that hung like wet dish rags, hadn't seemed important, still weren't.

She rushed to fill the growing silence between her and Thomas. "You have no idea about the condition of this area. Look at all the funding Toronto has received for resettlement and think, they expect us to shut down and leave with nothing; for goodness' sake, where is everyone to go? I'm still not convinced we need to leave. The local historians say this area was saturated with water in the early days too. It's a cycle. We need to adapt for a bit, not run."

"And the farmers, how can they make a living without any land?"

"Well, that's just it. The greenhouses are mostly hydroponic anyway. They just need more electricity to run the artificial lights. Cattle producers are looking for new livestock. Nothing with hooves does well, but the poultry alternatives look good. Ducks are the new chickens. Bamboo has been established, and years ago, someone brought wild rice in from the Nipissings. The Delaware will make a killing on it this year. They hope it stays wet. We deserve more funding and support for our initiatives."

"Exactly which ones, Catherine?"

"The rebuilding for one. Surely someone, somewhere, knows how to build things that float and rise with the waters."

She listened to Thomas clear his throat. Feeling smug, she left the straight-back kitchen chair, taking her cup of tea and the phone to the horsehair couch by the stove. He was immersed in explaining the principles of coastal architecture, sharing his experience of the floating homes and islands he'd seen in Holland and Dubai. She woke from a little catnap when Thomas suddenly broke off the call. "I have to get back to work."

Thomas called again the following morning to see how Catherine had progressed.

"I tried to reach you after supper last night."

"I had to go out," she said. "You must have been in bed when I called you back."

"You were driving those roads at night?"

"It's not like there's any traffic to watch for." Catherine sensed panic on the other end of the line and added, "Besides, Frank Dolsen picked me up. There was a Historical Society meeting at the tavern. Pretty important, don't you think?"

"Good God, what have you got into?"

"I've been asked to chair something very important. After all, it is the bicentennial year of the Battle of the Thames."

"Are you still hoping to find the bones?"

"Thomas, it's like you say—disaster is the surest way to bring out the trophies. If the bones are in the area, there will be movement. But for now, I need you to help with something quite different."

~

Last night, the party room at the Tecumseh Tavern had been full of community members keen to dress up and play a role from history despite the fact that they were barely afloat. As if invoking the past would pull them forward, the survivors of the flood voted to go ahead with the annual fall festival and re-enactments, *if it pleases the weather to co-operate*. Drinks would be poured after the meeting; a table by the bar groaned with baked goods.

"There is one remaining item on the agenda." The plump, friendly face of Madeleine French took on a no-nonsense look. "We will hear from each of the candidates, then vote for the Honorary Chair of the festival." All eyes shifted between TK Holmes, the middle-aged son of the biggest pharmacy owner in Chatham, and the interloper, as Catherine thought of herself.

"TK, would you introduce yourself and explain a little about what you would bring to the position of Chair?"

TK stood, cocky, yet slightly unsure of what was expected. He had been the Honorary Chair for the last decade. Catherine knew her challenge was unexpected, a bit like the flood. She watched his father prod him to speak.

"As you all know, I'm TK. There's been a son named after Tecumseh for generations, ever since the great leader came to this area and saved the lives of so many Loyalists. We were burnt out by the end of the war, but it would have been worse if it weren't for Tecumseh. Now it's our turn to give back." TK looked down at his father who nodded approval. "We, at Holmes Pharmacy—owned since before confederation by the founding family—are happy to be the Honorary Chair of the Bicentennial Festival and donate—not $2000—but $5000 this year. With all this rain, we are going to need more tents."

"And bailing cans for the canoes!" Matthew Crudge shouted from the back, bringing laughter to the room.

"Thank you, TK," Madeleine said as she stared down Matthew.

It was Catherine's turn to rise and face the room.

"I've known TK all my life and would like to thank him and Holmes Pharmacy for once again bringing not just words, but good hard cash to the festival. I know everyone appreciates their very generous donation. Let's give him a round of applause." The crowd, wary of her motives, joined her in polite appreciation.

"I guess you know by now who I am. I grew up on the First Line, not a quarter mile from the battle site. Like you, I spent my childhood hunting for arrowheads and rifle shot, hoping to come across some sign of a person of note in that battle, maybe Tecumseh himself. Not much remains after two hundred years. And despite the rumours, no one knows where Tecumseh's bones have been laid to rest." She paused to let some sniggers roll by.

"Now, some of you will forgive me for going away to earn my livelihood, and others will have to forgive me for coming back, but in the last thirty years I've developed a lot of unique resources and friendships that could make this a most spectacular bicentennial celebration."

"Have you considered that it's an international event? Tecumseh touched the lives of people from the American South to the North, and West to the Missouri River. A future president and vice-president fought Tecumseh in the Battle of the Thames. Johnson claims to have fired the mortal shot. Their political lives were built, in part, around this association with Tecumseh. Tecumseh campaigned tirelessly in the war against American expansionism— and for a native homeland. He tried to save his way of life but he saved us instead. I believe that we can build a venue that will draw all those people here. We can teach them and entertain them. And just maybe, we can claim this land from the rain and save ourselves this time."

The crowd roared with approval. TK shouted over the din, "Just how are we going to entertain them so they'd come here?"

"I have a special guest lined up who will bring Tecumseh to life."

"So who's the guest?" This from Irene Watson, the wife of the silent but dignified re-enactor, Aubrey, who had played the role of Tecumseh for as long as anyone could remember.

Catherine grinned, and through that grin, she also wondered who. Who would even come? She`d spoken with the bravado of a schoolgirl and must continue. "The guest," she said, "is someone from Tecumseh's past."

Irene Watson stared harder and Catherine hated her, the combination of parochial complacency and marital protectionism. Which one from history could sink that woman's ship?

"Well, if you'll have her, I was thinking of a direct descendant of Miss Rebekah Galloway, the woman Tecumseh courted back in Ohio."

"Yeah, she was worth what," heckled Crudge, "fifty pieces of silver to him? Will Aubrey be able to afford Irene after this?"

Aubrey Watson did not laugh. Slowly he stood up, one hand on his wife's shoulder, the other held out for peace, indicating that he was in the role of Tecumseh. He did not utter a word until the hall was silent. "Miss Rebekah Galloway and her father honoured the Shawnee by settling near their traditional home. They lived respectfully side by side for many years. It would be a great honour to see this Miss Galloway once more. The One-Who-Has-Returned has my support."

"All in favour of Catherine as Honorary Chair, raise your hand."

Madeleine counted the hands, a good number of them.

"All in favour of TK Junior, raise your hand."

Some prodding resulted in a few raising their hands a second time, but even with that, the winner was obvious.

"We have a tie. Co-chairs this year are TK Holmes and Catherine Blackwood, nee Lennon. The meeting is adjourned." Smoothly Madeleine scanned the crowd as it headed for the bar, then narrowed in on Catherine, who plastered a bright smile on her face. "You understand," Madeleine said over the din, "that we couldn't let TK off the hook for that donation."

Catherine genuinely beamed. Madeleine hadn't doubted her wild promise.

~ 4 ~

REBECCA CROSSED THE SPONGY GRASS to the barn with the same kind of sinking feeling she had when she criss-crossed the graves in the old cemetery. The earth might open to claim her.

Although it was past the usual time to furrow the fields, she wanted to try again before the Historical Authority volunteers came and challenged her abilities. She wanted to prove that she needed none of them. The horse stood patiently as she hooked up the harness for the plough. nuzzling her for warmth as much as for the soft apple in her pocket. Dampness had worked its way through the gelding's coat. No matter how much she curried and towelled him, sores developed on his skin. He hadn't liked her greasing every bit of his hooves and forelegs against the wet, but she must. Bloodsuckers were breeding in the fields.

The blade sank into the ground and created the furrow as it should, which acted as a canal for water to rush in, sucking the topsoil away with it. There could be no traditional planting. Like last year, seedlings would have to be set by hand. She'd get the volunteers to do that back-breaking work. At least the wheat berries, broadcast late last fall were coming up as green as grass. The wild geese liked it too. Every morning for a week, she'd been out to shoot the geese in the fields. Today she stopped, unable to pluck one more carcass.

The ground was too wet for barley to survive. There was little hope that beans or potatoes would grow in a summer as wet as the Almanac forecasted. The weight of the rain took all the air from the soil, and without the sun, the typical foodstuffs of her heritage would rot at harvest. As they had last year.

The horse was fed and stabled. On the flagstone entrance by the kitchen door, she pulled the hem of her skirt out from the broad leather belt where she had tucked it in, and shook clods of mud from it before going inside the house. In front of the kitchen fire, she removed and hung up the thick moleskin shirt she wore, a boy's shirt; the dirt would brush off easily but only if it was dry. She slipped on a starched cotton day blouse that had been warming on another hanger. Deftly she fed a strip of tiny seed buttons into the loops, one after another as endless as the falling rain. Always, women's clothing took time, but in two weeks, the volunteers would come and she would not offer any evidence of her grief to the gossips. She would make herself dress properly.

Even on the last Founder's Day, the day her parents were drowned, she'd been generous. She'd stayed home because of her pride. Because she'd had enough teasing about being an Indian lover from her classmates. At dinnertime, she banked hot coals in the kitchen hearth and spooned grease into a pan on the trivet over the fire. As she breaded chicken breasts and legs for frying, she heard rapping at the door. Quickly, she dusted the flour from her hands and pulled the apron up and over her head. She'd been reading a romance all afternoon, so the story of lovers in the wilderness lingered in her imagination. She opened the door.

There stood the town's mayor, holding not an offering of game but an umbrella. Beside him was the minister, rain dripping from the brim of his felted pilgrim hat, which historically speaking, was outdated by the time of the western expansion. To be charitable, he might justify it by its practicality, as the beaver pelt was superior in keeping his shoulders dry in the rain. Behind the men was a bevy of women in modern Sunday dress, appropriate for town but not on her family's homestead. They had the appearance of turkey vultures, faces flushed red. Rebecca stared. With their bare legs and painted toes, they looked like savages.

They asked to come in, but she'd stood square in the doorway, blocking their entry. Something about the women's red-rimmed eyes and anxious hand-wringing put her off. One doesn't invite misery inside.

Over and over, the pastor said, "There's been an accident. We're so glad we've found you at home. Could we please come in?" The grease Rebecca had left in the iron pan must have spit onto the hot fire. Acrid smoke filled the kitchen. The women took this as an opportunity to push their way past her, tut-tutting over the state of things.

"Get a fan," said one.

"They don't have power."

"But the chicken. The meat will spoil without refrigeration."

Rebecca stood aside for the men to enter and shut the door, then pushed past the women and their fear of the fire. She opened the flu wider and the smoke rose up the chimney again. She banked more hot coals around the pan, added more grease, and set the chicken parts in the pan. Those women didn't know a thing about her.

"Oh, you poor child. You'll come with us."

"Yes, we can't have you living alone. You might set the house on fire."

"Or you could die of food poisoning."

"Get your things, you'll come with us."

The minister told her that her parents were dead, and that two other families had suffered losses as well. It was best that she hadn't been there after all. "Very fortunate," he told her.

She refused to go with them. It was simply beyond her abilities. If it was true, she thought, she would discuss arrangements with the undertaker about getting Josiah Carpenter to make traditional coffins. She would see that her parents were buried properly, side by side, in the family burying ground at the hill on Massie Creek. With her back to the table, her hands holding the edges for support, she told them, "I will finish making dinner tonight and when the rain stops, I will go to town and see if my parents truly have drowned."

Her words had little effect. The mayor kept saying he was so sorry. "It's Founder's Day. Jesus! We always put a flotilla out on the river. We had no warning about a deluge. The weather just sprung up so fast."

The minister took her hands into his. "It's God's will."

"Like the twisters of 1974," said the mayor.

She pressed the minister's soft hands to comfort him, as graciously as she could, saying, "At least they went together." Not a true note rang in those words. Her parents would come home. What could she do in the meantime? A mug of something warm might settle them, and the poultry was frying up nicely. "Please stay for dinner. It'll be no trouble to bring in another chicken."

The women gasped. They chorused, "Get your things and come with us."

"I will not leave my home." She held back from adding that she would burn in hell first.

The mayor looked at her as though seeing her for the first time, with sudden understanding in the way a parent might have. He gathered the others and herded them out, leaving Rebecca to tend to her supper. The goose was young and fat, crisping nicely. She turned a breast over but it slipped from the tongs and a ball of grease shot from the pan onto her blouse. She cried out. She'd forgotten to put her apron back on. Now the blouse was spoiled.

She found her parents that evening in the church narthex, laid out beside the others who'd also drowned. It was all the people of Xenia, Ohio, could do in one day, the recovery of the bodies taking so much longer than the drownings. Rebecca went through the rituals she remembered from her grandmother's death. At eighteen years of age, she was still a child in the eyes of the state, but she summoned up what authority she could. After all, she would turn nineteen in three weeks. "It's just so sudden, so unexpected," people said, unable to console the stiff girl who stood before them.

~

On the exact day Rebecca turned nineteen, the Historical Authority sent their lawyer, Mrs. Claire West, to speak to her.

Rebecca was expecting it. She brought a bucket of coals from the kitchen into the Colonel's study, and she set a piece of hardwood on top. It was October. The rain had chilled the house as well as the land. If she wasn't careful, the damp would infect the homestead with mould. The two-storey, six-bedroom cabin was in as good condition as when the Colonel and his sons built it more than two hundred years ago, and she would keep it that way. A handful of green herbs tossed on the fire created a pleasant, fumigating smudge. Mosquitoes remained a problem.

She watched for Claire West from the eight-pane window in the study. The lane was a gumbo of mud, but it didn't matter. Cars parked out by the road to preserve the truth of the homestead. By the time Mrs. West made it to Rebecca's door, the rain had eased to a mere spit. The attractive lawyer wore knee-high rubber boots and carried her briefcase in one hand, high-heel shoes in the other. Originally from Minnesota, this fair-skinned woman had married a local man whose family had Indian blood. Rebecca's parents had mentioned her favourably, saying she didn't hold with local prejudices and neither did they.

In the study, Mrs. West pulled up the visitor's chair with the cabriole legs to the Colonel's desk, and spread her papers out on the polished ironwood. While she organized, Rebecca took her place in the Colonel's chair on the far side of the great desk, and studied the books that lined the room: classics from Europe in English, French, German, Latin, Greek, Spanish and Italian, treatises from the early colonies, and words from the statesmen who founded America.

The Historical Authority wanted her off the property. They'd always wanted her family gone so they could tell history the way they liked it, the way it was written after the fact to excuse the expansionist behaviour of the new American union. Rebecca and her parents kept to the earlier truth. Their reality lay between the lines of 1797 and 1820, in the house as it stood then with its outbuildings, when briefly, Xenia was the capital of the newly created state of Ohio, and the land to the west was mythical.

"May we begin?"

Rebecca nodded.

"You are within your rights to stay on the homestead," said Mrs. West. "However, I must read you the terms of the trust, as well as the offer of the Authority to buy you out."

"Yes, Ma'am," said Rebecca. Meek-seeming, she let the lawyer-words flow over her. When they trickled to a stop, she simply refused the buy-out by stating the words she had practiced, "I do not agree."

The complicated part came next, as she signed many papers to that effect, worrying that one might hold a fifth column and the homestead would slip away through legal treachery. Mrs. West had a lot of explaining to do, and Rebecca was pleased to find her beyond reproach, though the same could not be said of the Historical Authority. Mrs. West defended her employer.

"You come from self-reliant people, like my husband," she said, "but the Greene County Historical Authority has an obligation, moral and financial, to care for you, especially as you are living alone. Next, I'll go over your obligations to them and their obligations to you under the revised conditions of the trust. They are minor adjustments. You can agree to the new terms, or not, as you choose, but it would be wise to see this as a partnership."

Rebecca nodded, fearing uncomfortable terms might have been slipped in since her family lawyer had last advised her. He'd said there was no need for the buyout, as life insurance had left Rebecca with a comfortable living. It was her decision if she wanted to stay. Very aware that she represented the last of her family, she looked Mrs. West straight in the eyes; the woman smiled back, understanding that any unreasonable shackles imposed by the Authority would be hotly contested.

"As agreed to in 1832 between James Galloway, Junior, and the State of Ohio, and in 1887 between Greene County and William Galloway, *the homestead and lands belonging to Colonel James Galloway and his heirs will remain intact as a living history to the Northwest Frontier in perpetuity as long as a direct descendant of the Colonel shall remain living true to such conditions and so occupy the property, to the end that all subsequent generations of Greene County and the peoples of the Ohio Valley shall have access to such a living history. The upkeep of the property and livelihood of the tenants is to be funded by monies held in trust and these are to be matched by the state as such monies prosper and in keeping with inflation.*

"The trust has been extremely well managed and it remains viable. You have money and will have a say in the investments when you are twenty-five.

"The following are amendments. For insurance purposes, you are to keep a cell phone on the site. You will use a computer to keep records. Volunteer participation and public education has been scaled back this fall and winter to allow for a time of adjustment, but by the late spring, a full-time volunteer co-ordinator will work with you on educational programming, as well as to direct the volunteers in the daily operations."

Rebecca raised her eyes a second time to the lawyer's. She swallowed hard before nodding her agreement to this. A volunteer co-ordinator. That was her daddy's joB

~ 5 ~

OVER THE PHONE, CATHERINE EXPLAINED to Thomas that none of the locals were any the wiser about the fact that she had not approached the Galloways, or anyone in Ohio, about coming to the celebration. It was a promise made in the moment. The connection had just popped into her head.

"I simply accepted their best wishes."

"But why would you promise such a thing?" Thomas asked.

"Because, dear one, the other thing that popped into my head would have been disastrous."

"Tecumseh's remains."

"But this is brilliant!" Catherine said. "I called the Historical Authority in Ohio. There is a homestead where the direct descendants of Rebekah Galloway still live as historical re-enactors. Well, only the daughter is there. Her parents recently drowned and they tell me that she is going through a difficult time. Luckily she's nineteen."

"Drowned? What's luck got to do with it?"

"We're lucky she isn't a minor and doesn't need anyone's permission."

"Cruel heart!"

"Thomas, it's a once in a two-hundred-year opportunity."

"What did the girl say?" he asked.

"I can't get a hold of her. They gave me her cell phone number to call, warning me—if you can believe this—that the homestead is without modern connections *and* in a dead zone. Making contact would be the equivalent of winning the state lottery."

"Surely the girl leaves?"

"Not often. And she's a technophobe." Catherine smiled into the phone. "What they don't know is that we have the master of microwave technology on our side."

"You can't ask Hiram to interfere in this."

"No, but his side-kick James might offer to help. It never hurts to ask."

~

A short time later, Thomas called again. He demanded that Catherine pack up and leave as planned.

"Did Hiram call you?" she asked.

"Of course! James had the good sense not to agree to your little plan. My god! you told Hiram that you needed him to *use his magic waves to juice up the cell towers in Ohio.*"

"Oh, I wouldn't have said that. Not ever."

"He said those were your exact words. You've managed to worry him a great deal."

"I know it was wrong—the 'juicing up' part—as soon as the words were out of my mouth." Catherine felt her cell phone growing warm against her ear and held it away. "I did apologize."

"It goes beyond that. It is simply not safe to stay on the farm."

"Actually, it's more stable here than it is in Toronto," Catherine said. "Even Hiram said so. Anyway, you get used to it, the changes in the land. The roads are the same and the people too, only there's fewer of each. Besides, I have a backup plan if the girl can't come."

"Let me guess," Thomas said. "The bones."

"It is possible they are in a private collection."

"We have no leads."

"Humour me for a moment. It isn't *proper* for someone to own these things. They could never be displayed unless it was at a time like this—the bicentennial—when moral lapses might be less controversial if the collector was to put things right."

"Forget the bones," Thomas told her. "Focus on the girl."

"She can't be reached by phone."

"There are other ways. What would entice a girl of that background and age to come up to Flood Zone Four?"

"It's still Chatham County to us." Catherine thought for a moment. "You mean a gift."

"I could, say, get a hearth kit."

"New pots and pans?" Catherine snorted. "What teenage girl wants that?"

"Do you have a better idea?"

"Have all the crates been sent?"

"Not nearly."

"There is a colonial gown," Catherine said, "made in Boston. Hugely impractical for a homesteader but very romantic. Any re-enactor would die to touch it, let alone wear it. I'll look up the crate number and take care of the paperwork so that it gets through customs."

She could hear Thomas's breath labour as he wrote down the details.

"Will you come down and see me?"

"How are the roads?"

"Not bad. Mine is built up like the pictures you see of the roads in lowland Belgium during World War I, with marsh and mud on both sides and barely enough room for two farm trucks to pass. You'd have to back up if you met with one of those huge cultivators. But no one uses them anymore."

"Sounds lovely."

"Really, you should come. The air isn't as dank as Toronto's."

"You need to finish up and get out of there this weekend."

"Impossible. Too much to do. Cancel the truck."

Thomas heaved a mighty sigh, but no expletive. "I have meetings this week and the next. By the following week the ROM collections should be gone. I could bring some of our new materials down there and test them out—with your expertise. The kids are telling me to find a way to use the moisture, not fight it." Then he shouted, "Jesus Christ! You know this lengthy stay is not part of the plan."

"Have I ever told you that I love you?"

Thomas was silent, except for his breath, harsh, then softer. "You say that, my dear, but you've changed our plans. I don't want to lose you."

Catherine started to shake and tear up. Unable to speak, she coughed out a silly laugh and rang off.

~

Thomas was not laughing when he got off the phone. He had a missed call from Clementyne. She'd likely heard about Catherine asking Hiram for favours.

Hiram was aligned with law and order. The boy had grown up in a disputed land where he experienced war, the instant shattering of lives. His parents had been rather bitter immigrants, angry that they had to leave their land in the hands of "squabbling cousins" as they called their respective peoples. It made sense that Hiram should come up with a fair and elegant solution to stabilize border areas. It made him a good, trustworthy husband, and oddly, the most powerful counterpoint Clementyne could have found to himself. The Safety Net had stopped the flow of goods and this had set Thomas' trade back enormously. He had been angry at first. For Clementyne's sake, Thomas and Hiram had to set up a "do not ask" policy between them as one tried to close borders, the other to smuggle goods out. It was extremely bad form for Catherine to ask him to interfere.

Catherine should be in Sudbury protecting the collection and ingratiating herself into the new structure of the Royal Ontario Museum. They had agreed it was the best plan. Thomas couldn't go yet. He was working on a joint project between the ROM and the Smithsonian to refit the museum. Catherine should be at the other end to ensure her collection stayed intact. Just as artifacts became fluid in times of change, so did the hierarchy of experts and their positions in the bureaucracy. By staying in the flood zone, she risked her career.

He set the table for lunch and re-heated last night's beef curry in the microwave. A finger of bourbon was in his coffee mug. While the microwave hummed over the drone of the dehumidifiers, he turned his clothes on the open rack, examining them for signs of mildew. Satisfied, he pushed the rack into a storage closet, turned on the ultraviolet lights and shut the door. He sipped from the mug until the curry was ready.

He didn't mind staying behind. At least a million people still lived in the Greater Toronto area. According to projections, the weather would remain unstable for another five years. His fellow citizens would continue to struggle against fungal infections, the fouled water supply, bouts of dysentery and pneumonia, the unreliable and unsafe power supply, the structural damage to buildings and roads. Most who stayed were older, or poorer, either afraid or unable to leave the only home they knew. Others, like Thomas, were ready to take risks in order to profit. With food, water, power and medicine hard to come by, the underground economies had opened up. There were opportunities for speculators. And if Toronto couldn't dry out? Who would cull her treasures? Staying to refit the museum was an investment either way.

He washed up the dishes. Catherine had good instincts. She deserved some personal time. Perhaps this bicentenary project would capture the interest of the federal government. The idea of including Rebecca Galloway could strengthen cross-border ties. He wasn't sure that the dress in crate Col10434: drawer 511 would be enough, considering what Catherine was asking the girl to do. At least he was in a position to put out feelers for other artifacts that might help with the wooing.

In his field, old stuff was truly priceless; money alone didn't give things value. Public collections tended to be icebergs with only the tip on display. Ninety percent of any collection was submerged in storage vaults, held as leverage to acquire more prestigious items. Acquisition was a thrilling chase, the negotiations rigged with surprises. An aura of power surrounded the owner of the rarest items. Possessing an artifact could be transformative, the difference between knocking on a locked door, and having the key in hand to open it. Tecumseh's bones could be such a key. However, in the past when collectors took possession of that kind of relic, Thomas had seen more disasters than benefits. If the bones could ever be authenticated. So many skeletons had been presented but none had the right height, or the famed femur with the tell-tale fracture. Even Tecumseh could fall off a horse.

For Catherine's sake, he would ask around for a more enticing artifact to woo Rebecca Galloway. Everyone knew the spurious romantic story about Tecumseh and the girl's namesake, which would inevitably raise the question of the warrior's final resting place. A discrete strategy.

Thomas pulled the plug and watched the tiny bit of dishwater drain away into the clear plastic tubing and shrugged. His clothes should be disinfected by now. The big man stripped down to nothing and went into the storage closet to stand where the clothes rack had, his arms held high above his head, his legs apart. The bank of ultraviolet lights mounted to the wall would kill the fungal infections that constantly invaded his skin at a microscopic level. It was a ritual that had to be repeated, often. The process was aging him too quickly, he thought, eyeing the fine lines on his tanned skin and how they cascaded down his arm and crumpled across his shoulder. Having counted to ten, he turned, started the count again.

~ 6 ~

RAIN CONTINUES TO PRESS up against the soft belly of North America. Gently, gently rain washes up the funnel-shape left between mountain ranges and peaks in Ohio State, then rolls back down the watershed to the Gulf of Mexico. At the same time, rain continues to flood the Great Lakes, looking for the tipping point at which the two watersheds will join.

Earth churns magma in counter-movements against the pressures on the surface. She moans softly so that rain pauses to listen.

Rain falls and eases.

Again, again.

Falling. Easing. Falling.

Earth groans. This time, the stars hear her.

~ 7 ~

THE RAIN THINNED, THEN PAUSED for the first time in months, and so did she with the wonder of it. Shading her eyes against an unnatural brightness, Rebecca stood at the kitchen door. A wraith-like mist appeared in the weak sunshine and seemed to stroll up the lane like the devil himself. Wrapped in that impish mist was a man with a package under his arm. She hadn't ordered anything. The FedEx man side-stepped the puddles, had her sign a receipt, and then put the package into her hands. He turned and plodded back into the mist, mud from the lane balling up on the soles of his boots until his feet were encased and his knees showed the effort with each progressive step. Then he was gone.

Rebecca shut the door and set the box on the table. Carefully she teased the knots loose, saving the string and brown paper. Inside was a thick cardstock box, imprinted with the engraved name and picture of a Boston dressmaker.

M. Boyles
Mantua Maker from London
Established in Boston ~ 1797

Inside this, wrapped in tissue, was a nest of cream tulle over a light brown silk shot with threads of muted greens and golds.

"Oh my heavens!"

Rebecca put the lid back on the box and rocked herself. Pinched her arm hard. Be easy, young lady, she thought. This is exactly what I'd want if I was young Rebekah. At least, if she were me. I know she was so much better than me, not likely to have her head turned by fancy things. It'd be her duty not to covet what she'd seen in magazines or pictures printed from the Internet, but I am so much less worthy.

Rebecca wrapped the box back up and slipped it into a deep recess set high in the far side of the massive stone hearth, a place she'd been told to stay away from, and because of the childhood warnings, she reasoned this recess would be a good hiding place. The hearth would take away any dampness. The volunteers would never find it. As she slid the box in, it bumped against an old bundle. Some horrible thing that she wouldn't disturb, just push aside. There was room enough. Before the box went all the way in, she fingered the sender's fine penmanship, then impulsively kissed the return address, a readable if blurred script: Mrs. Catherine Blackwood, Chatham County, Canada.

Such temptation was hard to resist. Every day she pulled the box out to admire the tulle and silk. She made a sachet from a hanky embroidered with her initials and filled it with lavender and tucked it inside the box. She thought it might make the dress become hers. A week passed before she dared to lift it out by the shoulders to see if it would fit.

A note, hidden in the folds, fell to the floor.

Of course, there would be a note. No one sends such a heavenly item without an explanation and the terms attached to the gift. The writer stressed that it was a personal gift, the words clearly underlined on the vellum. Mrs. Blackwood was extending an invitation to a bicentennial celebration in Chatham County. Her committee had devised some play-acting events. They wanted to include an *authentic* connection to the man they considered a hero. Rebecca had been teased enough at school about this so-called "connection" to Tecumseh through her namesake that she was in no way flattered by the writer. Would Rebecca be the guest of honour? The dress was a gesture of international goodwill between nations to mark this historic occasion.

Sadly, for Mrs. Blackwood, Rebecca's family was in mourning, even if by family, she meant only herself. Reluctantly, she folded the dress back into the tissue and back into the box. Could she accept it without being obligated? Until she decided, the dress must remain in its place beside the old bundle. She needed guidance, a sign like a mass of Red Viceroys covering the privet hedge. Or a silky trail of moonlight across her bed. Or a hummingbird in the lower branches of the buckeye near the kitchen window.

In any case, with the arrival of this gift, the rain had eased up. The summer chores now seemed possible.

～

On the day before the volunteers arrived, the distant warmth of the sun touched Greene County, and a rainbow appeared over the river, spanning from one side to the other. Surely this was a sign she'd been waiting for, a bridge between shores, goodwill between nations.

Rebecca composed a brief letter to Mrs. Blackwood, blotting the paper often, then set a two-pound iron on it to prevent the ink from bleeding. She would keep the dress in the spirit it was given and counter with an invitation to Mrs. Blackwood to visit Greene County and see Tecumseh's homeland for herself. Did she have the right to do this? There was no one to ask, but hospitality was part of her family's creed.

～

To post the letter to Mrs. Blackwood, she had to go to Xenia, taking the deeply flooded rail lines all the way into town. They'd become her personal highways. Silently she made her way, skirting past businesses and houses like a ghost, paddling as close to the post office as she could without being seen. For some reason, it made people cringe to see her out on the water even so many months after the capsize of her parents' boat. To be fair, they hadn't been the only ones to die, and there had been a number of others drowned since. Classmates of hers. The very ones who had teased her every day while they studied Cooper's *The Last of the Mohicans*. In the novel, Colonel Munro took a native woman for his wife. Because of that native blood, the author proposed that Munro's daughter, Cora, was destined to love the Mohican Uncas. Who else would take her? Her classmates took up the idea, and wondered every single day, out loud, whether the hack, Cooper, wrote his novel based on the Galloway family and their friendship with a proud Indian firebrand, the last of his kind in Ohio. They badgered her with silly questions, but the way they asked was so personal. Why did Rebekah leave Xenia as the war broke out? Surely she could have married anyone, so why her cousin? Why did Tecumseh go off and die? Did she break his heart? Did she have Tecumseh's love child? Was Tecumseh's blood still coursing through Rebecca Galloway? It was a stupid book to study in school, thought Rebecca, a waste of time, Cooper's sad attempt at romance on a frontier he'd never experienced. Mark Twain was the better author, more honest the way he stuck to his own times.

And now the voices of so many classmates were silenced—the twins Gilbert and Mitchell McCoy, Ann Lindemood, Jesse Carpenter, Ellen Burch and her little sister Martha, Simon Kent, Zachary Starr and Rob Hannahs. There was no mercy for fools or innocents with this rain.

~

She tied the canoe fast to a clump of willows and clambered through them to solid ground. Setting her skirts straight, she stood and buttoned her good jacket tightly around her neck so the black worsted covered her white blouse except for a bit of the limp high collar.

She marched into the post office and asked for an international stamp. Business at the second wicket stopped. There was Mrs. Claire West, lawyer for the Historical Authority, eyes narrowed.

"It's good to see you, Rebecca."

"And you too, Mrs. West." She bobbed a half-curtsey.

"I don't see the buggy outside."

"No Ma'am."

"Did you get a ride in?"

"Yes, Ma'am."

"Can I give you a ride back?"

"That's kind of you, but I have a ride waiting for me as soon as I've finished my business."

"Another time, then?"

"Yes, Ma'am."

Rebecca pulled the coins from her purse and paid for the stamp. She felt eyes on her back as she left the post office. She made herself walk towards the library rather than back to the canoe. There, she looked up the War of 1812 and Chatham County. Nothing of interest. Loyalist deserters fearing more reprisals. American sympathizers run out of their homes, a few hung for treason against the British and their cleared land confiscated. Indians were pell-mell everywhere, fighting and falling when they should have stayed out of it. She spared a glance at the framed image of Tecumseh in the foyer as she left. Not the most handsome of men. He wasn't her hero and never would be. He hadn't died protecting his home, his people. He'd run.

~

By the time the first round of spring volunteers arrived, Rebecca was bathed and had applied the *3-C Ointment*—calendula, chickweed, comfrey—below her breasts and to other dark areas where her skin was raw and itchy. She applied talc from her dressing table across her chest, then toweled it off when it clotted. She pulled a comb through her dark hair before piling it on top of her head. Curls were teased out to fall alongside her temples. She was dressed in light cotton undergarments. A bit of pin tucking and lace edging was a sign of her family's status, that they'd come to the west from a more civilized place. The cotton clung to her skin. She'd rather wear woollens but it was getting harder to find the fine weaves that were "walked" into a cloth smooth enough for undergarments. All winter, she had spun yarn for vests, not needing anything better than firelight, her fingers so skilled. Plying it was a two-person job and hopefully one simple enough for the awkward teens that the Heritage Authority had hired. The boys always wanted to get fitted with flintlock pistols. They would strap them to their hips and wear them slung low and tied at the leg. This year, someone other than Rebecca's father would have to explain how long it took to tamp and pack the powder and ball. Thank goodness, it would be too damp to work. Did they know the odds of killing themselves were about as much as killing their enemies? Some of these boys would become good shots with their pistols. They'd be the ones raised by the re-enactment crowd, their parents fiercely fighting this battle or that against the South or British or Indians, though the battles were won or lost long ago.

The homestead had always been a place of learning and diplomacy, perhaps the only one in Ohio associated with an Indian hero that was not tied to a bloody massacre. The Colonel could be credited for that. In the coming months, it would be up to her to make sure the volunteers understood the real value of this land, why they'd come to live on it in the first place.

~ 8 ~

LEDGERS AND BOXES OF NUMBERED STICKERS were stacked on the oak table that seated twelve. The dining room was the least likely room to produce bones, a good place to start the tedious work of cataloguing, something any intern or student could do. But it was Catherine's history and the ROM wouldn't insure any help. She found the massive mahogany sideboard to be a world of its own with drawers, inset trays, cupboards and rails; it'd been hauled to the First Line from Massachusetts by her family in 1822, crammed with linens, silverware, and china settings ever since. Plates jostled on the rails.

She hated the job, but it took her mind off the problem of Rebecca Galloway. The girl had the gift; Catherine knew it from the tracking record. When would she reply?

The sideboard yielded one surprising find—a small packet of water colour paintings had been tucked inside the grandmother of all silver chests. In good condition, these tiny washes with quickly hatched lines showed the newly built farm house and outbuildings, out of place in a land of stumps. There was a nicer one of the river with geese migrating across a blue sky. Another was of a swampy field. Upended tree roots were piled into a fence along one side. Cows grazed in the pasture. It looked like the swampy field where Tecumseh had fallen, which hadn't been completely drained until the 1860s. The paintings weren't signed or dated, likely sketches by a family member stealing time from the work of a farm. Clementyne would be interested.

Catherine propped the bucolic scene of the battlefield along the back rail of the sideboard. "Where are you, Tecumseh?" She slipped the rest of the watercolours into an archival envelope and put them back into the silver chest, back into the sideboard.

Perhaps it wasn't necessary to pack everything up. She had the whole summer and early fall to enjoy a true family home. Everything that came next would be new, no matter what its age. Her things in new arrangements, in new places. For so many reasons it was too soon to pack up. What would visitors think if the rooms were bare? What kind of statement would that make when the bicentennial bureaucrats came out to see the battlefield? She needed to impress them, not frighten them. She would take an inventory, that would do.

She needed to impress upon Rebecca Galloway the importance of coming north for a few days. She rehearsed her pitch while she hit the redial button on the telephone and waited for a connection. A ring.

"Pick up, you silly goose."

An electronic voice droned on about the number not being available.

~

Everything in the dining room was recorded. Professional packers could crate it when she left. In the meantime, the wealth of good china would remain on display. Outside, the generators droned on, giving her the light she needed, but soon they would stop. An electrician had been working outside since early morning to restore the power to the house. She was tired of the pall of oil that hung in the air, not to mention the noise.

The good parlour was on the other side of a set of pocket doors. Today, she would tag the furniture in there, the ancient settees and tiny end tables. The cut crystal lamps with wildly sagging silk shades. The curved display case with its imperfect glass. The parlour stove would come as well. Thomas would know how to dismantle it.

The parlor was a room to inspire awe, good manners and morals in Sunday visitors. A smidgen of fear still reigned inside Catherine, of upsetting or breaking one of the many treasures. No wonder she'd gone into textiles with their sturdier kind of fragility. As a child, her job was to pass the glass candy dishes to guests, careful to avoid the pair of pewter candlesticks with tapers that stood almost three feet high. She must not touch the oil lamps with their deep red fonts and soot-edged chimneys. The ivory carvings and an engraved emu egg were okay to touch under supervision. In moments of weakness, the marvellous snow globe of the Eiffel Tower received her fingerprints. A great-great-great uncle brought it back from the World Fair in Paris in 1889. Her father had never been farther than Toronto, yet he could recount the wonders of Paris, recall the details of the Imperial Diamond and how the gentle music of Debussy played. His stories of a Negro Village with living people on display were barbaric and frightened her in a different way. She'd looked into it during high school and found newspaper articles cut out from the *Chatham Gleaner* stuffed in a trunk in the attic. Her great uncle had written diatribes on the gross mistreatment of African peoples. Her people had good hearts.

Was it likely that Tecumseh's bones were hidden in the house? The attic was stuffed with trunks and crates, but who would have kept them? If they were upstairs, how had they come there? As a favour, a safe-keeping, or a secret theft?

In the parlor, there were only tiny drawers to hold matches and wicks, coasters made of mica, too small to hide the bones. There was one other place, though, a recess under the floorboards just large enough to hide slaves from bounty hunters. A suffocating space but it had saved lives. She peeled back the rug and pried up the boards. Dust, a few buttons, a drawing by Clem of her father, and his favourite cap. She'd hidden it there after he died, after he had been crushed in a tractor accident. No one thought to stop him from driving at his age. Her mother lasted four years without him. Their bodies were buried side by side and their stone markers would remain with the land, but her memories of them were with the house. They would have been heartbroken to see the damage the water caused. How was Catherine to tag and classify and ship this?

She took a break on the back porch, her father's cap pulled down over her forehead keeping the soft rain from her face. The electrician came around to talk to her, tugging the peak of his cap in greeting, a cap with logo of the same co-op as her father's. She offered him a cigarette but he waved it away.

"The house is hooked up to the power lines again."

"All clear then?"

"The roof is good. No water in the walls. It's a well-cared-for house."

"We've tried."

"Other folks have too. The rain takes what it chooses."

Catherine looked at him, the lost look on his face fleetingly brief. He wiped his forehead and set his cap back on his head.

"I'll do the barn after lunch."

Catherine nodded. There was something else he wanted to say, and he hemmed, then started.

"Janice wants to know if it's okay to reuse towels that have been bleached but still have the black stains."

"If it's coming out of the dryer that way, the mildew is dead. Just watch for new spots."

"I'll let her know."

"Tell her to call if she has any more questions."

He nodded his thanks. "I'll shut off the generators before I go. You'll want to keep them filled with oil and ready in case the lines go down again."

Late in the afternoon, Catherine heard his truck leave. With the unholy noise of the generators turned off, she could hear the river lap against the sandbags at her back door. It was the loneliest sound she ever heard. She rang up Rebecca Galloway, listened to the cellphone ring, then cut off. Then her phone rang, strikingly loud in the quiet house. She almost dropped it. It was Madeleine French, the postmistress as well as the working chair for the Bicentennial.

"You have a letter from the Galloway girl. We stopped deliveries last year, so I'll hold it here until you come to pick it up."

Catherine checked her watch. "I'll be there before you close."

~

Simple and well penned, Rebecca stated her sincere appreciation for the gown but flatly refused to attend the Bicentenary. Her family was in mourning. Catherine sent a facsimile to Thomas with a query: *Have you been able to coax any treats from the Smithsonian?*

He called as the weak light of the day set behind the usual veil of mist. Not that she could see much of the transition from day to night from where she sat at the kitchen table. A swarm of iridescent beetles had pinned themselves to the west side of the house a half hour ago, blocking the windows with a dark wall of legs and underbellies. Catherine shuddered, took the phone into the parlour.

"I asked if anyone had seen trade silver that may have passed through the hands of Tecumseh," Thomas said.

"Apparently he offered thirty silver broaches to James Galloway for his daughter."

"Locally they say it was fifty pieces."

"She must have been quite the girl."

"Any luck getting one?"

"No. Besides, wouldn't she take it as an insult?'

"So why did you bother?"

"It got me a virtual glimpse into the vaults," he said. "All the relics involving human remains have been removed. No one wanted the place to flood and for this kind of artifact to float to the surface, literally. No razor strops cured from strips of human flesh were to be found. A favourite memento for some."

"Don't be ridiculous."

"My feelings exactly."

Catherine pursed her lips, and Thomas broke the silence.

"How are things at the farm?"

"Fine." At least he couldn't see the silent horde of beetles or wonder what other horrors lurked in the changed countryside. "So, the Smithsonian has nothing."

"Right," he said, "but my contact knows someone who picked up a locket from a pawn shop, of all places. She said the collector brought it in to be verified and it turns out this locket was an engagement gift from Rebekah Galloway to George Galloway, circa 1812."

"You bastard! You have a locket and you didn't tell me."

"We don't have it yet. According to my sources, it won't clear Hiram's blasted Safety Net. It's been registered somewhere."

"But you have a plan."

"If you're up to it, I do."

Catherine was to drive through two flood zones, cross the border into Buffalo and pick it up. Then she could post the parcel within the States to Rebecca. His contact promised it would make an exciting gift. Catherine whole-heartedly agreed.

She purchased more note cards from the Chatham County Historical Society and practiced writing with a quill pen. Of course, a lefty always smudged, with the result that her handwriting distorted into larger, rounder loops, impossibly long on the lower segments. Blotting was an art in this damp weather but finally a copy was made that approached Miss Galloway's penmanship. The girl on the receiving end must be impressed. This time Catherine made sure the gift came with a condition. Rebecca Galloway had to say yes.

If only she could offer the promise of higher ground or sunshine. The watersheds in Greene County, according to the Weather Network, continued to recede from their high-water marks, whereas they reported Chatham County waterways were incrementally rising. Not true. From the upstairs windows, she could see lines of sludge marking the high water points. To her eyes, the flood water looked like it was going down, and the shoreline was quite foul from the life and garbage it'd taken on its journey. As the weather grew warmer, it would stink. At least her parents had left bush along the river, and put in rows of evergreens to the north where the battle had been fought. The trees blotted up some of the excess water. And they blocked the view.

~ 9 ~

CATHERINE DROVE AWAY FROM THE FARM in the dark before
dawn in a race against the cycle of morning fog. James had laid
out this plan, and Hiram backed him up, saying it had the best
chance of success. It was up to her to carry it out.

Climbing out of the lake bottom, she took the 403
highway down to Niagara Falls where she would cross the
bridge in Fort Erie. The windshield wipers were steady,
slowly pushing aside the droplets, but failing to clear the
varying thicknesses of mist that slapped across the
windshield, at times like a monster, or like the curtains in a
carwash. As she neared the Niagara escarpment, the mist
thickened into a uniform fog. Veiled glimpses of a waterway
or the escarpment leapt out and disappeared.

Catherine wondered how Rebecca Galloway coped. The
family wasn't part of the consumption-based, guilt-ridden
broader citizenry and it must seem unfair to her to have lost
her parents to global warming. They'd hardly made a carbon
footprint. At least the homestead had survived the flood,
although it was likely in a similar position to her farm with the
fields underwater. How would that girl preserve herself if her
home was carried away?

She stopped the car in Fort Erie and stared out at the
Peace Bridge. The wide mouth of the river had drunk in more
of Lake Erie than one could ever have imagined. In the last
year of sunshine, almost five million cars crossed the Peace
Bridge. Not now. Cars trickled across, one at a time like water
striders, the surface of the road only inches above the rushing
waters. God-damned rushing water. Always rushing.

Nothing James had said prepared her for the state of the
bridge. This was the only route if she insisted on driving. She
told him that she hated flying, but she was really concerned

about the Safety Net restrictions and whether the items she took with her would pass through customs. She pulled out a cigarette from her pack of duty-paid and lit it.

The pilings of the bridge were submerged in the river. The bridge seemed to float, an effect amplified by a new system of cables suspended down its length. In the rear-view mirror, she watched a car slowly approach hers until it stopped beside her. The driver rolled down his window to say something but she couldn't hear him over the noise of the river.

"What?" Catherine asked.

"I said, 'I do it every day and it never gets easier.'"

He grimaced and drove on. She tossed her cigarette out the window and followed at a respectful distance.

Thomas had arranged for his contact to meet her in the European gallery of the Albright-Knox. It felt good to stand and walk, to let her legs shake out the tension of the drive and the perspiration fall rather than pool. She headed straight to the washroom where she checked in the mirror for damp spots on her wool suit. Like anyone these days, she was prepared to change her undergarments several times a day.

In the foyer, she noticed the Jackson Pollock was gone. Staff said it was in Alaska. By the time she got to the European gallery, she saw a clear pattern. The museum was hanging much lesser works. Paper had disappeared. Rembrandt had been replaced with Tintoretto, and the Poussins with pastoral scenes by Rosa Bonheur.

Catherine did not check her watch or make any other sign that she was waiting for someone. Security guards stood in the corners, a hovering presence even though every piece of artwork was coded for a security net that surrounded the building. Nothing could leave the building without the staff knowing it. James had explained that the Net wouldn't restrict little things like pens and pencils, hair pins and tie clips. She'd asked, "What if I wear my broach, the French one from the Early Empire? Would the scanners pick up on the gold, say, and restrict it?"

"No," he'd said, "they only scan for things already in the collection, or obviously dangerous substances—acidic or caustic things in amounts beyond what is normal."

Someone bumped into her. Catherine turned, saying, "I'm sorry," to a young version of herself from her student days. The contact shrugged.

"My fault, don't be sorry." She tapped Catherine on one arm while her other hand palmed something into Catherine's jacket pocket. She had been told to dress suitably for such a pass. Catherine wondered if the young woman appreciated the textured wool, a Canadian blend. However, the contact ignored her and opened up her paint box to continue with her copy of *Rowing Boat*. Catherine dared a curious glance. It wasn't bad. The sheep were half-sketched into the well-defined boat; the oarsmen were in their place, and the old Scot in profile. The distant shore was just a line. The water was a blank void.

Several miles away, in the privacy of her car, Catherine slipped the contraband from her pocket. It was heavy. The memorial-style locket did not open but had a face made of rock crystal. She stared at the thick lock of brown hair held against an edging of what might be silk needle-lace. A lock of brown hair. The back of the locket was soft yellow gold and engraved in curly, almost illegible script.

For George
A token of my promise
RG
Christmas 1812

"*RG.*" Rebekah Galloway. The locket was meant to sit in a man's vest pocket over his heart. George must have fingered it each time he dressed for church but not much more than that or the engraving would have been rubbed clear away.

Catherine strung a grosgrain ribbon through the hole where a chain would have gone, wrapped the locket in silk, then carefully slipped it into the small, jeweller-sized box that Thomas had made from aged Ohio walnut. He'd carved the flags of Canada and the USA crossed in partnership into the base. He assured her that these materials would pass through the Safety Net. She wriggled the box into a bubble wrap pocket, then forced it and the handwritten note into a courier company's cardboard sleeve. FedEx couldn't guarantee the delivery date but gave her a number to track the progress of the parcel on the Internet. It would take a week or more to get there. They were more concerned with the safety of their couriers these days than the speed of delivery. Then it might take Rebecca another week to write a card, and another two weeks before the surface mail delivered it to the Chatham post office.

~ 10 ~

THERE WERE A NUMBER OF THINGS Catherine forgot to tell Thomas. Sections of the highway had turned into a slurry of gravel and mud. Fog banks drifted across the lanes, wandering across without regard for his personal safety. When he finally reached her lane, the sedan fishtailed in, and he kept the gas to the floor as he ploughed his way up to the house, venting the tension of the whole trip as he fishtailed again. He got out.

"It's fucking Southwestern Ontario—not Bosnia or Pakistan! How the hell do you drive in this?"

Catherine pointed to the hose. "You can use that, or leave the car until this evening. It rains like clock-work every afternoon at five."

"You can't drive on these roads!"

"We'll put more weight in your trunk. It'll make the world of difference."

"And you, my heart!" Thomas said. "I can't believe I let you drive to Buffalo. I had no idea it was this bad."

Now that he'd finally made it to the farm, Thomas couldn't wait to leave. The house was claustrophobic. In Toronto, there was concrete and pavement. One could step out onto something solid. Here there was nothing but mud and water and stifling humidity as the weather grew warmer. Like clock-work, every morning a haze rose from the bush, then invaded the house. He could barely breathe. The air cleared somewhat with the five o'clock rain, as Catherine promised. His hair frizzed out; his groin was either itchy or burning from ointments and powders. A smell of cat piss pervaded the area between house and barn, and he, the city boy, knew which direction was north because of the psychedelic green moss hanging on that side of the house. The hall stand was filled with drippy, broken umbrellas. He threw them all in the trash. Catherine rescued them.

"Tipping fees are terribly high. Every scrap has to be shipped north."

"More artifacts for Sudbury."

"I can't even think about it."

The backdoor Thomas had painted five years ago was sticky to touch. The cupboards smelled of vinegar; the coffee maker was surrounded by a moat of black mould. At night, he swore he could hear the grass growing above the hum of dehumidifiers, pushing up between the floorboards of the parlour, for all he knew. From the bedroom window, he stared hard at the place where the moon should rise; a streak of spooky light ran across the water towards the house. He felt half mad from the lack of solid form, and sang under his breath, "*surely as the ghost that haunts this town.*"

In the morning he saw that Catherine was right. The car did drive better with the cement blocks. And besides the ghost of Tecumseh, there were enough sturdy threads of everyday life he could grasp onto when he needed a lifeline. A credit union kept the economy afloat. The municipal offices were open twenty-four hours a day in the upper rooms of the Tecumseh Tavern. There he met the agriculturalists, meteorologists, geologists and Canadian Geographic researchers who roamed Flood Zone Four in their boats and amphibious cars—helicopters some days—measuring and counting, photographing and recording. Proving the land was lost, the struggle worthless, though somehow stragglers managed to live here. He invited experts out to the farm to discuss the materials he had brought to test, while on the sly, he asked the Ministry of Natural Resources about their plans to divert the flood waters.

Of course, Catherine refused to believe that the diversion was real, that the farm and towns would be inundated by another ten metres of water by Christmas. According to her, the experts would find a plug and drain the bizarre leviathan of water away. The counties could dry out, and they would have their celebration and maybe plant crops next spring. Thomas couldn't shake her belief as long as all the levels of government supported the bicentennial celebration. It was her proof.

"See, there's no hurry. We'll ride this out."

"It only looks better on the Feds and the province to celebrate," Thomas told her. "They still intend to flood, like the Three Gorges Dam in China. They are making channels now along the Thames watershed."

"Never!"

It was like telling a four-year-old there was no Santa Claus.

Catherine made a point of introducing Thomas to the various stake holders in the festival who politely kept him at arm's length, as though he might utter a heresy and sink the project. The next time they were at the tavern, he made sure to buy enough rounds to loosen the Loyalist tongues. Stories of the days leading up to battle flowed as if it happened yesterday. The sightings of troops, of Tecumseh. A relative of Arnold, the miller, spoke of the destruction of the Chatham Bridge and how the retreating British had sunk their own bateaux and armaments to prevent the Americans from capturing the munitions.

"What kind of bridge?" asked Thomas.

"Wood. On cedar pilings."

"What kind of bateaux?"

"Flat bottomed. Stable.   The kind used on the small waterways all over the continent."

"We could build them," said Thomas, "and then blow up the bridge and sink the boats again."

"They never blew the bridge," said Matthew Crudge.

The table around him grew quiet.

"I've got an old set of plans for the boats," said a descendant of the old Arnold family.

"I've got enough timber," said Frank Dolsen. "No one's building houses anyway."

"The Colonel has some good sketches for the bridge," said another.

Crudge frowned. "We can build them, sure, but it's so sodding wet. We can't blow the bridge. They would have used powder."

The men around the table looked at Thomas.

"I might know someone who can help with that. I'll get Catherine to use her influence there."

"A toast to Catherine!"

She might, thought Thomas, still have an "in" with James despite asking him to hack the Greene County microwave tower a second time. Rebecca Galloway's phone still had no reception.

~

Catherine continued working in the house while he met with the men of the county, either at Dolsen's workshop or at the conservation area where the festival would take place. The roads were still a slurry of mud, but he stopped complaining. Like a boy, he came back with stories—like how Crudge had joked that the river was so thick, it would tempt Christ to get out of the boat and walk. They all wished that the water was clearer so the boats would be visible when they sank. Reserves Colonel Garnet Holmes, no relation to TK and an expert in the logistics of that old war, said that the murky water was a deliberate part of the scuttling strategy. The Americans were meant to come upstream and collide with the unseen bateaux. A pile up on the waterways.

In any case, Thomas explained, they decided the boats could be sunk off the current boat launch at the conservation area, but the shoreline might need some work to accommodate the crowds.

They were eating a cold supper in the kitchen, potato salad and slices of cold duck, wine from California where the sun still shone. Raisin pie for dessert.

"We're building docks too?"

"Makes sense."

"There aren't enough funds."

"Madeleine had a word with the Feds. The Army Engineer Corps is doing it as a special 'safety and prevention-rescue-launch-historical' project."

Catherine made a gesture with her wine glass to indicate that her nose was growing longer. "Liar."

"Their words exactly."

The bridge, she learned, would be tricky to place. Flood waters had made the shoreline risky to walk, and no one really wanted to go out in Matthew Crudge's little outboard to scout the best place. Thomas had been unable to wheedle a helicopter ride. Dolsen suggested viewing the river from the bridge that remained on Highway 2. They might see a solution by looking downstream.

"When we got there," Thomas told Catherine, "there was already a crowd and they were looking upstream. A mass of crate-like objects was bobbing in the water and coming our way.

"'Munitions on the loose!' Crudge said.

"'Caskets,' a bystander whispered. 'A sign of the Rapture.'"

"I warned you that they believed in it," Catherine said. "They keep calling me for advice."

"Do you believe?"

"Only that if they keep pressing their wool suits, the glare from the shine will blind St. Peter. They must remember to use a cloth between the fabric and the iron."

"They really have their best clothes out, ready to go?"

"Enough of them."

"If I stay here much longer, I might hope for the same escape."

"As long as you brought your best suit."

"In any case, it was true. The coffins were in amazingly good shape, swollen with the rain, quite buoyant on the river. Frank Dolsen pointed out the masses of drowned earthworms, like small islands and the air was thick with gulls."

"Thomas! You've become a storyteller."

He waved the comment away with his fork and continued.

"'Doesn't look at all like a second coming,' Crudge said, and he sniffed like a kid. 'More like a cattle break-away.' That was Dolsen."

"He would say that. His family is buried farther to the north in the same churchyard as mine. Higher ground."

Thomas nodded, looked at the pie, checked his watch.

"It's time for the news."

They listened to the radio for the official account of the floating caskets. Over the next few weeks, Thomas continued to follow the story as if his own mother had been unearthed. His reports became an irritating reminder of their precarious situation. It took the rescue service weeks to locate the last of the strays, some tangled in windfalls, others washing into fields. One casket made it past the mouth of the Thames into the big waters of Lake St. Clair. Long before then, Thomas bought a boat with an outboard motor and tied it to the back porch of the farmhouse.

~

Catherine finished cataloguing the ground floor—the parlour and dining room, the more often used sitting room and the kitchen. The bedrooms and attic were left. The barn would be left to Thomas. She found no signs of the bones, or anything native in the house so far. She often went to the attic where there was a widow's watch with a clear view of the land all around. Not a single thing rose up from the battlefield, no coffins or skeletons. Thomas cleared a storage area in the barn and rigged up some of the new conservation materials. There was no room in the attic to move. He'd been up to the attic again to take down another load: dressmaker forms, coat stands, lamps, tables and mouse-infested arm chairs.

"You're to leave any boxes of papers in the dining room. I don't want them in the barn. They're too irreplaceable to experiment on."

He stretched out his back. "If we're done here, let's eat out at the Tavern."

~

From the other side of the bar, Catherine and Madeleine French watched the men make their plans. Thomas had become popular among her people. Catherine wasn't sure that she liked this turn of events. She'd had to switch to iced tea, knowing she'd be driving him home. Unfortunately, he'd noticed that she'd started to smoke again.

"It stays on your lips."

"Damn." She had no higher ground to stand on.

Still, the big man was drinking a bit much. His new-found friends coped in the same way. She could hear them as they raised a toast to the dead, and to something else. Madeleine explained that they had found a site for the bridge.

"While the coffins were bobbing downstream, Colonel Hicks noticed they bunched together about a hundred meters upstream of the conservation area. The current narrows there. The Ministry finally gave us permission to build."

"Us."

"All of us are in this together." Madeleine clinked her rye and ginger ale against Catherine's ice tea, finished it off, and ordered another.

~

Thomas slept in the car on the way home, and Catherine would have left him in the passenger seat but he might wake up frightened and wander off and drown. She pushed him into the house and up the stairs. Half-way through getting undressed for bed, Thomas stumbled into the chair by the window. She turned the damp sheets down on the bed, then sat on the edge in her silk nightgown waiting for him to move again.

"Alright, then, let's talk," she said. "This building stuff is taking the edge off my whole purpose for being here. I want to place Tecumseh's bones in a grave on the day of his anniversary."

Thomas rubbed his eyes. "I've quietly—"

"Oh, quietly?"

"Yes," he said, "—asked after them. Guy St-Denis has a book on the subject, well-referenced. He concludes the bones are gone."

"Things like that don't disappear."

"I spoke with him too. Nice guy, local yet not too obsessive."

"Just last week there was a story about St. Anthony's finger in the papers—a perfectly preserved relic."

Thomas lurched onto his feet. "Holy Jesus, I hate the trade. To have the whole skeleton? Someone would have had to pick it clean."

"The book says the body was hidden in the river bank below the water mark. It was some time before his son came of age and could return for it."

"His son?"

"Who else would avenge him?"

"Enough of the apocryphuckal talk. If you would read the book, you'd know that story is bullshit." Thomas flopped back onto the chair and held his head between his hands.

"The Smithsonian?"

"They have nothing."

"Maybe a smaller museum, like the one in Illinois that stole the Inuit remains."

"I hope not."

"Some say he's wrapped in a beaded hide, possibly a wampum belt."

"And you can prove it?"

"Well, no. Just the book."

"Just the book?"

"The same one you read. It has a summary." Catherine swung her legs onto the bed, pulled a blanket over her. "Come, get into bed now."

"Realistically, what can I do?"

"Come to bed. Tomorrow we'll get Rebecca Galloway."

Thomas launched himself at the bed, rolled onto it. He turned his head to look at her.

"Would you be wooed by gold if your parents just drowned in the river out back? Would you cross many bodies of water to attend a festival taking place in a flood zone for a complete stranger?"

"You know damn well I would."

"Christ, I do know. Tell me, is it the idea of a man in buckskin that attracts you?" Thomas looped an arm across Catherine. She twisted to turn out the light but he pulled her close, his breath smelling of rye whisky. She giggled.

"Right, it's all about the sexy leggings and fringed jackets. The whole frontier Indian style. And him being buck-naked underneath."

"Quite the adolescent fantasy. Say more."

Into the dark, she whispered what she'd dreamed as a child. "He's riding a horse. He's like a wind that you want to catch. Then he's running silently by our open windows so that he could reach in and touch us without our knowing. He's telling us to be safe, warning us the Americans are coming."

"Hero worship."

"It was that."

She nudged him.

"You are my hero, silly."

Thomas had passed out. Catherine drew the covers over both of them.

~

In the morning before the mist could gather at the edge of the bush, she shook Thomas until he woke.

"Seriously, I want to do one thing right in this town. I want there to be one authentic event in my time that isn't disaster. I want the bones of this beggared warrior so that if I must leave this farm, the town will recognize me for putting an injustice to rest."

"Catherine, love, we don't know that an injustice has been done. Tecumseh would want you to look to your own safety. The rain will spare no one, however noble her intentions."

"The rain will hold off, I know it, until I find him."

~

On the warmer days, Catherine abandoned the attic for the coolness of the barn. Under her supervision, Thomas and two of Frank Dolsen's younger boys were packing up the old farm implements and equipment. The tractors and combines were auctioned when her father passed away. There was no son to take on the farm, and she had only a passing interest in that side of life.

They knocked crates together like it was play, then riffled through the tools. The boys knew the function of most, but not all. When they drew a blank, they called Frank up. Even Frank had to check with his circle of cronies and older relatives for some of the functions. Catherine made notes in her ledgers and passed out tags.

"What is the real value of this stuff?" Thomas was looking for a story for each tool, for some connection to history that would take it beyond the hard-scrabble life of a modern farmer.

The older Dolsen boy laughed. "You never throw anything out. As soon as you do, you'll need it."

"Exactly!" Catherine said. "Either way, it costs the same to ship to Sudbury."

"You could let it sink." Thomas hefted the small auger in his hands.

"Darling, we'll be done soon. Frank and the others won't build the bridge without you."

"No, they won't. Dad has to find more wood."

Thomas wanted to help in the search for wood. He didn't have the local contacts, but Catherine knew he had a way with bringing out the hoarders, and that she would lose them soon. She might get another half hour from them if she left now to make lunch. Frank's wife had sent over a generous amount of food, as the boys still ate so much. There was nothing to prepare really.

She went straight to her computer and pulled up the FedEx tracking on the parcel to Rebecca.

"She has it!"

Catherine dialed the girl's cell phone number.

~ 11 ~

LETICIA WEST, THE LAWYER'S DAUGHTER who claimed Shawnee blood on her father's side from way back, came quietly into the kitchen. No matter how she sneaked about, Rebecca could always sense her presence, awkward but not quite as foolish as the other young girls. Leticia had been two years behind her in school.

Rebecca tapped a fresh loaf from the last pan and turned to look at her. She did not resemble her older brother, the one the Authority hired to be the volunteer coordinator. He was dark-haired like his father, but had his mother's fair colouring and strong features. Leticia, on the other hand, was round-faced and brown as a berry. She handed Rebecca a small parcel.

"Look at how much it cost just to send it from Buffalo. Aren't you going to open it?"

Rebecca slit open the bloated commercial cardboard sleeve with a kitchen knife. An envelope from the Chatham County Heritage Society fell out, addressed to her in the same careful mature script as the dress parcel, but sealed with wax this time. Mrs. C. Blackwood from Chatham County. Why, then, was the package sent from Buffalo?

She looked into the sleeve, but whatever was inside was wedged in tightly. She shook it for Leticia's sake, who watched curiously but respectfully. Rebecca wasn't afraid to let her temper show with the volunteers. Even so, when Rebecca shrugged in defeat, Leticia reached out to take the parcel and give it a try.

Rebecca slapped the trespassing hands away. "You stay and set the table. I'll put this away." She took the package to her bedroom and closed the door. Inside the FedEx carton was a bubble-wrapped package and when she wriggled that loose, she found a box of wood, a jeweller's box from the look of it. It was swollen shut from the humidity. There was no time to prise it open. She'd have to wait until the others left. For safekeeping, she tucked the envelope and box under her pillow, then sat on the edge of the bed, popping the air pockets on the bubble wrap the way she had seen children do it. An amazing material. Even if the delivery van was caught in a washout, the package would float.

"Miss Galloway!"

"Rebecca!"

She heard Leticia's voice and another right outside her door. More shouts came from the kitchen, the panicked voices of frightened youth. It couldn't be a fire; the damp snuffed everything out. She rushed out anyway.

Leticia and her older brother flew down the stairs before her. They pushed aside the volunteers crowded in the kitchen doorway, gaping wide-mouthed at the hearth. Groans and gratings issued from the pile of fieldstone and mortar, yet the trivet held. The soup, though rocking, did not spill.

Rebecca flew around the table. She placed her hands on the warm stone hearth as though to take its great weight, her cheek turned towards the recess where the bundle and the dress were hidden. "You have that old bundle," she whispered, "and you have the gown. I don't know what's in the package but you will have it too. Just don't fall apart, not in front of them. I could not bear such a thing."

The kettle on the trivet stopped swinging; the hearth sighed, then was silent. Miles West gathered up the volunteers and the food for lunch and took them outside. He thought the kitchen might not be safe.

Speculation ran in circles around the table Miles set up on flagstones under the eaves of the barn.

"It was an earthquake."

"It wasn't a quake."

"It was a pocket of air in the mortar," Miles West said, but the volunteers had stopped listening to him.

"Remember the quake in 1812 when the Mississippi flowed north?"

"Remember? You idiot! You weren't even born then."

"I remember it from school, and this felt just like I read. Like we could fall into a crack if the earth wanted us."

"It wouldn't want the likes of you."

"My grandparents say it's the fracking. They have quakes all the time around Cleveland."

"That's my dad's job and he said that's horse crap."

"Your dad is horse crap."

Rebecca watched boys draw their pistols and pace off in different directions. "Fracking" sounded like coarse work, but it hadn't caused the hearth to shake, not this time. Thankfully Miles stepped in before she had to. From the kitchen window, she watched him direct the lunch cleanup and assign the afternoon chores. Then he spotted her and walked over, taking his time.

He'd been a year ahead of her in high school. His sister said that he had three more years of college ahead of him, and Rebecca wondered if this boy might become the permanent coordinator.

"Any more activity?"

"All's peaceful."

"Has it happened before?"

"Never."

"Any ideas?"

"Mass hysteria."

Miles laughed.

She kept her counsel and the day dragged out without much privacy for reflection. Others found the energy to speculate, even the Wests. She overheard Leticia whispering to Miles about how Rebecca hadn't yelled at anyone all afternoon, that the shaking must have frightened even her.

"She's just tired of us, and grieving too."

"She's had ages to get over it."

"She's been alone."

"Her choice. Don't you want to know what spared us?"

"The heat from the fire trapped moisture in between the hearthstones. I've got the mason coming out tomorrow to examine it."

~

The mist lifted in the late afternoon. Rebecca was prepared when Miles asked her to take the coals from the kitchen and lay them in the fireplace in the study. Without the haze of drizzle, the daylight lasted unusually long, making it easy to bed the animals for the night without lanterns and the insects they drew. Like the moths, the volunteers lingered no matter how brusque Rebecca became. They should have been too hungry. Who passed out the leftovers from lunch? Miles West? He came to her, said that his sister was willing to stay the night if she wanted some company. Rebecca threw up her hands in disbelief. "Get. Just get these people out of here and let me have my peace." Sharp as a hawk, she chased after every last person and watched them board the van.

Miles stood before her, speaking down to her, saying "The cell phone has been recharged and it's in the Colonel's desk. And I've left a box of flares inside the kitchen door. Someone might see them." Rebecca tilted her head sideways and gestured towards the bus.

"You are driving them home, aren't you?"

There were backward glances, especially from Leticia West. When the bus finally disappeared, she took a deep breath. It was time to act on her plan.

~

"Never mind how it seems," Rebecca addressed the hearth, "I'm only going to borrow your treasures so the mason can do his work."

She took the dress box, first, up to her room. If the house was reduced to dust when she opened the package, she didn't want to die wearing the black of mourning. It wasn't like she was dressing to go anywhere, but the gown deserved appreciation. She washed the day's work from her skin and powdered the unmentionably sweaty areas, changed into her best undergarments and stepped into the dress, fastening it one way, then another, unaccustomed to the fine closures. She kept her back to the mirror, and not daring to look yet, loosened her hair and brushed it into curls.

A whistling sound rose from the kitchen, not the high rising pitch of steam in a kettle or the hiss of a wet fagot releasing gas. The hearth was cold. It was a call, a note up and two across and then one higher. A question. She puckered her lips, found the right place between her throat and curled tongue, and whistled back something to the effect of *I'm coming.*

The whistle from below didn't surprise her near as much as her image when she turned to face the mirror. The light brown silk gown, shot with green and gold hung on a woman's body. The brocade shimmered with life and Rebecca blinked away her surprise. "I look lovely." Another whistle. Her hair must wait. She picked up Mrs. Blackwood's newest gift and letter, and carried them down to the kitchen.

"Dear Hearth, what makes you shake so? Surely not this tiny box. It weighs as much as a goose egg. How could it be anything to you?"

A clatter rose from the recess, sounding like old bones dancing, the way fiddlers play the sound of the dead rising, cracking their bows against the bodies of their instruments and sawing their horsehair strings until they snap and fly into the air like ribbons. In this case, cobwebs swung loose from the beams across the ceiling and spiders dropped in dizzy spirals. She brushed them aside with a towel, protective of her dress. Another whistle, this time clearly from the recess.

"Perhaps that old bundle wants rescued after all."

Cautiously, she put her hand up to it and drew it out. But in mid-air, it began to rattle so violently that her heart leapt and some kind of reflex made Rebecca press it against her chest the way she would have a thrashing child to keep it from doing itself harm. She scolded.

"Quiet there. Quiet."

Then she soothed.

"There, there, there. There."

She set the calmed bundle down on the table and looked between it and the jeweller's box. Mrs. Blackwell's gift held more interest, but first, she'd read the letter. Deftly she broke the wax seal and this time, Mrs. Blackwood begged her to attend the bicentennial in Chatham County. It gave no clue as to the contents of the wooden box. Yet this gift came with a condition, make no mistake. She would think about it later.

The box had no maker's mark, just an engraving of two flags crossed, American and Canadian. She slid the blade of a kitchen knife into the tight seal beneath the lid, working her way around each side until the pressure was released and gave her whole attention to the contents. Wrapped in blue silk cloth was a heart-shaped locket, a wisp of dark hair set under its crystal face. Instead of chain, a length of grosgrain ribbon was threaded through the loop on the back. Rebecca reached for the ribbon and slipped it over her head so that the locket hung against her chest. The table shook. The bundle! Rebecca slapped her hand down so hard that it jumped.

"Be still! Nothing beautiful comes to this house anymore and I will enjoy this."

Slowly, she turned the locket over and read the inscription.

For George
A token of my promise
RG
Christmas 1812

"It's from her."

The bundle growled.

"Whatever devil are you?" She reached her hand towards it as she would to calm a horse she didn't know or trust, and she touched the beaded wrapping tentatively. "I'm never to touch you, my mother said, but she's not here to explain. You be kind to an orphan and let me see what's inside. Though I fear you won't bring as much pleasure as this." She brought her other hand up and touched the locket. Electricity shivered through her, from locket to bundle, bundle to locket, until she quaked. She let go and backed away, then approached the bundle again. With shaking fingers, she attacked it, searching for a way to loosen the wampum that bound the deerskin. Inside, there were bones, as she feared, old bones: a jaw, a skull, ribs, scapula, feet and hand bones, long bones. The notorious fractured femur.

She stood back, held the necklace so that the lock of hair was in plain sight of the bones. "You loved her after all, didn't you?"

A noise sucked her breath away, the most frightening sound of the day—and it didn't come from the bundle or the hearth. Her cell phone was ringing in the old Colonel's desk, playing a popular dance tune she'd heard in high school. It made her feel faint in the head. The world as she knew it had come to an end.

The ringing would not cease. Her knees buckled as though the firm ground beneath the homestead was sliding beneath her. Rebecca walked like a drunk to the library and found the cell phone. A message flashed: INCOMING CALL.

A landline was easy to use. Just pick up the receiver and someone's voice was there. Or ignore it and the caller would go away. She shook the tiny phone but the ringing continued, a lewd string of words grinding at her, laughing at her. What kind of prank was this? It played over and over.

Rebecca crossed the yard by moonlight, the hem of her silk gown lifted well above the mud, the locket cool against her chest. With walls four feet thick, the milk shed should take care of the problem. Surely the batteries would be dead by the morning.

~ 12 ~

FROM THE BIG UPSTAIRS BEDROOM, and the attic above, they could watch for problems in the dyke, for erosion along the tiny elevation between the house, which stood at 188 metres above sea level, and the river at 186 metres. Wavelets lapped against the sand bags at the bottom of the slope where thick grasses languished like seaweed. On the highest bit of ground, Catherine had been talked into planting a new, water-based garden. They would eat lotus bulbs instead of potatoes for Thanksgiving.

They should have been in bed, asleep an hour ago. While she stared out the window, wishing she could smoke, Thomas pretended to read in bed. Lamplight joined the space between them. Catherine turned from the window, and they spoke at the same time.

"Let's call again."

She redialled the number. For the first time, she heard a ring tone, but after dialling for most of the day and getting nothing, she hung up automatically.

"Oh my heavens! We have a connection." She tried the call again.

"We have a connection! It's crazy, but it's ringing."

Thomas left the bed and stood next to Catherine with the phone between them.

"It is ringing," he said and kissed her.

Eight rings later, the connection cut out, and Catherine dialled again. Always eight rings, then a disconnect. Thomas tried calling on his phone. The same.

"The girl probably has it on vibrate in some drawer," he said.

Catherine nodded. "No voice mail."

He programmed Catherine's phone to speed dial and plugged it in. They fell asleep to the pulse of ringing, the disconnect, and more ringing.

~ 13 ~

A MOTH FLEW FROM HER HAIR to the only source of light and warmth in the kitchen, the oil lamp. It battered itself against the glass chimney until its wings were singed and it fell to the table. Rebecca watched the moth creep in circles, off balance, and then flutter into the exposed bones. It landed in the nasal cavity of the skull, wings beating in and out.

What had the family stories said concerning ghosts and restless spirits? She was no witch or medicine woman, but there must be a way to make the bones talk. That much was owed. When the winters were hard, her mother had gazed into infusions of roasted dandelion, deciding who to call on with small packages of food. Likewise, thistles had deep roots to call forth spirits. Mugwort and wormwood were herbs her mother had burned, but they exorcised the house of spirits. Rebecca wanted to call this one inside. She looked into the apothecary drawers in the sideboard. Musty smelling, then a whiff of lavender. Wasn't it said a cloth soaked in lavender attracted lovers? Could it bring out spirits?

Careful of the silk gown, she bathed her neck and arms with a handkerchief soaked in lavender, then reached under the bodice of her camisole to lay the damp cloth close to her heart, aware of the weight of the crystal and gold locket against her breast.

The bones remained still as stone. The moth looked all but dead. Wanting something to live in the night alongside of her, she bent over and blew on it. The moth flew up into her face, and she stumbled away from the table, putting a hand on the hearth for balance. An old woman, risen from the cold stones, transparent as glass, stared at Rebecca, examining her down to her very soul. Her empty eyes held onto the locket. Rebecca stepped back towards the table. The spirit stepped down onto the flagstone floor towards her in an old-fashioned colonial gown that rustled crisply, unaffected by the humidity. And lord, did that old woman have a voice, a sharp angry tone as fresh and bold as spring water from the well.

That locket should have been buried with George.

The apparition was too real, too detailed to be a hallucination. The ghost turned away and paced the slate floor, muttering as though she hadn't spoken to a soul in centuries.

I could have sworn the locket was buried with him. The carpenter must have taken it. May he rot.

She stopped beside the bones and fingered the beading of the wampum.

Think of my horror when I opened it. I tried to put him in the earth, but no amount of Christian prayer would take him. Dogs and foxes dug him out the same day he was buried. Then I put him in a box, under the shed floor, until the shed shook so much that all the nails fell out. Explain that to the god-fearing neighbours. When George died, I put the bones under my bed. A little strange, sleeping with him under our bed, a pillow of hops to bring me sleep, and horehound to stay the spirit's fascination, the scent on the sheets the only thing between us, a veil between living and dead.

"I think his spirit still needs some settling."

The ghost took up her pacing, long skirts swishing like reflective pools around her legs.

Nothing settled him in my day. Those damn Shawnee. They laid his corpse to air in the branches of trees, let the birds and beasts, the sun and rain, strip it bare, then carried it back to me because Tecumseh told them I could change their fate. He said that I would endure—Miss Rebekah Galloway—and that I would get a second chance. A chance to put the frontier on the right path, according to his heathen will. He was asking for the earth!

She stopped at the head of the table and stared down its length at the skeleton.

The yelping dog risks being shot. The wayward child is lost. We survived to build this home. His people are gone.

I never wanted the bones.

"Whose bones?" The ghost grew faint. Rebecca felt panic rise. She reached out for the spirit, still fading, then shouted, "Answer me!"

This one here?

Rebecca nodded.

He's the panther, the shooting star, the chief, the warrior, the enemy. He wasn't the only one among them who learned to read and write, but that man could talk.

"I knew it was him."

She looked up in triumph but the ghost had disappeared, absorbed back into the cold empty mouth of the hearth. The lamp flickered. The moth had fallen in among the bones, was trying to climb out. Rebecca reached in with her fingertips and picked up the brown moth and set it on the table. Its wings collapsed, flat and open. Round, grey eyes stared back at her.

~ 14 ~

THE MOMENT MILES WALKED UP THE LANE to start his day, Rebecca Galloway took him aside by the arm and marched him into the milk house. He knew he was blushing. The other volunteers watched, mouths open in surprise as they straggled out of the bus, shifting their historic garb to a neatness acceptable to the girl who ran this place. As Miles was pulled away, he could hear the comments.

"Ooh, he's in big trouble. She'll whip him for something he forgot to do yesterday and we won't be able to hear him scream. The walls are four feet thick."

"Or, maybe it's a booty call. And he'll come out with legs of rubber."

"Unless she kills him afterwards."

"Yeah, like a black widow spider."

In the dimness of the milk house, Miles could hardly make out what Rebecca was thrusting at him. Then he saw the glow of a cell phone. There was always a logical explanation, he found, when it came to Rebecca. At least she'd kept it. Still, he hesitated to take the phone because she was so rude. "It won't bite!" She held it out in a way that suggested otherwise. "That's what everyone tells me. But now that it's ringing, I can't make it work."

Miles reached out for it. This time, Rebecca pulled back from him, and he wondered if maybe the phone wasn't her only problem after all.

"It's been ringing?" he asked, hands by his side.

"All night. And when I tried to answer, it stopped ringing but I couldn't hear anyone talking. If there was a plug, I would have pulled it."

"No offense, but who would be calling you like this?"

"*Incoming.*"

Miles dared to smile. She softened, the panic leaving and she offered the phone again. When he took it from her, he noticed that her palm wasn't rough and calloused like people might think. She was a freak, maybe, but a girl too.

The phone flickered enough to show that the reception really was working. The same number was flashing, time again. "Do you want me to call it?"

"Yes, please."

"The battery is almost dead, but we can use mine."

Rebecca nodded.

Miles pulled his phone out from a deep pocket in his dark serge trousers. Rebecca didn't look the least surprised that he kept his phone on him. It was one of the worst crimes according to her. "Remember," his parents had said, "you are responsible for everyone's safety. Use your common sense around Rebecca Galloway and she'll respect you in the end." He'd kept his phone, not believing it would ever pick up a signal out here.

It took four rings for someone to pick up.

"Hello? Hello."

Miles held the phone out to Rebecca so that she could answer. She turned to speak at it. "Hello," she said tentatively. "With whom am I speaking?"

Then Rebecca cupped her hands around it, and his, and pulled the phone close against her ear.

He could make out a name, Catherine Blackwood. An older woman with authority in her voice.

"You are the one who has been sending gifts."

The rest of conversation was one-sided, at least he only caught some of Catherine Blackwood's words.

"I am grateful for your attentions but unsure of the meaning."

"... battlefield where Tecumseh fell ... flooded soon ... honour ... our past ...."

"Oh my, I thought it was a flood zone already."

"It's still Chatham County to us!" That came through clearly.

Rebecca stood straighter, took the phone from Miles. "I had graciously, I thought, explained that such an expedition was beyond my current situation. I am a young woman in mourning with many responsibilities. The timing falls during our harvest and I must oversee the many volunteers who keep our traditions alive." Then she paused and turned her back on Miles, as though it would exclude him from what she was about to say. "However, as I have the opportunity to speak with you in person, I would like to convey my great appreciation for the little parcel I received just yesterday. It is immensely meaningful, and I take it gratefully as a measure of your appreciation of our pioneer history. I will be sure to have the historical board set up a proper display."

"That ... is for you ... you alone."

"Oh my, a personal gift?"

"Who else ... come ... here ... three days."

Three days? This woman was asking Rebecca to leave the homestead and go to Chatham County. What state was that in? Rebecca started to tremble. Helplessly, she held the phone out to Miles.

"Hello? This is Miles West speaking. Miss Galloway has just been called away. She runs a busy farm and has to oversee the activities of many volunteers. They're rather new at this time of year, a big responsibility." Miles checked to see if this was the proper message to give. Rebecca nodded. "I loaned her my phone for this call. You see, we don't normally get reception out here. We're kind of surprised to see so many missed calls from you."

"We had to be sure Rebecca got the parcel we sent. May I say goodbye?"

"I'm sorry Ma'am, but she's already gone to adjust the kitchen flues. The damp makes it tricky to bake bread." He paused. "I'll just say goodbye for her."

Miles hung up and slipped both phones into his pocket, Rebecca darted for the door. Miles blocked the way. Cocking his head to one side, he asked in a tone his mother might use, "Someone's been sending gifts. More than the parcel that came yesterday."

"Who told you about a parcel?"

"Leticia did."

"You people pry into everything."

"We work with you. We used to go to school together."

"You can't tell anyone. You and Leticia can't say a thing, especially to your mother. I will not have the Authority meddling with my life."

He couldn't believe it. Rebecca was shaking like she was afraid. "What's going on?"

"The phone rang all night. It's a terrible sign, somehow, getting reception here."

"Slow down and tell me about it."

In the dim light of the milk shed, he examined Rebecca as she related selected facts about Mrs. Catherine Blackwood. Despite the humidity, the shed still smelled sweet from the cream and fresh butter. Her face reflected that wholesome diet, not that she was exactly wholesome. She seemed to burn like a wick. A bit of a firecracker was a better description.

"Do you swear not to repeat a word I've said without my permission?"

Miles stiffened. She must have sensed her mistake, this bossing of him, for she tilted her head and rephrased the order.

"At least promise that you'll give me time to think."

"For now," he said, "I can't see why anyone needs to know. But no matter what, you have to learn how to use the phone. Every call on it can be tracked by the Authority because they pay the bill. And Rebecca, I know you're not asking me for advice, but I can't see why anyone would invite you to Chatham County, where ever that is."

"It's in Canada."

"They're drowning up there. There's no reason why you should go, gifts or not. It's too risky."

She looked somewhat satisfied with him, a bit too much like Leticia whenever she conned him into doing something against his better judgement. He added one last thought before he stood aside from the door. "I'll be thinking on this as well. I can only give my word that I'll let you know before I share this with anyone else."

~ 15 ~

SHE WAS WEARING THE LOCKET around her neck, the ribbon lengthened so that it sat low between her breasts and was covered by her shirt and apron. It was a comfort to her when the mason came to check on the hearth. He was efficient if nothing else. Some of the mortar was loose, small wonder with his tapping and picking at it. He filled a few small cavities and stood back to admire his craft. Not satisfied yet, he brought out a ladder from his truck and checked the hearth from the outside, climbing all the way to the top of the chimney. He nodded and shook his head as he worked, confusing Rebecca with his meanings, and she worried that he'd found something else hidden there. Miles stood by her side throughout, nodded or shook his head in response to the mason's gestures. The men seemed to speak a common language. When the mason had poked at every nook and cranny and put his ladder away, he addressed Rebecca.

"Damn fine construction, Miss Galloway. Your kinfolk knew how to build."

"I believe your family had a hand in the upkeep over the years."

"There's a lot of history on this homestead," the mason said, as he turned to Miles and explained his findings. Of course. He likely knew Miles' mother also worked for the Authority, likely handled the purse strings as well as the legal affairs. Hadn't Miles known a lot about how the phone bill would be paid?

When the mason left, Miles turned to her, and though she had listened to the mason's every word, he summarized like she was an idiot. "The hearth and chimney are sound. He wants to come back in the fall to give them a thorough going over from the inside."

"He always cleans them in the fall. Don't let his attentions go to your head, Miles West."

Rebecca left him there with his mouth open and went about her chores. Besides the problem of the phone last night, there had been the bones. She had wished there'd been a moon as she struggled to carry the bundle upstairs, along with the lamp while holding up the skirt of the new gown. As she made her way up in the dark, she had kept turning to see if anyone followed. There was only her and what remained of him. That bundle trembled when she set it on her small bed.

"Stop it."

He looked larger against the quilted counterpane than he had on the kitchen table.

This won't do, she thought, so she had to make room in the bottom of her wardrobe and set the skeleton inside, shut the doors, and twisted a leather thong around the knobs, feeling like his jailor. He might not like it, but she couldn't think of a safer place. She certainly wouldn't sleep with him under her bed.

She undressed in the dark, finding the rows of pearl buttons easily against the warm silk, and then draped the new gown carefully over the back of a chair. The locket only came off once she'd crawled between the sheets. She cupped it in her hand and laid her cheek on it.

The bones rumbled in the wardrobe.

"Enough! Be still or I'll throw you into the fire."

He rattled a moment, then took to tapping lightly, the sound like a twig hitting the window, but just a bit louder every time she was about to drop asleep. When she finally rose from her bed, he took his rest. She wrapped a quilt around her and sat with her back against the wardrobe, then curled up on the floor, sleeping but not daring to dream.

In the morning, the toggle she'd placed around the knobs of the wardrobe doors had loosened off and it and the knobs were on the floor. The doors were slightly ajar.

~

The day felt endless once the mason had gone. Rebecca dismissed help whenever she could, and stood quietly in empty rooms, trying not to wonder about the night before and what might happen this night. Finally, the last of the volunteers were gone, Miles West included, and a renewed fire was banked in the kitchen hearth. Rebecca went upstairs to her bedroom and carried the bones back down. They weighed as much as a healthy toddler.

The fire blazed in the kitchen. In the long licks of the light it cast, there stood the ghost. She drummed her fingers on the table, setting off sparks until she almost disappeared because of it.

I'll show you how he likes to be treated.

She swept past Rebecca, beckoning with a nod for her to follow.

Bring those bones.

She was compelled to carry the bundle back upstairs. The ghost waited in her parents' bedroom and gestured towards their bed. *After George died, I laid the bones on his side every night—the long bones, the backbone linked together with cat gut then. A gloss came on them from my handling, and now they're yellowed into smooth ivory. They have passed from woman to woman through the Galloway family for better or worse. It's his bones that keep generations here as witness to the frontier.*

Be a good girl and lay them out one more time.

Rebecca placed the bones as she was instructed. She trembled, not to handle the old bones, but because she suddenly, sharply, missed the warmth of her parents.

"Can you see him now that you are passed over?"

The apparition lifted her hands in horror. *We are Christian, my dear. Of course I haven't seen him.*

"My parents then?"

And so they live, and pray, and sing, and tell old tales, and laugh at gilded butterflies, and hear poor rogues talk of country news, who loses and who wins; who's in, who's out.

"Can't you tell me more, more than lines from the bard?"

What happens in the Hereafter is of no concern to you as long as your heart beats. I'm not a spy for God. I can tell you that when your grandmother was old enough to play with dolls, her mother thrust the bundle into her arms, saying, "These are the bones of the Shooting Star, and now they are yours." She packed and left. Hope you aren't a scaredy-cat like her.

"You've watched over us, then, all this time."

It's you that's called me to him. I will not be staying. I am not weak for him, nor did I ever yield to him.

"They all say you loved him."

Balderdash! I failed to make him Christian, that's all. The living rewrite the past to serve their purpose.

"Why? Why would they say you loved him?"

Young fool, the beating of a heart is not a sign of love. It is the count-down to death, the steady erosion of a finite resource. Lub-dubh-lub-dubh. A cacophony in motion inside the human body.

I remember him predicting that without peace between nations, the earth would shake. I countered by predicting a fireball would cross the sky for days, sent by powers greater than him or me. The earth did shake, and a comet crossed the sky. We are the vessels for our beliefs, his resonating with the earth, mine with God in heaven. Here he lies, still waiting for his judgement to come.

At the foot of the bed, Rebekah made herself taller than was natural and cast a shadow over the skeleton, raising chills up the nape of Rebecca's neck.

I stand with the Chosen and await to manifest Destiny.

Her arms stretched out, as long as tree branches, then swung towards Rebecca and the locket she wore. The contact was electric.

Rebecca fell back into a chair by the window, set it to rocking madly.

The old spirit let loose a shriek and addressed the bones.

Now it's her turn to serve you. You should be happy. She's a namesake at last.

Rebekah shrank back to her normal size, then floated over the bed and settled next to the bones where she rested her shadowy form, hands crossed over her chest. The bones beside her chuffed softly, as would a rig next to a pasture of mares. He longed for her. With a beatific smile, Rebekah Galloway faded into the layers of the centuries old wedding quilt that had been stitched from the cutting scraps of her trousseau.

Cautiously, Rebecca moved to the side of the bed where the ghost had disappeared. She lifted the edges of the quilt gingerly and looked under. The apparition was gone. Nor was it under the bed. Then she thrust the quilt over him, to make him decent for the night. She couldn't bear the thought of touching him again.

At dawn, a ray of sunlight touched Rebecca's hand on the arm of the rocking chair. *My father and mother watch over me,* she thought. It was the kind of sign she'd prayed for all night.

Before the volunteers came, she had to bundle the Indian up. Each bone had a certain weight, the ribs, the spine, the tiny tarsals and rounded skull, as she placed them back onto the deerskin. "God Bless," she said to each one. They had the power to gaze up to her now, or more likely, at the locket with Miss Rebekah's hair. The gaze had a proprietary feeling. Perhaps he had bonded with her as it could happen with the goslings. They set eyes on you and you become the caregiver, like it or not. She wrapped the bones in the deerskin, tied the wampum. She picked him up, the weight of the whole man much less than a sack of feed. Beads of perspiration from the summer heat rolled behind the locket to pool in her bodice. She smelled of lavender.

Take care of the shooting star. He belongs to you now.

It was *her* voice, coming from somewhere in the rafters.

"You should have buried him."

If you have the strength, you will find a way. If not, perhaps your daughter. It's of no concern to me.

~ 16 ~

THE QUALITY OF LIGHT CHANGED with the arrival of summer. Massive clouds squatted over the short, fish-bowl horizon of Southwestern Ontario and cast deep purple shadows. TinTin had just finished telling her that he'd seen sunlight on his walk home for their breakfast date. It had illuminated the breaks between the clouds, but he had to admit that he hadn't seen it touch the ground directly.

"Too much water vapour." He stared at his poached egg on toast, then stabbed it with his fork.

"I would love to see the sun again." She passed the tomato chutney. "The rays always seem to be shining somewhere else. Maybe somewhere, someone's been lucky. Like you today." In her sketchbook Clem drew a pot of gold touched by a very tentative finger of light. A leprechaun danced in rain. Such was her attempt at lightening his mood.

"Give him a life raft, it's more valuable than gold." TinTin smiled apologetically. "If this is my lucky day, I'll find my sense of humour."

The kitchen faced east and had once been their favourite place for their favourite time of day. But the window of the kitchen hadn't been warmed by sun in over a year. Like everything, it had become depressing. By nine a.m., Clem thought, the brightening of the day would sink into twilight and more rain would fall. Sometimes the rain was heavy, then it radiated its own sick green light, washing across the mid-morning in torrents, a yellow-green piss of some rude giant emptying his bladder with sweeping glee, flicking the final drops. The air would smell of flowers decomposing on their stems, petals falling and fermenting in puddles warmed only by the tilt of the orbital plane towards the sun, so the science boys explained it. Everything would turn brown. By noon, the summer sun would only draw up a chilly haze, a white light, a cloak of death that could stun people blind. In the face of such a light, she had the eyesight of a mole. She may as well leave the canvas primed and white, put her nose up to it and stare. When Pi heard her complain, the dear lad devised sunglasses modeled after Inuit goggles, traditionally strips of bone that fit tightly over the eyes, with tiny horizontal slits to prevent snow blindness. He got the idea from the Flash comics he collected, and her dad had helped design and fit them. Pi was sure that the fad would catch on, only he didn't know the arch-villain, Captain Cold, was copy-righted and the glasses would become uncomfortable to wear.

By late afternoon, dark clouds would assemble again over their fish bowl, calling people from their work, rushing them home before the next deluge. Rain would fall in short episodes, but this time the darkness would last. The premature twilights messed with circadian rhythms, so TinTin explained. Clem felt she was in some kind of stoner-vision. It would be easier to crawl into bed after breakfast and miss the agony of another molasses-atmospheric day. In sleep, the sound of rain was reassuring. All was normal. Who doesn't like the womb?

Thank goodness TinTin had come home.

Then TinTin told her that the engineers were going ahead with the canals that would divert the runoff from their area to the flat lands of the lower Thames watershed. Fiercely, she drew a rainbow over the pot of gold and blended the colours so that the arc twisted into a Mobius strip. Her home in Toronto was gone. Next, the farm. Soon her mother's farm would be left to sink or swim, to float all the way to the Gulf of Mexico. Anything south of London would be lost.

She turned to a blank page and drew a tiny life raft and a line across the horizon to support it. Very small, they were, in the watery world.

~

TinTin, on a morning like this, tried to remember the brilliant dome of sky over Jericho, how the crystal light created intense colours, pure lines. Sunlight sharpened form in the desert, dust created mirages. The sun warmed everything with a bone-soaking heat he missed. He was sorry for the news he delivered about the farm, but how could he not tell Clem? He touched the raft on the page in Clem's sketchbook. "Put us on it." Then he flipped back to look at Clem's boats. Water dissolved form. Persistent, it reduced all to nothing. Sunlight, at least, left a raisin in place of a plum. Or something like that.

Breakfast was over by silent agreement. He washed up the dishes while Clem dried. All he wanted was to crawl into bed with Clem and by circling her body, feel her warmth creep into him. He wanted the friction of their bodies to spark new life, a child. Was it even possible in this grey world to create a new and discrete form? A tiny being with no agenda and no responsibilities. Or would their love-making be doomed to clone the rain, soaking the sheets and bed, pooling on the floor into some kind of amoebic jelly that might learn to walk in the next geologic age, if it picked up the right genetic strands.

He took the tea towel from Clem's hand.

"Let the rest of the dishes air dry."

"You've just said the oxymoron of the day."

Happily, she slipped her hand into his. They walked to the university, quickly, before it rained. There he would worry, under banks of full spectrum light bulbs, about the effect of transferring molecular weight from one part of the world to another. There had to be checks and balances on the Sprinkler System that could shift mass with the immediacy and sensitivity of a high-wire performer. They hadn't shared the theory yet, but he and Pi had drafted a rather vaguely described project, and asked the fellows in the theoretical institute to construct models, each based on his or her speciality. Pi would crunch the results and mesh the best applications together. If anything practical came out of this round of possibilities, TinTin would be surprised. He was expecting a mess and more questions to arise than answers.

He dropped Clem at her studio. She was painting on canvas again, golden colours in the dark days. On canvas, she could brighten the hopelessly vertical and depressing form of rain. In fact, the rain was beginning to look sexy and inviting. As though it was a lover. For so many reasons, rain was such a bad choice if she was going to cheat on him. It was after all, water, and water sought the easiest way, opened small cracks into chasms, rushed in without thought or permission.

All he saw out the window that overlooked the campus was erosion and instability. Rain had no fear, no boundaries. Rain had claimed the earth and more than its seventy-percent share of the human body. It sucked at their top-heavy civilization from below. Rain would level everyone's game. The mother of all sink holes was waiting for them. That Clem might be courting it brought a tightness to his gut.

She was water-proof, he told himself.

On his way out, TinTin picked up an old carpenter's level from Clem's work table. He walked across the campus to the lab, trying to balance it across two fingers. The bubble flew from side to side, each time taking the opposite direction to the tilt. Motion and counter-motion. How does one balance a spinning globe with a molten core and continental plates without disrupting the fragile life in human settlements? Clem would cry if she knew what was in his heart. He wanted to let it all go. Let the earth and its core balance take care of redistributing the surface. Who was he to mess with the system? He was not a saviour, just a computer geek who got lucky with one application of wave-particle theory. The earth's relationship to weight and water distribution was beyond him. Atlantis sank, as much of America would. Geology cared little for the clumsy bacteria that crawled into human form on the surface of the planet. There were plenty more variations hatching in the core.

TinTin wandered past the common room.

Simple Pi shouted after him to stop. Did he have time to get his ass kicked in a friendly game of Ping-Pong?

~

Clem brought a late lunch to the lab, much appreciated by Pi and TinTin. It turned out to be a bribe. "My mom needs a favour."

"Your mom needs an intervention," Pi said.

TinTin nodded. "I also hate the thought of her, and Thomas too, down there. It is a flood zone."

"You know," Pi said, "we've packed everything up and can run our program on an undisclosed site up on the Canadian Shield, as well as on two other continents. The situation is that unpredictable."

Clem nodded.

"Did you tell them that the government is still planning to flood the region?"

"I told them." Clem played with the carpenter's level. "Mother's favour is a little bit interesting this time. She wants you to stop the rain for a few hours in Chatham. Dad is planning a re-enactment of the destruction of the British flotilla. Just some small flat-hulled river boats, and a bridge. The powder has to be dry enough to ignite."

"He should have asked. I'll get him some gel if he wants. Humidity won't affect it."

"No, no, it has to be historically accurate."

"Stopping the rain by inventing a convergence of G- and microwaves is historically accurate?" Pi asked.

"What did you tell her?"

"Only that you are brilliant. Please, baby. Use it as your test site. The place is literally drowning. No one would suspect. They're all watching the New York shoreline. No risk to you. From what I hear, you can't make it worse. They're going ahead anyway. They've built floating boardwalks at the park. Think about the press."

"The press?"

"Yes. Plan ahead this time. Make a trial at the farm first, then work up a bigger plan for the anniversary of Tecumseh's demise. He would have predicted global warming. It could relate. The indigenous way is ignored with consequences, but TinTin fixes it."

"No press."

"Then make the experiment so small that it just clears the area where the bridge is to be blown. The people of Chatham will be intoxicated at the time and think nothing of a clear moment."

"Yeah. Pi and I will need to discuss it first."

Sadly, his best friend loved the idea.

"It's brilliant."

"It's risky. We can't know the side effects or how it might interface with the outside world."

"We didn't when we set the Net in motion. It sorted itself out nicely."

"This is different."

"This is a baby step and you know it will work."

TinTin capitulated. "Baby steps first."

"Exactly. We have the perfect opportunity to experiment away from prying eyes. Clem is right. No one is measuring rainfall in Chatham County. They're looking at the capacity for holding water."

TinTin felt the pressure of the role of Quaker Chair more than he thought possible these days. Maybe he had become far too cautious. After all, they did have a solution. Another chill stole into his gut but he would commit for the sake of his friend. He trusted Pi and Pi trusted him, that's all there was in the world.

"Okay."

Pi nodded like he knew the answer all along. Clem had been watching from the hallway to give them space. She came in and hugged them both. TinTin held her in front of him, his arms around her waist, rocking her from side to side. "Catherine's farm is a good place to start, and if we screw up, I hope she has everything packed and the life boat ready."

"Don't listen to him."

"We'll need the time and date of the event—and the exact location."

"Yup."

"It'll be all natural stuff, right? We'll need the precise humidity ratio for the gunpowder that Thomas is using."

"Yup."

Clem broke away from TinTin and picked up her phone. Before dialling, she whispered to Simple Pi. "Mom's also after some historic Indian bones. Is there any way to scan along the river for them?"

"Another small favour for Catherine?" Pi whispered back, rather loudly.

"Shush! I'm curious, too, especially if it's all to go under water. If I had the skull, the bones, I could do a reconstruction. No one's ever painted a likeness."

"Hey, I can hear you guys whispering." TinTin stood between them. "What Catherine suggests amounts to messing with someone's ancestors. We put family in the ground and that's the end."

"Lighten up. It's not like it's your grandpa or uncle," Pi said.

"He belongs to someone."

"To all of us at this point. He was a relic in his own lifetime." Clem put her hands on TinTin's shoulders. "The Brits had already given away the continent with the Treaty of Paris. By 1813, the loss was unavoidable. He knew it and offered himself up. Better to die than live as a ... I dunno... a refugee?"

"Low blow, Clem."

TinTin waved Pi's defence aside. "The European Imperialists and their treaties. Once I reverse the rain, I'll work on an antidote to that problem. Everyone should have a homeland."

"Then you'll do it?"

"The rain?" TinTin shrugged. "Sure, I said I would try."

"The bones?"

"You'll need to beat Simple Pi at Ping-Pong first. I've already wagered that you can. But no promises. The bones creep me out."

~ 17 ~

THE BONES, THOUGH BUNDLED INTO THE NICHE of the hearth, seemed to follow her everywhere, even into her dreams. Dark pools where there should be eyes. Luckily, Rebecca had no time to reflect on the end of her world. She was too busy with the summer tasks. During the long days, blue eyes followed her every move. Miles West.

She pushed the cast iron kettle into the back of the fireplace and wiped her hands on her apron. It was damp, not from the steam of the hissing fire, but from the continual cloud of haze over the land. Her hair was limp and her stockings soaked inside her shoes. Moving through the humidity that rested so heavily on the Ohio Valley in normal times was heavy work; now it was stifling from so much ground water, so much rain. Drips, too diluted to be called sweat, rolled down from her brows and caught on her long eye lashes; beads formed dew along her hair line, and trickled into her ears, down the front and back of her dress. The ribbon holding the locket was never dry and chafed her neck raw. Even the slate floor wept and puddles formed, making it easy to slip in her leather-soled shoes.

The day's chores were done, and normally she would sit on the front stoop in the good light and sew, but her thimble had rusted. It left blood-like blooms on the cloth when she plied the needle up and down through swollen cotton fibers. The stitches of her normally tidy hand had become monstrous, childish. A drizzle of condensation fell from the rim of the kettle and dropped into the fire, hissing like a cat.

Miles looked up from his computer as though waking from a dream. With the wireless connection working, he could work on the accounts from the homestead. He'd even found another person to drive the bus so that he could stay after the volunteers left and teach her about spreadsheets and such. He'd been adamant she learn this since she'd taken him into her confidence about Mrs. Blackwood.

Rebecca had been watching Miles. He was detail-oriented with the bookkeeping, but also had more understanding of her culture than she'd thought. The lifestyle settled on him naturally. He even ran the volunteers with an efficiency she grudgingly admired. He could sense the meaning of a chore but always asked how she would approach it before offering his own suggestion. Maybe he didn't know in so many words, but she was sure he understood how her life was linked to a time when the frontier was alive, before people washed over and killed it, just as surely as they had those bones in the hearth. May they rest in peace.

"Everything is quiet for a change." Miles tipped the kitchen chair onto its back legs and rocked as though to cool himself. He slicked his hair back from his forehead. "Even the rain has eased to a mist."

"We wouldn't be sitting idle now if it weren't for the wet. The planting would soon catch up with that soft city-body of yours." Rebecca buried her face in her apron to wipe a bothersome streak of sweat from her face. Miles was quick to reply.

"You'd be surprised at how many of us town-folk enjoy the work out here." He paused. "So many of us are thankful for how your daddy shared his talents with us."

Abruptly she dropped her apron and stared at Miles, recoiling from the mention of her father, as though a horse had kicked her in the chest. She hadn't known how to react to similar observations at the Memorial Day service for the drowning deaths. She had to attend because of her parents, but refused to speak to a soul and left before the social. Her way of remembering was to canoe out to her parents' graves at the Massie burial ground and lay her own flowers. *But praise! praise! praise! For the sure-enwinding arms of cool-enfolding Death.* The year of mourning wasn't over, but she'd torn a strip from the hem of her black dress and draped it across the stone. No more dressing like a crow, she'd said to that black stone, and immediately felt guilty at the pleasure. Afterwards, she reasoned it was too hot for black crepe. An armband was enough to show respect.

Miles, from the look on his face, must have felt he could risk a few kind words, that it'd be better than to seem indifferent to her tragedy. He looked at her with genuine care, yet he knew her well enough to settle his chair back to the floor, ready for a fight. Was that her daddy's voice? *Easy now, think girl.*

"Well." She swallowed hard on anger, felt a sense of hope with the inward breath that followed. It wasn't Miles' fault, and the sound of him speaking of her daddy wasn't so bad. "Well." She started again, "I suppose my daddy might say that you deserve a little extra butter on your bread for all that you've done. So how about we leave off the accounting today and I teach you to canoe in the Galloway tradition?"

"On the river?"

"On the milk house floor, you fool!"

He coloured at the memory.

"I'm just surprised," said Miles.

"I won't let you drown. It's not the same river as took my parents. That river passed to the sea ages ago, haven't you read the Greeks? I'm going to take you out on today's piece of river. That is," she said, "if you are interested."

"You know that my father teaches the canoe guides at the National Park. I've learned a thing or two from him."

"Have you indeed? I've heard he's darn good."

But she wasn't sure how good Miles was. His sister had been a junior guide in the national park where his father worked. Leticia told her she was only at the homestead because canoeing was banned there on account of flash floods. She seemed to be warning Rebecca, even as she had looked longingly at Rebecca's canoe.

Out on the river, Miles sat in the bow, a bright orange life jacket over his traditional garB Rebecca tucked hers into the centre of the canoe.

"All you need to do today is get a feel for these waters."

Rebecca guided the canoe into the swells of the Little Miami and let the swiftness of the current carry them quickly downstream. Every now and then, she swung the paddle into the current and when she did, the canoe settled nicely. Miles could lessen his grip on the gunnels. She watched his shoulders, how he moved with the river, and how he softened after a while to its flow. His dark hair had grown longer and he'd tied it at the nape. He had the ruddy complexion of the families who'd been in the area since the founding days and married into the melting waves of back country settlers. He looked good, she had to admit.

Miles' sister, on the other hand, was plain as could be. "A shame," Rebecca's mother had said, "that the Lord had not matched her looks to her talents." Leticia's face was flat, her brows dark, her hair straight as a board. With eyes round like dark moons, she had that open expression of a doll that needed to lie flat for the eyes to close. Rebecca had been on the swim team with her and knew she had been nicknamed "Muskrat" by her teammates. Leticia hadn't cared. Her close friends called her "Muskrat" just the same. Historical garb hid some of her worst features, but made her look like a native in domestic service. A shame. Leticia would like it out here, but she still had her own daddy to teach her the ways of the canoe.

Miles, she noticed, had picked up his paddle and was waiting for the right moment to dip it in. She took the canoe into a lesser tributary and he turned to smile at her.

"What now, Boss?"

She let him take the canoe up the small inlet against the current, then back down to feel the difference. Before long, Miles had the knack. When they put the canoe up into the rafters of the boat house, she could see a new respect on his face.

"I have to admit the Galloways have some skills with a canoe that surpass even my father's."

He wanted more lessons.

That summer, Rebecca took Miles out on the muddy creeks and roiling rivers, travelling farther as Miles became more reliable. At first Miles worried about the canoe filling with rain but Rebecca showed him how to spread oiled cloth across the gunnels to keep the worst out. They travelled upstream until they were spent, then rested, letting the currents take them home. It helped to share the load. They travelled the big river sparingly, as industries bulked out into it, and like Huckleberry Finn on the Mississippi, they risked being tipped by the wake of a barge, or sucked into a pool of effluent. The river had its sounds and looks, its own strong skin on which the canoe glided. But the creeks were better, more intimate. Her father taught her how to find them along the overgrown banks and where to swim and which pools would hold her body spread-eagle for ages, slowly turning. With all the rain, it was too cold to swim, so they let their heads fall back and the canoe turn in lazy circles until their heads spun too. And then Miles dipped on the wrong side and almost capsized them.

He flushed crimson up the back of his neck. "That was so stupid of me. I could have killed you."

Rebecca quickly righted the balance without a word and swung the canoe towards home. They were half-way downstream when Rebecca thought about how she had taken charge. Her father had always let her fix her own mistakes and maybe this was a time when she should have let Miles.

"It could have been worse. It's about knowing the water and your craft, even when your head is spinning. Now dip your paddle in and give my shoulders a rest."

Miles hesitated. "This canoe is so sensitive. There's no room for mistakes."

"We made it through that one."

His necked coloured, and Rebecca softened up. "My daddy said this canoe is like a leaf gliding on the water, or a fish darting in the currents. It's too swift to think what's next."

"Like it has a mind of its own. You've got to guess what's next."

"Shame on you, Mr. West! I never guess." Now she'd made him tense up and he was leaning forward as though he'd get there quicker. "If you keep that up, you'll spill us right into the drink. Let your spine be as supple as a fish's, your paddle be the fins. Your head is set perfectly now to cut the current straight and true." Rebecca felt a sweet taste in her mouth. "Dip quickly side to side with a light touch. Now twist deeply on the paddle to set us into the current."

"Some days, it feels like me or the river."

Why had he brought up death out here? She would be gracious, she'd change the subject.

"It's not a contest. In fact, and I don't say this lightly, but I wonder if you have a natural talent. Folks say you have Shawnee in your blood line."

"Really? And folks say that your namesake had a baby with Tecumseh."

"That's not true! It's a fact your old man West took an Indian for his wife."

"Oh my god, Rebecca Galloway!" Miles' back shot up straight.

"Easy now. It's true. Look at your daddy and Leticia."

"I have, and unlike you, we don't consider Indian blood such a bad thing. In fact, this is too weird. Here I am, the educated civilized guy with a year of college, hanging out on the river with you—who lives in the past. And you're teaching me to canoe like a freakin' native and saying I must get the skill from Indian blood."

"Like a native?" How dare he bring up the teasing again after all the kindness she'd shown him! How dare he imply she was no more than a rude Indian! She slapped her paddle on the water, bringing the canoe to a dead stop.

"Get out."

"You're kidding."

She repeated.

"I'll drown."

"I could care less. I'm not native. The line never married and the temptation was all rumour with no truth. I come from true-blood Kentucks, and don't ever say different. My great granddaddy-three-times-back was a frontiersman with Daniel Boone. This skill was taught to him and passed down. White to White."

"Explain then, where did Daniel Boone learn it? In merry old England? That's where your family came from, all the way across the Atlantic Ocean, and your great granddaddy had the grace to come and teach the natives how to do it. Right?"

"That's ridiculous."

"So is saying I catch on because of native blood."

"I mean you're good."

"I read the Greek philosophers too. You're better, so logically, more Indian than me."

"Get out Miles."

This time Miles turned back and stared at her. How ridiculous he looked, his eyes dark as cobalt and his mouth turned up at the corners, smiling despite the serious line of his jaw. "I'll tell you this truth, Miss Rebecca Galloway, no matter where the skill comes from, if it weren't for you, I'd surely have drowned out here on this crazy river."

Rebecca didn't take her eyes off him. She held the canoe stable in the rushing water, barely moving off the mark. She must decide whether he was mocking her or not. With a quick twist, she drew the paddle out of the river and plunged it back in. The canoe rose out of the main current like a sleek otter and rode the waves to shore. Miles kept his balance, and when the bow lodged against the soft bank, he scrambled out before his weight could sink it. She followed, and together they pulled the canoe up on solid ground. Miles flopped into the long grass. Rebecca laughed, then her land legs gave way too and she spread out beside him.

"He courted her with this canoe, so that Rinaldi woman wrote." She touched her foot against the side. "If I believed that story, I'd tell it another way, like Whitman might. This canoe still remembers the blood pumping through his veins, his feelings shimmying and skimming wide and deep. But you can't make love to a human in a canoe. You must get back on land and that's where my daddy said my namesake always found her legs. She wouldn't go one step further into the native ways."

"You love this river as much as they did. Like in the story. Don't take the teasing so hard. You're famous through no fault of your own."

"It's my bloodline."

"It was a long time ago."

"Long ago is my time."

She watched Miles rest between the overgrown stalks of hay seed. Had she made him into a character from her imagination? She wasn't sure about his true identity, or his place in her life, but she felt she could trust him. "They both loved this land, and so do I. At least what the rain hasn't taken. Tecumseh was stubborn in ways, and naïve about those French trappers and British sympathizers who got his help for pie-in-the-sky promises. They used him."

"They did. And Rebecca, you come from good people."

She turned away to hide a tear running down her nose, and they spent a while in silence. Miles broke it.

"Talking about British sympathizers, I had another phone call from Mrs. Blackwood. She'll never take no for an answer."

Rebecca turned her head back. Miles spoke again.

"She'll keep calling until the tercentennial."

"I've been thinking about that," Rebecca said, "thinking that maybe I should go. Maybe it's time to see some history from another point of view. Something started here and it ended up there." She jumped up and rubbed her face, shook off the grass that clung to her clothes, and held out her hand to him. "Will you go with me?"

Without missing a beat, Miles took her hand and pulled himself up. "The Wests crossed the Alleghenies, so I guess I could cross into Canada for a day. I'd have to ask my parents for the car."

"Oh, I don't want to drive." Rebecca smiled. "I thought we would canoe."

~ 18 ~

LATER IN THE SUMMER, TinTin and Simple Pi drove down to Catherine's farm. As they drove, a report came up on the radio that four houses along Tecumseh Park Road in the small city of Chatham were lifted from their foundations by the flood waters and carried into the greater Thames. The sleeping owner of one house, an unemployed pipe fitter, didn't wake up until rescue workers dropped from a helicopter onto his roof. He dreamt he was on a boat, as he had many nights before. The other houses had been abandoned months ago.

They called Thomas. "You'll have to revise the plans for the waterfront. Anchor the docks three lots back from Tecumseh Park Road--it'll give you almost 3 meters in elevation." Southwestern Ontario was filling more quickly than it could empty into the Great Lakes. The rain wasn't to blame, but canal work to the north.

They passed large warning signs announcing the diversion, and then one to mark the official beginning of Flood Zone Four. TURN BACK, it read. TinTin felt grim as he drove through, but the shaking that started after the news report had stopped. Flood Zone Four looked much the same as anywhere else these days. Pi tried to keep the mood upbeat by playing tunes while he monitored the emergency channels and weather networks. They both kept a close eye on the live feed GPS that tracked their route. Catherine's farm was miles upstream from the town, but the elevation wasn't much higher. Just in case things went wrong, they'd packed portable flotation devices and survival gear. There was no higher ground to escape to.

TinTin spotted a grove of evergreens still above water by the road. "The battlefield is just ahead. We're almost there."

Pi lifted his eyes from the monitors. The bush to the north of Catherine's farm was underwater, maybe by a metre. Old corn stalks massed like rafts along the trunks. Some clung even higher in branches, the trees looking like crazy scarecrows. The high water marks had left black lacy edges on some trunks. TinTin drove slowly enough so they could look, but not so slow that they'd get stuck in, or slide off, the gravel slush on the road. Pi tried to sound casual.

"Apparently otters have replaced the raccoons."

"You're a brave man, Pi, coming down here like this."

"I know, though, I'm beginning to wish I'd learned to swim."

"Wouldn't matter. The currents would suck anyone under."

The farmhouse was set in from the road on a deep lot, on a slight rise some ways from the river. In mid-day, the mist was a uniform gray but the clouds were at least 25 metres above the ground. The little lookout on top of the house, a widow's walk it was called, rose above the steep roof. Simple Pi pointed.

"What's that for?"

"The pioneer ladies liked to watch both the road and the river, especially during prohibition. For their men. A lantern still hangs there—Clem showed it to me."

Pi shrugged. *Water, water everywhere*. It's like something from a Goth tale. Do you think we'll find the bones?"

"Shut the fuck up about the bones, will you?"

~

"What happened?"

TinTin had set up a video link for Clem in her studio in Waterloo so she could watch the experiment with them. It turned out there was nothing to watch for the longest time. Instead, they watched Clem paint curled strips of paper with acrylic resin, then cut the bottoms into the shape of tear drops. She hung the strips from the lid of the barograph case, which she had taken from the lab the minute TinTin left for the farm. This move was something of a guerrilla tactic, TinTin thought, but the theft was slightly ameliorated because she replaced the sarcophagine case with a clear glass cake cover from her side of the basement. They watched Clem hang the curled drops over a series of stalagmites she made by chewing paper up into spit balls. Little wave-like tongues of rain seemed to pock the stalagmites, drip by drip, eroding instead of building them. Such was the way of this rain. Then the video link broke down.

An hour later, they had it up again.

"What happened?" she asked.

"Clem," TinTin said through tight lips, "I think that scanning for the bones led to an anomaly."

"I'll tell you what happened." Simple Pi was half-laughing, half-crying. "TinTin's experiment broke all your mother's bone china."

"What?"

"I don't know how to describe it." TinTin pushed Pi aside from the monitor. "The moisture was wicked from the room and created a vacuum. You know how it is when central heating dries out furniture. The wood shrinks and the glue comes away."

"And the chairs and drawers fall apart."

"I told your mom it was the same principal for fabric shower curtains. A close weave gathers enough moisture so the moisture itself creates a barrier and prevents puddles outside the tuB Water actually holds many things together."

"But dishes breaking?" Clem asked.

"Crashing. Picked up and dropped. Bam!" Pi waved his arms behind TinTin to illustrate.

"Anything else?"

"No, just that," TinTin said.

"But the room is okay?"

"Yes. We sucked the curls right out of my hair."

"Maybe too dry?"

"No, it was wonderful. It's the first time in ages I've been able to breathe through my nose."

"So, where did the water go?" she asked.

"It rose fifty feet and was wicked above the tower lines to Sandusky."

"Then it followed the Mississippi."

"It ran along that corridor like a series of beads. Bring up the video feed and show her."

Pi did, and in the corner of her screen he used the cursor to show her the sequence. "Then it reached Oklahoma and we shunted it west."

"We're still waiting for it to drop."

"Still aiming for Uncle Walter's pool in Phoenix?" Clem asked.

"Ha! He'll wonder where that came from."

"Actually, Pi, he'll never know." TinTin said this with relief. "He's visiting my folks in Jericho. He heard they're getting rains and he likes the idea of a green desert. We've tapped into his home security cameras. This small quantity of water should evaporate in less than two hours. Such is the arid state of Arizona."

"It's worked!"

"Except for the china."

"The good china?"

"Only the best bone china."

"Everything?"

"Everything that was in the cabinet and boxes in the dining room."

"Weird."

"Something about calcification. We think it's related to the scan but just in case, we'll make sure there's no bone china around in the next trial. Anyway," TinTin said, "I think that you should call Catherine. She's pretty upset. She has, for some illogical reason, transferred the blame to Thomas and threatened to drown him. He says she should have had everything packed up and shipped north, and it's her own fault for getting involved with the bicentennial. He accused her of running after bits of quilts and tatted tablecloths that her neighbours are still using but that have no value."

"She came right back at him," Pi whispered, "and said she didn't know that his demolition committee would commandeer the good parlour and blow up her irreplaceable china."

"Oh dear, I'll call."

"Before you do, watch the monitor for a moment."

A ribbon of rain fell from a clear blue sky and dropped into Uncle Chaim's empty concrete pool, the first drops steaming as they made contact. They watched in awe.

"You have made me very happy." Clem threw the boys kisses. "Next stop, Somalia!"

She heard Simple Pi laughing. "What?"

"TinTin has a list of things that can go wrong and it only takes ten to the power of eight gigabytes of memory to hold it."

"The bone china anomaly is disturbing."

"I'll speak to Dad and he'll apologize. He'll make it right. Besides, she must know that she's to blame for asking for the scan."

"I mean scientifically. There will be Fossils at this event— all the old folk in Chatham and the surrounding townships, clinging to the sinking ship. Who knows what they'll wear or bring. Something set up a vibration that broke the bone china."

"On the bright side, my genius love, it works. Look at the rain fall in the desert!" A dark patch was spreading across the bottom of the concrete pool. "We can share the water, the web of life, with your little sprinkler system."

"Yeah," Pi said over TinTin's shoulder. "We'll have to publish quickly. It'll cause another crazy-go-round in the world of geopolitics." He sighed. "Imagine the proprietary rights this application would bring."

Like Pi, TinTin also had some regrets about giving up control of the Safety Net, though not about the wealth it might have brought. Sharing the principles had created some strange problems. Open software, like any open market, he had told himself, was self-correcting. Then he tried to buy a soft drink at a small town variety store not far from Catherine's farm. He was kept out by a security net. The owner stood in the doorway laughing. "It's programmed to keep you curry-eaters out. Go home, Paki!" The man laughed even more when TinTin shouted, "I'm not from Pakistan. And I built this Safety Net!"

TinTin had thought, rightly, that the Net could not profile races. Humans shared the same genetic structure. But to make assumptions about diet and then to regulate for volatile oils in food, that was pretty sophisticated, and effective, it turned out. He might have seen the possibilities to create fragrance-free workplaces but not that. They all knew that the system would be hacked and perverted. While they wrote up the Sprinkler System, he wanted to keep it quiet, to consider all the angles. Thomas might be a help there.

Before they left the flood zone, Thomas insisted on driving them down to the conservation area and what was left of Tecumseh Park Road and the docks. What struck TinTin was the beauty of simple technology against the power of the water. He filmed it to share with Clem. Geometric solids, cylinders, hemispheres and rectangular solids repeated in the forms of floating docks and boats. At this point, the powerful river easily dominated. On the surface, the river was a series of perpetually changing furrows and rounded eddies, blending like quicksilver. Colourful water-safety equipment lined the edges of the docks, and someone had stationed a number of powerboats at intervals downstream, perhaps anticipating the speed of the various currents and how body mass might travel. Mere toys in the flood plain. The land had shrunk. Thomas pointed out what had been the shore, where trees still stood, their tops bowed over in matted blobs, the trunks disappeared. He pointed to where viewing towers would be added. The site was amazing and idiotic at the same time.

~

Clem found the video fascinating. She drew an analysis of the river on her studio wall and began her own inquiry.

"Bring me more data on the river," she said.

From actuarial tables, she painted the plotted drownings in orange first, then the water currents as seen from the video, then GPS-recorded voyages of rescue craft. A paper scale version of a body was crafted and rolled over the surface. There were too many twists and turns to track, too many sudden reversals to predict. Despite the science, the most successful water rescues were those guided by intuition, people linked to the water-mind. The best firemen were said to think like fire and the best police officers to think like criminals, so Clem concluded that the water rescuers who thought like the flood waters had the best outcomes.

While Clem painted, TinTin needed to protect his applications from the prying eyes of his colleagues. To distract them, he picked up on Clem's idea and wondered aloud about linking the Net to the intuitive aspects of rain, to follow rain before it even manifested, then feel the build-up, the turning and wonder of the mass, the need to release. So many variables, he told his colleagues, so much intuitive feedback and response to track.

Across the world, the theorists quickly came to a consensus.

They needed a rain whisperer.

~ 19 ~

PEOPLE ALL OVER THE WORLD claimed to be in touch with the rain, but Clem believed the whisperers who gathered the most media buzz were liars. Sure, small miracles did happen. Some prayers were answered, how many out of millions? The genuine survivors told how it felt like they'd died and only when they had given up all hope and struggle, only then, had the water, or the weather itself, carried them to safety. They had submitted.

Clem stopped asking for data. She surrendered to the rain.

On her first try, she spread every colour she possessed out before her, laid out brushes and rollers, buckets and water, mediums and gels. She stared out the north window of her studio into the rain and thought of everything that made her sad. Sweating was too involuntary, and other than peeing herself, she thought crying was the closest human mimicry to the phenomenon on the other side of the windows. She gave into the crying and it felt good at first. Then it became tiresome, but she continued to let the tears flow. She squeezed her eyes hard and bent forward so they puddled in the palm of her hand. At body temperature, the impact of tears falling was almost indiscernible. She licked them; she sucked them up and stopped crying. Just one colour matched the rain, Payne's grey. Clem pried open the lid and picked up a roller. She felt like rain.

She didn't remember, but afterwards, TinTin told her everything. That he had come along later in the night and saw a canvas painted grey on the wall and another on the floor. "You were naked." She was holding a tray of blue-grey paint horizontal to the floor, and jumping up and down on her toes so that paint fell in drops onto the canvas. The back wash from the tray streaked across her arms and chest, splattered down her belly and legs. So many smudges crossed her face. "Your eyes were the only thing I recognized as you."

She was in a trance, and didn't hear or see him. He called her name, then again and again to the rhythm of her hops. She noticed him and smiled, but didn't stop.

"Clementyne, I called out pretty sternly."

"It must have been the judgement in your voice that broke my trance."

"You looked like a guilty child." Her pleasure was simple enough, but not acceptable. She responded by sharing, offering the paint tray to him, hoping he might decide to remove his clothes and join her. He shook his head. "You let me wrap you in a piece of canvas."

"I remember thinking it was funny, and then you took my hand and we ran down the halls."

"You left grey-blue footprints on the linoleum."

TinTin took her to the showers in the laB He rubbed her hair and face with white foamy institutional soap. The paint washed out, "like rain" they said together, and they laughed. They howled as the grey ran down her body, as though she was the window surface, and the rain poured over her.

"Then I wanted the real rain." She pulled TinTin out from the shower, towards the door. "I saw a look of fear on your face.

"You were heading outside."

"Outside."

"You ran off like a spooked horse. I apologize for not covering your nakedness." He'd used the towel to cover her head. "I had to block the sight and sound of water."

"I felt your touch then, and heard your voice, the love."

"You came back to me. You remembered you loved me."
He took her back to the change room. Shyly she dressed in
front of him, in the white lab gear he'd found.

"I thought of joking," Clem said, "of asking where you kept
the straightjackets but you looked tired. I was tired."

"It's over. It doesn't matter now."

~

The next time Clem painted, she went back to using data.
She listened to the sounds she'd recorded of Laurel Creek,
swollen to the size of a small river as it cut through the
campus. Her goal was to match the noise with colours and
shapes. She painted the higher pitched sounds first, lightly
streaking the huge canvas pinned to the wall, climbing up on
step stools to reach the sound. She painted deeper sounds,
thoughts almost, embedded beneath the rushing water and
used buckets, slopping colour from crotch level, watching it
splash and run. She stretched another canvas across the floor.
All she could hear was the river, relentless, implacable noise.
She made guttural sounds in her throat and dropped paint
from the top of the step stools.

Clem wanted to get into the river. She jumped and landed
on all fours on the slippery surface. Scraping a mix of black
and burnt umber, some viridian green, Prussian blue together,
she pushed the sworls to the edge of the canvas, and they bled
to the underside. She shimmied under after them, and in the
dark, brushed the colours on from inside the river. Dull thuds.
Swishing. The brush struck the canvas. It wasn't good enough,
she wanted more paint, more rain, and she punched the
canvas with a utility knife, pierced it. Ripped it. Rushes of air,
drips of paint.

"I didn't know you were there, then I saw you lift a
corner."

"I was trying to coax you out."

"I wanted to stay in the river." She'd be damned if she'd let him interrupt her.

"You growled at me, hissed too."

"It wasn't me, it was the rain on the creek."

"I kept talking anyway. I thought you'd bite me when I touched your face."

"You were in the river with me."

"I had to crawl under to talk to you."

"I knew you. I said, 'You are my husband.'"

"I asked you to come home. I told you it was time to come out."

"I couldn't move."

"You said you didn't know how."

"I'd been trying to cut through for ages."

It hadn't been easy to convince the seventy percent water part of Clem to follow him out, but thankfully, the thirty percent mineral part was hungry. At least she had kept her clothes on. Streaked in paint, they walked home. She ate breakfast without talking. Afterwards, they watched the video recording of her process.

TinTin copied the sound waves onto his laptop, the colours Clem had used, and then her kinetic responses. These were overlaid one onto the next. The result was an image of the creek, just as it had looked where Clem recorded the sounds. She watched the way the creek and the rain came together, how the rain broke the surface tension as though with a thousand-thousand tiny knives. TinTin looked uncomfortable. "You don't know how it looked from my point of view in the studio."

"The creek wanted the rain, wanted to dissolve with it."

He didn't say, but it looked and sounded like a violent kind of love making.

Upstairs, Clem fell asleep to the sound of rain outside, and Laurel Creek playing in her head. She dreamt of a large wave coming towards her. As she calmly waited to be engulfed, she anticipated, like a full kiss that would take her breath away. She remembered the dream clearly, but didn't share it with TinTin. He would ask about the meaning of it, and she didn't think she could explain.

For a week, she stopped painting. She filled her sketchbooks with thoughts and images from her memories of her recent experience.

The rain is watching us, slithering through our world, piling up weight, sodden garments, soggy lawns, beating on the roof, searching for a way in. What does it want? It shouldn't be here. It's up to no good.

The charity calendar on the kitchen wall would be flipped to September the next day. Augusts of the past had been hot and dry, electric with the sounds of cicadas and the bleached colours of dying grass. If she looked deeper into her frontal lobes, as TinTin called memory, the black soil of her grandparents' country garden had been hot enough to scorch her bare feet. Beet and carrot tops were tall enough to hide her from the practical world as she, a city girl, sketched the amazing topography. Soon her grandmother would call her from the back porch and hand her a basket. For the next hour, she would strip back the succulent leaves and silk from ears of corn. Back then, that's where all the water had gone. Into ripe seeds, fruit, roots. How nostalgic. She was thinking like her mother. Would September bring the cold, the thunder and storms to dry her world out and bring her mother home?

～

Mid-day on the first of September, TinTin left for the campus and Clem spent that night in the backyard, which was still grass-covered but drowning in the pouring rain. She had stripped naked. Rain plastered her hair so it flowed down her back, a waterfall skipping over vertebrae until it stopped at her midriff and the rain ran to her butt cheeks and into that channel before it fell to the ground, splashing back up on her ankles and calves. She tipped her head back and opened her mouth wide. At first she struggled, choking on the water before she thought to breathe as if she were swimming, to tip her head to one side, then the other. The rain was delicious. All flavours, changing, striking the epiglottis, bringing oxygen, pelting it down—popping—and the smell, the nuances, were incredible. The downpour fell vertically straight like the warp of a loom, marched across her like a scanner reading barcodes. She sensed the rain tasting her. It wavered as though to back up, perhaps finding her delicious in turn.

By dawn, her heels had sunk deeper than her toes into the muddy clay of the lawn. She fought to keep her balance, working her toes among the grass roots. Worms and their castings floated in the pool above her ankles. She held her arms and hands out. Her skin might have been the colour of Payne's grey but for what looked like a touch of luminescence, ultramarine blue. She and the rain were one.

~ 20 ~

TINTIN CALLED TO SAY THAT HE WAS COMING home for breakfast. To start the day together had been their only marriage vow. When Clem didn't answer, TinTin thought perhaps she was in the shower. He'd already checked the studio. He walked to the house in the now familiar rain, bath-tub warm, not too bad for getting soaked despite his rain coat and the rubber boots that knocked against his bare shins at every step. He no longer side-stepped the puddles, but tested them with a walking stick that had replaced his umbrella. People in this city had been swallowed by sinkholes, even along the sidewalks. It had happened uptown when Laurel Creek broke free of the culvert system and infiltrated areas below the infrastructures taken for granted, destabilizing human concourses in such a stealthy way. He tapped the sidewalk, could have been a blind man on a grey morning on a familiar route, comforted by the sound, so solid compared to the rain.

They no longer locked the house, as keys rusted so quickly. Some kept their keys oiled, but telltale circles of grease soaked into their coat and pants pockets. Besides, the door was swollen shut. They'd been forced to break the basement window to get in a number of times. He put his shoulder to the side door and turned the handle. In the natural pause between the push-twist action of entering, TinTin heard a voice in the backyard. A mere drizzle this morning, it sounded like the rain had taken up singing.

Of course, it was Clem. To be honest he wasn't surprised to find her completely naked and blue. Her belly and breasts heaved with her song. The rest of her was frozen like a statue. On closer inspection, the blue was not paint, but likely physiological. She was very cold to touch. This bothered him almost to tears. He called Simple Pi. "How do you deal with hypothermia?"

"You mean in the Arctic or Antarctic?"

"There's a difference?"

"A big one to do with medical contacts."

"I'm looking more at a backyard situation. More like someone's been standing in cold water for a number of hours."

"Another Clem experiment?"

"She looks rooted in the yard. She's cold as stone. I'm afraid to move her, that she'll break."

"Just talk to her. She'll listen to you."

"What about hypothermia?

"Call the doctor, man."

"I'm afraid if I do, he won't understand. She's naked and singing."

"I see," Simple Pi said. "Maybe start by drying her off. Give her something sweet like honey in hot tea. I'll conference with Theo. He's had hypothermia. Then I'll be right over."

"Thanks, Pi."

"No problem. Is that her singing?"

"Yeah."

"You should record it. Make it worthwhile for her later. I've heard that when the circulation returns, the pain is agony."

TinTin quickly found Clem's video camera on the back deck, guided by its *whirr*. It was tied up under the eaves of an old bird feeder hanging beneath the canopy of wisteria that grew beneath their bedroom window. She had the video set up to feed directly to her computer so memory wouldn't be a problem. How long had she been standing there?

Before he picked it up, he faced the camera for an editorial shot. Water from the wisteria dripped down his face.

"Fuck you, Rain!"

The words were shouted loud enough to set the neighbour's dog barking, and to stop Clem in mid-song.

Crossing

ഇരു

~ 1 ~

EARTH HAS COME TO FEEL THE WEIGHT of rain on her vast soft belly as consolation, pressing and filling, spilling and receding. Human forces thrust deeply into Earth's sedimentary layers, replacing oil with a liquid she has no memory of tasting. The pressure has set up vibrations. She is receptive but she won't let go her deep waters, the black oil. The shale and aquifers hold. She is spread wide and lets rain flow between the layers of pressed, organic sediments and porous limestone, mixing and churning ancient bones and new matter, squeezing with the muscle of her shifting plates. Contract and relax.

In the cradle of two vast continental watersheds, she rocks the floodwaters of rain so they slick up the slopes higher, higher. Tongues of mud draw down humans, their structures. Earth groans; she shakes beneath the high mountains to the west, and beneath the low ones to the east. She breathes the water up from the south on a quivering inhale; on the exhale, northern debris washes into the sea, the ocean. Ships are tossed to her pleasure, some swept underwater in looping graceful curves of tidal waves. She squeezes marrow from the bones of maritime souls. Tangy. Sweet.

Rain rises from the eastern ocean spiral-armed, and hurls itself onto the continent, but just short of the mark in size and strength. It isn't time, not yet.

With great anticipation, the Earth spins.

~ 2 ~

IN MID-JULY, CATHERINE RECEIVED A LETTER from Rebecca Galloway. She whisked it away from the curious postmistress, Madeleine French, and opened it in the car. The linen envelope with the carefully blotted address hadn't run with the humidity, though it felt limp and clammy like a damp face cloth. Glue seeped where the envelope had been sealed. A round of dark blue wax held the contents securely. Inside were linen pages with the same beautiful penmanship. The letter stated that Rebecca, in her grief, had not considered the benefits to others that attending the bicentennial might afford, and how such a journey might be a suitable occasion to represent the memory of her parents. She went on to say her year of mourning had just passed. And with the rain, being home for the harvest wouldn't likely matter.

> *Rain and heat have saturated our spring plants, forcing them to grow beyond their strength, pushing more flowers out than we've ever seen. But the blooms rot. The sear browns that should come in August will most likely remain lush and green—same as last year—and the native crops will soon rot and smell of carrion. Garish, bright algae blooms continue to spread over pools of standing water in the gardens and in the fields. Forgive me for such a dismal portrayal. Instead let me close with a thankful heart. Not only for the distraction from agricultural concerns and the opportunity to commemorate our victory in battle, but to celebrate the after-effects of that old war: our lasting ties of neighbourliness.*

Catherine returned to the post office and shared the letter with Madeleine French, who only commented, "Such a formal child."

Catherine filled in some of Rebecca's history, explaining it had taken this much time to get her acceptance in writing.

"Such a tragedy," Madeleine said, "the loss of her parents. We will honour her family." She looked Catherine in the eye and lowered her voice. "Now that you have proved your claim to this guest, I'll book a nice suite for her and her friends at the Holiday Inn."

Catherine met her gaze head-on and matched her whisper. "Would you mind, given her rather delicate circumstances, if they stayed with us? It's my impression that she isn't used to modern conveniences. I'd like to personally make sure she's comfortable."

"You'll be so busy."

"Clementyne will be down by then. She's offered to help."

"The driving might be too much."

"Our guest will want to spend more than the allotted time at the battlefield. We have the best location. No need for anyone to drive her."

The President of the Historical Society and Bicentennial Committee surrendered, likely under the pressure of the four o'clock line forming behind Catherine. "It might be for the best."

"In what way?"

Madeleine raised her voice ever so slightly. "I mean, her people did win the battle. She made sure to mention it in the letter. She sounds like she might gloat over the victory."

"Surely not. She is our personal connection to Tecumseh."

The postmistress waved her hands in the air, as though helpless to get Catherine to understand, or move on. "I'll leave you to vet her speech. Make sure it emphasizes the goodwill."

Catherine tapped the letter, waved it for everyone to see. "Rebecca Galloway seemed to get that point on her own." She turned and headed to the door.

"How are the 'fireworks' progressing?" Madeleine called after her, smiling brightly to disguise the intended sting. Catherine was well aware the community had more enthusiasm for Thomas' project. The county residents would come in droves to see the bridge blown up. So much for historical accuracy. The bridge should be burned. Given that the wood would be too wet to burn, the men decided that blasting it to Kingdom Come would be much better. She smiled across the crowd and left without the last word.

～

Catherine found Thomas sitting in the Tavern with his cronies. He acknowledged her with a nod as she hovered beside him. She caressed a handful of his thick hair, wound her fingers in it. She pulled his head back to look at her, then tugged his humidity-softened beard towards her lips. She whispered in his ear, "We did it. Crazy plans don't work out? This one did. What I want is not crazy."

"I'm not so sure of that, my love and life," Thomas whispered back.

~ 3 ~

MILES HAD A BIT OF SUNSHINE in his life these days, and her name was Rebecca. He could push aside dark clouds of worry when he worked with her. She never mentioned the trip to Canada again. Mrs. Blackwood kept calling him. Until he figured out Rebecca's intentions, he let his phone ring. Finally, he took Leticia into his confidence.

"You cannot go in a canoe. Not only would you drown, how would it look to your Mrs. Blackwood? She'd think we're backcountry hicks, that none of us believe in cars." Leticia shook her head sadly. "You'll be living two hundred years in the past before you turn twenty-one, Miles West. Are you soft in the head?"

"You're just jealous because I'm out on the water, and Dad has grounded you."

"I've spent more hours in a canoe than you. You know I'm better."

"Not anymore. Rebecca is that good."

"Rebecca is leading you on. She examines you like a bug under a microscope. It makes the hair on my arms stand up on end."

"Just shut up. I thought with your brilliant mind you could help me out, but no, you're just my dumb little sister after all."

"Don't be heartbroken when she dumps you for a purebred cousin named George."

Miles made to punch Leticia in the arm and she turned to him as though to take it. He pulled back. His sister took enough from the town over her native looks. God knew Rebecca was more prejudiced than most along those lines. Leticia was just giving back.

He didn't think the town was racist. They had their way of sorting people, of keeping them honest. The Wests had

Shawnee blood from the frontier days and the genes popped up in random generations—two in a row with his dad and his sister. It wasn't a big deal but it wasn't something the town let them forget. Even with his fair colour, he got his share of teasing. Rebecca, well, she got teased about everything. Maybe the link to Tecumseh was just the last straw. The Galloways, they'd climbed the social ladder right on up into the early government. The family had always taken a hard line that nothing happened between old Rebekah and the Shawnee, that Tecumseh's offer of marriage had been just that, nothing more. None of their generations had come out brown-skinned like his father, Owen, and his sister, so maybe it was true. In the end, Miles believed what mattered most was how people treated one another.

His mom was a first-generation immigrant, her family from Sweden. She had a different view of American history, through a background of socialism and a different set of prejudices. What bothered her most were bullies, and the idea of anyone being superior. And then came the recordkeeping in Greene County, the lists of generations, the idea of the unblemished family tree. The Daughters of the American Republic tracing their beginnings to the founders of the United States. "So, what about intermarriage, the mixing of blood?" she'd say.

But the people of Xenia quoted family history like it was the Bible, chapter and verse. Some in the town snickered at her marriage to a West from Benjamin's branch. The first time it happened to her face, she'd been ready to litigate. His dad wondered if it would be better to move to the city. The state capital was just an hour away. He would commute to work in the park. In the end, his mom had accepted apologies while squarely addressing the history of her husband's family with pride. The town learned to tread cautiously around her, and she had more business than she could handle.

Every year, he and Leticia came home with a school project on local history, and the Grade 10 project was always on personal ancestry. Claire acted more like a lawyer in The Hague than a mother. They spent more time on these projects than any of their friends, and they didn't necessarily get the best marks. The county teachers didn't take to their mother's revisions of history. The problem was, there had been another Leticia on the outskirts of the family tree, and she wanted that old Leticia counted into the family, no doubt about it.

Last year had been Leticia's personal history project. They were both studying at the dining room table, he for math. His mom beamed when she heard Leticia was working on her family tree.

"Why not tell the Wests' history from the Indian point of view?"

"Sorry, Mom," Leticia answered, "there's none around here to ask."

"And you say that as though you have no native blood. You can speak for your own."

"Mom, I'm not going to say how my great-great-great Shawnee grandparents kidnapped Benjamin West's two little girls."

"Let's be honest, this country was built on the labour of kidnapped children and families from Africa, and other countries too."

"Ohio never condoned slavery."

Claire returned to the kidnapping. "Culturally, kidnapping was acceptable among the various nations along the Alleghenies. How would the Lenni Lenape know that this incoming tribe of Englishmen preferred, religiously, to keep their gene pool insular?"

Leticia faced their mom. "Let's see. How would the Shawnee have known? Perhaps they might have asked, given the difference in dress code? Or the different language might have been a clue? They'd dealt with the settlers long enough for everyone to know the settlers didn't like Indian ways." Leticia worked her jaw, clamped her mouth shut.

Claire narrowed her eyes. "Perhaps the Shawnee believed, rightly, that the law of the land was theirs." She leaned towards Leticia. "A frontiersman assured the Wests that the Shawnee would raise the girls as though they were their own. Not as slaves."

"The same guy told Benjamin to pack up everything and follow the Shawnee. He said Benjamin's only chance to get his daughters back was if those girls snuck back home in the night. So, Benjamin West moved his whole family close to Shawnee land along the Little Miami River, and that's how we put our roots here."

"Point granted. And happily, a return was brokered with the help of Colonel Galloway."

Leticia sniffed. "It was more likely the work of the Indian agent, Simon Kenton."

Claire allowed a broad smile. "You have done your homework."

Miles knew their mother's pride was in logic and what she called fact, but sometimes he hated her for it. No one wants their noses rubbed in history. It's not that anyone in the room had been a player in it; they were just the offspring of decisions made centuries ago. He knew his mom, knew the story, and Leticia was going to have an even rougher go in the next few minutes. Thinking he might distract Claire, he mimicked her tone, and stabbed the air with his pencil, saying, "Notice this, Leticia. Our family negotiated where others would have murdered the thieving Indians to get their children back."

"Point noted on the defense, Miles, but out of order. Now, Leticia, what comes next?"

Miles left his math books and stood up from the dining room table, as though to stretch. He wanted to leave the room but only a coward would leave his sister alone.

Leticia looked at her notes, though she didn't have to, and read in a careful voice. "Just before the massacre at Raisin River, the Wests took in an orphaned Shawnee girl from the family that had taken, and then returned theirs. It was a risky gesture, given the uprisings and reprisals on all sides."

"Have you addressed the context of the so-called uprisings?"

"No Ma'am. The teacher just wants our family's history."

"I'd like to know why the hostilities?" asked Claire. "And why didn't the treaties work?" She included Miles in the questions. Leticia looked to him for answers too. Between them, they did their best.

"The federalists didn't know the reality of life on the frontier."

"The excitement of the expansion took over common sense."

"Cultural differences led to misunderstandings."

"There was room only for the one great white vision."

His mother shook her head. "Was there something beyond race," she asked, "that made the invading peoples so mad with greed that they had no sense or compassion? After all, they destroyed everything that didn't serve their purpose. Peoples and habitats. We're reaping the consequences today. This flooding is a result of the European idea of progress."

Leticia just hung her head.

"Then what happens in our family history?"

"Benjamin was an old man and a widower when he registered two sons as being his. He gave the mother's name as Leticia. There are no records to say exactly who she was."

Claire sat across the table and stretched out her hands towards Leticia, and said softly, "This is the bit of history I want you to claim without prejudice: Leticia was the adopted Shawnee girl, and she'd borne Benjamin two fine sons."

Leticia's jaw was popping with tension. She had that look of something going on inside her, something he hoped would resolve itself without harm to anyone. She kept her hands on either side of her notebook, like it was a flutterboard she'd use in the pool for practice when her arms gave out. She read out loud one last line. "Benjamin gave the boys a good name and my family is descended from the eldest son, William, and his wife, Selah. Selah is my middle name."

"Leticia Selah West, never be ashamed of your native history."

"But Mom, he never married the girl. He was ashamed."

Miles jumped into the breach. "No, Leticia, he wasn't ashamed. He was likely shamed." He'd grown up with teasing about bastard sons. "What no one says is that if Benjamin had done right by her, his house would have been burned to the ground. Hate ran high against the Indians—the British too—whether it was justified or not."

"Thanks Miles," his mom said, and she smiled at them both, holding her hands open. "Despite right or wrong, we can't try people in the past against today's standards. It would be at least fifty years before the emancipation of slaves." Claire looked at him with such deep respect.

"Ohio never had slaves." Leticia was repeating herself.

He had gathered up his books. For him, the discussion was over. The town didn't think as much as his mother, and didn't mean much of what they said. He would always defend his sister against any of the local bigots, but his parents were part of the problem. Leticia's mud-coloured skin, thought Miles, might have been ignored if not for her name. He knew the coarser ones in town referred to her as a mongrel bitch, a smile always present to soften any offense. Why name her after the woman who was the source of the trouble in the first place? It was like calling a daughter Delilah or worse, Jezebel. Names carry history that can add to, or lighten a burden. He thanked his lucky genes there was no brown cast to his skin. His mom would have called him Tecumseh.

His parents didn't have a clue about Leticia. His sister kept her head down, getting sympathy and respect. He doubted that she saw herself as any different from anyone else. The only reason she went to work in the park with their father was because she was a Daddy's Girl. It had nothing to do with being an Indian and loving "nature." Leticia was smart in ways their parents didn't know. *The sum of my parts,* as she called herself, was alive and well in the Age of Technology. He found out she had joined several online hacker communities after someone stole his term paper and handed it in before he did. Luckily, Miles ran it through the college's plagiarism site before he turned it in. It rated 100% plagiarized. He'd had to rewrite it, losing precious marks for a late paper.

"It could have been much, much worse," he'd told her. "You let hackers use my computer."

"It was a glitch."

"I could have been expelled."

She'd reset everything and then booby-trapped it with her own firewall magic, but he had this to hold over her. That's why he told her Rebecca's plan.

Rebecca rubbed Leticia the wrong way. Miles could see they were like opposite sides of the same coin. One had the "wrong" history but didn't care. The other was apparently "unblemished," but touchy on the topic. For him, the confusing part of liking Rebecca was that she lived so far back into the past she didn't know she held onto the old prejudices too. Something like slinging their gear into a canoe and crossing to Canada didn't mean the same to her as it did to him. He wasn't sure what he was getting into, but even after talking to Leticia, it still felt right.

~

They were out on the backwaters in an eddy where they could let the canoe spin. He'd settled himself in the bow of the canoe so that he faced Rebecca, their feet tangling with each other in the middle.

"Rebecca, I'm going to speak to my parents about going to Chatham. Tonight."

She looked so grateful that it pained him.

"I'll have to tell them our plan in stages. They'll get used to the idea of us going into a flood zone first. Then I'll work on softening them up so they'll be okay with the canoe trip."

~ 4 ~

LETICIA HUNG AROUND AFTER SUPPER, circling like a hawk as Miles carefully, casually, described to his parents the trip he would make with Rebecca. He mumbled about it being a gesture of goodwill in a time of instability. A noble cause.

Her mother continued putting dirty dishes in the dishwasher. Her dad washed up the pots, scrubbed hard at the edges of a pan that still held burned bits of apple crumble. Behind their backs, Leticia mouthed a countdown that she mirrored with her fingers. At *ONE!* the explosion she predicted failed to materialize.

"Uh huh," her mom said, like her thoughts were somewhere else. She put soap in the dishwasher and turned it on. She picked up the just washed pan, inspected it, found a spot. Her dad scrubbed the bit off, pulled the plug, and dried his hands.

Miles shrugged, playing it cool, as though it was nothing more than a weekend trip to the state capital. "So, I'll keep you up to date as the time gets closer."

Her dad flicked the tea towel at him, playfully. "You don't have to go to such extremes to date that girl. We'd be okay with you taking her out to a movie, even in the neighbouring county. It's not that people will be surprised. You get along with Rebecca when everyone else has failed."

Leticia gently punched Miles. "See, I told you they'd be fine with your plan."

"Well, like I said, I'll keep you all in the loop. I've got to get Trevor now for the ballgame. We're playing Yellow Springs."

"Isn't that game tomorrow?" His mom looked to Leticia with her lie-detector x-ray death-stare. "Is this trip for real?"

Leticia shrugged.

Miles nodded, his head a loose yo-yo, and suddenly his mature, calm voice was gone. His hands were shaky despite all his preparation. In the end, Leticia had coached him about the obvious questions the parents would ask, and some that weren't so obvious. Southwestern Ontario was a disaster area, obviously. In fact, the states of Ohio, Michigan and Illinois were fighting against the Canadian diversion project to save good old Toronto. The Great Lakes were sure to rise because of it. Any miscalculation in the water flow—all guess work according to everything she'd read online—could inundate the state, sweeping them away. New York, on the other hand, was supportive.

But, as she predicted, less obvious questions arose. Claire went directly after the character of the people who would dare to invite Rebecca. "Where is the certificate of sanity for this Blackwood woman?"

Miles couldn't speak. He agreed with his parents. Leticia would save him. On her laptop, she'd bookmarked pages to show her parents the professional links to the Blackwood family and the bicentennial. Catherine Blackwood was as *bonafide* as they came. Miles looked somewhat relieved to have that much settled. A little grateful too.

"I want to talk to this woman," her mother said. Owen was still reading the pages, hoping to find the whole idea was joke, that a page with "haha!" and a funny picture that would save them from discussing such a crazy proposal.

Miles produced his phone. Mrs. Blackwood answered on the third ring. From her mother's expression, Mrs. Blackwood was taking the barrage of questions in stride. A good sign that she was prepared for an interrogation. It meant she knew the idea was crazy. As she answered questions, Mrs. Blackwood sent emails with current photos of the bicentennial site. Her father zoomed in and out, looked up GPS locations and cross-referenced the information with databases he could access through his work software. Mrs. Blackwood sent itineraries and guest lists with dignitaries from high political office. On the lists were more First Nations than Leticia thought existed in any locality outside of Oklahoma. Her mother's eyes narrowed, hard to say if that was a good thing. In the end, nothing was resolved. Her parents would sleep on it. Leticia settled down to what was left of the evening, pulling Miles into the living room to watch an old television show with her. She knew he wanted to talk to Rebecca, but it was too late to drive out there. Rebecca still wouldn't use her cellphone. He looked drained, like he might die tonight if things weren't resolved. After they'd all gone to bed, Leticia heard a hiss of whispers, and went down the hall to the bathroom where the heating vent connected to her parents' room.

"I want her to see how other Indian Nations made out, the ones who escaped the American conquest. Not that colour makes you one of a race, but it shows in Leticia like a waving flag."

"Claire, it was one woman in a line of many who passed on those genes." Then her dad must have hit a pillow. "Just tell me, how is sending both our children into that flood zone going to help?"

"I believe they have the right stuff in them."

"And suppose they make the trip there and back, I don't believe they'll find the Indians are treated any better in Canada."

"According to the guest list, Owen, they've done much better."

His dad whispered really softly, like it was a secret that he should keep, but had to share. "I don't want Leticia exposed to trouble. Natives fill Canadian prisons. They live on isolated, underfunded reserves. There are problems, not with everyone, but enough that we should worry. And now they're losing their land again, this time to the rain."

"Everyone is losing their land. Wouldn't it be good for her to see native nations included at a time like this?"

Leticia could imagine her mother, how she must be sitting on the bed, her back straight, chest out, hands clasped in the pose of a Norse queen ready to die for her tribe. For once, she was rooting for her mom, not that she cared so much about the Indian crap, but she'd hoped it might work this way. She really wanted in on the canoe trip, which they didn't know about yet.

Then her dad played dirty. "Remember the drownings on Founders Day?" he whispered. Leticia felt her stomach drop. "Rebecca has no one to come back to after this trip."

"Rebecca was always a good girl for her parents."

"I don't mind Miles and her as an item, but this trip is all wrong, and you know it."

There was silence, and Leticia wondered how she would survive if anything happened to her parents. Sure, she could fend for herself and she had Miles, but how could she replace the love of her parents? Then her mom spoke softly, as though for her ears alone.

"Let's start with treating Rebecca like a valid person instead of a 'crazy backwards' girl. Let's see where the idea goes."

"We don't even know if a trip is possible," Owen said.

"If we give permission, we'll have control over the trip in a way that Rebecca will respect."

"Like with Miles wanting to drive there on his own."

His parents actually chuckled. If only they knew.

At breakfast the next morning, Owen and Claire gave permission to Miles to attend the bicentennial, with the details to be shared and worked out. Miles' eyes shone brightly, so pathetic. Then they explained that Rebecca needed a travelling companion, a girl her age. That her parents, if they were alive, would insist on it.

"Leticia, we'd like to ask you to go along as well."

Miles nearly choked on his breakfast. He glared at her, shaking his head like some old fool.

"If that's the only way Miles can go, I suppose I better."

"It is," her mother stated.

There was a flurry of pretended excitement all around. The parents weren't really keen on the idea, and Miles didn't want Leticia, but Leticia already knew she'd be asked to go. As she'd hoped all along. She repeated, "Oh, I understand. I understand," like she was doing everyone a big favour, each a deeper dig at Miles.

At least this morning Miles knew enough to bring up again how he wanted to drive, and argue with just enough resistance to make it sound convincing. There would be a real argument about canoeing later. She would be ready for that. When it seemed like everything was said and settled, Leticia had one last request. She had thought hard through the night of how to word it, but maybe a direct approach was best.

"Mom, you know I'm okay with going, but I'm not going all dressed up like a pioneer for the day in the car to get there, another day to get back, and the whole time between. Miles likes to play dress-up, not me."

"No one would expect it, honey."

"Would they expect it of Rebecca?"

"She lives the role." Miles was so defensive. "So who cares? People like that kind of stuff."

"Wouldn't the people in Chatham," Leticia continued, "think Rebecca was a weirdo if she dressed in the role the whole time?"

"She does dress that way the whole time, idiot."

"It's weird. She'll look like a weirdo, like Laura Secord, that's who they'll think she is up north. A girl with a cow going to rat us out."

"Maybe you should stay home." Miles' voice came out like a low growl.

Her mom frowned at him, then turned to her. "Would you be embarrassed to travel with Rebecca?"

"No."

"Honestly?"

"I would feel sorry for her. She is treated like a freak here, and it won't be any different there."

Miles face flushed right into the roots of his hair. "It's amazing that Rebecca even agreed to travel so far. You lay off her."

The parents waited for his breath to return to something like normal. Anything to do with explaining Rebecca left him floundering like he was in a pit of quicksand. Oddly, some of the redness from his face migrated and flushed across their mother's.

"I understand what you're saying," she said to Miles, "but Leticia has a point—poorly stated though it may be."

Her dad nodded in agreement. His eyes were filled with sympathy for Miles. The boys in this family had to stick together, and there'd be a chat later about how being a man meant standing down sometimes, listening when his heart shouted otherwise.

"I don't think Rebecca really knows what she's getting into," Leticia said to Miles.

"I agree." Claire made it sound like a judgment was passed. It was over for Miles. Leticia would have some control over the crazy Galloway girl—if Rebecca really wanted to go.

Ever the peacemaker, her dad reached out to both her and Miles. "You're family, of the same blood and bones." He held them both by the shoulders until they looked at each other, then at him. "I'm going to trust the two of you to discuss the full implications of this trip, and the modern world, with Rebecca." He pulled them into a close hug, kissed each one. Before he let Leticia go, he whispered into her ear, "You'll use this power in a caring way."

~ 5 ~

"THERE, IT'S YOU."

Rebecca didn't know the girl staring back at her in the mirror, hard as glass and shaking like an aspen at the same time. Into the silence, a long sough escaped her open mouth. She hoped Leticia didn't think a demon had made it.

Leticia's body quivered too, so excited that Rebecca had accepted her challenge on the spot to dress in modern clothes. Not that clothes made a person, they agreed, but after all, one had to play their part. At the homestead, the historic garb put everyone on the same page, reminded them of the time and the ways of Rebecca's world. They didn't have zippers, or Velcro, and Rebecca thought their manners changed, just a bit, for the better. What convinced Rebecca to wear modern clothes was not Leticia's argument that people were more than their clothes, that how one looked depended as much on what was inside. Demon sighs? It was the challenge more than the argument, and how Leticia would hold it over Rebecca if Rebecca failed to meet it, that made her agree. She would rise to the challenge and strip the girl of any power over her. But like the volunteers at the homestead, she held to the knowledge that she could shuck the garb as soon as she got home.

Leticia put her arm around Rebecca's shoulders and took a quick picture of them together. They wore the same type of tight-as-skin sweater and pants that revealed every anatomical part. Their hair had the same sweep of loose curls. Kohl around their eyes gave them a sleepy raccoon look; their lashes were made up dark and long. The flash of colour about their eyes was brighter than a shiner. Rebecca's skin was pale. Leticia's summer colour, despite the lack of sunshine, was like a milky tea. They had the same cherry red lips.

"Look at us!" Leticia made a dancing motion, a victory move. "You like?"

Rebecca forced a grin, nodded her head, and squeezed a tear back into her eye. She'd never felt so naked. She was shivering from cold. Leticia put her arm around Rebecca's shoulder again, and turned them for a new pose, holding onto Rebecca too tightly. Rebecca shrugged her off. Enough.

Leticia smiled straight at her, another challenge in it.

"Let's go shopping."

The girl pulled a clutch purse from her closet and thrust it into Rebecca's hands, and tossed a pair of jeweled sandals at her feet.

"They're flip-flops from Florida. You'll love them."

Rebecca felt the yoga pants stretch across her private parts as she bent to get the shoes, felt the pants bind up with her underwear as she stood. The shoes slid sideways on her feet.

"The secret is to curl your toes every time you step." Leticia demonstrated how she walked in hers. "You'll get used to it. I have bandages in case you blister."

Rebecca balked.

"Hey, if you can chop wood, you can walk in flip-flops. Right?"

Another challenge. Rebecca would get back at the girl, would have her muck the stalls and clean the chicken coop, would get her plant seedlings in the rain in a full set of petticoats.

Leticia pulled her into the hall; Rebecca barely kept the shoes on as she went down the carpeted stairs and then along a tiled hallway. The 'flip-flop' sound followed her like a horse down a hard road.

"Hey, you!" Leticia called out to Miles in the living room.

～

He turned his head to return the greeting, then leapt from the couch to his feet, upsetting the laptop he'd been using.

"Rebecca? Is that you?"

He was shocked, and it must have shown. Leticia laughed at him, then laughed more as she put her arm around Rebecca, and they struck one of the poses that he'd bet they'd practiced in her bedroom mirror. Miles knew she did it with all her girlfriends, but with Rebecca, it seemed an act of evil. Rebecca had the cornered look of their cat. His sister still got her kicks out of dressing it in doll clothes. Mom should have had another baby for her to play with. He spoke for the latest victim.

"You can't take her out like that."

"She looks cute."

"She looks like you, not herself at all. You've gone too far."

"Everybody wears this."

"She looks scared."

Miles noticed Rebecca's grip on Leticia's arm had become like a hawk with a mouse. Her body language was shifting towards anger, and Leticia noticed it too and let go.

"She's nervous." Leticia looked at Rebecca. "Right?"

Rebecca stepped away and stood at her full height. "You may both stop talking about me like I'm not here."

Rebecca was back, unmistakable, if a little choked.

"Miles, your sister and I are going shopping at the mall for maybe an hour." She looked to Leticia to confirm the plan. Leticia nodded. "I need to buy a pair of jeans. Leticia's don't fit me and these *tights* are uncomfortable. Then she'll take me home." She turned to Leticia, as nice as pie, saying, "I think I forgot my things upstairs, would you please get them for me?" Rebecca looked down at her feet. "I'm not sure the flip-flops will make it *up* the stairs."

Leticia grinned, and raced off. Miles knew his time was limited, but said nothing. He stared at Rebecca, keeping his eyes on her face.

"Gee," he managed to say.

"Not what you thought?"

"Too much of my sister for my comfort."

"I have to start somewhere."

He thought her eyes filled up, but no tears fell, so he couldn't go to her, couldn't rescue her. "Call my cell if you need anything at all."

"Thank you, Miles."

~

Rebecca concentrated on walking from the car to the mall entrance, the flip-flops sucking up bits of grit from the wet pavement and spraying her bare feet and ankles. Waiting for them in the entrance was Mrs. West. It so happened she was also shopping at the same mall on that very afternoon. Her busy lawyer-schedule was clear for a few hours. "A rare thing indeed," Leticia said to her mother, but the girl looked relieved.

Mrs. West's guidance was greatly appreciated. Apparently, there was ample money in Rebecca's bank account, but first she needed an electronic card to access it. Mrs. West took care of the matter in such a way that Rebecca left the bank feeling like the heiress she was. Leticia seemed happy enough, giving no evidence of jealousy or malice over such attentions being focused on an outsider. The girl was generous. She was the same when Mrs. West insisted on taking the girls for ice cream and spoke about fashion and how hard it was to find your style right away, but how a girl could mix the styles to get the best of all worlds. Leticia would have known all this. Leticia had a very worldly mother. On the way out of the mall, they stopped by the news depot where Mrs. West picked up several fashion magazines. "Remember, you can mix and match styles across the years. I know you're clever. You'll figure it out." Rebecca was about to pick up a magazine with an attractive full gown on the front. It was *Today's Bride*, and she passed over to pick up another about food. Shyly, she nodded at Mrs. West. "I'll do my best, Ma'am."

They spent longer than the one hour she'd promised Miles. Rebecca was surprised at the relative comfort of the shopping mall. The lighting was unnatural, but the humidity was half of what it was outside. A person could forget about the rain in that place. By the time she left, she'd bought several good pieces of clothing, including the necessary jeans. Rebecca left the store wrappers and bags in the Wests' car, saying she had no means to dispose of them, and carried a folded bundle of new clothing up the lane and into the homestead, trying to decide where to hide it. Her parents would not approve, of that she was sure.

~

As she'd predicted to Mrs. Blackwood, the early harvests were scanty or rotting. Rebecca made use of the last weeks of the summer holidays to inveigle her way into a place of trust and respect with Miles' parents. Miles would soon be off to college, and she wanted to show them that she could negotiate both worlds.

Rebecca tugged on the now familiar jeans and pulled a V-neck sweater over a lace-trimmed but simple camisole from her traditional wardrobe. She had noticed when she dressed in these clothes, she was all but invisible at the mall. Sure, there were gawks, but not stares of sympathy or curiosity. They were looks of admiration, the same kind paid to Leticia's mother. Everyone said that Owen West had married a beauty.

The colour of her sweater matched the grosgrain ribbon holding George's engagement locket. She slipped into brocade flats embroidered with a Woodland Indian pattern and looked into the bubbled glass of the mirror at her face and hair. A hint of colour hovered around her eyes; her lashes were darkened with blacking from a makeup wand. Her thick hair was braided to one side. A slight bit of bangs wisped across her forehead. She liked the disguise. Her earrings came from her mother's dresser, simple bits of trade silver. Last of all she slipped into a body-hugging leather jacket.

"Your parents wouldn't know you," she whispered to the reflection. "You're a modern girl and you're going to see a moving picture today with the entire West family."

~

After the matinee, Rebecca nudged Miles. His parents still didn't know about the plan to canoe to Chatham. Leticia noticed the nudge and looked eager to broach the subject herself. She'd been in on the secret from the start, though according to her, there was little to suggest that their parents would agree. Miles steadfastly maintained that if there was any hope at all of getting permission, it was better if he was the one to begin the talks.

They were finishing dessert in a quiet corner of a restaurant and lingering over coffee when Miles presented what he called "a slight change in plans."

His parents paled, they were horrified. For the first time, Rebecca's conscience struck her. She wished she could take back his words. It really wasn't right to risk the lives of the Wests' children. In her orphaned state, she just hadn't considered that impact, that she had been willing to risk everything to get rid of the bones, even Miles.

Miles carried on with grim determination, ignoring the emotional pull from both her and his parents, losing point after point to Claire West, who had a mind like a steel trap. Matters couldn't get worse. He looked to Leticia for help.

"Our family has a right to cross the waters freely," she said. "Natives on both sides of the border will be doing it this fall, as they have uninterrupted for hundreds of years. Who will represent the Shawnee, if not Miles and me? Haven't you been drilling that into me? That our Shawnee blood is something to be proud of. Wasn't that what the Battle of the Thames was about? The military chasing out the Indians? This might be our only opportunity to learn how it feels."

From a large handbag, she produced a laptop and the research she had done for their proposed trip—the roads, the launch site, the border crossing and Safety Net restrictions, the logistics of weather and currents. She backed up her brother's arguments. Leticia even spoke highly of her brother's canoe skills.

Rebecca nodded encouragement to Miles. He jumped on Leticia's idea of honouring their Indian blood.

"If nothing else," Miles said, "I've got Rebecca to thank for making me proud of both sides of my heritage. Every time we go out on the river, we take an Indian-made canoe, the best craft I've ever paddled. The skill is our heritage. We're taking Tecumseh's canoe."

The course of the discussion changed. Claire West found finer points to quibble over, but Rebecca could tell the mother was bursting with pride, that she wanted her children to win. And they did. More coffee and dessert were ordered. The siblings shuffled their feet under the table in congratulatory kicks. Rebecca flinched from a stab of guilt. Her acceptance of the Wests' Indian line had been necessary to get Miles' cooperation. Her purpose was not, as Leticia had stated, to relive the trek to Canada, but to quietly slip Tecumseh's bones into Lake Erie, and let them scatter on the currents as surely as the tribe of the Shooting Star had scattered across the continent. As she listened to his family argue, she heard love and respect. She wished her parents were here to counsel her. All she could do was borrow the political sense of her forefathers and misrepresent her purpose to achieve her goal. Did anyone need to know about the personal if the historic could be argued?

The rain let up on the drive back to the homestead. Miles wondered aloud if the weather echoed his gratitude for his parents' permission. Rebecca nodded. She was certainly grateful. She would have let Miles come without it, and she could see how wrong that would have been.

～

During the few days before Miles went back to college, no one commented on how the rain had stopped, as though to comment would bring bad luck to such good fortune. It was the same about the trip. Life shifted back to the normal tasks at hand. Throughout September, Mrs. West kept Rebecca extra busy with plans for the trip, and what the Historical Authority thought was appropriate to take for gifts, who should pay for them, etcetera, etcetera.

Rebecca looked forward to the weekends when Miles came home and they canoed on the river under the watchful eyes of his father. Mr. West finally gave up the romantic notion that his canoe skills came from Indian blood. He said that he wished he'd spent even a day on the river with Rebecca's father. He gave his blessing for Leticia to take part in the canoe training. No one mentioned how well she fit into the routine, that many times, she'd already slipped out on the river with them. It was important for Leticia to learn in case some ache came upon Miles, or her, unlikely as it was. For their part, Rebecca and Miles had to get used to the new balance of a third person. The added weight sank the canoe deeper into the river.

~ 6 ~

MERELY TEN METRES ABOVE the broad and fast Thames River, Catherine stood still for a moment in the farm house's cavernous attic and listened. The ever-present patter of rain had ceased. Water dripped from the eaves. The rain had stopped.

Relief showed suddenly at the corners of her eyes. For a moment, she could picture herself as a child and the attic packed as it had been. She held her arms straight out from her sides and slowly turned in the space beneath the lantern. The last time she could do this without hitting anything, she'd been six years old. Fans, the background noise to all human activity these days, wicked perspiration from her body but not fast enough to stop the river that soaked her shirt. She squeezed her eyes shut. Hard blinks. Her tears fell and fell.

She had emptied the attic of all its treasure; the four windows of the widow's walk in plain view above her, pried open so that, in theory, the air would circulate. Just one trunk remained. Minutes ago, she'd had Frank Dolsen drill holes into it a few inches below the leather-bound edge to save the contents from rust and rot—a brass spy glass, a lamp and its wick, a woolen blanket.

"Is that it?" he called from below.

"Yes, Frank. I'll be down in a minute."

Her eyes filled again. Blink. Lifetimes sorted and removed. Tears streamed down her face, as natural as rain, mingling with decades of black farm soil that had sieved into the attic and found her skin a good medium for mud. Her arms and legs were streaked, her face now too. She heard the footsteps below, climbing up the ladder, felt the weight of them tug against the floorboards, a weight heavier than Frank Dolsen's slight frame. She did not open her eyes.

"Thomas."

He reached out his fingertips to touch hers, and slipped a fresh handkerchief into her palm. Catherine turned aside, ran the soft cotton under her eyes, over her cheekbones and down to her chin. She blew her nose. When she looked again, Thomas had climbed the ladder and was sitting on the ledge up in the lantern, looking through the spyglass. "It's changed so much that I don't even think of it as the Thames. Your Thames never had a personality like this."

"It was a rather comfortable river." Catherine turned in the empty space again, unwilling to climb from it to enter the view above. She shut her eyes again and remembered. "Just a trickle of molasses at this time of year. Half the time you didn't know it was there because of the thick brush along the banks. You could see it from up there. Mostly I looked past the river to see the other side. Who was getting their hay before the rain. If the Morley and Bechard kids were chasing each other through the corn. We were never allowed. Sounds carried across the water. Once the corn was off, I could see the Callwood yard, the mother hanging laundry, half of it dragging on the ground, her mouth working. She was known for belting out country songs, and the wind might snatch them, like an old Victrola, and play them across the river."

Catherine stopped turning, and climbed up beside Thomas, nudged him to give up the spy glass. She turned it onto the battlefield. The memorial site was above the floodwaters, but not the battlefield itself, originally a swamp. She pointed to the edge of the river. "His bones were supposed to be in that river bank."

"That was a public school girl's fantasy."

"Who says?"

"St-Denis."

"Oh him."

"I'm thinking," said Thomas, "of taking the author with me to Ohio to see the warrior's birthplace. He's never been. We'll leave early enough to stop at the museum in Columbus on the way and see if they have any flesh trophies from the battle."

"After the scandal over the Field Museum's collection of Inuit remains? Would anyone talk?"

Thomas stroked his chin. "The smaller places have a hard time with past collections. They tend to ignore any remains. It's ghoulish to look, but they might be happy to unload some human souvenirs if they weren't asked any questions."

Catherine took the spy glass away from her eye and touched Thomas gently on the leg, the microfibre fabric of his shorts strangely dry to her touch. "Two centuries later, what would a strop made from a man's thigh look like?"

"I'm told that if it was cured properly in the first place, it would look and feel like leather." He took her hand in his, and ran it along his thigh. "If it was cured properly, it'd feel supple. Of course, there'd be a sheen if it had been used."

"St-Denis thinks a part of Tecumseh is in the trophies?"

"If you'd read his book, Catherine, you'd know he, and every other historian, clearly say that the bodies were stripped of ornament and flesh. The remains on the battlefield were so badly mutilated that General Harrison refused to identify anyone. He ordered the natives all buried without markers. It's possible that Tecumseh could still be buried in the field." Thomas took the spy glass from Catherine and twisted so he could see the battleground.

"If it wasn't so bloody wet we could get a grant for a proper dig."

"Too late now."

"I, for one, haven't given up hope. The bones could surface. Even Frank Dolsen's pet cemetery worked its way into the light of day."

Thomas wiped the spy glass down with the loose tails of his shirt. "Is this staying up here?"

She nodded towards the trunk.

Thomas slid down the ladder and placed it inside. "Someone's drilled holes in this," he said, his fingers finding rough edges on the outside.

"I asked Frank to."

"It will sink, should the house go."

"No, it's stopped raining."

Catherine slipped down the ladder too and handed the balled handkerchief back to Thomas. As though she were a fragile artifact, he covered her hands with his, then drew them into his chest. He didn't kiss her, or say he loved her in the way she liked, which really meant he liked her spirit, her resilience. Instead, he looked at her seriously, grief tugging at his face. "I came up to tell you that the Wests have called again. Claire wants to speak to you about a new development."

Her reply, *I love you too,* withered and died on her tongue. "What now?"

Downstairs, Catherine got down to business on the phone with Claire West, pacing the rooms, from kitchen to parlor to dining room to porch and back through, a path of questions and defenses worn on the now bare floors. How was Catherine to know that the Wests had native blood in the family, or that the reticent Rebecca Galloway felt she had to honour her friends and First Nations' treaties by *canoeing* across Lake Erie? Canoeing? It was bad enough driving.

Of course, thought Catherine, once the situation was explained, it was perfect for so many reasons. Go with the problem, she'd always told Clementyne, which meant with the water in this case. She reasoned that a boat was safer than a car. But how safe was a canoe? There was no highway patrol on the lake should anything go wrong. On perhaps the seventh time she passed Thomas, he made a sign—his hand cutting across his throat. Catherine let Claire West know that she had another important call to answer, then flopped down onto the couch in the kitchen, and set the phone on the recharger. Ten minutes later, a cup of tea in hand, she shooed Thomas out on an errand. It was time to call Hiram's friend for advice.

"James, how is the weather in Waterloo? How is the rain experiment going?"

"Quite gloomy, but there's good news in the forecast. The volume of rain is easing up. And tell Thomas the sites for anchoring the truss bridge look secure."

"Wonderful news for us all! I do have another favour to ask."

"No more scans, Mrs. Blackwood. TinTin said so."

"I couldn't agree more. A whole dinner set was lost because of that fiasco. If only Thomas had done his homework earlier and read St-Denis, that possibility would have been ruled out. His bones were never buried in the river bank. This time I need information about the safety of Lake Erie in early October. I've just received news that our esteemed guest from Ohio will be boating to the Canadian shore. In a canoe crafted by the hands of none other than our lost warrior, Tecumseh." Catherine paused. "Would it even be possible? Would it be safe?"

"Mrs. Blackwood, I have no idea how things around you get so complicated. Until recently, I thought museums were dull and boring, but you constantly show me that in times of trouble, it's quite the opposite. It's not something I've investigated before. If it's alright, I can get back to you in a couple of hours."

"James, you are a dear. And I'll return the compliment. I never knew that science could have so many practical applications."

James found out that people made the 92-kilometre journey all the time in the summer, even amateurs. While it was true that crossing the lakes was part of a long-standing treaty right, the usual Safety Net custom and excise laws would be in force. Most importantly, such a trip looked like it would be safe, given the current weather patterns.

A torrent of new exchanges started up between the Wests and Blackwoods, with Thomas and Owen exchanging technical expertise, Catherine and Claire pouring over the words that would represent the risky journey to the world. In the end, their spouses thought the journey would be better left unpublicized. Too many people might put their fears on the children and sink their hopes. Thomas had to tell St-Denis he couldn't go with him to Ohio, that there wouldn't be any room for him in the car. To Catherine's disappointment, he would still drive down to Xenia. The Galloway girl was bringing gifts, too many to fit in the canoe.

~ 7 ~

TRADITIONALLY, AUTUMN IN SOUTHWESTERN ONTARIO fired the trees to burning hues, Clem thought as she lay on her side in bed waiting for the dawn to come, for TinTin to wake up. On cloudy days, the fall trees were even more beautiful, the colours seen through the prism of water drops. She could remember that. And she wanted it again. For a second autumn, colour was soaked out, leaving the rust of death and decay. Everything drooped, and the membrane between water and air disappeared. The trees were blob-like sponges, saturated, and still they produced more leaves and branches to sop up the excess. Maples were unseasonably laden with chatelaines of rotting malformed keys; branches drooped low and smelled of rot instead of sweet leaves bright with sugars.

Then, just three days ago, the sun had come out. Light was the cure, surely, but the beauty of autumn was beyond rescue. All the sun did was dry the keys up so the whirlybirds dropped mouldy spores on everyone. Leaves fell from trees in clumps, like hair after chemotherapy treatments. As she watched the window, waiting for the sun to crack through the curtain, she couldn't shake the feeling of suspicion that the lack of rain gave her. The wisteria painted on the wall brightened, sinister after so many months of soft chiaroscuro, of smudges rather than form. The celebratory feeling the sunshine brought was wrong. What, it rains until we want to die, and then suddenly stops? It felt like a set-up. She imagined what might be coming: Sunday-school pictures of Judgment Day came to mind, bodies rising and the bones of the chosen dancing across graves. What next? Everlasting life? Joyous zombies with smiles stretched across their teeth. Bodies returning to dust, disintegrating on those very shouts of joy, and like the rain, obscuring the air. Motes rising and twirling, all dead, all death. What was really coming?

This rain wasn't over, she thought. It was up to something, and she turned onto her back to stare at the ceiling. Often the empty space above let her scry the best answers to her questions.

Three days ago, the barograph in TinTin's lab had gone wild with the differential pressures from the heat of the sun (TinTin's terminology, not hers) as it cleared the heavy skies of nimbostratus clouds. New clouds. Cumulous. Stratus. Cumulonimbus. The changing pressures created sudden downdrafts. Pockets of wind (her terminology) rushed and slapped the land and trees, sped across pooled water and pushed it over dikes. TinTin and Pi had called her parents every hour to warn them of the latest assault. While the boys crunched the science, she followed a newsfeed on rainbows. Softly, so she wouldn't wake TinTin, she whispered the hilarious words of the local weather anchor. "Now the rain romps among the clouds, flirting with the sun, creating sudden, dazzling rainbows." She and the boys had laughed: Science knew the angles made it *seem* there were many rainbows. Be that as it may, this playfulness of rain had her stumped. Her rain had always been serious.

Darn, she'd woke him up, and he was whispering their jokey response, "Maybe it's all the same rainbow."

"Maybe," she whispered back, and turned her head so their lips brushed. He held her face square to his.

It had been very hard to watch the winds trounce Chatham County. After almost two years of the same old rain, any change in the steady and depressing humidity was frightening, yet exciting. The anchors on the weather service cheered it on, calling the high pressure system a "sun dome." Her mother and father were excited too. The oldest maple on the farm, with a trunk the diameter of a small car, held firm. Then they could have cried as they watched Thomas' live video of a strip of fir trees to the northwest, the oldest in a series of windbreak plantings, fall like a row of pinwheels in child's play. "Bowled over" was how the anchors described similar events throughout the county.

White caps whipped across the Thames and over the top of the sandbags. Thankfully the river didn't breach them and the farmhouse held. Most houses withstood the wind, as they had withstood the water. In fact, TinTin thought maybe the humidity itself was responsible for holding things together. That would change if the sun stayed around.

"Talk to Catherine again," he said to Pi. "Tell her to get out."

"They have a huge outboard ready to go. She's ready to leave at the drop of a hat."

Clem waved her arm between them. "How is it they say they've seen five rainbows?"

"Not the same one, either," Pi said, nodding like he was high on something, likely the same thing as the weather anchor.

"Stop encouraging her, you idiot," TinTin said to Pi. "They really should be leaving."

"Catherine appreciates me. More than you, some days."

"It's sad enough without you egging her on."

"Guys!"

All the dull routines had been disturbed by the lack of rain. Their whole sense of survival was turned upside-down. Light waltzed in, creating havoc. There should be rules. One rule that never changed was remember to eat. Clem ordered pizza. The bickering stopped.

Before that first day of sunshine ended, they picked up one last interesting newsfeed. In a newer subdivision to the south of her mother, the windows in every house blew out in sequence, the new houses being hermetically sealed, so that as the wind trounced, a vacuum was created. They burst like corks from the differential pressure.

That was three days ago. The "sun dome" was still a big deal. She hadn't found an answer to rain's disappearance, and the sun was about to come up again.

Clem lay on her side, looking into TinTin's steady brown eyes. "I haven't really processed this sun stuff enough. Tell me it'll be alright."

TinTin stroked her cheek with his thumb, drew it over her lips, down her neck, brushing her fine hair back. "Everything will be alright." His voice didn't quiver, his eyes never blinked.

She sighed, rolled over and snuggled into the curve of his body, tugging his arms around her. She closed her eyes and remembered the last call she took from her mother after midnight two days ago. Tired and deflated, Catherine said that with only twelve days until the celebrations, Chatham County had a lot to clean up. The Premiere of Ontario wanted to declare the county a disaster area, and proceed more quickly with the controlled flood. There had been an emergency meeting in the upper rooms of the Tecumseh Tavern.

"'Typical of the province to overreact,' that's what Madeleine French said."

"You were there?"

"Your father drove. We picked up Frank on the way."

The council discussed their options. They would have liked the military to aid in the cleanup, but not if it meant calling everything off. Her mother mimicked the voice of TK Holmes saying, "Wouldn't something like that turn aside the tourists?"

After a short debate, so her mother said, the council came to a unanimous agreement: given that the local infrastructure was accustomed to brown-outs and disaster, given that none of the major highways was washed out, given that they had developed some extremely resourceful alternatives to utility maintenance, they would cope with the troubles on their own.

"Good on you, Mom!" Clem had said with as much enthusiasm as a wet blanket. A night of nightmares followed. What were her mom and her neighbours doing?

TinTin shook her gently. She opened her eyes. Sunshine flickered across the wisteria carpet. It touched the bed covers, crept closer and closer to them. TinTin reached his hand over her body, into the light. The sun touched his pale skin.

"Tell me again," he said in a sleepy voice, "why your parents won't leave the sinking ship?"

Clem whispered a childhood story to him, how every October the County of Chatham held a festival dedicated to all things early 1800. Mead and hard cider replaced beer; storytellers and town criers wandered the streets. Punch and Judy puppet shows entertained the adults and frightened the children. British regiments lined up against Kentucky militia. Indians wore red jackets and native headdresses. And in the thick of it, a stately, yet quiet character moved. Tecumseh lived. It was a magical transformation, and at the same time, not too far removed from the daily life on her grandparents' farm. The costumes, the gear, the old way of talking turned ordinary people into historic players.

"They never act. They become the past, somehow."

'It's the bloody pioneer spirit." TinTin rubbed his eyes. "It's the same people intermarried generations later."

"I'm one of them."

"Thomas seems to have become one of them as well. I hope to stay on the outside."

"Aw, you're fresh blood."

"The town hates me."

"It would be the same if I went to live with you in Jericho. A newcomer waltzes in and they think she wants a share of the pie she hasn't yet earned. I will spend my life fitting you into my arms, my heart, my life. But the town has to work you among the many into its fabric until you're seamless. Only recently has Dad been that pliable and willing to spend the time."

"Your parents do realize that the whole area is sunk after the bicentennial."

"Mom says there's some kind of genetic programming that makes her return like a spawning salmon, and that's why she won't give it up easily."

Clem pretended to scoop up sunlight by the handful, let it trickle through her fingers onto the covers.

"The weave of Catherine's childhood is rotting," TinTin said. Clem rubbed her warm hands on his arm. "This social fabric of which she and you are a thread, would it perhaps be another kind of Net worth studying?"

"I think it's been studied enough. There's no culture more documented and headstrong than my mother's."

~

After breakfast, Clem sat in the sunlight and remembered before the rain. Not merely nostalgic, but remembering the goodness of sun in her life. By the time she walked hand in hand with TinTin to the University, she was enjoying the warm sunshine, and feeling like they were springtime lovers. A delicious feeling. TinTin, in this happy groove, was taking his time to get to work, still cautious of dangers but his head up more often than down.

They were a block away from campus when she saw Pi walking towards them.

"I couldn't stay in the lab any longer."

"So, you had to find us?" TinTin said.

"Give him a break." Clem made room for Pi to join them. "We're happy to see you."

"I've just had coffee with the last guy in Botany Bay. He's been filling me in on tree activity."

"Relax, man, the wind has died down."

"No, according to Keith, there's more to come."

Still holding Clem's hand, TinTin picked up the pace. She kept dragging him back, interested in what Pi had to say. Pi talked fast.

"Trees are generally less than fifty percent water. The rest is cellulose. That ratio and the cohesive properties of water help them to defy gravity as they reach for the sun. Keith looked up the ratios yesterday: spruce twenty percent, willows forty percent, maples as much as thirty. Those are just the trees he thought I would recognize in the park. When it was raining, these vascular plants bloated their leafy boughs in an attempt to transpire more water, but the evaporation couldn't keep up with the rate of rain. Now that the sun is shining again, the trees are instinctively pumping the excess water to their extremities so they can raise their heads again. The older trees, sadly, are affected by embolisms. The sudden sunlight is too much, and they are popping like champagne corks—exploding from a combination of heat and water vapour. I'm on a mission to film it. Keith says the event should peak any time now. What a show this will be!"

"We've got work to do."

"I've already been in the lab for hours, so screw that. For the next while, you'll find me filming the Kingdom *Plantae* in action. Keith would, but he's got a conference call this morning."

Pi pulled his sunglasses from his shirt pocket and ran his fingers through his hair so that it stood up in spikes.

"You still look like a geek."

"I'm happy with that."

As Pi veered off towards the park, TinTin shouted, "Did you put on sunscreen? You know you always burn!"

Pi shrugged and kept walking.

"Don't be an idiot! Get a drone to do it! What are you doing chasing after trees, suddenly Nature Boy?"

"Like you were once, bending microwaves around G-waves at the brickworks."

"That was different. You could get hurt."

"Not me. I've figured out a Net pattern to ward off the assault."

"Let him go," Clem said. "I'll follow him once I drop my gear." She dropped a kiss on TinTin's cheek, and took the short cut across the quad to her studio. On the way, her phone buzzed. Simple Pi was messaging her.

>*I've stripped down to my tee-shirt. Can you believe it?*
>*Disgusting.*
>*Come join me. The corks have started popping and the sounds are crazy-mad. You'll love them.*
>*Record them. I'm on my way.*

Then she messaged TinTin.

>*The party has started. Come join us.*
>*I have a meeting. Soak up enough sun for both of us. Love.*

By the time Clem got to the park, the walkway was almost impassable with chunks and fragments of exploded bark and lost limbs. Black willows, with their tendency to lean anyways, had split from their bases and split again along the length of their trunks. They lay on the ground in massive tangles.

>*They look like beached whales fallen from the sky.*
>*Pi, where are you?*

~

TinTin left the meeting without an explanation. The messages from Simple Pi had stopped, and Clem's had become incoherent. Evidently he had gotten lost somewhere in the campus' few acres of Kingdom *Plantae*.

>*Clem, wait at the edge of the park for me. I'm tracking him down through the GPS on his phone.*

The park looked like a disaster zone, like it'd been bombed, but the smell wasn't of munitions. It smelled of fresh wood and something more astringent, like chlorine. Clem was waiting off to one side, clear of anything taller than three feet. She was drawing, her phone pressed under the thumb that held the sketchbook.

"Still haven't heard from him?"

Clem shook her head, no.

TinTin messaged Pi.

>*I'm at the park now. Shout so I can hear you*

Silence.

TinTin shouted out Pi's name, and his given name too.

Silence.

He nodded to Clem, and they walked into the debris, careful of anything still standing, following the GPS signal from Pi's phone.

>*Pi, we can't see you on the path*

"Pi!"

>*Are you hurt?*

"Pi!"

>*Where are you, man?*

He couldn't possibly be at the same location as his phone. TinTin pointed it out to Clem. "There, on the ground under those branches."

Before he could stop her, Clem was climbing through. She couldn't find it.

"It's there, just move some stuff."

Beside Clem, a great old willow heaved and creaked. It'd already been split apart, an embolism blasting the top off, steam rising from it.

"Sorry, sister," Clem said, "you smell pretty bad."

"It's the ozone."

"Come here and tell me that. The tree's already exploded."

TinTin picked his way over and gagged. "It smells like bad barbeque."

>Pi, where are you??

"Pi!"

"The GPS says the phone is here. Pi should be here."

"This is weird, even for Pi." Clem dialed Pi's phone. It rang above them, from the steamy opening of the great tree. TinTin boosted her up to get it. In a flash she had it, and he reached out for it, hung up on the call.

"We don't want to know how it got there, do we?"

"The phone will tell us. Let's see what he's done." TinTin scrolled through the functions, found the most recent date stamps. "He was recording, not even paying attention to our texts."

They looked at each other. "Play it."

Crackles, pops. *It's ozone man, coming from the ground. It stinks like a bad connection on an electric streetcar.* Violent pops. The unmistakable sizzle of electricity. One, two, three explosions, like artillery. Four, five, six. Seven. A hit, no warning whistle to proceed it.

TinTin felt ill. The Net should have protected Pi.

Air whizzed, burred, drilled, sucked. *I'm picked up, some kind of vortex. I'm levitating, man. My hair is standing on end. My arms—the capillaries are popping on my skin like tree branches. Traveling up. Burning in. No pain. no worries, man.* A huge concussive boom.

TinTin dropped the phone and grabbed Clem, pushed her to the ground. Silence for a full minute. Another minute of silence. He twisted to look at the sky, the hair at the nape of his neck standing on end. All clear, but then a drone doesn't come with a whistle. Tears streamed down Clem's face. TinTin began to shake. "Fuck you bastards!" He reached for the phone again. The digital counter ticked on. At four minutes, seven seconds, Pi spoke again, the hiss of venting steam making it hard to hear him.

Sooo hot in here. Inside a tree. In a mother of all trees. Like a sauna. I'm burning up. Creaks and hissing. Gasps. Sobs. A back and forth rocking sound. *TinTin, man, I can see the sky. I'm gonna toss the phone so it doesn't fry. And buddy, remember the bone china? It's like the Herge book, you know, The Calculus Affair. So be careful, man.* A thud, sounds of wood or bark splitting. Ricocheting. More thuds like footsteps hitting the ground. High pitched *Ahhhgh!* The wind, or was it a human voice? A sing-song voice. *Lalah lalalala, lalahhh.* Creaky rocking.

"Pi, where are you?" Clem shouted, struggling to get up.

TinTin pulled her back down. "This is so fucking not funny! Pi!"

The recording counter had stopped, but the creaking sound continued. TinTin turned the phone off. He listened. Nothing but that creaking old tree, and now a layer of cirrocumulus clouds above, cooling the air slightly. A ridge of cirrostratus forming to the southwest, about to cover the sun with a thin blanket. And a creaking, rocking sound behind them.

The coroner said that Simple Pi died of compressive asphyxiation, similar to deaths experienced by farm workers in silo accidents. The tree collapsed in on him. How he'd managed to get inside it was a mystery. TinTin wiped the recording from the phone.

~

Simple Pi's funeral took place three days later, a simple trip through a gas kiln in a cardboard box. The box had been printed with a facsimile of Pi's social network home page, with photos and comments of friends and colleagues, his Likes and favourite links, all in his preferred colours. He would have liked it, thought TinTin. The company did a good joB After the cremation, Simple Pi's mother and father took the ashes up in a small aircraft into the milky blue sky. TinTin watched the sun glint off the wings as the plane banked. His best friend's remains lifted in a mass, spiraled in the aircraft's wake, then dispersed over the university. Today, with the prevailing winds, we breathe him in.

"There was no one who could obsess over a problem like Pi," he'd said in his eulogy at the crematorium. "James was the real TinTin, truly the blond hero who knew where to go and what to do next in any sticky situation. I have had the privilege of being his lucky sidekick all these years. And now without Pi, I'm not sure how the story will go. Or if I'll ever get to the bottom of the Theory of Everything."

Afterwards, back at their house, Clem's mother gathered him in one of her sensory hugs. It reminded him of the old tree, grabbing onto Pi and suffocating him, but he stood still and took it. He wished his parents could have come too, but with the flooding, seats on airlines were scarce, and getting visas would take too long. As TinTin stood in Catherine's circle, motionless, he sensed a neediness in her. He patted her shoulder in a way he thought might comfort her. She held him tightly for a moment, then pushed him away to look at him at arms' length.

"I'm sorry to ask," Catherine asked anyway, "but did James get the research done, the information about crossing Lake Erie?"

TinTin knew what she was thinking, of her responsibility for the lives of the Ohio teens who were about to get in a canoe to visit her. He knew she'd asked Pi for this favour, and was glad she brought it up, instead of waiting for him. *This little project* as Pi and she called it wasn't something that Pi had hidden from him. They'd both contributed to the data. Catherine would miss James so much. Though he was no James, he'd have to pick up the slack.

"I'll get it for you."

He handed Catherine a manila folder with the rough notes he'd printed out earlier. Let her get a feel for the process of research, he thought, for all the variables that we can see and the ones hidden between gigs of theory and data. She read from various pages out loud.

>The lake: freshwater, vast body of organic particles, various industrial chemicals, and motion. The motion/wavelengths that could get them through, a Zen practice of becoming "as the lake" and "of the lake." Tecumseh's canoe would help. The randomness of the lake's actions would too—waves come in varying intervals, create sound; sound might help the crossing. Pythagoras' theory that music ruled the world—long wavelengths holding life together on the planet. Rock music and grunge and screaming techno all indicators of earth stress. The Japanese shakuhachi flute saving us all. Physically, water in us = water outside, pressure in us versus pressure of

water at 174 metres above sea level. The canoe carrying air, space and how to hide it. Or will that air flow in and over the gunnels just as lake water flows around and beneath the canoe below?

>Other life: fish, lamprey eels, turtles, water animals from the river that cross from shore to shore. Algae, gill nets, diving ducks, gulls, shipwrecks. Bones of shipwrecks lie below. Bones are dense, settle in silt where the sedimentary stage of rock formation occurs. Will become pressed and one day pushed into a shore line like the cliffs of Dover. To be made into new china dishes for Catherine. Or to become shale, compressing gasses, sinking carbon.

>How the kids cross without being detected: Diet should be organic, traditional and they'll read like a water animal, the regular splashing of old wood paddles nothing remarkable, unreadable to the Safety Net which is forever tuned to the future, to the next artificial substance. No plastic bottles, no life preservers. No complexity. Simplicity is the way to hide; purity of thought in the context of myth, in terms of drug quality. Eat local fish, not breaded or fried. Mercury fillings ok and silver in the amalgam won't be detected. Lots of mercury in the lake. Plastics in composite fillings may not pass if in large quantities.

>Willows and scrub will mark the river's mouth at landing. Look for sea rocket and spurge, burr cucumber and beach pea. Algae bloom will also mark entrance if the waters are calm. Depends on the amount of manure in the runoff.

>Cool nights but water still warm enough from the summer to modify temperature. Comfortable on the surface, too cold for swimming. Fog a strong possibility so take a compass made of iron and quartz. Electronics won't pass through the Net. Avoid passing over shipwrecks which can set a false north reading.

>Take willow leaves, not sharp, rather gummy. A chew will ease muscle aches. Or labour pains. Just joking. TinTin wants children, as if no one knew.

"His life, it was too short, so short." Catherine closed the file, waved it in the air, as if she could conjure him back. TinTin wished she had that magic, to bring back lives just as she brought life back to her artifacts. "He was the dearest soul I know, and never had a chance." She looked to Thomas, and snuffed with her emotions. Clem and Thomas curled like brackets on either side of her, handing out tissues, murmuring kind words. Under her lashes, she looked his way, and TinTin knew she wasn't looking for comfort. Like him, she was looking for those bits of Pi that she could carry forward. His work, his life, his thoughts—curated and alive because she bothered, and knew he would too. Shit, he'd finally been drawn into Catherine's orbit, and from the looks of it, his first job was to rescue her.

"Look," TinTin said, "you guys are staying for the night, so let's forget this until the morning. The project is good. I say we order in beer and Chinese food, and work our way through the vintage games. Pi would like that."

Catherine lifted her head. "Vintage games?"

"Yes."

Thomas laughed out loud. "He means video games."

"There are vintage video games? I love them already."

~ 8 ~

SHE MOVED CAREFULLY IN THE GLOOM of dawn. The oil lamps were extinguished, the last candle put out and placed on the hearth. She had let the fire die out yesterday, but stirred the ashes anyway until she was sure there were no embers that might re-ignite and start a blaze in her absence. Despite the chill of the house, she was warmed by her nerves.

She reckoned there might be another hour before Mr. Blackwood and the Wests came by for her. Her portmanteau was packed with both modern and traditional clothes. The formal gown Mrs. Blackwood had sent was perfect for the dedication. It was folded back into the tissue, and back into the maker's box it had come in, wrapped again in the thick brown paper and tied with string. Everything was stacked by the kitchen door. The paddles for the canoe were waxed and the oilskin tarps rolled up in compact bundles. Hard biscuits and cheese, pumpkin corn bread and jerky were set in tins. Fresh water filled skins, except for one, which contained sherry for emergencies, everything her daddy would pack. Gloves and hats and buckskin jackets were in another pile. She wore a boy's shirt, and breeches made just for the trip, which fastened at the back so she could pee into the bailing tin. She'd come up with the idea after eavesdropping on an argument between Leticia and Miles—not about peeing—but how likely it was for women wearing traditional clothes to drown. They'd been heating pitch by the boathouse to waterproof the canoe. She'd been down by the water running her hands over the bottom of the canoe, tapping, tugging. It had to be perfect, then tightly sealed.

"We have to wear garb," Miles said, "to cross the Net."

"Those clothes are a death sentence." Leticia's voice rose to a whine.

Miles shushed her, but Leticia hissed back, "Can't you still see her mother going under, the weight of those skirts pulling her down?"

Miles groaned as though his belly ached, and Rebecca stayed stalk still, waiting to hear his reply. Leticia broke the silence, whispered, sounding like she was in tears. "And her dad, how he stayed with her mom. He could have made it to shore, but he stayed with her."

Rebecca didn't have that memory of the drowning, of the helpless witness. She hadn't been told that bit, not when she'd washed her parents' bodies, so careful not to press on the bruises. Gently she'd eased out fragments of cloth and river debris from gashes and scrapes. Inch by inch, the soft flannel washed over their blue-grey flesh, hoping to warm it back to pink. They might really be alive. People just made mistakes, even about death. But when she washed their faces, she saw Death, not Salvation. She'd cried then, the only time, and prayed for their souls to return. Souls were eternal, right? It was unconscionable that they should have parted that day with just a regular kind of goodbye, when she really needed something grand. Some direction and blessing on her life. Now she believed maybe Miles was that blessing, and his sister too, for all her stubborn ways. Rebecca had rested her face against the side of the canoe and looked out at the turgid river. They would all wear breaches, and coats that were easy to shuck off. No one need drown.

The rain, it seemed, could not say good-bye. It had returned just moments ago, not as a downpour, but a drizzle. It brought the slugs out, large and fleshy. Her face pressed to the window, she watched their pink underbellies crawling up past her nose, leaving trails of slime. She should pick the pests from the wall and take a bucket of treats into the chickens and geese, but she'd already been to the barn and done the chores.

She'd crated the fattest Pilgrim, picking the goose's warm, sleep-heavy body out of the straw. It was her contribution to the Canadian Thanksgiving which would be celebrated the weekend after the bicentennial. Herbs and a current cordial for dressing were packed in a small box with the other gifts she had chosen.

While she was gone, Mr. West promised to take good care of the homestead, and Mrs. West had promised to distract the Heritage Authority from making improvements or interfering in any other way. They'd be gone for five or six days. It could turn into a week. Still, an opportunity to put an uneasy past to rest was rare. Rare as sunshine, but not unheard of.

Rebecca had one last piece of business to take care of. She took up a cloth soaked in lavender water and laid it over her face. "It's your last chance to come out." She turned towards the kitchen hearth. Nothing there. She loosened her shirt and dipped the cloth in again, then placed it over her heart by the locket that had set the bones rumbling like morning thunder a few months ago.

"Come out, you lazy Indian, and talk to me."

Now there was movement from high at the far side of the hearth. Inch by inch the bundle worked its way to the edge of the crevice and beyond, teetering like a fulcrum in an alchemist's laboratory, the kind of place where Boyle had turned sand into gold. Rebecca willed the bones to transform into a proper man, or ghost, one she could converse with rationally. The bundle wiggled and shook—with love or hate, which was it? She wanted his side of the story, to see him stand on his own two feet. The bundle wavered at the critical point, dipping towards the floor, then pulling back, only to tip dangerously again.

Fool! You catch those bones!

Sharp like a knife, the words pushed between her shoulder blades, causing Rebecca to leap forward as the bundle fell. It struck her breast and she brought her arms around it. Shaking with anger, Rebecca swung about to protect her back. That ghost again. Old Rebekah had aged over the summer, more wraith than ever, but lost none of the vinegar in her.

You treat him with dignity. Hasn't he been through enough?

"Him? What about us? Me?" Rebecca nodded to the bundle. "If you'd married him, you would have been up there in Canada already, and I wouldn't have to leave. Maybe you'd have stayed with the Mohawks."

Not the Mohawks, he'd have none of the Six Nations.

"Brant's family lived like lords."

He wouldn't live like them and their white ways. I wouldn't live like him.

"You have no obligation to care for him. He's no relation to us."

Girl, you don't know the half of what you're saying.

"You stabbed me in the back, I know that. You put him before family."

No! No, I never, not even now. What I'm saying is, you don't want to stir him up. That's not the way to get peace.

"Almost two hundred years of molly-coddling these bones. That's not peace."

Don't you complain to me. I have tended them, listened to them shake, rattle, disappear into sullen silence, then sub like crickets on an August night. They scratch, scrape, struggle, jump, twitch, sneak, bang, lurk, stealthily listen, openly eavesdrop, tantrum, sing, keen, tumble. You barely know him, and now look at you, dressed like a boy. I know what you're up to. Throw them in the lake for all I care.

"Well!" Rebecca looked down at the bundle, her heart jumping against the deerskin; the bones remained still in her arms. "I will put him to rest, and you too."

She stepped towards the apparition, squared for another attack. The ghost flared up, then faded back as Rebecca tried to thrust the bones into the dead one's arms. There must be some way to do it, she reasoned, and then they could all stay home. But old Rebekah crossed her arms over her chest, and jinnied herself out of the kitchen, leaving the bones curled in the young woman's arms, warmed again after a night in the cold hearth. "You better get used to the cold," she told him. No movement.

There was nothing left for Rebecca to do but roll the deerskin-wrapped bundle up in the last oiled tarp. As she did, the words of the old woman sang in her head and burned on her cheeks. *Throw them in the lake for all I care.*

She was still flushed when car headlights shone through the kitchen window. Mr. Blackwood had arrived. The introductions passed quickly. He seemed reluctant to load the goose in the car, but he sure did admire the canoe.

~ 9 ~

THOMAS LEFT THE HOMESTEAD with the goose and suitcases, and wondered how the children would fit too. On this part of the trip, the children, as he called them in his thoughts, despite their ages and expertise—and Rebecca's old soul—rode with Owen West. He followed the Wests' car with the canoe on top to Highway 75 and drove north to Maumee Bay, then along the back roads to the place where the canoe would be launched.

The Galloway girl was clearly the leader of the expedition. As soon as the cars stopped, she was supervising the removal of the canoe and cargo from the Wests' car. Father and son carried the canoe with Rebecca leading the way. She snapped willow twigs beneath her boots, pushing them deeper into creek banks, where they would root and spread, as willows do throughout the world. She announced as much to the expedition. She commented on the "civilized grace and elegant shade" of the location. According to her, they were heading to a *near* perfect launch site.

Thank goodness she was happy with it, thought Thomas. In the dark of early morning, it looked a miserable place. He held his flashlight high, knocking water from overhead branches. The shoreline was hidden. The woods were as lush as a tropical forest. In a normal fall season, in a normal climate, access to the rivers and woods would be easier; the plants would have died down long ago. Catherine said the fall of 1813 was miserably wet like this, but much colder. He was sweating beneath his jacket. He imagined the damp chill the children would have to endure once they were out on the lake.

Rebecca, despite the undergrowth, kept up a running commentary. "Have you noticed, Mr. Blackwood, how the skunk cabbage has risen in the wrong season. Perhaps the recent sunshine is responsible." Next, she warned him quite sternly not to touch the towering water hemlock on either side, then followed up with a question in a more conversational tone. "How is the mosquito situation in Chatham County, Mr. Blackwood?"

"Much better now, thank you."

She plucked some stalks from shoulder-high plants. The tall leggy plant broke wet and bled a sticky sap that clung to his clothes. "Spotted jewelweed, also in its second flowering. It's the antidote for bites." For the trip presumably, thought Thomas, or perhaps for an infestation that may be waiting on the Canadian shore. He wouldn't ask.

She stopped and pointed. Thomas heard the water lapping before he saw it. Feeling useless, he watched Rebecca and the Wests prepare the canoe in an easy, practiced manner. He'd read of slaves and rum smugglers navigating by the stars and following the Dipper. The protective cover of night for all things clandestine. In darkness, one didn't see the details, one wasn't seen by others. Yet the darkness had lifted since they left the road. The grey dawn offered a different kind of cover, a suffocating flannel blanket of fog. He could see over the top of it, standing on the shore, but the children would be tucked into it out on the water.

Leticia pulled out a compact SLR camera, caught her brother and Rebecca lowering the canoe into the undergrowth, the bow sliding forward to touch Lake Erie. At the moment, it wasn't raining; water lapped the shore regularly, tiny touches. Rebecca held a compass and pointed out across the lake. "North East." Another picture.

Owen took the camera, a Net-restricted article, and pulled Leticia in close for a last hug and kiss. Miles had climbed to the bow of the canoe. He and Rebecca seemed patient with the delay of the embrace; then Rebecca was quick to guide Leticia to her place in the centre of the canoe. Leticia would hold the compass from now on, facing Rebecca and the Ohio shoreline, and guide them to Ontario. They should cross before evening. They had a full day.

Before the fog could swallow them, Owen called out to Rebecca to turn the canoe towards the shore so that he could take a picture. Leticia was barely visible over the gunnels. He caught the three children gliding under the blanket, a record of a rather startling disappearance, Thomas thought, as West showed the photos to him. Both were struck by the fact they could have been taken two hundred years ago. No matter what the era, it was a lonely scene.

West led the way back to the road and hastily, they said their goodbyes. It was up to Thomas to make it to Ontario by road, and then find the children on the other side. So far, the roads had been in good repair. He'd get updates from Hiram along the way.

West handed Leticia's camera to Thomas.

"She will want this on the other side."

Thomas nodded.

"And call us."

"When I get there. And the moment I see them."

As he tucked the camera into his coat pocket, he thought of the images, or what some might believe were their souls, as being in his protective custody for the journey. Thomas doubted that he would ever let Clementyne do anything this risky. Hypocritical, he knew. The night before, he'd spent hours talking circles around the idea of Owen following them in another canoe. There was a saying about angels and a fear of treading, which he couldn't quite express during the long night, but everyone felt it. The timing was right, the artifacts accurate. The reasons seemed pure enough. The West children were exercising their rights to cross the international border. There were no controversies surrounding it. Even his son-in-law had said that the very youth of this mission would be the best insurance for its success.

It was the strangest artifact shipment he'd supported. Living children in a canoe rumoured to be over two hundred years old. He'd get a better look at it on the other side.

~ 10 ~

PASSING THROUGH THE WHITE FOG gave the impression that the canoe stood still. There was no receding shoreline for Leticia to judge the speed or distance. Her shoulder and neck ached from the tension of holding the compass out for Rebecca to navigate by. She couldn't imagine how badly Rebecca and Miles would hurt by the time they reached the Canadian shore. The needle swung as they hit incoming swells and crossed the shore currents. Once out on the cooler deep water, the fog finally lifted. Wraiths of mist swirled around them.

"It's like stepping on a grave. Doesn't it give you guys goose bumps?" The alternating warm and cold was disconcerting in another way—she needed to pee. "Miles, can you not see a way to go around them?" She hadn't meant to complain. It was just that in the silence, she could hear them breathing hard on each stroke, but not the paddles cut into the water. It was getting to her.

They both answered at once. "We'd go in circles," and "Keep that compass direction true, or I'll throw you in and let the fog get you."

"No way!" Leticia squealed despite herself. "There are monster eels in the lake!"

Miles must have turned and caught Rebecca's eye, for Rebecca shook her head sharply with a look meant to shush him. It wasn't a look for her, and Leticia said, "You may not believe this, Miles, but I know you guys are making fun of me."

She hated being the baby on this trip. She shivered again and resisted the urge to pee. They'd had her practice with the bailing can on the roughest parts of the river, but she didn't want to be the first to go. More silence followed, and she wondered why they had adjusted their technique to reduce the break on the upswing. Maybe the wake of their paddles had already caught the interest of eels. Thankfully, she was too low in the canoe to see.

Every movement they made told a story from where she sat. The canoe was that sensitive. When they moved past the initial turbulence, Rebecca relaxed somewhat about seeing the compass heading. That girl, thought Leticia, already had a sense of the lake below her. Now there was just the tedium of steady stroking. Once she'd peed, there was little to stop Leticia from nodding off as long as she kept the compass outstretched. She jerked awake whenever the rhythm broke, and checked the bearing. Rebecca nodded that things were okay. At one point, she woke to a discussion of Miles' weight training plan, how their arms were aching to the point of numbness despite it. Such pitiful complaints raised her spirits. She announced that it was snack time, and passed the water skins and unwrapped the pumpkin bread. It must have been hours since they had eaten and in the excitement, it hadn't been much.

Without any notice, the canoe hit turbulence and lurched into what looked like the wake of a ship. The stern swung wildly as Miles tried to correct their course. Miles' portion of bread floated out past the left gunnel. All he achieved was to splash Leticia. She opened her mouth to complain, but the food suddenly wasn't sitting well. The canoe rocked violently and she grabbed onto the sides.

"Leticia! Are we on course?"

"Yes." She gestured the heading with her arm.

"Don't take your eyes off it. You must tell me if we go off course."

Leticia held the compass, but the swinging needle gave her a sense of vertigo. She could only glance at the compass in small doses. In between, she focused on Rebecca's knees in front of her, counted the strokes as Rebecca swung the paddle from side to side. Whenever the turbulence took them off course, she shook her head and swung her arm out in the direction of NE. When it stayed true, she nodded, hoping her arm matched the bearing of the needle accurately enough. Then Rebecca pushed the paddle into the water and held it there as a rudder. Leticia could feel it. It was as if the canoe had a sail and the wind skippered it forward. The current was carrying them.

"Leticia, you need to watch the compass, but in the meantime, Miles and I can finish eating."

"Did you know about this?" asked Miles. He reached for more bread and cheese. Being in the bow, thought Leticia, he should have seen "this" coming.

"I'd heard there were currents in the lake, that the Indians and traders knew them. There's no guarantee of finding any. They change depending on the season, the moon."

"Whatever is doing it, it feels weird to be pulled through."

"Pulled through faster than we could paddle."

Leticia set the compass on her lap and returned to the provisions. She passed the tin of dried apples to Miles and offered more biscuits to Rebecca. Rebecca shook her head against another bite. Leticia packed the tins away, and stared at the compass cupped between her knees. She looked out at the flat, calm lake, then at the rippling band of current that ran alongside them, just below the surface. It rubbed against the hull, spreading and twisting like ribbons unravelling behind them. Hypnotic. After a while, she needed to break the silence again.

"Do you believe in the rumours about vortexes, the kind that suck boats down to the bottom?"

"I suppose that if another band crosses this current that the intersection could create a vortex. We'd sink so fast. You'd better say your prayers now."

Leticia heard the tease in Miles' reply and didn't respond, didn't look up from the compass. She nodded her head to the right. Rebecca swung her paddle into the lake to place the canoe a little better in the current. Even though it was a free ride, Leticia felt the adrenaline running in her legs. She hadn't thought of the lake as having such a strong personality. She was used to seeing trees on the horizon of Greene County's small lakes. *We're sitting ducks out here.* She could swim, but where to? Blue eyes, green eyes, brown eyes scanned the lake in all directions. This time, Rebecca broke the stillness.

"Listen up, Miles. If we see a vortex, we paddle deep and hard. We hit the currents just right, then we jump it."

"Oh shit!" said Leticia. "You're too funny! You can't pop a wheelie in a canoe in Lake Erie."

Miles laughed so hard the canoe trembled. "I hope she can. It'd be a pleasure to be part of it."

"If we survived and didn't end up on the bottom of the lake."

"A little pessimist, aren't you?" Rebecca made as if to splash her. Leticia held her hands out for mercy, and Rebecca smiled back.

She had to pee again. It was all the sitting still in the damp air. Another amusing interlude for Miles to tease her about, as she jostled the canoe very minimally. Rebecca's version of pioneer boy pants were working just fine.

"Something smells. Is that you Leticia?"

She turned the contents into the lake and rinsed the can, then turned and hit her brother across the back with it.

"You better have rinsed that out!"

"Maybe I did. Maybe I didn't. Afraid of getting wet?"

"Seriously, don't you smell it?"

He was right: the quality of air over the lake had changed, as though all the smells from human and wildlife activity had gathered into one place. It smelled of fish mixed with oil with fugitive whiffs of smoke, cleaning agents, paint, car exhaust, grass cuttings, sewage. Some spots carried only one smell. They started a guessing game, with the winner having to chew a hard biscuit and whistle a tune.

At one point Rebecca stopped. She said to Leticia, in her serious way, "You know that without a compass bearer, we couldn't cross this lake."

Miles grunted. "I smell sentimentality. Must have followed us all the way from the Galloway place."

"Sweet, isn't it? Even if it's not for you."

The sound Miles made got Rebecca laughing so hard that she had to gesture for Leticia to pass the bailing can. Then more smells to guess.

Everyone figured it would take ten hours to cross, but they didn't carry a watch. It might set off the Safety Net. If the current continued on course, Leticia thought, they might be about half-way there. By the vague angle of sunlight, it looked to be around noon.

"Do you think we've crossed the border yet?"

"There's no way to tell."

"We'd know if Leticia's hair dye didn't grow out."

"Or if you cheated by eating at McDonalds."

"Like I would."

"You so would. You can't help it."

Rebecca enjoyed the teasing. She hadn't at first. She had taken sides, maybe natural for an only child to hear their teasing as disrespect. She didn't know that it was their way of noticing the other without it being sentimental. Leticia's mother had to explain that proper teasing was very respectful. With practice, Rebecca found her own wit and threw it in without taking anyone's head off. Like she had earlier, about jumping the vortex. Leticia decided it was good that Miles' girlfriend could be both funny and sentimental. Lately, she had begun to dream of replacing Miles with an older sister, someone who might understand her worries, her pleasures. Maybe if he chose to marry Rebecca, she might consider keeping him too.

The current tugged them on. It spread out into wider bands of grey, the only colour to reflect from the overcast sky. The lake around them had become littered with garbage. More smells. Bottles of sunscreen, water bottles, bits of foam buoys and pool noodles, take-out dishes, bits of feathers and oily fish guts.

"Inner tubes ahead!" Miles called out.

They passed through an island of medical supplies and floating IV bags. She hoped there would be no needles. No body parts. She didn't like her intimate, eye-level view. Leticia watched the compass more closely.

"I think I see the border ahead," said Miles.

"You think that's it?" Rebecca asked.

"See the line where everything bunches up. The current that's been carrying us is from the south, so that stuff must be caught on this side of the Safety Net."

"But we can pass through?"

"Of course. Unless Leticia has smuggled some chocolate bars."

"I have made sacrifices for this trip, I tell you." That made them laugh.

She was disadvantaged, faced backwards, and made the mistake of asking how close they were to the border. Miles began an annoying countdown. The current got more and more sluggish. At "One- Zero-" Miles had to go into the negative numbers. He and Rebecca dipped their paddles and pushed them deeper into the filth. Gulls cried and soared overhead. Leticia started glancing over her shoulder.

"Keep still," warned Rebecca.

It was too late. Leticia had seen the border: a mountain of garbage piled against an invisible wall. It was the point where some gulls passed through but most stayed on one side or the other, their gullets full of enough coded material to restrict their crossing. All of her school's Environmental Club's worries had been real. If they made it through, she would write letters to Washington about this mess.

Miles grunted and shoved aside the larger pieces of garbage with his paddle. Rebecca provided the power from behind. He shouted, "Hurrah!" as he passed into the open lake on the Canadian side. Free of the garbage, the canoe lurched forward, and Leticia was through. The tail end of the canoe, however, was stuck. Leticia lifted her head. Rebecca had set her mouth stubbornly and paddled hard. The canoe lurched sideways.

"What the hell? Leticia!" shouted Miles.

"It's not me!"

"You idiot!"

"It's Rebecca."

"No way."

Leticia looked around. Relatively clear water to one side, garbage piling up against the canoe on the other. As she pushed the plastics away from the canoe, she teared up.

"Yeah? All this time I've been getting lectured and she's the one who doesn't pass through." Leticia bit her lip. Rebecca's status had dropped back to being Miles' annoying girlfriend.

"She never eats anything or does anything that wouldn't be, like, pure."

"Pure?"

Leticia stared at Rebecca, trying that description on her. Rebecca was a misfit, in some ways like her. Pure or innocent wasn't a word that she'd use to describe either of them. What was that girl hiding? she wondered, and stared even harder until Rebecca glanced away in guilt.

"I did bring something that wasn't on the list." She reached underneath her seat and pulled out something wrapped in a tarp. Definitely not on the approved cargo list. She passed it to Leticia.

"Let me turn the canoe first." She looked apologetic but a little excited too, like a wish was coming true. "Take the extra paddle, Leticia, and push back the garbage. When we're ready, pass the bundle at my feet up to Miles. I think it's holding us back."

The strange bundle passed through the Net easily, and so did Leticia a second time. Rebecca looked stunned to be held back in home-waters for a second time. The canoe slewed sideways. This could get funny, thought Leticia, if she wasn't facing a wall of garbage, and beyond that, a wall of rain to the south. It was still some miles off but it was heading their way. Rebecca suggested taking another run at the border.

"Put more power in the stroke. Leticia can keep the garbage from piling in."

"Even if we could get our speed up, something at your end is holding us back. What else could it be?"

Rebecca's look of frustration turned to tears. "It has to be the bundle. Just throw the thing over. It's okay with me."

"There is no problem with this bundle."

"Throw it, Miles. I'm sure it'll get us through."

Leticia could see that Rebecca didn't understand the practical nature of the Safety Net. "Something else under your seat, or something you ate, or even something you put on today, is being registered as restricted. We won't cross the border until we find it."

Rebecca sniffed.

"I understand."

She back-paddled again, calling out instructions to Miles, so that the canoe pointed NE.

"May I have the bundle back?"

Leticia held the bundle for a moment, curious. Rebecca prodded her with the grip of her paddle to give it up. She set it by her feet, then reached through layers of clothing to fish out the ribbon that had hung around her neck all summer. The ribbon held a locket and she pulled it over her head, holding it out so that the locket dangled over the bundle. It swung like a pendulum, madly one way, then another. Leticia checked the compass. The needle stayed true.

The canoe rocked on the verge of moving sideways. Swiftly, Rebecca passed the locket to Leticia and picked up the paddle again.

"It's gold, isn't it?"

"What's gold?"

"This locket."

Just a lock of hair under a simple crystal face. On the back was an inscription:

For George
A token of my promise
RG
Christmas 1812

Reluctantly, she turned and passed it to Miles. By then Rebecca had the canoe stabilized. They moved forward through the garbage. The tip of the bow passed through, then Miles' knees, but he had to lean back. The locket was holding them back. With a scowl as black as the sky to the south, Rebecca took the canoe back several yards, out of the height of the garbage. She rested her paddle across the gunnels and leaned her forehead against it. The canoe bobbed gently;

plastic containers of all sorts bumped against the hull. Something moved at Rebecca's feet. Leticia put her hand on Rebecca's arm to warn her.

"If I wanted your comfort, I'd have asked."

"You don't have to be rude," said Miles. "We all make mistakes."

Leticia couldn't speak. The bundle was definitely creeping towards Rebecca.

"Who is George, anyway?" Miles asked. "Is he historical or, um, someone in the present?"

"Read the date, silly. *1812.* George is long dead and buried."

Rebecca raised her head, then followed Leticia's look. Cool and calm, she pulled the bundle up against her knees and ignored it.

"The locket was a gift from the Colonel's daughter to her cousin George. We talked about this before."

"But you didn't show me the locket."

"Someone gave it to me recently. It's not part of the Galloway collection. It's mine."

"It's registered somewhere," said Leticia. "The Net is reading it."

"Who gave it to you?"

"Someone who thought I should have it."

"I'm tossing it over."

Rebecca lunged forward. Leticia pushed her back down into her seat. The canoe tipped from side to side.

"Quit it, you two!"

"Pass it back, Miles."

Leticia took it from him and held the locket out to Rebecca, who whispered, "Hold the locket while I untie the ribbon. That was something I replaced."

She tossed the ribbon over. It fell across an international brand name water bottle.

"Before we make another try, you might tell me who gave it to you."

Miles was in a groove now. The suspicious boyfriend. She felt like the antebellum character, Melanie, sitting between Scarlet and Rhett, neither of them caring that Atlanta burned around them. Rebecca held onto the locket, and touched the crystal, wishing she could touch the lock of hair inside.

"Hers?"

Rebecca nodded.

"I never thought of the forbearers as having romance, or the cash to pull off something like this. It must have been important."

"She was the colonel's only daughter."

"It was more than that."

"Shut up for once, Miles."

"Maybe George wasn't Miss Galloway's first love."

"Not this again!"

Leticia looked from Rebecca to Miles. His shoulders were hunched towards the Canadian shore. Brooding.

"Who are we talking about?" she asked.

Rebecca had that guilty look again. It shifted towards the creepy bundle touching her breeches.

"George was brought in to break up the romance between Rebekah and Tecumseh."

"Ah." Leticia suddenly understood what people meant when they said, *and then the penny dropped*. "What I find more interesting is that the secret of the shaking hearth and mystery parcel is revealed to us in the middle of Lake Erie."

"What?"

"Don't be dense. That day, shortly after the summer work started, the hearth in the kitchen shook."

"That was water vapour."

"No, I think it was something else."

The canoe caught the wrong way in the current and rocked from side to side. In unison, Rebecca and Miles put their paddles in to counterbalance it. Junk washed against the canoe, oil and bilge garbage rose with the plastics to a dangerously high level against the hull.

"We have to get going." She would say nothing about the rain approaching. It was still somewhat distant, but like a chill creeping in.

Rebecca did not move. Leticia thrust the locket into her hand, then picked up the bundle and unwrapped the tarp. It was deerskin tied with wampum. Something old and sacred. Shells instead of beads. Hard shapes inside, like bones. She dropped it into the space between them.

"You bloody idiot! Do you know what you're playing with?" Rebecca's face was red, her voice high. "This locket meant that Tecumseh had no hope. He was courting Rebekah. After Raisin River, it was clear that Tecumseh's confederacy would not hold, and she chose George. She had a right to choose."

"And, Tecumseh had nothing to come back to," said Leticia quietly. "Is that what happened?"

Rebecca stared at the locket. "It wasn't her fault. What happened after that was not her fault."

"What's in the bundle, Rebecca?"

"The bundle?" asked Miles.

Rebecca looked up. "You mean *who*."

"Who?"

"It's *him*!"

"Holy shit!" Leticia jumped back, and the canoe rocked. Garbage spilled in. "Is he pissed at me?"

"For dropping him? Yes! You better hope that nothing broke."

It was too surreal, thought Leticia. She made herself sit still and breathe in time with the quick slaps of water lapping against the hull. Rebecca, with a major yuck-factor look on her face, picked the fish guts off the bundle, and dropped them over the side.

"We've had his bones all this time, our family, but I only just found out. It was on the night the hearth shook."

She looked at Leticia with respect for guessing right. Leticia smiled weakly.

"I knew the stories about him coming to the door with gifts, maybe a side of venison or a string of fish. About him learning to read. It was a bigger relationship than cousins, bigger than a regular "let's-get-together-and-make-babies" courtship. The bones came to life the day the locket arrived."

"Why is the locket so special?"

"She made her choice but it seems his bones still want her. Dead or alive he's got to understand that I can't let it go. It's all I have. This is where my family began. There has to be a way to get it across the border."

"I understand about the locket. But why bring that bundle?"

Rebecca started to shiver until her knees shook like a dog's.

"The bones are the reason you agreed to go to Chatham, aren't they?"

Rebecca nodded. Miles asked, "What did she say?"

"Yes."

With his voice as neutral as he could make it, just like their father did at work in serious situations, Miles pressed the issue. "What made you decide that?"

"To put him to rest. History didn't go right for his people, we know that. It's not my fault. All I know is that the bones have stuck to us."

"And?"

"I want to drop them in the lake." She sat up straight. "Rebekah Galloway had a right to choose her destiny. And I have a right to choose mine."

"Supposing we do have a bundle of bones in this here canoe," said Miles. "You understand that it's the locket holding us back. How did you come by it?"

Rebecca compressed her lips so hard that the edges turned white.

"It was Mrs. Blackwood," said Leticia. "In that package post-marked from Buffalo."

"Did she warn you not to bring it?"

"Okay, so I shouldn't have brought the locket. We can go back now."

"We're not going back." Leticia's voice came out sounding incredibly firm. She pointed south. "There's a wall of rain behind you. All three of us and the good Indian couldn't bail that much water fast enough. We cannot go back."

"Rebecca, you've got to trust," said Miles. He spoke so softly that Leticia felt embarrassed to be listening. "Think about what you told me out on the river."

"Go on."

"Be in this moment. We can't keep the locket. It won't pass through the Net."

"It's her hair inside it. I can't throw it over."

"Maybe you can take the lock of hair out."

"Maybe if the gold is soft enough."

"Rebecca, use your knife to pry up the glass. Keep the hair, and pass the locket to Leticia. Let's try to cross again."

In a minute Rebecca took the canoe forward. It stopped at the locket.

"We have to throw it over."

"I'd rather throw the bones over and go home."

Rebecca reached for the bundle but Leticia slapped downwards, hard. The bones fell to the hull again. Stung, Rebecca looked around.

"Is this where Tecumseh deserves to be buried?" asked Leticia. "In our culture's garbage?"

"But George is family."

"You have other reminders of George. You have his DNA inside you."

"Rebecca," said Miles. "Please. Do the right thing."

Rebecca sat like a stone. She touched the lock of hair to her cheek, then slipped it into the bundle.

"Are they really his bones?"

"I can show you later. There's a fracture in the femur."

"Put the locket overboard."

Leticia had never seen Rebecca look so naked, so honestly hurt and lost. A ghostly look crossed her face just before she dropped the locket over the side. With its weight, it tumbled easily through the plastic rubbish and slipped into the water, releasing a spiral of tiny bubbles as it sank.

Rebecca slipped her paddle back into the lake. This time, they passed through. The water on the other side was clean; the current pulled the canoe forward, slowly, then quicker. Leticia watched the line of garbage recede until it was a brilliant band of white across the horizon. A breeze picked up and sent shivers through them. Miles asked for the bailing can. Leticia kept one eye on the bundle at Rebecca's knees as she passed the skin of sherry around. She held the compass level.

"The current's still headed NE."

"Hey," said Miles, "look ahead!"

Leticia turned, expecting to see a rainbow or a vision of a warrior walking among the clouds. She sighed. A light rain hovered in the north east. She passed rain gear out to each of the paddlers, then pulled out the oiled cloths and spread them across the gunnels. The rain approached and receded, then caught them gently. Rain pebbled the surface of the lake. Thunder vibrated through the canoe before she heard it in the distance. An uncommon sound these days, she thought. To the south, a wall of yellow-green light moved towards Ohio.

"Someone's in for a big storm," she said, "but at least it's not us."

~ 11 ~

"I DIDN'T KNOW IT WAS THIS BAD."

When they turned onto the highway south of London, she folded her sketchpad shut and clasped her hands across her chest in the crash position. TinTin, she saw from the corners of her eyes, drove white-knuckled but confidently. He'd done this trip before with Simple Pi. TinTin drove along the higher, northwest bank. They were at Wardsville now. She marveled that there was a road at all, yet here they were on it, buttressed by sand bags and fallen trees. The rest of the flotsam was hard to look at: a child's pram, family vans, hockey equipment, furniture, snarls of hydro and telephone wire, homes and sheds. No one had prepared her for this. There was nowhere to stop or turn back. The crossroads were washed-out.

The last time Clem had seen the Thames River, it was a shallow ditch a bit larger than a plough's width. If you dropped the *h*, it became the Tame River. It had never rushed between high banks, like the Don did in Toronto, falling over itself in tumult. It wasn't a burly thing keeping more or less between steep banks, like the Credit River in Waterloo, fed by creeks that burrowed under the city in culverts. The river before her was broad and purposeful. Nile-like. *She* ran alongside the car like a long hungry tongue slurping up property and crops, trees and landmarks. *She* poured herself over the land so there could be no place for others to plant a flag. *She* smothered it with a placid love. A selfish love. It was hers and no technology could hold her back. Except for a few places along the road, the townships were under water. The government's plans to flood the whole area made sense. Clem saw that. The Thames would take it all anyway.

They passed a large sign bobbing on a buoy among lush grasses in the shallows on the north side. "Rice," said TinTin. On it was the number of the Moravians' band office and their sea rescue unit. "They have reclaimed the north side of the river. It was under water anyway. They've built houses on stilts. I hear everyone has a canoe or an outboard."

Clem nodded. She unfolded her arms and took up her pencil. She scribbled the outline of the sign onto the cover of her sketchbook and copied the telephone numbers. This was the first thing that made sense, she thought. Out loud she said, "We shared this land. Now it's gone. Where will they go when the big flood comes?"

"Good question."

"No answers?"

"Nothing I like. Basically, if the various groups, the Chippewa, Oneida, the Delaware and Anishinaabe, move without permission, they will lose their treaties. They will become a people without land, and without the status land confers. The government is negotiating, very slowly, a game of chicken."

"Sounds familiar."

"Pi says—said—that natural catastrophes are a method of renewal, and that we are but bacteria on the crust. The Europeans coming here was a natural disaster of sorts, an invasive species that swept the continent. They consumed resources and overwhelmed the native system of checks and balances. He used to say, *When the world so teems with inhabitants that they can neither subsist where they are nor remove themselves elsewhere, that the world will purge itself in one or another of ways.*"

"Funny, you quoting Machiavelli."

"Me quoting Pi quoting, then."

"And repressing others was one of his ways?"

"Actually no, just flood, famine and plague. Repression and genocide came later. What we found interesting about the present time was that members of the invasive overgrowth have the means to remove themselves, and yet they remain attached to the location."

"Like my mother. What did you say about her?"

TinTin clenched his jaw and stretched it out.

"What did Pi say?"

"Pi proposed that the ones who stay behind, for whatever reasons, believe that extraterrestrial life forms will save them. Gods, angels. It's not about the land. They stay to force a miracle, a healing, to bring the Rapture."

"Rapture?"

"Pi called it a form of hysteria. A collective delusion about a parent-figure from the Bible. The believers will be gathered up before any judgment, aka, world disaster. They rise on a cloud and are saved. Gathering together, like they are for the bicentennial, just strengthens this kind of psychosis."

"Everyone's entitled to their beliefs. It doesn't make them sick."

"Maybe they aren't." TinTin's voice broke with a tight, small anger. Clem slowly let go of her pencil and sketchbook. She touched his shoulder gently. Though they were talking about Chatham County, Clem guessed he was thinking of his parents' exile, and then their return to occupied lands. He took a long breath and exhaled. "On the other hand, maybe this group is exceptionally adaptable and they have become locavores within just a few generations. It took my antecedents a few thousand years. The problem with any imprinting is they don't adapt well to changes."

"This is your theory."

"My parents grieved for the dirt of Jericho every day they were in Canada. I enabled them to return with the Safety Net.

It gave them a better way to handle aggression and to protect the land they loved. They weren't whole when they lived here."

"What about you? You were born there too."

"Any place outside a lab is foreign to me."

"Liar."

"Pi said that we literally are the dust we breathe. We share the breath of the trees and plants. In the daytime, we breathe air designed for us. In turn, they breathe us in, what we cast off. *It's so fucking beautiful*, he'd say."

"Yes." She curled her hand up to his ear and caressed the lobe, bringing a smile to TinTin and a decent breath.

"What I'm afraid of is the miracle, the answer to the prayer that we're—I'm—bringing here, will make things worse. The Sprinkler System is interference, and I don't know how the interference will play out on a large scale. I'm afraid of what will come anyway."

Neither finished the thought. *After all, Pi was taken like a hostage and we didn't get there fast enough to save him.*

"Look, we're almost at the farm."

The great She-river hadn't swallowed everything. The public site of The Battle of the Thames, where between fifty and sixty fighting men were killed, was still recognizable. The banks of the river were steeper here, a good place to fight off an enemy. Clem saw that another monument had been built on a raised cement pad. Not high enough, she thought as they passed by.

TinTin slowed down and turned into the long laneway of the family farm. She pinched him on the neck so hard that he stopped. A sudden flash of memories washed up inside her, and were tumbling over her heart like polished stones.

"I've been imprinted too."

TinTin reached up and took her hand down, and held it. They sat, each with their own thoughts, the car windows steaming up from their breathing.

For Clem, the sudden pang had come on seeing the five-seated glider with its faded olefin cushions on the front porch. A five-year-old girl had waited there for sleep to come. She'd counted shooting stars from the tip of her grandfather's finger. When cool air seeped up through the spaces in the porch floor boards, she had curled her legs up on the cushions, leaning closer into her grandfather's lean body. He scooped her onto his lap. She struggled against the warmth and comfort to keep her head up, heavy as it was with sleep. Finally, she let it fall against his chest, wedging it under his chin so that she could watch the lane for her parents to come. They had promised to return that evening. In her sleepiness, she confused the headlights of her parents' car sparking down the lane with the transient flashes of the meteor shower that streaked the sky above.

Another stone. A seven-year-old girl walked past where the car was idling. She carried mail up the lane to the house, tall corn on one side, pasture on the other. Her grandmother stood up from weeding the garden to wave. Onions and cabbage grew on the slope towards the river. Sweet carrots hid beneath the black, mysterious soil, the result of some agreement her grandmother had made with them, she'd thought.

Then a ten-year-old looked out from the lantern of the widow's walk, wondering whose trucks were parked in the lane. Most days, all she saw were fields filled with a maze of paths that must be seen from above to be understood. She had to memorize them or she would run blind. She drew secret maps of the shortcuts, the cul-de-sacs, the places where men who smelled of peppermint and machine oil might gather.

Those men had a too easy tease ready on their lips. They were about to take the hay off the front field.

"Whose boy is this?"

"It must be another one of the Dolsen boys."

"Sure is growing up fine."

"He'll be big enough to help with the corn by fall, for sure."

A round of winking made it worse. The ten-year-old girl stood her ground in the field, the message from her grandmother delivered. She knew to wait politely, that she was expected to wait for the reward. Her grandfather pulled a tin of mints from his shirt pocket and offered "the boy" one, so proud she belonged to him.

By the time she was twelve years old, there were different errands. The attic and windows in the widow's walk, which had given her a map to the farm, became a source of pain. She did not share her mother's love of old things. Yet her grandmother used the same tactics on Clem, as she had on Catherine, to indoctrinate Clem into the past. Suddenly her grandmother needed a parade of mothballed history.

"These old legs don't do stairs as well as they once did. Perhaps, Clementyne, you'd take this key and see if the *name-that-item* is in the *name-that-colour* trunk."

The twelve-year-old opened trunks with the care of a snake handler. Pinched fingers picked out lace, wool, china, tin toys. She spit with anger at the tiny spiders that bit and left itchy welts, squealed at the sight of earwigs that raised their pinchers when their nests were disturbed. Photo albums, photos framed, silverware and cups, and medical devices— including enema bags and rubber doughnuts for the sufferers of haemorrhoids—required more fingers. The books. She hated searching the book trunks. Small grey moths flew out. Their sticky cocoons bound the pages together. The smell.

They smelled of yellow, wrinkled old stories that should have stayed locked up in trunks forever. And more teasing.

"Hasn't she found his bones up there yet?"

By her fourteenth summer, the past had been conquered, and she was allowed downstairs again. The kitchen door had a lovely weight as it swung shut on the dining room where working men ate huge dinners at noon. She'd swing the door open and confidently set down platters of meat and bowls of vegetables, enough to fill the men after a long morning cutting hay, or taking off the wheat. Silence reigned while they ate the main course. Conversation came with dessert and coffee— grunts about the weather, figuring and questioning about the neighbours' plantings, silences ending with "Jeezus!" followed by the clatter of cutlery. They saw her as a woman, and they must have thought long and hard on suitable topics to bring up when she entered.

"Hargrave," a neighbour would say, a honeyed innocence in his voice as she remembered it now. "It's too bad you don't open that field to the south. Then we could get Jackson's binder down there."

"South is still too wet in June. Daddy said he would lose the binder down there, don't think he hasn't thought of going down himself."

"Oh, *Daddy* has? You don't say?" The sun-burnt men laughed, poking fun at the seventeen-year-old at the table, so that he turned even redder in front of the fourteen-year-old girl who served their dinner.

The swinging door rocked back and forth between rooms, then quieted. Clem ate at the kitchen table with her grandmother.

"They can shout if they need anything else."

Poor Hargrave was sent to the kitchen to ask for more sugar, poking his head through the door and offering the empty bowl, but not daring to step in despite the men's encouragement.

"Go on, she won't bite."

Soon enough, they went back to work. Her grandmother put the white tablecloth into Clem's hands and sent her out to shake the crumbs. Sparrows fought over them before they hit the ground. The birds had to be quick. Not all the barn cats were out chasing deer mice in the newly cut fields.

"Okay?" asked TinTin.

Clem started to say yes, but then the hardest memory in her life tumbled through her heart, a large polished stone the colour of jet. A memory of the good parlour. Her grandfather's accident. He had lived in that room for three weeks after the tractor fell onto him, propped up in a hospital bed by the west window where he could see the bare branches of the sassafras bush, and look up past the branches of a sugar maple to the sky and the stars at night. His body was injured beyond repair. It only needed time to learn how to die. At dusk, moths pelted the window. The lamps were draped with scarves.

An arm chair was set beside the bed, always occupied by a knitter, a reader of scripture or almanacs, a scribe to the lists of business that cultivated her grandfather's mind. He spoke slowly to those in the chair and listened to them as though he had all the time in the world. Clem took the late shift. She could hear her mother and grandmother, the visiting great aunts and uncles and cousins tossing on the bedsprings upstairs. In the night, no one came down to interfere with her *impractical* sketching. Her grandfather didn't mind the reading light behind the back of the arm chair as long as it didn't cast a glare on the west window. The girl chewed on the ends of her hair, looking for things to draw in the shadows cast by the lamplight, darkly smudging in the radio cabinet, the sideboard, the over-sized sofa, a bear's head mounted on a heraldic shield. Her grandfather dozed and woke. He asked her to draw Jack, dead for twenty years. She sketched the dog from her memory of photos—sleeping, eating, jumping in the long grass of the pasture, hunting mice and moles, howling at the moon. *Draw that day the storm broke just after we got the sweet corn in.* She sketched dark clouds, a wall of rain coming in streaks towards the red combine, which was lit up with a pool of god-given light. Some nights he tossed, but if he was still, if he seemed to be really asleep, she'd sketch his bloodless hands, the fingers swollen like sausages.

The stone came to rest on the night he stopped breathing altogether. She had turned the lamp onto his face and gently closed his eyes with the eraser tip of her pencil so they became pools of shadow, as though he slept. She drew the web of deep lines that mapped his features. His hairline, still full around his face. One ear, the tip pressed over from birth.

The stairs behind her creaked, the sound coming down, not going up, ghost-wise. Clem still wondered how her mother knew the sketch was done. She turned to a fresh page, turned the light so her grandfather was in shadow again. Her mother reached over the back of the chair to kiss her hair and squeeze her shoulders.

"I think he died."

She cried into her mother's hand.

She had been seventeen. There were no more summers on the farm. Her grandmother had a stroke and passed away soon after. The farm was rented out until the rain came and made the land useless. No, she thought, the land had been taken. There were no fields, no corn, no grain or beans to harvest. Just the river everywhere.

TinTin, she noticed, had turned off the car. His head was tilted back, his eyes shut. He squeezed her fingers. She squeezed his hand back. All was quiet, not even the sound of generators. A dream world.

"I have breathed in more of the dirt than I thought. It's the only reason I can think of that would make me feel so bad that it's gone."

Neither of them mentioned that there was only one car parked in front of the house. Her father hadn't come back from Ohio yet.

~ 12 ~

THE CLIFFS ALONG THE NORTH SHORE OF LAKE ERIE were unstable at the best of times, a series of millennia-old dunes made of sand, clay, silt. The weight of the rain had brought large sections of the cliffs crashing down. Flash floods carved deep gullies and sucked away more of the shoreline. Since the rain had begun, the shore had receded almost three hundred metres inland in places. This was not the coastline Thomas remembered from summers spent on the farm with Catherine. Between Wheatley and Wallacetown, Highway 3 had fallen off the map and into the lake.

Hiram explained to him that the recent sunshine made the situation worse; the sandy soil dried out more quickly than the hidden pockets of dense clay that retained water. The weight difference could tip the balance. Even before the rain came, the sandy cliffs were known to fall without warning on sunny midsummer days. Hiram provided satellite maps to show where the erosion was worse. He and James had looked over every inch and gathered statistics on the historical occurrences. He gave Thomas a military quality global positioning system that updated every ninety seconds. "A gift from Pi," he'd said.

They had narrowed down several possible landing areas by linking the canoe's route to currents in the lake. Hiram marked the sites that would be accessible to Thomas from the current roads, and mapped several possible routes to each. In the days before he left for Ohio, Thomas went to the three main sites and left behind waterproof boxes with flares and a disposable phone at each one. Catherine had tucked in chocolate bars and water bottles as well. The children were given photos and a map of the shoreline on Net-approved paper to take in the canoe. They'd all done their homework.

Thomas' stomach was in knots. His right knee ached from sitting for hours on end in the car. His drive to the Canadian border was uneventful. The 401 was still open. It would have taken him quickly back to Chatham, but he had to turn south onto Highway 3 until it disappeared. The backroads had softened again in the recent rain. Turkey vultures soared overhead. Along the lakeshore, the landscape was surreal. Abandoned farms, houses and parts of houses tilted out over cliff edges. Some lay cracked open in the gullies, like eggs. Trees clung to the edges of washouts as though arrested in a mid-air leap. Rough trestle bridges were set up over gullies and churning creeks. Although Hiram had tagged the bridges to trust, Thomas stopped before crossing each one to check it thoroughly against the latest GPS information. He stopped again near a bluff that Hiram had marked as relatively stable and parked the car. Here he had an unobstructed view of the lake between the two most likely landing points. Out on the lake, there was nothing to see with the naked eye, and not much more with the binoculars. The grey of mid-afternoon was a depressing sight. He pulled his phone from his jacket pocket, wanting to call the children and ask how they were. Their phones were in his car.

"Owen, it's Thomas."

"Where are you?"

"On the north shore. The weather is looking good at this end, calm. No sign of them yet."

"You're there already? We hear there's a storm developing."

"Everything is calm, just the usual drizzle. The storm is headed your way, thankfully."

"The kids would have missed it, you think?" This was Claire.

"No worries there. Just wanted to let you know I'm here on the shore looking out for them."

"You'll call as soon as you see them."

"I'll call."

"As soon as you see them." Claire again.

Thomas could hear her concern. It made him feel worse.

"Of course. And now I should go. I want to make sure I don't miss them."

He tucked his phone back into his pocket and picked up the binoculars that hung around his neck. Sweet Jesus, he thought, the families of fishermen must have felt like this, the fear in their bellies reaching up like hands to choke their hearts. Sea monsters and sudden storms vivid in their imaginations. Did the Wests feed each other's fears, or ease them as Catherine did his? Yet, he couldn't call her, not until he had something. She did care in her own way. He remembered when she asked if he needed anything else. He'd said a Saint Elmo cross might help. Catherine had told him not to be ridiculous, that everything would come together without tears, that he was the best man for this bit of work. Still, someone had hung a St. Christopher cross in his car. A better saint for this crossing business. It had been days since he'd seen Catherine, and he missed her. Their whole marriage was one of comings and goings. It was getting harder in the past few years. As he'd set out on this journey, she'd kissed him lightly, saying, "Don't make me come look for you."

"Believe me, I don't plan on dallying." He'd kissed her back with more passion. "And don't you do anything that might land you in the grave, or I'll be forced to crawl in and carry you back out like bloody Heathcliff."

"Such a romantic."

"Behave, Cathy." He found himself blinking. He'd buried his face in her hair.

The clouds over the shore were rent apart like a cloth, and the west-tracking sun burned through. A goddamned rainbow sprung from the gully to the south of him. It arced out over the lake as though painted with a sponge. The colours were brilliant. He shivered, wondering if it was a cruel harbinger of destruction, like the rainbows two weeks ago. But what if it was a portent of incredible good fortune? Thomas patted his pockets and pulled out Leticia's camera. He could delete the photo later if things didn't work out. Quickly, he snapped a picture, as dark clouds from the west closed in on the rainbow. Sunlight shone through the cracks with the strength of a god's finger. Brilliant, angelic light.

A canoe paddled into it.

Thomas clapped his head in disbelief. The canoe was approaching the shore at a good clip. He fumbled for the binoculars, his phone. If they stayed on course, they would come to the gully where the rainbow had started. They were hours early. He ran for the car. He dialed Catherine's number.

"They made it."

"You sound upset."

"I've been running. I'm relieved beyond belief."

"Thomas, why are you running? What's happened?"

"I'm getting into the car to go get them. I had to share it with you."

"You're safe, then."

"Yes, I parked far back from the cliff. I'm driving towards the creek where they'll land."

"Concentrate, my dear love. It's up to you to get everyone home safely. Right?"

"Right. Stay on the phone until I get there."

"The parents will want to know."

"I can't call them now. It's too perfect to jinx."

~

He stood near the mouth of the creek and cupped his hands to call out to the children. They couldn't hear him over the surf. With the binoculars, he could see Miles and Rebecca searching for the mouth of the creek. They were paddling into the rainbow. Rebecca must have glimpsed the sun reflect on the binoculars, because suddenly she raised her paddle to him. A victorious gesture. He waved back wildly. Then Miles saw him, and the two paddled even harder with spare, but powerful strokes, toward the shore.

Where the currents of the lake and creek joined, Rebecca could be heard calling out instructions to Miles. They made it look easy, keeping the canoe on course, riding the swells inland. Leticia's head was barely visible in the middle of the canoe; the fore and aft were covered with tarps. The sun inched along with the canoe's progress, closing the gap in the clouds. Stitching the grey clouds back together.

Rebecca made a gesture upstream. It looked like they would take the canoe up as far as they could, where he'd left the box marked by an orange flag. Thomas ran down the dune, sliding, balancing, cursing, and thankful.

When the canoe finally bumped against the sand and gravel scree some twenty metres upstream, he was there to take a photo. Then he ran into the water to help.

~ 13 ~

THE SUN SHINING OFF THE WATER refracted and shone like a halo on the droplets in Rebecca's hair. Rebecca glowed with triumph. She had just seen a tiny black spot in the sunlight waving at them. When the sun hit Leticia in the face, it gave her a headache. She pulled her rain hat lower.

Behind her, Miles shouted, "Almost there!"

"Not yet! The cliffs aren't stable. We should go upstream as far as we can before landing."

Leticia couldn't see the shore behind her, just a rainbow arcing over the canoe. She put away the compass, started folding the tarp in front of her. Then she grabbed the gunnels on either side, pulling into a crouch, as the canoe tipped and rocked over the shore currents. Rebecca rose above her, an Amazon woman.

"Steady, Leticia."

Leticia didn't usually imagine things, but she knew a journey could take place on many levels. On this journey, with just the three of them and a bundle of bones on the vast lake, she felt out of time and place. She felt an urgency to pull into the shore. She wouldn't be surprised if a local militia was there to meet them, and worse, that the bundle at Rebecca's knees might rise and lead them to the battlefield. A hero's death, he'd asked for. Every fibre in her cried out, "No, I will not follow."

The canoe hit gravel.

"Now!" Miles called out.

The bow popped up as Miles jumped out. Rebecca was already jumping out to help Miles lift the birch bark canoe onto the beach.

Leticia swung sideways, getting the right momentum before she jumped out, but the large, hippy-looking Mr. Blackwood was in the water beside the canoe, hauling her out.

The baby again. When he set her on the ground, Leticia would have fallen but for Mr. Blackwood's grip. She saw Rebecca nod, satisfied that she and the canoe were safe, then watched her collapse Indian-style on the dry shore. Miles tried to help her, but the rocking motion of the lake was still in his body too, and he fell flat on his ass beside her, laughing.

All the way to Chatham, Mr. Blackwood gushed about the trip, at how quickly the canoe had travelled, how the rain had held off for the landing. Had they seen the rainbow? he asked. Leticia kept him talking, letting the two in the back seat, with a Thanksgiving goose between them, sink into sleep. They had paddled a long way together. Even the trials of the border and the wall of garbage, even the secret of the bones, hadn't put them out of sync.

She glanced back. Rebecca held the bundle in her arms like a pillow for her head to rest on. The bones rose and fell with her breath. She looked exhausted, no more colour to her than a ghost. Miles rested his head on his arm stretched across the back seat so that his fingers almost touched Rebecca's shoulder. Leticia turned towards the front again.

"How are the preparations for the re-enactment going?"

"Everything is set as long as we can keep the powder dry."

It began to rain. At one point, rain poured buckets over the car. Mr. Blackwood peered intensely through the windshield wipers, glancing between the road and his navigation system. He smiled grimly at her.

"It's just a local squall. First in days. We'll be out of it in another minute."

All the way to Chatham, Leticia stared out the car windows, wiping at the condensation and trying not to gasp at what she saw of the countryside, or what was left of it. It was worse than Ohio. The pictures that the Blackwoods had emailed must have been taken years, not months ago. Her parents would be horrified. She fingered the phone in her lap, wondering what she should say. They had been so relieved to hear they arrived safely. She couldn't worry them when there wasn't a thing they could do about it. At least Mr. Blackwood had been honest when he said it was better to leave the driving to him. If, or when, her parents discovered that Chatham County had become a watery grave, she would blame everything on Miles.

They passed a "Welcome to Chatham" sign. It tipped backwards as though reaching towards the strip mall whose roof barely rose above the water. The drive through the town became a game of hunt and find. They had to cross the river. The route Mr. Blackwood took just two days ago was no longer *feasible*.

"Unfortunately, the roadways flood with little notice."

She grunted. He must have taken that for enthusiasm.

"We are a little ahead of schedule. Do you want to drive by the conservation area? Everything is set up."

"Sure." Leticia hoped the sarcasm was clear. It was unbelievable that anyone would gather a crowd by a river these days. This, she thought, will be hard for Rebecca. But wait a moment, Rebecca hadn't been there when the Founders' Day boats had capsized. She and Miles had been the ones to see it.

"It's very safe," said Mr. Blackwood, as though he knew what she was thinking.

"That's what they said about our Founders' Day picnic two summers ago."

"I'm sorry for your town's loss, and for Rebecca's too."

Leticia shrugged.

"No one is going out on the river. The boats," he continued, "will be sunk, and a bridge blown up with explosives. We'd normally set it on fire but the wood is too wet. That should be fun to watch, right?"

Leticia was suddenly bone weary, and decided she'd had enough of stupid ideas. She didn't reply.

When Mr. Blackwood pulled into a parking lot looking over the conservation area, her eyes nearly popped out at the sight of the docks along the river. Without thinking, she got out of the car to follow him. She had to admit it was the most beautiful, solid thing she'd seen in her brief time in Chatham County. They had built a floating city, with little lookouts with railings. And two beautiful new boats bobbing up and down in sync with the currents of the river.

Mr. Blackwood bounced up and down on the planks of the dock to show her how stable it was, even by the edge. It must have covered half an acre of flood plain. Laughing, he told her the old parking lot was underneath their feet. What was the word when someone behaved like this? Jovial? Did it mean a kindly sense of humour in the context of disaster? Maybe there was a better word. Deluded? Insane? Maybe she really had crossed into another land. Maybe these people didn't fear water. They might even be hiding gills, for all she knew. Maybe there was a set hidden under Mr. Blackwood's long side-whiskers.

Local people, she assumed, strolled hand in arm along the docks, drawn to the marvellous boats. They stared at Leticia in her travelling breeches and smiled when they saw who she was with. Everyone had a hearty "hello" for the man beside her. Mr. Blackwood drew her along with the others to look at the boats, smiling like a proud father.

"They're the real thing, with cork and oak plugs. Fresh pitch on the hulls. Up close, they smell of cedar."

"They look like the bateaux that some people still use on our rivers."

He smiled, taking it as a compliment. "Why don't you take a picture of them?"

He pulled her camera out from his coat pocket. Then he pointed upstream to the new truss bridge. A bridge to nowhere on a flood plain. Her parents would freak out.

"We built that over the summer, a replica of the bridge at Arnold's Mill, further downstream. Your countrymen burned it down."

"I'm sure they meant no harm." Leticia had another moment of grave doubt about her sense of reality. Why was she apologizing? Arnold, if she remembered the story, got away safely. She looked back towards the car. Miles and Rebecca, her anchors, were awake and stood outside the car with looks of wonder. She shrugged helplessly at them, then waved for them to come and rescue her. By the time they wandered over, Leticia had become giddy about *les bateaux* and babbled on to block out any more information Mr. Blackwood might share. Strangely, she didn't mind when Miles focused on getting her to be quiet, blaming her behaviour on the long canoe trip.

"She must be dehydrated. We should get her back to the car."

That got Mr. Blackwood to drive them onwards. He took a road to nowhere, where great fields of milky brown water lapped at either side of the road. She closed her eyes, prayed to wake up from a bad dream. Yet with her eyes shut, the grey waters of Lake Erie surrounded her again. The remembered motion of the canoe carried her towards a shining bridge. Just as the canoe went under it, the bridge exploded.

Leticia opened her eyes. Miles had his hand on her shoulder. "We're here."

Fulfillment

೫೦೦೩

~ 1 ~

THE EARTH CHURNS IN HER CORE. She is the gyre that compels rain, the gravity that holds everything together. In return, rain gives her a sense of self. Without rain, she is blind to her own body. Rain continues to fall softly, trickling joy and whispering of journeys, of hungers yet to be filled. Unfixed and lively compared to the body of Earth, rain breaks into countless fractal waves, slanting north, then east and west and south, gathering continuous filaments into splendid, surging bodies.

Rain touches every ridge, cries into every valley; rain drums against stone, pounding her surface into sand until she is clothed with dunes. Algae blankets ponds, binding edges, and sphagnum carpets weave through wetlands. She is covered.

In a mere breath of geological time, rain ceases to fall.

Across a great, shallow inland lake, bones skitter, delicate, a gossamer strand flying across a loom. A mass of bipeds gather on the edge of a minor river valley, a mere trench. Rain teases up loose currents of water.

Earth sucks in her breath more deeply, extending the moment, a pause before the exhale. Over the eastern ocean, fierce winds fill the sky: saline waters whip into towering swells. Rain rises higher, shouting over booms of surf, and urges Earth to join in, to run with riotous abandon through space.

On her axis, she teeters—the pause of a pendulum.

On the cusp.

Rain quivers. The fabric of desire is nearly complete.

~ 2 ~

CLEM SPRANG UP FROM THE PORCH SWING when she saw it really was Thomas, when he heaved the door open and got out of the mud splattered car.

"Dad, you've got to get her out of here. The whole place is morose and decaying. It's a disaster waiting to happen."

"Don't worry. Mom's—"

Clem gripped the porch railing, the painted wood milky soft in her fists, and she leaned out further. "I am worried that she won't go. Don't let her think that TinTin can fix everything. It's all theoretical. Nothing has ever been done to control the weather. Mom is insignificant when it comes to the big stuff."

"Give us a few more days."

Beside her, TinTin pulled on her arm. He was trying to tell her something.

She saw that her father was struggling with a crate. It sounded like there was a squawking goose inside it. Three strangers in pretty rough-looking historic garb got out of the car as well. They carried good looking carpet bags. She closed her mouth and smiled. Her dad smiled hugely, and passed the crate to TinTin, and pulled her face down to his for a kiss. He smelled, beneath the mint of gum, of coffee and worry.

"Welcome, welcome everyone." Her mom was on the porch stairs. She pulled the guests into the house with a wave of her magnetic hospitality. Thomas followed with their additional luggage.

TinTin took what he could and went where he was directed. Only an hour ago, he'd unpacked their car and set up his equipment in the good parlour. Not a piece of bone china was to be seen; just a carpet and the bare bones of furniture remained.

Clem didn't lift a finger to help. She leaned on the porch rail, pulling whatever strength it may have into her palms. She stared hard and long at her father's sedan. It looked too small to have disgorged all that stuff. She examined the birch canoe lashed on top. Even she couldn't imagine crossing the lake in such a fragile craft.

~ 3 ~

REBECCA FOLLOWED MRS. BLACKWOOD, a mature and attractive woman of means. How would this sender of wonderful gifts react if she were to learn the gold locket she sent lay at the bottom of Lake Erie? Rebecca paled at the thought, and Mrs. Blackwood noticed, kindly saying, "You must be tired. I'm sorry about the stairs." She opened a door to a large bedroom. Besides the bed and dresser, there was an upholstered chair and a large wardrobe. The room was mid-Victorian. Electric lamps were discretely placed but fitted with period glass or silk shades.

"Of course, if you need more blankets or towels, or anything at all, just let me know."

Rebecca had not let go of the bundle since they'd lashed the canoe to the top of the car. She crossed the room to the far side of the big double bed, and set it on the chair, then walked slowly back to the door where Leticia lingered beside Miles, who looked unsure. Mrs. Blackwood pushed Leticia gently into the room, and took Miles away. Leticia closed the door and leaned against it.

"Guess we're sharing," she said.

"I've never slept in a bed with anyone but family."

"I have."

Rebecca had not expected this. She was the star of the visit, the Wests merely companions. "Miles is getting his own room?"

"You'd rather share with him?"

"Lord no! I was thinking you would."

"Not in my world, and thankfully not in the Blackwood's either." Leticia nodded towards the chair. "What are we going to do with *him* in the meantime?"

Pain radiated from Rebecca's shoulders; her back felt bent as if she had paddled for a hundred years. She wished she had a room of her own for reasons Leticia wouldn't understand. The bones were supposed to be at the bottom of the lake by now. They weren't supposed to be here. She wanted him out of her life, but there he remained, like a talisman around her neck. Her hand went to her throat. The locket was gone. He was to blame. She sank to the floor against the door and pointed. "Perhaps there's a trundle bed."

Leticia looked. "No luck."

"Then that's where he'll be."

"It'd be the first place anyone would look." Leticia flung open the doors of the large wardrobe. Inside was a pile of well-used toys and old blankets. "He'd fit in here. Our gowns would cover him."

Rebecca gestured to Leticia to place him inside, but the girl didn't want to touch the bundle. Rebecca had to pull herself upright again. The journey across the room seemed long and tedious. She was confused by the mix of modern and traditional things. An hour could have passed before she got to the chair. All she wanted was to flop on the bed. She lifted the bundle and lurched to the wardrobe. On her knees, she emptied everything from the bottom of it. Leticia looked at the pile on the floor in horror. Perhaps Miles' sister thought she was a messy roommate, but it had been her idea.

"You go ask for a box, or something, to put this stuff in."

As Leticia left, Rebecca forced herself to stand again. She opened and turned out the contents of Leticia's travel case, and stuffed the hero inside. Now Leticia would be the messy one and that wouldn't do. Hurriedly, she put Leticia's clothes into dresser drawers. She laid out the girl's gown for this evening on the bed, a poor copy of a dress from a popular painting—machine made of unnatural fibres. Certainly not silk. Leticia had chosen it against Rebecca's advice and refused Mrs. West's offer to spend more. At least it was of the right period. Trying not to feel proud or vain, Rebecca opened her dress box.

M. Boyles
Mantua maker from London
established 1797

The gold in the gown shone warmly in the electric light.

Leticia returned, and noisily announced she'd brought Mrs. Blackwood. Mrs. Blackwood was full of apologies and carried a box. Both of them fell quiet when they saw the gowns on the bed. Leticia gasped. "It sure is beautiful." Now that she saw the real thing, maybe next time she would choose better.

Mrs. Blackwood smiled like her face would split, looking from Rebecca to the gown and back. "It really does suit you. I'm so glad you brought it."

"It's silk," Rebecca said to Leticia. "A gift from Mrs. Blackwood, from her collection."

Leticia looked a fool, her mouth open as she looked from Rebecca's gown to hers. A poor cousin. Rebecca smiled graciously. She may not have known how to dress in modern clothes, but she knew what was of value in her day. Mrs. Blackwood reached over to smooth a fold.

"It makes me so happy to know it will be part of living history again."

Then their host turned to the goods strewn across the pine floor. "I meant to have Clementyne clear this out before you came. This was her room." She set the box down, then sighed each time she placed a toy in it. The blankets went on top. Leticia cringed when Mrs. Blackwood reached into the very back of the wardrobe, "Just checking," and pulled out an old cradleboard stuffed to the brim with dolls of every shape and size. She clapped her hands with the joy of a girl as she spilled generations onto the floor. "That's where they disappeared to. I couldn't find them in the attic."

Rebecca picked up a fair-skinned, porcelain baby doll and pulled away the cocoon fixed in a web across its eye lashes. Mrs. Blackwood must have seen her distaste. Taking it from her gently, she tried to smooth its tousled curls and tidy the rumpled clothes. "I'll make sure this one gets cleaned up."

It made her feel dizzy, this casual treatment of so many dolls. She remembered her own, of youthful French elegance from the time of Independence. Marie's beautiful wax face had melted somewhat with the heat of so many Ohio summers and by being warmed by the winter fires, but her mother had been clever about pushing the features back into place. The gown had been replaced, several times, and the real hair, though still stylish, was thin. Her Marie was still well-loved.

Only the cradleboard was left on the floor. What kind of girl was Clementyne that she would play Indian Mother? Had she gone about the house kidnapping baby dolls? There was nothing to indicate maternal feelings, not with the way the dolls had been stuffed in. As though reading her thoughts, Mrs. Blackwood explained.

"It was in the barn for ages, then Clementyne brought it into the house. She must have tired of the pram. And dolls in general, I think."

Leticia, who should have let the conversation go, picked up the cradleboard. She fingered the designs painted onto the hide, and gingerly touched the beading and the worn smooth wood. She asked, "Would this have ever been used for a real baby?"

"Yes. Look at how the toggle on the end of that tie has been chewed. Someone was teething."

"Do you need to pack it up yet?"

Mrs. Blackwood looked at Leticia in surprise.

"Would Clementyne mind if it stayed here a bit longer?"

Mrs. Blackwood nodded as though she understood. Rebecca didn't. Leticia was too old to play with dolls and too young to have a maternal instinct. Worse, perhaps she sympathized with a native culture that bound their babies to a board.

"Maybe we can stuff it with a blanket so it doesn't look so sad now that it's empty."

Finally, Mrs. Blackwood made her way out of the room, taking the toys, dolls and blankets with her. Rebecca shut the door behind her and leaned against it.

"Now that she's seen our hiding place," Rebecca said, "we can't very well keep him in there."

"She won't disturb the gowns. And under the bed is worse."

"He won't like it in there. And he won't like being in there with a baby's thing."

"She'll find him under the bed."

"Well, he's got to stay where he is, at least until we're dressed."

Leticia looked around the room. "Where is he?"

~

Soon enough, Miles was knocking on their door.

"Is it just me, or is this all a little surreal?"

Rebecca, her forehead pressed against the cool window pane, cocked her head to one side. Miles looked different in his dress breeches and a loose white shirt. Cleaned up. Good. His hair was still loose; a dark ribbon hung around his neck. She remembered the one she dropped into the lake, and bile rose in her throat. He'd been wrong and yet right. She swallowed.

"All this water?" he said.

Rebecca stared at him dumbly.

"This place shouldn't even exist. A flooded land."

She heard a shake in his voice and looked to Leticia.

"*Flooded land*? If it's flooded, there is no land. We shouldn't be here."

Dusk, the time for regrets. A heavy mist veiled the view. No familiar landmarks. No livestock in the barn, no barking dogs. Even the goose was quiet. She pulled the curtains closed. She hadn't looked at the photos the Blackwoods had sent. They hadn't interested her. It left her with nothing to compare. Her thoughts had always been about the bones.

"I always thought Mrs. Blackwood was a little crazy," Miles said. "This just confirms everything."

"Although, we did canoe here."

They both glared at Leticia, and she had the grace to be quiet.

Miles pulled the ribbon at his neck from side to side, as though sawing through a trouble. His hands shook. He must be as tired as she was. Then he asked, like a child, "Rebecca, why did we agree to go to the banquet tonight? I don't know if I can take any more."

I don't think I can either, she wanted to hurl back at him. *I hate this place.*

Do not let your friends take the brunt of your despair, her daddy's voice came to her. *Do not let the enterprise fall apart now. You are the Captain and they will follow.*

But I'm weary, she wanted to say, *and wish I could rest in your arms.*

Rest is a reward for later. Do your best now.

That's what her daddy would say. She thought for a moment. Miles still held the ribbon for his hair, as though to tie up his hair would take the last bit of his strength, but he'd do it if she wanted. He'd do what she wanted, but he needed to hear it from her.

"Listen, I wanted to turn back out on the lake but you two said there was no turning back, that there was only one proper way to settle this. These bones need to be put to rest." She looked over at Leticia's case. Nothing moved or shifted, but she suspected he could hear. "I certainly share your opinion that Mrs. Blackwood is not worthy of our trust. We must enlist others in our goal to inter his remains." She paused, waited; the bones did not stir. "We must attend the banquet and talk to the mayor and such politicians as would have some say in these matters."

"To network," Leticia said.

"Lobby," said Miles.

"I think the historic term in this case is *glad-handing*. We need to get them on our side."

Miles and Leticia nodded.

"Now, let me tie your hair properly, Miles, and then you must leave so we can dress."

~ 4 ~

CATHERINE CAME UP BEHIND CLEM so quietly that Clem only noticed when she felt her mother's weight on the railing beside her. The floorboards were that soft; the old wood holding despite the damp. The railing, however, was rotting. Between them, they could push it over.

"Dad's having a lie-down with a warm cloth over his eyes."

"Headache?" Clem asked.

"No, just tired."

He shouldn't have been on those roads, Clem wanted to say, but if she started down that path, more would come to drown them all including TinTin, and she'd sink with shame for not having seen it sooner. Float. As long as they remained on the surface, no one would drown.

"The girls found your doll collection in the bottom of the wardrobe. I wrapped the babies in a blanket and left them in your new room. You can go through them and clean them up while you're keeping Hiram company. Leticia was fascinated with the cradleboard."

"I used to desperately wish I had a sibling to stick in there."

"Ah."

"I used to wait for you and Dad to come for me every day I was here."

"You were with your grandparents. We didn't abandon you."

"I know. I loved them too, but it was better when you were around."

"We're all together again, Clemmie. Everything will be alright. You'll see." Catherine's hand lightly touched hers, warm. Clem slid hers away.

"If you need me, I'll be with TinTin."

"Don't forget about the banquet tonight," Catherine called after her. "I've set out a lovely gown on your bed. There are breeches and a shirt for Hiram, and a rather dashing jacket."

"Your guests won't mind you leaving them behind?"

"They're coming too."

Clem stopped on the threshold. "Mom. Really?"

"They want to."

Clem shrugged and went to find TinTin. She passed her father in the hall.

"Dad, about that banquet."

"Good timing, isn't it."

"Aren't they tired?'

"As are we all. They insist on coming."

"Beats me." Clem dodged his outstretched arms and slipped into the parlour.

"You've got another half hour, then it's dress up time, Pioneer Boy." She laughed at TinTin's expression. "For the banquet, silly."

"Just where will this banquet be?"

"At the Tecumseh Tavern. The high ground in Chatham County."

~

Her father smiled like an idiot. Historic garb made him goofy. He couldn't resist coming right in, oblivious to the wires and cables, the delicate state of the electronics in the Victorian parlour, which thankfully was up to code. He bowed to them both, a sweeping gesture from such a big man.

TinTin hit a series of back up keys, then stood to bow in return. It was rather cute, thought Clem. Seated, she extended her hand towards Thomas, feigning delicacy. She might really need help to rise from the settee. Her gown had wrapped itself around her legs. Before Thomas could barrel in, TinTin had his arm out to help her. It brushed against her skin like a wet dog's nose. As he leaned towards her, the frilly front of his shirt wafted past Clem's face. In drier times, it would have tickled.

"How kind of you, sir."

"Milady."

Thomas cleared his throat. "Lady and Gentleman, the Mistress of the house desires you to come and meet our guests. We are gathered in the sitting room."

Clem laughed, and rose with TinTin's help.

～

Across the hall, lamps were lit to ward off the evening gloom. The setting sun was hidden behind a thick haze. There was an atmosphere of casual neglect in this room, more used than the good parlor.

Rebecca Galloway was seated on the camelhair sofa like a duchess. The girl was stunning in her gown, a vision bathed in golden light. She remained seated and barely stretched her hand towards Clem when they were introduced, just enough so their fingers touched. Was it tiredness after the long trip, or was the gesture calculated? Clem was about to test her when the younger girl, Leticia, jumped up. She took Clem's hand warmly and babbled greetings from Ohio and from her parents and wasn't it a lovely house and they were so happy to be here.

"I hear you came by canoe." TinTin was speaking to a young man in colonial shirt and breeches who stood staring out the window, looking into the dark. The temperature dropped at night, and the window ran with what looked like rain.

"A fine birch bark." He paused. "There's a lot of water here, even more than back home."

"Yes!" Her mother's tinkling laugh, a lively, brassy gesture from a seasoned politician. "We're featuring the waterfront prominently in our celebrations. You saw it on the way here."

A round of polite chuckles. Then an awkward silence. Still as liars. She wondered where the lie had started.

Had to be her mother.

Young Leticia jumped up again, suggesting that she take a picture of everyone. That girl had to be pleasant—her features were placed so unattractively. Clem hoped for Leticia's sake she was a late bloomer, that she'd become an irregular beauty. Catherine took over organizing them for the photos, first her family, then the guests, then all seven of them counting to five for the timer, smiling. That bit was over rather too quickly, and the early awkwardness was about to return. TinTin, of all people, saved the moment by offering the guests a laptop.

"It's loaded with the software for your camera. Take it with you up to your room."

How sweet. He was saving them from her family. The boy with the all-American good looks certainly looked grateful. "I would like to send some photos to Mom and Dad. If there's time before the banquet?"

Her mother looked at a loss. "We're leaving in five minutes."

"Actually, Catherine, I think it's closer to twenty." TinTin pushed the boy along towards the stairs.

"We won't be long, I promise. Thank you."

Catherine let them go. What else could she do? But before Leticia escaped from the room, her father placed his bulk in the doorway and asked to see the recent photos. He gushed for a moment about Leticia's technical ability, then waved her upstairs.

"What was that about?" Clem asked.

"I was hoping the windows weren't included in the shots." He looked at TinTin. "Or anything else that might worry their folks back home."

"I heard them express surprise that the land-to-water ratio was not quite what they were led to believe. I set up the laptop with a delay, so I can monitor their accounts."

"Hiram?" Catherine was beaming to the point of tears.

"Pi would have done it for you."

"I won't expect you to make a habit of it." She kissed him, and he didn't even flinch.

Twenty more minutes until they had to leave. Clem pulled TinTin towards the good parlor, whispering, "You are a surprise, Pioneer Boy."

He lowered his head.

"What did you just call Hiram?"

"Nothing, Mom. We'll meet you shortly on the front porch."

~

They drove in two cars, her mother leading the way. At the tavern, the guests from Ohio were claimed by Madeleine French and the bicentennial welcoming committee. Thomas held onto Catherine's arm in a rare gesture of possessiveness, at least it might look that way to a stranger.

"There's lots of time to hover," he said, then he joked to Clem about how they had spent the summer and early fall at the Tavern in *meetings*. Catherine laughed.

"I can't drink another beer, or rye and ginger ale. I've switched to Tom Collins, but I'd kill for a properly mixed cocktail."

"There's a job for me." Clem grabbed TinTin and started for the bar.

Catherine called after them. "Wait a moment. I have better plans for you. I need you to be sober, to be my eyes and ears. Everyone still wants you to marry their sons."

Clem kept TinTin in motion, but he pivoted to face back to Catherine. "She is married. To me."

"A fact that gives me joy every day. However, out here in the backwoods, it hasn't sunk in. Give them a few more decades, Hiram, before you register with them. If that's what you want."

TinTin narrowed his eyes.

Catherine almost fussed with his shirt ruffle. "What benefits us is that you aren't a threat. You'll be able to find out what nasty secrets they've been keeping from me. Find out who the rumour-makers are and trace the sources. The weather is bad enough to deal with. Why would it start to rain again so close to the festival?" She waved a hand to stop TinTin from answering. "It's beyond most of us." She smiled, wickedly. "But the human element isn't."

"Do we start with anyone in particular?"

"If you wouldn't mind, try the local politicians. Let Clem introduce you as an important scientist. They flip-flop about too much, and we want to know what they're really thinking. I need them on our side. The budget is overrun. It always is for these events. And if you could, would you watch TK Holmes? He's still a bit miffed about sharing the Honorary Chair with me."

"Of course."

TinTin took the instructions to heart. He bowed his way through the first flurry of introductions to the engineers who had originally come to consult with the First Nations about rebuilding. Despite the plans to flood the area, the engineers hoped to sell the town on a floating infrastructure. They quickly pulled TinTin into their circle and introduced him to the Deputy Minister of Industry and Development, a tall man. He looked discretely down Clem's dress front, and was the first to buy her a drink. She dutifully accepted and flirted to get the whole story on how an actual Minister was suddenly available for the festival's opening ceremony. They were soon joined by a throng of local town councillors, led by none other than TK Holmes, perhaps as a result of one too many rye and gingers. They all flirted with Clem, like always in an alternate reality. They challenged her about being married. TinTin overheard, and made his way through the circle of men, his face flushed, a sign he was about to get really huffy. Clem could tell. Her mom intercepted TinTin, spun him into another orbit, introducing him as the genius he truly was to a bevy of matrons and elders. He had his own problems now.

Clem gradually wriggled her way to the back of the hall where Hargrave's dad, Frank Dolsen, was sitting at a table watching the crowd with his usual good nature. Sitting next to him was Clayton Lawes, the manager of the farm co-operative. They were talking earnestly. Frank motioned for Clem to join them.

Clayton was worried about signage. Everyone thought that the flotilla of wood was paid for out of the Holmes' family's pockets. "The co-op is bridging more than the river," he was telling Frank. "The costs are crazy with all the price gouging. Not to mention the premium put on anything shipped into the county. We aren't shipping much out these days."

"I thought we had enough lumber locally. There's a ton of old stock lying around."

"People are donating their wood just fine, all kinds, all varieties and sizes. But who's milling it so that everything fits? Who's paying for the nails and hammers? That's coming out of the co-op's pockets. It's got to be thought out more carefully.

The docks seem to expand every week. We've had marine glue on back order for months."

"Must be those Moravian Indians using up the glue," joked Frank. Clem didn't laugh, but he kept on. "Only the natives are crazy enough to build houses. Doesn't it figure they'd get government funding for housing now. Makes you wonder whose judgement is worse, the band councils' or the governments'?"

Clayton ignored the comments too. "There are still families living here, though you wouldn't know the government cares. The only reason the Minister came is because we're selling advertising on anything that still stands above the water line. There must be an election in the works."

"Clayton is thinking of running for mayor, just to put things into perspective."

"Damn true. This rain is a once-in-a-thousand-year event. The water will subside as it always has." Clayton appealed directly to Clem. "We've got to have some hope. They can't flood the place. Like we're some damn hydro project up north. Or in China."

She had to change the subject. "Mike is still the mayor?"

"Yes." Then Clayton remembered his manners. "How's Toronto?"

"I'm from Waterloo these days."

"How's Waterloo?" asked Frank, smiling.

"Wet, like everywhere else."

"Water and loo. Going down the can."

"Chat and ham. Lots of big fat talk."

The men laughed silently; Clem giggled.

"You haven't lost your spunk," said Frank. "I remember you serving up dinner on your summer holidays. Too bad my boy never had a chance."

"As if," said Clayton. "Now your mother's got you down here to help with her big do."

"Not much to do, really, but cheer her on. Gran was the same. Self-sufficiency runs in the family. I'm just trying to figure out who's stayed, who's had babies, that kind of thing."

"Hargrave married the vet's daughter. She went into the family business. Damn good with livestock, she is." Clayton hesitated. "They lost their son in a flash flood last spring."

"God, Frank! I'm so sorry to hear that."

"He was caught between the sandbags for the house and the pump out back." Frank spoke as though he was watching it happen. "Not much of an incline but they say the pump suddenly discharged and some kind of undertow held the child under. Against the sandbags." His eyes teared up but the pleasant look on his face never slipped. "They saved that new house and they're still out there with the surviving child. We're working on some way to keep the road banked. She's afraid of the next washout, that it could take them house and all."

Clem had the same fear. And she realized there were more reasons why the instinct to run to higher ground had been lost in this area. Some were past waiting for a miracle. They had stayed too long already, dug themselves in too deeply. The best ones refused to leave anyone behind, including their dead.

Late into the night, she nodded, smiled, grimaced, kept her tongue behind clenched teeth as she listened to more stoic stories. It was the way all news was delivered, good or bad. She had nothing to record the events and histories—no sketchbook or pencil, just her heart—of those who stayed and those who would never leave. The loss of livestock was staggering. Enough cattle, poultry and pork had died to feed a small nation. She tried not to picture the bloated carcasses, how they were corralled by motor boats into booms, and floated downstream where barges on the lake could haul them somewhere drier to be incinerated. Herdsmen hung themselves by their leather belts on rotting barn timbers, or turned their shotguns to head or heart. The land slipped away and so did hope. So did life. Ghosts lived in the depths, and those remaining slipped between grey worlds, between mud and sky, mere shadows in the mist as long as they stayed.

Clem followed Frank outside to where a group of smokers stood under the eaves of the tavern. Her mother was there, and silently the three stood together. Clem took the cigarette Frank offered and let him light it, let the smoke swirl into her eyes so she could cry for a moment. And still a misty rain fell. Lucky rain allowed to pour its soul out, for that's what rain does best.

~ 5 ~

SHE CARRIED A TRAY WITH TEA to the front porch, tapping on the door of the good parlour to let TinTin know it was ready. To call him out from the wired madness and to have another human being sit with her before *the great void*. Clem stared out at what she knew was a landscape only because a horizon line hovered in the distance. It had not been visible earlier in the day, blotted by a mist rolling off the river and just recently withdrawn. The horizon line, she noticed, might be fat or thin, far or close, depending on how dense the air was. It was like watching Penelope at the loom, creating and unpicking the weft threads she had cast in the day. Sometimes, sunlight struck through this veil and all she saw before her was an endless flat sea. Without a horizon, there was no landscape, only a void to be filled by the imagination. There was nothing to draw upon but sadness or fear. Her fingers gripped the tray for a moment longer, then she set it on the table.

She rocked alone on the porch swing, feeling a new sense of herself in the world. Even if the farm should disappear in this dream-like way, Clem still existed. She couldn't be unpicked. She had enough of the dirt and fields in her, the crops and livestock, the lives of the neighbours and their farms and kids. She had been mocked on her visits for not knowing the country, but even that was an acknowledgement of her existence.

Perhaps the neighbours had powers beyond hers and— they still saw the land. Even now as they looked out from their sheds or barns, or the windows in their kitchens as they ate their lunch, they must see more than *the void*. Could they look into the veil and conjure everything they had lost? Hadn't their families broken through the forest to find the soil, survived fires set by militia and sometimes neighbours, as well as floods and taxes and sons sent to the wars? Hadn't they smelled land from where ever they'd come from and settled here for a better life? Last night, Frank Dolsen had pictured a future despite his losses. Today he would watch for signs of fair weather, though the soil had been smothered by rain. No one would be able to plant crops in the spring. Yet, he was planning, thinking—*if only the rain holds off, the fields could be dry by then*.

In the city, in Waterloo, she'd been safe to sink into the lawn of her backyard up to her ankles in the mud and lush grass. The experiment had chilled her almost to pneumonia, but her future hadn't been dissolved by the rain. In Chatham County, there was no network of grass to hold Frank up; he would drown with his fields. His life, his "Frank-ness" was invested that much in the land. The land didn't have that hold on her. She was Clem, not the land. She was a bubble, floating as long as the membrane held. Frank didn't understand how the rain competed with him and had won. It had harvested the land before his very eyes, and it had taken his grandchild too.

Even if the rain stopped, the river had become the rain's commodity merchant, pushing trade, pulling in debts, dislocating and selling wares downriver, rushing by with the latest acquisitions to tempt the desperate. It made her afraid.

Not so that stuck-up girl, Rebecca Galloway. This morning, she had pushed out in her canoe onto the misty river with her friends, putting more grey hairs on her parents' heads. She said they would follow the shore, they'd go upstream to visit the Moravians who'd invited them. She said she knew all about rivers from the ones back home. But that girl didn't have a clue about what lay beneath this one. Thank goodness, they'd come back safely—the three of them pink with effort and whatever their real business was—bubbles intact.

Last night, from the back of the hall, Clem had watched them, watched Rebecca pull aside committee members and talk so earnestly that the members had been sympathetic and crossed their hearts in some kind of promise. She'd seen her mother follow, and how the West kids intercepted her— Leticia with a vivacious question or Miles moving to protect the star quarterback. At one point, her mother must have found out the secret, for she smiled like a barracuda. She looked energized. This morning, Catherine had let loose with a cleaning spree, chasing after mud and any other dirt she thought the vacuum might pick up, rolling it over the floors until she stopped in the girls' room for what seemed forever. Clem was about to go upstairs when the Hoover finally started again and moved on.

Clem lifted the tea cozy and touched the pot. It was still hot. She tapped on the window behind her for TinTin to hurry up. She watched the lane. Nothing but one line of horizon parallel to the road in front of her. She forgot about tea, about TinTin, and flipped through her sketchbook. Then he was beside her, though she kept turning pages.

"Have you noticed that we only focus on the rain? We're looking at the rain, living in the rain but we aren't water creatures. This obsession doesn't help us. We aren't fish."

"Fish, that's interesting. Pi described the kind of wave we're using to pull the rain along the Sprinklers' pipeline as the way fish move."

"Are we becoming fish, then? I want to stay human."

"The unending rain is what's fishy, not us. Rain normally is a beneficial precipitate. As the rain falls, it pops out oxygen like crazy. Because of rain, we don't need gills. We can stay human."

"The farm around us has disappeared."

"We won't. There's lots of solid ground left."

"And oxygen." Clem gulped in the cool moist air. She drew a line across a fresh page. A solid horizon. She could relax.

Then TinTin spoiled it, saying, "Thomas has bought another boat. He asked if I wanted to drive with him to pick it up."

"You said no!"

TinTin gestured for her to lower her voice, nodded yes. He slipped his hands underneath the tea cozy.

"It's still warm."

"It was hot, once." *When I tapped at the door,* she thought, *and needed you to sit beside me. And now you are here, a miracle.* She stared back out at the road, listening to TinTin as he scooped spoonful after spoonful of sugar into their cups to suit his taste. Clem took her mug from him. She smiled at the first sip.

"Sweet."

"Oh, sorry."

She set her cup on the table and lay on her stomach on the porch floor, so that she was looking through a veil of water dripping from the eaves. She reached back for her sketch pad and box of charcoal sticks, twisting awkwardly. TinTin's chilled fingers met hers. Receptive.

Propped up on an elbow, her belly pressed against old floorboards, one shoulder and arm cradled her head. Her left hand curled over the page to draw the surface tension between the rain and dirt. Above, TinTin noisily sipped his tea, snuffing in the heat the same way the rain took up the earth. Greedy. She felt him watching her; she felt her diaphragm pressed into the floorboards and moisture rising up between the cracks. She watched rain drip and oxygen pop along the edge of the porch, and she breathed it in at a count of one for nine falling drops. When TinTin left, she would try to match her breath more closely. But TinTin came down to her level and matched her fast breathing, then slowed his down. Hers followed. He poked a finger at the sketch of exploding rain.

"It doesn't fall like tears."

"You should have told me that long ago."

"And ruin the poetry?"

"Damn Science."

TinTin cupped her hand, then held it to illustrate. "The bigger drops are spread out like little parachutes because of the drag of the air." He pressed her fingers open, his fist in her palm, supportive, a firmament. Then he took his hand away.

"They catch the air."

"And pop!" said TinTin, "The air flies out as each rain drop hits something."

"The rain is destroying the earth with its oxygen bombs."

TinTin shrugged. "Rain gives the Earth oxygen so she can grow things. The earth, she watches from her bedroom window at night, listening to all the sounds of rain and she nods, like she's saying *well done*. And she turns over for another good night's sleep."

"Nice fairy tale, science guy, but I think you're misquoting someone." Clem flipped to a clean page and smudged in a layer, then pierced it with parachutes of rain. "Tell me more science."

"It's all on Wikipedia."

"Tell."

"When rain falls on water, the sound we hear is created by the bubbles forced below the surface. The softer the surface, the deeper it goes."

"Even the rivers and lakes are broken by rain."

TinTin rubbed a circle into the smudged layer on the page. "The Earth is our medium for growth, baby. She changes but is never lost." He rolled on his side so that he half-covered her, and she knew he would be solid and forever the same man. "When we're done here, I'd like to go home, to my parents' compound in Jericho. When we get there, let's test my theory. I'll be the rain and you can be the earth."

Clem turned so they faced each other. He took the blackened tip of his finger and drew a dark bar underneath each of her eyes. "You'll need to bring your sunglasses."

Her eyes brimmed. "We will go to Jericho. Let the rain have this bit of earth." She pushed TinTin onto his back, wondering how the dry ground of the desert would feel beneath them, how it and the sun would pull the water from them. She rested her head against his chest, let tears fall across the smudge lines TinTin had put beneath her eyes, a silty feeling to the streaks running down her face. Would any of the tear drops be large enough to open like parachutes before they hit his soft shirt, releasing oxygen so they could breathe?

~ 6 ~

SHE SAT ON A BENCH AT THE TOP OF THE STAIRS, looking out over the porch roof to the road. Miles was in their bedroom, propped up on her side of the bed; then he'd gradually stretched out to be closer to Rebecca, not so innocent really. They both kept sighing and saying how they were *so tired* after all the canoeing. Miles had almost touched Rebecca at least three times and Leticia couldn't watch anymore. He'd either end up dead or her lover. Same result either way.

Last night, the bundle of bones had been in her travel bag. Rebecca threw it into the bottom of the wardrobe just as they were leaving for the banquet. When they got home, it was clattering to get out. Rebecca gave her a look—*See what I have to put up with. We should have tossed him in the lake.* Rebecca hid the bundle under the bed. To be fair, there was no other choice, though she doubted anything would have kept her awake. But Mrs. Blackwood would have heard the noise, and wouldn't have hesitated to investigate.

Nothing moved out on the road. Not even a breeze crossed the flooded fields. She went downstairs towards voices. Quiet, intimate voices. Clementyne and her husband, the front door propped open, but she couldn't see them. They were always touching each other, always in their weird little world, hand-holding and making funny promises like the one she'd just heard. And why would anyone go to Jericho these days? That city in Arkansas was overflowing with water. Someone had sounded the wrong trumpet.

She moved back into the house.

The door of the good parlour was partly open. They had been warned, subtly, to stay out. Leticia stared into a room so full of computers and monitors and strange machinery that she couldn't even pretend to know what it was all for. Wires crisscrossed the carpet so it looked like a snake pit. Hiram's laB She couldn't help pushing the door open a little wider to look in.

Someone tapped her on the shoulder. "Guilty," she almost said.

"Come on in."

Hiram nodded to the one chair free of equipment, a nicely upholstered antique. From there she could see all the monitors in what looked like a central control station. Hiram pointed to one. "Watch."

A satellite picture of the docks at the conservation area. On another screen, close and distant views of weather from radars. A dry prairie grassland.

"My lucky task these days is to keep an eye on the weather."

"I'm sure you're good at it."

"I had a friend who was even better at this kind of monitoring. He was my detail man."

"No offense, but your friend is better off for not being here."

Hiram turned pale.

"We shouldn't be here, should we?"

"No."

The first true thing any of them had said.

"I promise you'll get home safely."

No one could promise that. She shrugged like it wasn't a worry.

"You seem interested in this stuff. When I was your age, my friend and I invented the Safety Net. We really didn't know much."

"Who exactly are you?"

"I am the Quaker Chair of Peace and Security at the University of Waterloo."

"You're the guy they call TinTin? Here?"

"Despite the titles and nickname, I still don't know much. For one thing, I don't know how we're supposed to solve the world's problems with science."

"Hence all the equipment?"

"This is nothing. You should see my real laB Not so many wires on the floor, but lots of toys."

"Tell me about your real joB Why is all this here?"

Hiram smiled sadly and tapped a monitor, bringing up a picture of a guy, round-faced and blond. "This was my best friend and the co-creator of the Net."

Was. Leticia leaned forward to look. She recognized him: Simple Pi was all over social media. *Maybe she really was sitting with the reclusive TinTin, not good old Hiram, not so ordinary.* "Did you guys end up fighting, like Zuckerman or Steve Jobs?"

"No, we stayed really close." Hiram played a series of slides. "It's just that he loved life so much, and thought about the science so much, that he forgot to watch out for himself. Clem is like that too."

"Did he ... ?" Leticia clapped a hand over her mouth when she realized the implied question.

Hiram shook his head.

"He did die in an accident; *an anomaly,* he would have called it, it was so far out from the expected. No one could have predicted it."

"I'm so sorry."

"Me too." He switched the monitors back to the weather, and turned to tap a machine that pushed out a steady stream of lines. "Our barograph."

"Atmospheric pressure?"

Hiram nodded, distracted. Leticia got up to leave, but he interrupted her. He spoke to her in a way few did. "I've got no one to work with who'll get my ideas. And my worries. I'm thinking, since I saw you lurking in the doorway, I need to take another part of my job more seriously." He smiled like a crocodile at its dinner.

"And what might that be, Dr. Frankenstein?" How stupid was that?

"The movie or the book?"

"The book, of course."

"I'm just getting into it again." He pulled out a paperback. Dog-eared pages fanned out across the top and he read aloud,

We *must penetrate into the recesses of nature and show how she works in her hiding-places, then ascend to the heavens.* We'll *discover how the blood circulates and the nature of the air we breathe.* We *will acquire new and almost unlimited powers.* We *shall command the thunders of heaven, mimic the earthquake, and even mock the invisible world with its own shadows!*

"I don't remember the *We* in that passage."

"You and me and anyone else I can find. I need people with an original way of looking at the world."

"You should talk to Rebecca then. She's the most original person I've ever known."

Hiram laughed out loud and clapped the book shut. "Rebecca is original, but not the freshest. She's just coming into the 1950s, maybe?" Leticia blushed. "Let me tell you something I hope doesn't offend you. Before my friend died, he researched into the backgrounds of our Ohio guests."

"The details man. Simple Pi." She watched him blink after she said his name. Why hadn't she known he died? Stupid canoeing on the river, stupid to blindly follow Miles and Rebecca.

"It was part of his nature to want to know everything. Pi told me you have a nearly perfect grade point average. The History essay pulled you down. Perhaps you were too busy with a little side project?"

"That was my mom's fault. She and the Greene County historians disagree on lots. As a mere high school senior, I'm not allowed to rewrite history without losing marks."

"Honest and loyal, that's good."

A dig from anyone else, but it was a compliment, and he made it sound cool. She nodded.

"In a clever bit of pay-back, you collected DNA through cheek swabs, claiming they were for an organ donor drive. But your real project was to examine the genetic makeup of Greene County. To use science to test whose version of history was less skewed?"

Leticia gulped. His friend had been good at digging.

"Very smart not to use the results for your science fair project. You would never get into college, or find work after that stunt. And still, you couldn't resist publishing the results online through a company you invented. Then the State Department started looking at it, and you pulled the information faster than anyone could say, *Billions of bilious blue blistering barnacles!* The software you developed to make the genetic models was impressive.

"You—Leticia West—have a social conscience. And you're quite sophisticated in your hacking and programming abilities. Where did that talent come from?"

Leticia felt the blood leave her face. He really knew everything about her.

"Anything to add?"

"*'Bilious blue barnacles?'*"

"Perfect. Our first interview is over. You're officially on the recruitment radar."

"I have another year of school. I'm going to MIT."

"If it's still there in a year. Just joking. Is it okay if we keep in touch?"

She nodded. TinTin, alias Hiram, Catherine's son-in-law, smiled, tapped his fingertips together, seeming satisfied. Then a monitor beeped, and he shooed her towards the door.

Leticia went straight to the ground floor bathroom and closed the door, shaking, almost crying. He really knew her. She looked in the bathroom mirror. "I am Leticia West." Breathe in, breathe out. "And proud of it." The red flush faded and her milky brown colour returned. TinTin was doing more than monitoring the weather. She looked in the mirror again and nodded, yes. "Today, Leticia grows up and follows her own path."

Where to first? The floorboards squeaked outside the bathroom door.

"Leticia?" Mrs. Blackwood tapped at the door. "Leticia? Are you okay?"

"Yeah."

"Come join us in the kitchen, when you're ready."

～

Mr. and Mrs. B. had their heads together, looking over lists and blueprints that covered half of the large kitchen table. Mrs. Blackwood looked up.

"Are you of native heritage?"

Another crazy Chatham County holiday moment.

"A long time ago." Had Hiram said something? "Like in 1800 a granddad married a Shawnee."

"Your parents mentioned something like that, but I can see it in you."

Where was this coming from? Pretty racist, and from her parents too. Or her mother, anyway. Had their trip to the

Indian Nation this morning offended them? Would there be re-enacted reprisals, or some other gummy bit of history stuck to her, centering her out? Her skin a little too brown? Or maybe it was to do with the "gift" to be placed in the monument to Tecumseh. Rebecca would have to handle those questions.

"I only mention it because the Delaware chief called us after your visit. He wondered why you were dressed like a white settler last night and offered, if you are interested, to lend you traditional garments."

"Native gear?"

"Leggings, a skirt and blouse. I could get him to throw in trade jewellery as you are practically related to Tecumseh."

"Not related."

"We'll call it the Shawnee connection. There are descendants who will play Tecumseh's wife and son. We're all so proud of the hero in our midst." Mrs. B. smiled that warm smile again. These people were complex. She seemed genuinely to care.

"Okay, I am interested."

"Good. We'll drop by for the garb on the way back from getting the dory."

Mr. Blackwood looked up, a little concerned. Mrs. B kissed him up—it was what these people did.

"Don't worry," she told him, "the bridge to Moraviantown is still good. It's a minor detour off the highway. We're picking up a little seaworthy boat that Thomas has named after Clementyne." She planted another kiss.

"Only if the bridge is good. The roads are bad enough. It scares the hell out of me, how you kids do it in the canoe."

"Something about being young and foolish, if you remember?" said Mrs. Blackwood.

"You have to promise me, no more canoe trips while we're out."

"It's all good, Mr. Blackwood."

He stared at her the way parents do when they want to drill common sense into a child. It made him look quite comical. Mrs. B. swept her bunch of papers from the table, a cue for him to do the same.

"We should go now. I'll call the chief on the way and let him know we're coming. He'll be so pleased."

~ 7 ~

Thomas felt good after collecting the Ohio visitors and about his part in the celebrations. Yet pangs of doubt harried him. The sunshine of last month was overshadowed by misty rain, as though, along with the children, he had picked up the clouds.

On the good side, the dory builder from Newfoundland that Thomas had brought in to build the bateaux said over and over how happy he was that he'd relocated to Southwestern Ontario. Boat building was a lost art in this area, and he'd had dozens of orders for bateaux since the first ones had been moored along the docks at the conservation area. He'd had to hire local cabinet makers, as well as bring in his brothers, to meet the demand. Thomas insisted that the Newfoundlander personally build his dory, the *Darling Clementyne,* to which he happily agreed. It was a beauty, and not a day too soon. In a few minutes, it would be loaded onto the trailer behind Thomas' car. He wasn't sure whether to be pleased or disturbed about this fall backwards into history, where the artifact had become useful in present-day circumstances. Inanely, Catherine questioned the value of a dory at all. "We are moving to Sudbury," Thomas said, "and if there is one thing this province doesn't lack, it's waterways."

"You've never been a boating person before."

"I like the dory. It sits like a tea cup in the water. So Clementyne."

"It'll sit in a warehouse and you know it."

He sighed as Catherine pulled him away to one side of the boat yard to show him notes she had made from her conversations with Rebecca. Twenty pages now.

"These are just from talking with her while touring the farm. She's a living history."

"The girl's an anachronism. She brought a live goose as a gift. Don't you worry that she seems to be two hundred years old? She's young, for God's sake. We would never have done that to our daughter."

"I wonder what James, dear boy, would have made of her. Another anomaly?" Catherine lowered her voice. "Sometimes I wonder if he isn't still among us, in another plane of existence. We could turn a corner and there he'd be."

"Raised from the dead, or time travel?"

"Don't make it sound cheap!"

Thomas kissed her hair.

"And be supportive when we get to Moraviantown. They see the children as heroes for crossing the lake. No one hereabouts has the skill for this kind of thing."

"Or lack of sense."

"Don't laugh, but the chief also commended Rebecca for her modesty."

"Our Rebecca Galloway?"

"She doesn't see that she's different."

"I wonder."

The builder called Thomas to bring the car around. A good excuse to leave the conversation.

On the way to Moraviantown, Catherine brought up Rebecca again. "She is, I believe, more than a keeper of knowledge. She carried a bundle when she arrived. You saw it too. She's told the committee that she wants it interred in the new memorial for Tecumseh."

"Interred?"

"Her words exactly. Perhaps not so strange, because the bundle clattered when she moved it. And it clattered just sitting on the floor."

"Clattered?" Thomas asked.

"Like bones."

"For God's sake!"

"This is exactly why I hesitate to say anything to you," said Catherine.

"Did she say it was remains?"

"No, she did not. Just that it was *something sacred and not to be shared at the present time*. You know how formal she is. I found it when I was cleaning the girls' room. Under the bed. Inside that oilcloth. A bundle of hide tied with wampum. The deer skin looks as soft as a baby's bottom. There are signs of wear and tear on the wampum shells. There's newer gut repairing some loose edges."

"A pretty good look. How old?"

"Easily two hundred years by the shells. I want to compare it to some of the artifacts in the Moravian collection."

Thomas let out a long, long sigh. "You say the bundle clattered?"

"Like the bones of a skeleton. It's the length of the toddler mummy I disrobed at the ROM."

"A little short for a grown man."

"But the right size for long bones," said Catherine.

Thomas' hand twitched on the steering wheel.

Catherine squeezed his arm and hung on. He kept his eyes on the road. The turn-off was coming up.

"How close were you to it?"

"I almost touched it. Then it shook." Catherine quivered with excitement.

Thomas shook off her grip to run a hand through his hair. "God-damned Gothic imagination."

She clapped her hands, little happy taps.

"Cathy!" He reached out and curled his large hand over hers, while making the turn onto the road to Moraviantown, slewing the trailer after the car. It never ended, the mud and risk of sliding into the ditch, or the river in this case. "It'd be a long shot after all this time, that girl having Tecumseh's bones. In possession of the very people who denied Tecumseh his nation."

"The ceremony is tomorrow," Catherine said. "If that bundle contains the remains of You-Know-Who, it should not be shoved into the base of the memorial, sealed with cement, and left to the flood waters."

"Or maybe it should."

"It goes against a lifetime of collecting and preserving."

"Would laying claim to his bones at this late hour do you any good?" Thomas asked.

"Don't you at least want to know?"

~ 8 ~

"YOU WON'T TELL ANYONE."

Laid out on the Lone Star quilt in the light of day, the deerskin bundle looked shabby.

Miles was insisting on knowing more, now that he had rested and had his fill of Mrs. Blackwood's sandwiches. Rebecca wavered. Out on the lake, she'd had to let George go. The bones had won that battle, no matter if Miles and Leticia said the problem was with the strange Net technology, that throwing the locket over hadn't meant choosing one side over another. But it felt like the natives had won, and even their bones were free to cross the lake. Meanwhile, a good American, as represented by the locket worn by George, was denied. Everything else of the time had passed through: her father's watch secretly tucked into her vest, an inkstand and papers to be used should the direst circumstance arise, the various buttons and stays in their garments. Only the locket had held them captive. Divine Destiny had brought her to *his* place of death. She didn't know how many other battles must be fought before he was interred, and she was running out of time.

"I've come all this way, trusting you, Rebecca. When will you trust me?"

His eyes, his fingers reaching out to touch her.

She looked at the quilt stitched by the fingers of great-great-grandmothers from the maiden side of the Blackwood family, Loyalists who fled the new Republic. So much in this house was of that age or older. Mrs. Blackwood lived with the past and made her living at it. They shared that much in common. However, that woman was a collector, which set a gulf of differences between them. Miles had been tested this summer; he understood the difference. He would understand about the bones. That they weren't hers, that they should be released.

"He was never buried. Not like we Christians bury people. The Shawnee brought him back to Greene County. They laid his bones in old Rebekah's arms alongside her new baby." Rebecca touched the wampum lightly. "I don't know what this means, some kind of promise. He's been in the care of my family all these years."

"Have you opened it?"

Rebecca nodded, looking at Miles carefully, but he didn't flinch.

"He's all there?"

She remembered setting him out on another quilt, on her parents' bed, while the ghost of Rebekah took comfort beside them. She remembered putting the bones away, blessing each one. The tally just short for a human skeleton.

Rebecca shrugged.

"I'd like to see them."

"It's not right," said Leticia, the little sister, interfering again. That girl could be quiet, invisible at times. It was none of her business. It was Rebecca's future, and a chance to put it right for all the kin who'd passed. For her parents and all the way back to sour old Rebekah. "At least, don't touch them. I saw them move."

"We won't open the bundle here," said Miles, his tone against his sister clear. "Too many prying eyes. We should take them out to the battlefield."

Rebecca weighed up possible problems. Miles, for his part, stood too close to her, distracting, and she meant to move away, but she liked the feeling. If her mother were here to guide her, she might say *this young man likes you. It's up to you to say, or show him, that you like him back. A man can't cling to a hopeless cause.* Miles had to know she trusted him. He had to see the bones. As cool as she could, she touched Miles' arm in appreciation.

"It might be just the thing to settle him. One last airing out."

~

She paused at the top of the stairs, listening to the house. Leticia said the parents would be out for several hours. The other two were in the parlor where her hostess hid all the good china and furniture, relegating herself and the Wests to second best. She thought she'd be worth more than that to Catherine Blackwood. Miles said, to be fair, this house would be lost to flood waters soon. The best was likely sent away. The Moravians said their best had been taken over the centuries, with the last removal a year ago, when anything of value was shipped to a great cave up north. The next time they saw their culture, they'd be charged admission. They smiled like it was a joke.

The bundle was wrapped in the oilskin. She held it in her arms like a load of firewood, and walked softly down the stairs. Miles followed, his footsteps heavy. She didn't know about Leticia, if she followed.

Rebecca walked down the graveled lane toward the road, deep waters on either side. As though the road was a jetty hovering above a vast sea, and she did not like the feeling. She wanted the canoe, the safety of a vessel to carry them, wanted the power of her body to keep her safe. The road was precarious, crumbling. Untrustworthy. Soon enough, they were at the site of the battlefield, a cement slab with markers and plaques, and the new memorial still attached to a crane. She found a bench between the memorials, hidden from the road, a place for trysting, she supposed. The river flooded across the battlefield, drowning the rows of cedars and black spruce, barely rippling. A vast mud pie oozing a foul smell. A small group of sycamore were stripped bare of leaves, taken over by cormorants. Like figures of death, their wings were shouldered high to dry out, as though waiting for the right moment to swoop down on the souls lost in the waters of Hell. She began to shake.

"Are you alright?"

I need a moment, Rebecca wanted to say, but Miles was standing behind her, his hands on her shoulders, sliding them down to her elbows. Soon enough he'd see it was the bundle shaking, not her. The sister came around to look, eyes dark and fingers working the air helplessly. She would reach for the bundle in a moment, or Miles would. And Rebecca did not know what might happen after that. She twisted away to face them both.

"He gets like this. I'll put him down on the bench. That should settle him."

It didn't quite, so she sat down beside the trembling bones and opened up the oilskin to let the heavy air at him. No rush of wind, no breath exhaled as her fingers touched the deerskin, still warm from her body. If God cared about her at all, or her parents were watching from heaven, she'd like a sign to show her all was well, that the curse would be lifted. Miles sank his weight on the arm of the bench beside her, hovering.

"The bundle is a burden," he said. "I know you've been troubled by it."

She didn't need his comfort, yet he leaned forward and spoke calmly into her ear, his breath warm with life. "Tell me how I can help." Miles had been sent to her. Even the sister. She'd come around to sit on the other side of the bundle, wary, but ready to help. Help with what?

Rebecca loosened the wampum that bound the deerskin. They would look at his bones, then they'd go back to the house and eat some of the casserole Mrs. Blackwood had left over from lunch. A late migrating heron flew parallel to them. South. They would follow it home soon.

Leticia jumped, shifting the bench so Miles had to hang on. The bones were moving.

"Lord bless us all, you heathen coward. You came to die here, yet you won't rest. You want the battlefield one more time? One more time to take more American lives? Then I'll give you the field. What's left of it!"

Miles was saying to his sister, "Stop being a drama queen, keep back, let Rebecca handle it, she'll know how."

Leticia whimpering back, "It isn't right, it isn't fair, it isn't supposed to move, she'll be the death of us."

Rebecca focussed on the old warrior on the bench. He wasn't going to keep her from Miles. Let him have the field again, if that's what he wanted. Let the Lord resurrect him for all she cared. Saint or sinner? Let God be the judge.

The bones shook fiercely. The bolts on the bench would work loose and they'd fall in a heap. Miles tried to pull her away, and up against him. She pushed back and finished unwrapping the bundle. Small brown bats darted out from the cedars, swooped over them. Leticia covered her head, then ran for Miles, and he hugged her like they were three-year-olds.

Let them cower. Let them witness what she'd do next.

Rebecca put one hand on top of the skull, and clasped the lower jaw with the other. She brought the skull up to her face. "What do you have to say for yourself?"

Nothing.

She walked to the edge of the cement pad, to the place where this world ended and the watery grave of the battleground had sunk among black fir trees. She lifted the skull so the old heathen, if he had eyes, could see the field. His desire, or hers, there was no difference.

"You bring the clavicles, Miles."

But would he? She couldn't turn, couldn't beseech him with eyes filled with panic. She couldn't tell him that if he didn't, she'd remain on this spot frozen forever until she turned to bone herself. A fine memorial. A pillar of salt because she forced *him* to look back. A shudder rippled through her, hands to shoulders to neck to heart. The skull almost dropped. But Miles was there beside her, placing the bones on the moss-grown cement; placing his hands over hers; guiding the skull to the right place.

"What next?" he whispered.

"Ribs."

And so they put the bones out, the major ones at least. And when he brought the long bone of the thigh that proved him to be Tecumseh, the pelvis shifted of its own accord to take it. The shin bones came last, but they refused to lie down with the rest of him. They jumped from Miles' hands to stand in the murky water at the edge of the field. She resonated with an ache for sinew, for muscle, for the rest of him to be revived.

In horror, she saw Miles about to step down onto the field, obliging. Was that bit of unseen Shawnee in Miles offering itself? Or was Miles' Kentucky blood fired up to chase the renegade one last time?

"Miles!"

He didn't turn. The bones quivered at her feet. She felt like her bladder would rush, her stomach disgorge, her legs fall out from under her.

Where are your brave words now? Old Rebekah's voice was in her head. *What have you done to this innocent boy?*

Tears streamed down her face. She reached out for Miles. The shin bones danced in the foul floodwaters of the battlefield, taunting him.

"Miles," she whispered.

His teeth were chattering, *click-click*, and he shook with an urge. Or was it the cold of the grave beckoning him forward, opened but not yet filled?

Miles.

The stealth, his sister's, surprised her. So did her brave act. She had swooped up the skull and was putting it back in Rebecca's hands.

Rebecca shook with a livid anger, raised the skull over her head. "I'll dash you to pieces if you don't let him go."

Then warm hands closed over hers.

"No, no, not this, don't hurt him, let him rest, let him know it's over, let this be the end, let's put him away. Let's put him back properly."

Leticia. The girl broke the spell, and the shin bones jumped into Miles' possession, and he turned, goofy, with one in each hand. He looked at her with the eyes of a wily old man.

"Let's put him back, Rebecca."

All her sorrow. The tears of generations. The flood waters, and she without a compass or vessel. Then there was Leticia, and Miles. Those two would be her salvation. Her hands dropped to her breast, the skull splashed with a salty warm rain.

"Let's put this man to rest." He brushed against Rebecca, his shoulder lingering against hers. "Who knows what's in his heart? In mine, I am truly sorry for any grief I've caused you."

She leaned into him, her vessel to carry her onwards. "I am the sorry one, to have brought you here. But I needed you."

All was still. Nothing moved, then a random bit of sunlight shot across the memorial site, stark against black clouds gathering behind them. She turned and gave the skull to Leticia.

"Put him back."

The three stood in front of the bundle, the bones resting quietly. There was something else to do before he was put to rest. The lock of old Rebekah's hair had fallen through the pile of bones, and she reached in for it, then held her breath. *Now what do you want?* A grim smile curved across her face and quickly, before she could change her mind, she pulled a knife from the pocket she wore on her belt and cut a lock of her brown hair. She bound it to Rebekah's dry old hair with a bit of ribbon from the same pocket, and placed it on top of the bones. Her jaw set, Rebecca wrapped and fastened the bundle tightly. Each action the act of a conjuror. A lock and key, chains, magic incantations, blessings, each binding the bundle more securely than the last. To her best ability, the bones were secured.

Gently, she touched Leticia on the shoulder. "You have real strength." Then she pushed the bundle into the dumbstruck girl's hands. Unencumbered, Rebecca turned to Miles and melted into his arms. This was how love should be.

~ 9 ~

WHEN THE BONES TOUCH THE SOAKED FIELD, the ground where he last stood—sinew and muscle on his frame—charges of electricity pass between Earth and rain.

Sharp. Deep.

Earth begins a slow exhale.

Then pluck! The bones are no longer in contact with her soil.

Rain flashes needles of discontent across the sky, the thunder counting down to the bottom of Earth's breath.

She wants those bones returned to her.

~ 10 ~

THE TENSION IN TINTIN'S VOICE was taut like a bow.

"The barograph."

It was moving like crazy. The little nibs scribbling up and down the roll of paper, fast. *Anime. Allegro.* Crazy music on a scroll piano. *Allegro assai.*

"Go up to the widow's walk. Look to the—" TinTin flipped through the various weather channels. "—to the east. That's upriver."

Vitissimo. Clem blew him a kiss and raced up to the attic, hauled on the trap door. *Release the ladder.* Up top—empty— save for an ancient trunk by the window by the ladder to the cupola above. This was good, Mom really meant to go. Clem lifted the trunk's heavy lid and saw a lantern and matches. The spyglass.

Upriver was east and dark. The new monument, a crypt-like thing, was brilliant white, dangling from a crane. All too appropriate, she thought. The concrete would be lowered into the dark silt, buried. Over time and millennia, it might be opened by archaeologists who would wonder at the undersea culture and their burial customs.

A movement caught her eye.

Three tattered figures stood at the edge of the concrete pad. Storm clouds chuffed and roiled in the east; god-finger sunshine rays beamed down on her mother's house guests. Clem squinted. In their hands, there were bones. A skull held up by the girls. Some kind of pagan worship? The boy held long bones, dripping with mud, one in each hand. Then a collapse, the skull lowered, and if only the spy glass was stronger, or she could fly, she'd know what they were saying. She could only read the relief in the softening shoulders of the Galloway girl. The brother and sister hovered; he loving, she glancing up to the threatening sky. Bones packed into a bundle on the lover's bench. A skeleton captured from the field? Who had those kids conjured? She caught a glint of wampum shells on the bundle, now wrapped in another layer, now put into Leticia's arms.

A storm from the east boiled towards them. A whip of lightening snapped. A long percussive boom of thunder harried them down the road.

Over the din, Clem shouted downstairs, "It's coming this way."

Another lightning strike and the power was knocked out.

TinTin swearing in the parlour.

Darkness fell with a smear of thick mist. She couldn't leave her post. She must light the lantern and hang it in the high windows. The guests must make it back to the farm and they did, barely ahead of the worst of the storm. A rush of wind through the house as they entered, running sounds up the stairs. Doors blown shut in the gusts that followed them.

Just as the deluge started, her father's car, hauling a boat, fishtailed up the lane.

"*And God said unto Noah, make me a boat of finest gopher wood, three hundred cubits by fifty cubits and thirty cubits high.*" Clem whispered the words. She memorized them a year ago when she built her boats of clay. "*And pitch it within and without.*" That cagey old Jehovah promised Noah not to send another flood to wipe *everyone* off the earth. Maybe just some, if she had read between the lines correctly. The vessel on the trailer behind her father's car was no ark. It looked like a dory.

"Rub a dub-dub, three men in a tuB"

She slid down to the attic floor and leaned back against the trunk; footsteps and voices swirled below. Thunder outside, and rain battering at the glass above her from all sides.

Somehow, the guests have brought him home. His bones are in this house. And now the rain has found them.

~ 11 ~

THE DELUGE STOPPED AS ABRUPTLY AS IT HAD BEGUN, but it didn't clear the air. That would have been the best outcome, thought TinTin. Instead, sheets of lightning and echoing thunder booms occupied the sky above Chatham County. He watched the monitors, wondering how he could have missed this. He hadn't seen it coming. At least the emergency power had cut in when it should. He still needed to check the systems, and put to rest the fear that prickled up the back of his neck every time someone entered and asked where Clem was.

At last she came downstairs and into the parlour, silent, with a more other-worldly glow than usual. She rubbed his shoulder. The hairs on her arm were standing on end. She must have received a charge. "Don't touch anything, okay?"

She curled into herself, a tight unit, standing close enough to him to whisper into his ear. He thought she said, "I've seen Tecumseh," but his ears were popping with the sound of static electricity, like he was hearing her through old television tubes.

"Our guests have his bones."

He looked up for an explanation but she placed a finger on his lips. Sparks. He yelped.

"Alright in there?" Thomas called through the shut door.

"All's well. Just need to check the systems, then see where this weather came from."

"Clementyne is with you?"

She bounced into the one chair, retaining her discrete ball shape and picked up her sketchbook. TinTin smiled.

"She's sketching like mad."

"Let me know if I can help."

Leticia was the only one who had any of the skills approaching what he needed. He weighed up the option of asking her. There would be questions, and the project would have to be explained. Then she'd have to explain her absence to her brother, at the very least, which would start a game of whispers, the story being bent each time it was passed on. Those things always ended. He would concentrate on finding the origin of the weather pattern, tracking the sudden downpour through layers of data to the source. Lightning had struck the river only half a kilometre upstream, resulting in what looked like a mass of dead fish in the satellite feed. Pi would have set up a Net to catch them, so they wouldn't pollute the conservation area. TinTin didn't have time. The bloated bodies would surge through town overnight. Problem solved for tomorrow. At least the conditions for rain seemed to be limited to this one isolated cell, nothing broad enough to cause flooding downstream. Intense, but brief. And quite strange. His teeth began to chatter. Fuck, not a cold.

Clem stared up at him. The prickles on his neck became shivers. She'd said that thing about Tecumseh. Maybe she'd finally had a psychotic break. But no, she was waiting for him to say something.

"There's no more rain," he told her, "not here, or anywhere upstream in the watershed."

"Look." She passed her sketchbook to him. A macabre dance of bones played across the pages, rough cartoons set out like in a graphic novel. There were no captions but the gestures were clear. Each cell morphed into something more unbelievable. He recognized the guests from Ohio but not the main character. He could guess, though. It was beyond belief.

"Haha, put some captions in and we'll publish it on the bicentennial website. A great ghost story for a stormy night. I assume it's meant to be Tecumseh."

"His bones. This happened."

TinTin gulped back a soB *Clem.*

"And then the deluge."

He reached out to turn the monitors off. He'd turn everything off and get her out of here. Fuck it all.

An electric shock jolted him the moment he made contact with the equipment. *He* was the source of the static charge. A current raced up his arm, became a fist, a punch to his solar plexus. An implosion. He cried out in pain, tried to get his breath.

"Are you okay?"

"Don't touch me. Residual electricity. We never planned for this. Not one electric storm in the last eighteen months."

TinTin broke into tears. "Why now?"

"His bones are here."

No Clem.

She set aside her sketchbook. "I should call an ambulance."

"No. I need to turn everything off. Clean up the room."

She moved to touch him.

"Stay away." *Let me think.*

"Okay."

Now she was crying with him.

"Okay," she said, "What if I get you some electrician gloves, some rubber soled boots? They're in the back room."

He nodded.

"I won't touch anything."

As though playing a child's game, Clem picked her way through the snake pit of wires. She used a pair of cork-backed coasters to turn the brass handle on the door. Beautiful, smart Clementyne.

He dropped his head into his hands while he waited for her to come back. His heart was still racing, but not as much. He'd be fine. Through his fingers, he looked at Clem's sketchbook. Bones pulled from the flooded battlefield dripping with mud, a skull cradled against a young woman's chest. He thought of his birthplace where the dead never rested, where their names and the battles are recited over and over through millennia, as if the quiet after the wars was impossible to bear. The ghosts were called up, revenge plotted. Could the dead never rest?

TinTin rubbed his chest. He had to stop thinking like this.

He made a list in his head of what had to be done: the computers turned off; the room properly grounded. No, he'd have to sweep it for static charges first. It would be hours before he could turn the juice back on. Dr. Frankenstein was shut down. Messing with Nature had its price. If those sketches held any truth, then animating the dead was Rebecca Galloway's thing. The whole Ohio crew was messing with human remains—bones—while he duked it out with the rain. The Sprinkler System wasn't even running, so at least that wasn't to blame.

And Clem? She was fine. She'd been far too quick to realize he was in trouble. She was taking care of him. His heart still hurt, but the knot in his belly was loosening.

~

He looked at the kitchen clock. Almost nine. Another hour before he could reboot the computers. Catherine and Thomas sat at the table, poring over papers, taking phone calls. The radio played in the background. Clem was preparing food. She could have been mistaken for her grandmother, a large apron wrapped around her, the strings looped from neck to back and around her waist to the back again. Flour smudged her hands and face, sat like snow on her fairy hair. The kitchen couch groaned when he got up to stand near her. She smelled like cinnamon. He picked up a rope of fresh apple peel from the counter beside her.

"I saved it for you," she said as he leaned in to kiss her. "When the peel comes off in one piece, you'll have a long life."

While he nibbled at it, she spooned batter into muffin tins, put them in the oven, set a timer, and ran water into the sink to wash up. She did these ordinary things in a graceful, slightly awkward but focussed way. They hadn't spoken about what she'd seen. He'd handed back her sketchbook, nodding to show he believed. A bubble of concern faded from the corners of her eyes. The flurry of baking was her way to put in time. He picked up a tea towel to help, an ordinary thing to do. Thomas turned up the radio to hear the nine o'clock weather report.

A meteorologist from the Ministry of Environment and Disaster Preparedness explained that the present disturbance was the result of the meeting of two warm fronts in a low pressure area. As each tried to settle, they met the next front and so they circled, causing the thunderstorm.

Bullshit.

Catherine and Thomas looked up at TinTin. Had he sworn out loud? He shook his head.

"It's a 'wait and see' game. There is enough activity in the clouds to cause electrical disturbances. The activity is cycling off itself right now. Unfortunately, the sort of front that would clear things up and bring in dry air is over two thousand kilometres—"

Thomas hushed him. Jay MacDonald, the radio newsman, had begun a list of announcements for the next day. At dawn the Christian Moravians would lead a prayer session to offer an alternative to the tribal sunrise ceremony being organized by a traditional native group. The Canadian Coast Guard had moved most of the small ships from the border to Chatham, leaving the cities of Windsor and Sarnia in the hands of the Americans. Local militia volunteers were told to wait at the

Main Street Bridge where they would board the Coast Guard ships. The HMCS Prevost, the only representative of the Canadian Navy posted along the Thames, had commandeered rescue units from the London Yacht CluB Jay veered off into an impromptu description of the history of shipless naval bases or "stone frigates" as they were called in navy jargon. Back on script, he read that unauthorized craft were reminded not to launch on the river, and that included traditional native craft. They were allowed to launch their boats into a well-marked section of standing water upstream of the conservation area where they might safely see all the events. No one, Jay MacDonald repeated, was to launch a boat into the fast-flowing river. A detailed call-out to the local fire and rescue units followed.

Before regular programming resumed, the usual disclaimer was played, the voice of a disembodied woman:

This bulletin is accurate for 9:00 pm, October 4. The Disaster Response Team will continue to monitor conditions and recalculate projections throughout the night. Citizens are warned to stay tuned to this station's half-hour updates and it is their responsibility to monitor the emergency radio band. All reports are subject to change without notice.

TinTin could recite it by heart.

Thomas looked down at his papers. "The engineers say the floating docks in the conservation area can hold fifteen hundred people safely. If it rains, the river can rise one half meter before the safe load is reduced to half that number. If the river rises two meters in the next ten hours, in a gradual manner, the dock can stabilize, but must take half as many spectators again." Thomas paused and looked up at TinTin before he read on. "If the water levels rise more quickly, a two-meter rise would instantly take the structure downstream. In the case of such an emergency, we are to remember that the docks are reinforced below with flotation devices and that they will stabilize in units of four."

"Thank God for the engineers." Catherine smiled wryly. "Everything is going as planned."

The station played another Public Service Announcement, this time the "disaster jingle" read by a younger woman.

> *Gather and carry at all times your vital documents on your body: passport, birth certificate, bank information, insurance policy numbers, medical and prescription information. These documents are to be placed in the water-proof wallets distributed to each household.*

Finally, a warning from Jay MacDonald to remember that only these items were of any value. "Apparently some of you folk are sewing coins and jewellery into your jacket or coat linings, which can only weigh you down. You'll only drown faster, you silly buggers."

Thomas got up and turned the radio off. "What do you think, Hiram?"

TinTin was thinking about the historic costumes they'd be wearing tomorrow, the weight of them if they got wet. He'd make certain Clem didn't layer up on the petticoats.

"I won't know anything more until I turn the computers back on. However, I am pleased with all the telephone calls. We were worried about attaining the needed threshold of super- and ultra-microwave frequencies when people are, quite rightly, leaving the area."

He smiled to soften his words. Clem smiled back, then bent over to take the muffins from the oven. Such an ordinary thing.

Catherine looked cross. TinTin held his hands out to her.

"The influx of media has helped. Good work. We reached critical mass this afternoon, and it should only get better. The powder will be drier than it was two hundred years ago at the actual event."

He tried to sound happy. If only the sky would clear, as Catherine's face did, making his intervention unnecessary. Every small detail sat on a razor's edge. Yet, the people around him were impressive with their grasp of the physicality of the situation, and their planning for contingencies. Thomas had even brought in a Tibetan explosives expert. The poor guy needed Canadian work experience. What a place to come for that. Despite all this, the guests from Ohio were their best asset. Only they had the skills to survive on the river.

~ 12 ~

REBECCA'S GOWN HUNG IN THE OPEN WARDROBE, ready for tomorrow. It was beautiful and she was beautiful no matter what time she lived in. Miles might have told her so, but Leticia had wiggled between them on the double bed, nervous because of the storm, or so she said. She had become a little cocky since Rebecca gave her the bones to carry home. What a weird kid. Tecumseh was nothing to her. Holding his bones didn't make her anything special.

The ringtone on Leticia's phone made them jump. Leticia answered.

Their parents had seen the storm cell on the Weather Network, she reported, then he listened to her side of the conversation.

"Yes, we are fine. It's sheet lightning, not a real electrical storm. There are too many scientists around for it to be threatening. They'd be the first to pack up, wouldn't they?... No, I said we had no problem crossing. You can see us landing. Mr. Blackwood's daughter posted a video. I look like Laura Secord. ... Yes, we are well rested, and you wouldn't believe the food. It's all home cooking! ... No, the Moravians are actually great people. Not one bears a grudge about the massacre at Gnadenhutten. ... No, I think they are also recovered from the burning of Moraviantown. It was 200 years ago, and no one was hurt. ... They actually moved to the south side of the river. Real troopers. ... Everyone loves Rebecca and her connection with Tecumseh. I swear we should have made dolls. We could have made a fortune. It's not too late for an online project, if you or Dad has the time. ... They do have the Internet. How do you think I sent the pictures? ... No, Mom, I won't forget to call before we leave. We won't go out in the canoe again. ... We promised to let Mr. Blackwood drive us back and he will.

We're tired of canoeing anyway. ... Don't come up here. You don't have time. And no offense, but I trust his driving over yours. ... He's been very good to us. ... I love you too. ... Miles? ... Miles is passed out in his room, sleeping. ... He is sleeping. I'm ready for bed too. ... No, you wouldn't believe how much we are eating. It's too much, really. ... We're good. Mom, don't worry. ... Give Dad a hug from me. ... Bye."

Miles raised his head. "She wanted to drive up here?"

"It was more a threat than a promise."

"Don't send any more pictures. She would have a fit if she saw how bad it was."

"Not sending pictures would worry her more. I'm sending interiors only. She liked the ones of the party last night with the mayor. Perhaps we can take one of us eating tonight? She thinks we're starving for some reason. There's a smell coming upstairs now that reminds me of Rebecca's kitchen."

"Apple pie." Miles and Rebecca said it together.

Leticia groaned, and rolled half on top of Miles to get her camera. He pushed her all the way off the bed.

On his other side, Rebecca stretched, and Miles forgot about Leticia. He rolled across the bed to her side as though from the momentum of pushing his sister out. Rebecca frowned at him. Was he being *too forward*? She swung her legs off the bed, ignoring him completely. He rolled back to "his" side.

"We should get a picture of the bundle," Rebecca said.

"I agree. I need something to hold onto when the nightmares come later."

"I should hold them one last time, not that the bones are personal to me, but more so to my namesake."

"You should wear the gown you wore last night. That would make a good picture."

"Let's use the sitting room downstairs. I doubt they'll even notice we're there."

Miles raised his head to protest, but before he could say a word, Leticia reached over and messed up his hair. She snapped his picture.

"Delete that!"

"You look so natural, so cute and rumpled."

"You make me sound like an old geezer in a raincoat."

"Why don't you get out of here so Rebecca can get dressed?"

"If you're making everyone dress up, Little Letty, what about you?" He pointed to the colourful blouse and deerskin skirt and leggings that also hung in the wardrobe. "Mrs. Blackwood would love to see you in the Indian outfit."

"Then she shall. Now get out."

Leticia pushed him across the bed. He bounced out, and tried to open the door. It was swollen shut. Miles gave it a heft the way he'd seen Mr. Blackwood do it on other doors in the house, and he was out.

"Don't be long, ladies. I smell pie."

~

While the girls were dressing, Miles did some push ups and tried to shake off the excitement he felt from being around Rebecca. There'd been days of these feelings when he'd gone back to college, when he would have rather been on the homestead with her, working beside her.

He did another series of sit ups until his gut ached, then collapsed on the floor and rolled onto his back. He ran his hand over his face. The stubble on his chin grew in thicker every year. He thought about shaving again, but worried that the power might go out before he finished. He better not risk it. Better to look a bit rough than be laughed at, half-shaved.

Once they got home, he would buy a straight razor and get the barber to teach him how to use it. When he got home, he would buy Rebecca a new locket to replace the one at the bottom of the lake. The inscription on the locket would take some thought, for it had to be fresh, yet delicately reference the best of what she lost. He pulled on a clean shirt and combed his hair, tying it back with the ribbon Rebecca gave him last night, remembering how sure her fingers were the night before.

He made his way to the kitchen, thinking everything was the same here, just reversed. He was on the wrong side, on the wrong side of a border these people fought to keep. He'd thought the Canadians were just like Americans. Not anymore. The bones and the Loyalists were anti-American. Time and history had changed them. His father would disagree, saying his favourite cliché, that underneath they were all the same people. That it was the only way to think in times like these— or maybe anytime.

He glanced at the good parlour door. No glow from the computer screens seeped across the hall carpet. Down the hall there was a warm crack of light under the kitchen door, and voices. He would have to enter noisily so as not to seem like he was spying.

A farm-sized tea pot sat in the middle of the table, just like the one at the Galloway homestead. There were mugs and makings for sandwiches, a large pan of muffins cooling on a rack. Apple muffins, not pie. Hiram and his wife cuddled in a corner of the old sofa. She had a sketch book open, as usual. Catherine and Thomas jumped to attention when they saw him.

"We were just about to call you." Mrs. Blackwood said in a way that made him smile. They had forgotten all about their guests. Their cell phones sat on the table. One vibrated. "It's the mayor. Again." She put out her hand to pick up the phone.

"Don't you dare touch it!" Mr. Blackwood tapped the top of her hand like she was a child. "He can give you an hour. He agreed to that."

She looked over at his phone, also vibrating. "It's Colonel Holmes for you."

"It can wait."

"He'll have an update on the weather for you."

Mr. Blackwood wavered, saw Miles, and the food set out on the table. No one had touched it. Their plates were all empty.

"If it's about the weather, then I have another solution. Miles, would you look out back and tell me if it's started to rain? Then we shall eat in peace."

"Yes, sir. I'd be happy to."

"See, my dear, no need for the Colonel's update."

As Miles passed the table, Mrs. Blackwood turned towards him, gripping the large teapot in one hand. She placed her other hand on his arm. "We must seem silly."

He shrugged. "Nothing silly about getting weather reports."

Back home, bugs would have been pummelling the screen door, trying to beat their way to the light. Here, the air was too cool. He pulled the kitchen door shut behind him. His eyes had to adjust to the pitch black. In the distance, some granddaddy bull frog let out a croak that made him laugh. Maybe there were bugs. To the west, sheet lightning flashed over the town. There was a reflection of light from the kitchen out on the river, refracted into a fuzzy blob that refused to be carried downstream.

The weather was overcast, much as it had been everywhere for the last year. If someone was getting rain, he hoped it wasn't upstream. The river was less than half-a-football-field's width from the back door. He shivered and went back in.

"No rain in sight."

"Try to imagine," Mrs. Blackwood said, "that it is two hundred years ago. We would be watching for the Americans, wondering if our barn, our house, was safe. If they'd set us on fire."

"No fear of this American setting fire to things, Ma'am."

"I'm so glad you've all come."

"And, it's wet enough to dampen any lightning strike, if you had any worries on that account."

Mr. Blackwood looked at the son-in-law.

"The powder will be fine," Hiram said.

Miles wanted to know how they hoped to achieve that miracle, but suspected Hiram's solution was something his sister would understand better. He certainly wouldn't ask; it would only delay eating. The spread on the table had taken a different shape. There were enough plates set out for everyone, American guests included.

~ 13 ~

REBECCA SLIPPED QUICKLY DOWN THE STAIRS into the sitting room, and sat in a chair that commanded the room. The bundle across her knees. Where should her hands go? Folded and set neatly across the wampum? Too prim, not respectful. Perhaps she could avoid touching the bundle all together by hiding her hands on her lap. But the bundle might tip forward. If she held the bones across her forearms, her hands turned up to secure them, her shoulders sagged. It was tempting to hold them upright as if they were a child on display, but she had too little love of him for such a portrait. Besides, the locket no longer hung against her breast, ending the heathen's comfort there.

Leticia whispered, "Stop moving."

Rebecca threw her shoulders back and sat upright, one hand resting loosely on either end of the bundle. Leticia nodded and took pictures from a few angles.

"Enough?"

"Just a moment longer?" The daughter was sketching like a fiend from the doorway. Hovering behind her was the rest of the Blackwoods, and Miles in the shadows with them.

"I was just about to call you for supper," said Mrs. Blackwood.

Rebecca felt obliged to remain where she sat, to watch Mrs. Blackwood creep into the room, all *her* attention focused on the bundle. Her host inched down the sofa opposite to her, to sit as close as she could. Did she sense the bones? Would Mrs. Blackwood be pained to know the bones had never settled here, that her farm was nothing special to him?

Leticia and Miles broke the cobra's spell, speaking at the same time.

"Rebecca sure looks great in that gown, doesn't she, Mrs. Blackwood?"

"We smelled food in the kitchen. Don't let us keep you."

Rebecca took advantage of the confusion and polite laughter to stand and walk around the coffee table that stood between her and Mrs. Blackwood. Miles reached out for her arm and Leticia flanked her rear. They made it to the stairs.

"There's no need to rush," called out Mrs. Blackwood.

"Rebecca doesn't want to crush the gown. We won't be long."

Miles pushed the girls up the first steps, then turned back towards the kitchen, shouting out, "Those apple muffins sure taste good when they're warm. Don't be long girls!" He sounded like an idiot, but his heart was honest and so was his reference to the food. The others would surely get the hint and follow him back to the kitchen. *Nosey Parkers.*

"Let's get changed," said Leticia, "and get the second set done while they're still eating."

Rebecca stared at Leticia.

"The before and after. You in modern dress next."

Rebecca didn't move. It was too risky. Then the girl said, "I'll put on the native garB"

By the time Rebecca had slipped into her blend of modern and traditional clothing—tight jeans, a fine lawn shirt and a wool vest embroidered with Jacobean designs, Leticia was still turning the Indian blouse and skirt around and around to find the front and back. She put them down and held the leggings out from her like they were a reptilian skin. It was Rebecca's turn to transform the girl. Soon enough, Miles' sister looked Shawnee from head to toes. She turned Leticia towards the vanity mirror. "Mrs. Blackwood has a good eye for this."

"That she does."

Rebecca picked up the bundle and they tiptoed down the stairs a second time. All was quiet but the tinkle of cutlery and the Indian silver on Leticia's arm. Too late, Rebecca saw the Blackwoods were waiting for them in the sitting room. Drinks were set out on the sideboard. Plates of food covered the large coffee table.

"We may as well eat in comfort," said Mrs. Blackwood. "It's not a proper supper, anyway." Leticia made to turn back but Rebecca pushed her forward. "Go in."

"We should go back up."

"They've seen you."

"What about you?"

"I'm in your shadow. I'll try to sneak away."

She pushed Leticia forward again and stepped back. The word *sneak* made her pause. It was cowardly behaviour for a member of the Galloway family. She could feign a headache but at some point, her hosts would question her about the bundle. There was no getting around it. In other circumstances, in fact, it would have seemed an affront that the hosts had not asked her about such an obvious artifact of Indian origins.

Then she gave up her troubles and enjoyed everyone's response to Leticia as she walked softly into the room, graceful despite the rub of deerskin leggings. The skirt and leggings, the soft moccasins with fine Moravian Mission embroidery were unmistakably foreign in this European-style sitting room. Leticia had a presence, even as she held out the camera to Miles.

"If you wouldn't mind taking a break from stuffing your face."

It was the right thing to break the silence. Everyone laughed, even Miles. They had been caught off guard, expecting herself, not this transformation. Mr. Blackwood stood quickly and held his hand out for the camera. Leticia was forced to let him have it.

"Not just brilliant," said the son-in-law, "but beautiful. Seriously, call me when you're done school. Otherwise, the Smithsonian will get you."

"God save the Smithsonian!"

"Miles!" Mrs. Blackwood scolded.

"I know what he's thinking." The son-in-law was also laughing. "What kind of trouble will a smart girl with an Indian heritage make there?"

"Exactly."

The common ground for teasing between the young men made no sense to her. Rebecca narrowed her eyes and looked past Mr. Blackwood as he took photographs.

Leticia had sat on the edge of the same chair as Rebecca. Her dark hair was pulled tightly against her skull and plaited behind her ears. She wore no makeup. White teeth flashed in a smile when her brother reached out to tug the end of a braid. She looked happy, Rebecca thought. Perhaps it was time to bring the Shawnee connection out in the open on the homestead. Perhaps this journey was not about winning or losing, but about softening the line as it had been before the frontier was breached. Before the damned war. Greene County land had been Shawnee land once, and the Mound Builders' before that. The Colonel had fallen in love with it just as they had. Surely, he would approve, even her marrying Miles, as long as they stayed civilized.

A peek at Mrs. Blackwood gave her honest pleasure. The host was rightfully proud of placing Leticia in the Indian garB No more would Leticia be the ugly little servant.

The daughter was also transfixed, pencil in hand, then turned to a clean page and raced her lines across it.

"The bonnet," said Mrs. Blackwood. "Leticia, wasn't there a bonnet as well?"

"She won't wear it." Rebecca couldn't help stepping out from the shadows, the bonnet in hand. "She's like this on the homestead too." She held it out to Mrs. Blackwood, the bones propped in the shadow of her leg. Mrs. Blackwood smiled and took it from her, then approached Leticia as sure as thunder.

"You'll need it for tomorrow. To keep the damp away, if nothing else."

"Fine." Leticia accepted the bonnet from Mrs. Blackwood. She tied it loosely around her neck so that it hung behind her like a hood. Charming, even the flush on her cheeks. "No one wears a bonnet when it's this warm indoors."

Rebecca felt a chill. Mrs. Blackwood had circled the sofa and now blocked her path to the stairs. Warmly, Mrs. Blackwood drew her into the room, nodding for her to pick up the bundle again. "You look lovely as well." She turned to her daughter. "Doesn't Rebecca have a great look? Both eras are becoming on her."

"A traditional beauty no matter what, Mom."

Mrs. Blackwood asked about the lace, the shoes, the vest and leather jacket. She said nothing about the bundle in her arms.

The daughter hadn't really looked at all. She was sketching Leticia's face, bringing it into ever-clearer focus, the costume only roughly sketched in. The portrait taking shape on the page was of a different Leticia than the one Rebecca knew, even accounting for the Indian costume. Not Miles' baby sister, not an Indian princess. So who? She wanted to touch the drawing, as though it would speak and explain itself.

Rebecca was seated on the sofa beside Miles. Mrs. Blackwood quickly took up the seat on the other side, effectively blocking her in the middle. She set the bundle upright between the legs of her jeans, and clasped her hands on top. Miles offered her a plate piled with finger food. The bundle became a table. Reaching for a napkin, Rebecca put her hand on Miles' knee for a moment. Ever so briefly, Miles twined his fingers with hers. She wasn't sure who was more surprised, but he let go first. The napkin was real linen, crisply starched despite the humidity. Rebecca asked how Mrs. Blackwood had managed that trick.

A detailed explanation followed, but Rebecca barely listened. The others passed plates and poured tea. The son-in-law stared at the clock, vigorously stirring a huge amount of sugar into his cup. The bread was home baked. It tasted like her mother's. If it weren't for the bones and the flooding, thought Rebecca, Mrs. Blackwood might become a kindred spirit.

Finally, they could eat no more and the plates were gathered up.

"Rebecca's turn," said Mr. Blackwood. "Leticia, will you do the honours?" The girl leapt up from her seat and pulled Miles off the couch so Rebecca could escape. Before Miles could sit again, Mrs. Blackwood had moved down the sofa to be closer to Rebecca. Miles was left standing behind Rebecca's chair. They asked him to move. Lights flashed from two sides. In the seating shuffle, Mr. Blackwood had found a camera of his own.

The daughter held her gaze. Rebecca felt like a bug under a glass, then both their stares fell upon the bundle Rebecca held across her lap. She stiffened her backbone and waited.

Mrs. Blackwood commented on her slippers. "They're Plains Indian."

"No Ma'am. They're actually from a store we have back home. A Sears promotion, if I remember correctly."

"The hide looks genuine."

"I've waterproofed them with duck grease. A little trick to bring out the better qualities of the materials."

A clock chimed the tenth hour from the hall. The son-in-law set his mug of tea down. "You girls look really great, but I've got to get the juices flowing again." He kissed his wife and waved goodbye. Everyone remained quiet until they heard the door across the hall pulled shut. He, a possible ally, had escaped.

"Tell us, dear, about the bundle."

Mr. Blackwood sputtered and lowered the camera. The daughter kept drawing, likely used to her mother's ways. Equally direct, Rebecca started her prepared speech, the same one she told the entire county the night before.

"This bundle, you may be assured, has remained unopened for nearly two hundred years, as promised to the Blackfoot and Shawnee who handed it to my seventh great-grandmother when the frontier opened up. Our family was well respected by folk of all creeds and nations."

Undeterred, Mrs. Blackwood asked, "What do you think is in it?"

"I have no idea, other than to speculate that it contains native Indian artifacts that would mean more to the deliverers of the bundle, but not so much to its Christian keepers."

"May I look at it?"

"It's not meant as a museum piece." Miles blurted this out, direct and rude, but so was Mrs. Blackwood. Seeing the horrified looks, he added, "No disrespect to you or Mr. Blackwood, Ma'am."

Rebecca smiled at him, a direct, serious smile to let the others know he had it right. He moved to stand guard behind her chair, and she felt not so much like a pioneer protecting her family, more like a girl trying to protect her future—even as she wore lace made by old Rebekah's hand on her collar.

The bundle must be kept a secret or she would be stuck in the past with it. If people knew, his struggle would become hers. A strategic man, his spirit would be just fine with all the attention and jostling for photographs. The centre of attention, the place of an orator and nation builder.

Mrs. Blackwood leaned forward and said, "Surely it is a museum piece."

"It's never been that. My family have been stewards of the land, of our history, and we were asked to be stewards to this bundle as well. You invited me here to show respect for those who fell in a war where neither side profited, and Indian nations were undone." She stopped a moment and wished she could see Miles' face, for this is what she wanted to tell him, that she had respect for Indian relics, and that she meant to do what was right. When his hand touched her shoulder, she took a great breath. He was with her.

"Sadly, two centuries ago, my countrymen did not show respect to the warriors who fell on the battlefield by your farm. It is my hope that by placing this offering in the memorial, it will bring peace to all the nations." Rebecca paused. The smell of lavender in the air? A chill came over her. The next moment, she was pinning Catherine Blackwood with the stare of a 220-year-old woman. "There is to be no interference. This bundle will be interred tomorrow as agreed to by the Mayor and Ministers of Church and State, without further comment."

A clock ticked loudly.

Dazed, Rebecca sat ramrod straight and watched the Blackwoods look from one to the other. Mr. Blackwood recovered his wits first and mutely asked his wife for permission to speak. Mrs. Blackwood lifted her hands in bewilderment. The large man sighed, and spoke in a congenial tone.

"We will see that you get your wish."

Mrs. Blackwood's composure broke. Her worldly expression fell away, her shoulders shook, her hands turned on themselves as though they could mend time past. She looked for all the world a broken-hearted child.

The vinegar taste on Rebecca's tongue was fresh and strong. She dared not speak until she felt in control of herself. Mrs. Blackwood's interest in the bundle went beyond professional acquisition. Hers was as personal a quest as Rebecca's. She could sympathize with that. But the lavender was stronger than both of their desires.

Leticia responded for her, her hand over her heart on the Indian. "Thank you, Mr. and Mrs. Blackwood. It means so much to us to hear you say that."

The focus fell away from the bundle. As though from a distant shore, a familiar voice announced, "I'd say it's time for bed." A shadow fell between Mrs. Blackwood and her, and a face brought itself level to hers. "Rebecca, are you coming?"

She recognized that face. Miles West and his blue eyes.

She would marry into his family, she was sure of it. They would have babies and she would pray there were no brown ones. But if one should come, she'd accept it and guide it until it struck out on its own. It was the only way, no matter what time you were born.

~ 14 ~

CATHERINE ROLLED OVER ON HER SIDE OF THE BED, carefully so as not to disturb Thomas, but turning towards him. It was tempting to tap his shoulder. She turned back again, her nightgown sticking and twisting, and bunched her pillow into a wad, then mashed it flat and lay on her back. One foot stuck out. She crept the cold foot up to find the edge of the sheet, and wriggled about to pull the sheet down more securely. When she thought she had it, it sprang free. Rather than embroil herself deeper in a fight with the bed clothes, she turned again toward Thomas, tugging her twisted nightgown with her. She drew her knees up and rested them squarely against the centre of his lower back.

"Do you mind?" He sounded weary but quite awake.

She rubbed his shoulder in a circle. "Sorry."

"Settle down and sleep, Catherine. We haven't got much of the night left."

"How can you sleep when his bones are just down the hall?"

"We don't know for certain."

"We've got to stop her."

"That thought," Thomas said, "would certainly prevent me from sleeping."

"If you hold the flashlight, I could take the bundle and we could open it in the barn."

"Oh, Lord!"

"What else would the girl like?"

"She wants to be rid of the bones. Properly."

"Really, Thomas?"

"It's pretty clear if things don't go her way, we'll end up cursed. We'll wander the world homeless with a skeleton hanging around our necks, telling *his* story. Professionally and personally ruined. He should have been buried years ago."

"But why is he here now? In our house?" Catherine cried onto Thomas' shoulder. "You of anyone knows, I wanted him and he's here. Not be able to say, or show the community—it's beyond bearing!" She felt him shift, but still he did not turn toward her.

"Dearest Cathy," His voice was muffled by the pillow, or perhaps his fist was in his mouth. "All your work has paid off. Tonight was for us. To think, on the anniversary of his death ..." Thomas heaved a sigh and rolled to face her in the black night. "... to think he has been returned by the namesake of his love interest, and a pair of siblings who likely carry his genes. You couldn't have arranged it any better."

"I didn't know it would work out. So, you understand, I need proof."

"We have pictures of the bundle. Fantastic ones."

Catherine choked on a large breath, tried to hold back her tears, frustration really. She pushed away from Thomas and faced the dark room. Between sobs, she planned how she'd wait until he fell asleep, then get up and sneak into the girls' room and take the bundle. Thomas put a hand on her waist. She twisted against his pull and sat up.

"Who the hell do you think you are," she heard herself saying, her voice rising into a snarl, "making a decision like that for me tonight? I deserve to know. I brought the girl here. I risked my life and all those I love. Now you dare tell me to let it go?" She beat Thomas' hand away with her fist. "I won't!"

"Shhh!" He sat up and held her at arm's length. "Enough." Catherine pumped her fist towards his face. He caught it, her rage, in his large hand. He closed his fingers over hers, sliding his other arm up around her shoulders. She stiffened.

"Not going to forgive you. Ever."

She tipped forward, and her head would have rested against his chest if she'd let it. She wanted to bite or scratch, but couldn't decide which. Her nightgown was so twisted it felt like a constraint, and Thomas wouldn't let go of her.

"My dear love, something great has happened, but now we have to leave this place. Before it's too late."

"Tecumseh came *here*. He protected us, all of us."

"He's had two hundred years to think. It's time for surrender."

Her head sagged against Thomas' chest, and he gathered her close. Tears fell hard and fast, pooling onto Thomas' pyjama top, a little lake over his heart. They lay back on the bed, she in his arms, the fight gone out of her. Soon enough he was breathing deeply; she was weft on his sturdy loom. She was the colour, the one who raised or lowered the heddle for the shuttle to pass through; she was unable to achieve anything without this man.

Still, she had nothing. She would be left with nothing but rumour. The only thing to show might be a thickening of the yarn, a slub, in the weave in this autumn's fabric. Then a void. A bloodless hole. There would be no one left to care about Tecumseh. No one would care about her family, the farm. She'd always had this place. She'd dedicated her life to elevating Chatham County, and the settlers who changed the land around them, so like a quilt, the best bits bound together—farms and fences, families and friendships—each patch filled with the hues and textures of homes and fields and businesses. Yes, some pieces were covered with new bits of cloth—oil and energy, chemical industries. Some lines had changed, but she appreciated the layers and handled them skilfully with her curatorial gloves.

The land was the given that would survive them and keep them. *Place* held cultures together as much as language, kinship, dress and food. How dare they drown Chatham County to save Toronto. Arrogant, selfish capitalists! The land, according to them—and Thomas and Hiram—was without value. This rich fabric had become a mere bar cloth to sop up the mess they'd made.

Would this night, as Thomas predicted, become part of a fantastic tale where history turned and the land disappeared? There would be no *place* left. Like others, her culture would continue in the Diaspora section of the ROM, as boxed-up artifacts that held vaguely remembered purpose; she could make sure of that much. But the pieces would never beat again with one heart. Catherine could cry until her heart broke, but she remembered James putting it all into perspective for her. James had explained the farm in geological terms: billions of years as a great sea, millions of years weighed down by ice, and then covered with silt from receding waters. Mastodons and mammoths ate up the lush grasses that grew on alluvial soil, and from them, mighty trees grew up, living for thousands of years. People came to hunt; the big game disappeared. The people didn't. They were resilient and roamed as the land warmed; people came and went. Then they built settlements, they traded, and they chased each other along.

James told her, "What you think of history, Catherine, is only a mere two centuries of Loyalist settlement." After this, he told her, there will be a freshwater sea for an unspecified time.

"And after that?" she'd asked him.

He couldn't say. Their moment was so tiny, didn't she see that? A fine layer of silt, maybe some fossils, to show up at some later time, sandwiched between greater epochs.

Thomas still held her fist.

She uncurled it into his hand. His breath smelled of mint and coffee, Gently, she kissed his pyjama top. She may have to surrender her land. She understood now, the linens and silver, the precious bits of home life that women had clung to as they fled from famine and wars, and crossed oceans, and scraped a living from any land that might take them. The broken bits of china she'd found in among handkerchiefs and towels. Interesting professionally, but now much more personal. She'd rolled the best bits of her broken china into silk stockings she no longer wore. The fragments of painted clay were enough to remember, and they were real. The memories were real.

She understood the fight in peoples across the world for a homeland. A real home. She had a job to do, to continue to preserve the surviving bits, so the homes that men and women created would remain real, undisputed. That she would do. But in her, another scheme was taking shape, another section to fill on the loom. There still existed in the southwest of the Great Lakes, a land where the water was receding. While she could never be buried beside her parents, Tecumseh's bones could certainly reclaim familiar territory. And maybe they would refuel a culture. She had the contacts: between them, she and Thomas could make sure it happened.

She would rescue those bones from their ignominious end.

~ 15 ~

CLEM WOKE EARLY. TinTin was in bed beside her. She didn't know what time he had come upstairs. They were holding hands under the quilt. Without thinking, he had been stroking her skin so that the soft web by her thumb felt raw.

"We better get up," he said. "It's going to be quite a day."

"What's going on inside that head of yours?"

"Just last minute thoughts about what we've missed—I've missed. Disaster readiness, I guess. There are variables in any experiment and unintended results. We're fooling with the rain in a big way this time."

"Mom packed the china and put it in the barn, if that helps. I've scoured the place for anything else that might explode."

"One can only hope it was the scan that caused the china to break, but I have to take it into account until we can prove it. The parlour is no longer a concern. The actual site is, and it can't be regulated. I can't set up a Safety Net to keep out unwanted items. There are too many variables. I can only estimate the antler and horn in the settlers' gear, and the percentage of bone in the native gear. Pi already crunched the numbers for the general mass of porcelain broaches, earrings, buttons, cane tops, snuff boxes and candlesticks, as well as more modern appliances, like the old electric insulators still on a number of hydro poles in the area. Do you think anyone would bring a bone china service? They didn't have paper plates back then."

"They'll eat at the Tavern. Mom said that in the current circumstances, there's no way they could handle food preparation on site."

"I've added another five percent anyway."

"I trust you."

"What worries me is that bundle of bones. We don't know the state of ossification and what a large mass like that might do."

"You're worried about the spirit in them."

"I believe what you saw, Clem. I wouldn't want to hurt him further."

"Then I'll have to see to it that the bones stay here."

"Oh, if you wouldn't mind. It does mean keeping a sharp eye on them."

"You mean Mom could be a problem. Dad swears she will back down. But listen up, my worry man: the critical time when she might be a little emotional—"

"And impulsive."

"—will be after lunch, long after your job is done. She will beg for a look before the bones are placed in the memorial."

"Rebecca is doing the right thing."

"She's doing what she has to. She's been battered by those bones, perhaps many times. And that girl is possessed by at least one ghost. Did you hear her last night?"

"You don't like her."

"Actually, she reminds me of my mom."

"How interesting. A young Catherine. Did your mother see the drawings of what you observed yesterday afternoon at the memorial site?"

"No. She would have a fit that she missed out. She would never give way. It'll be years before she sees those sketches."

TinTin nodded. He threw back the quilt. As Clem had suspected, he was fully dressed.

"I'll put the coffee on. No one seems to be doing that yet."

"And I will take care of the bundle. You say that it really doesn't matter if there are bones in the parlour."

"Not anymore. The desiccation will take place along the docks."

"Then I have the perfect hiding place, right under your nose."

~ 16 ~

THOMAS SMELLED COFFEE DOWNSTAIRS. He had fallen into the deep kind of sleep that's rife with dreams that feel real. They were in the new dory, part of a fleet paddling in the wind. Paddling in the sky. There was no ground, only space. When he shook his head at the sight, drops of sweat fell. The drops turned into more rain. He shook his head to clear the view, again and again, until the air was filled with rain. The dory floated over a watery globe that he had created. Catherine was using the only paddle, and so they spun in circles. It seemed ridiculous now that he was awake.

He checked his itinerary against Catherine's so they would remain as near one another as much as was possible. The events would begin at the docks with the sinking of the bateaux by the British soldiers. Then they would blow up the truss bridge. Catherine would be on the raised platform with the members of the bicentennial committee and the invited guests. His work would be done. He would drive her and the Minister of Culture to the re-enactment of the skirmish, farther upstream at the fairgrounds where there was still solid ground. Technically, the battle took less than an hour, but with speeches and due reverences to the actors and dignitaries—and lunch—it would go longer. By mid-afternoon, they should be able to go to the actual battleground for the unveiling of the new monument.

He glanced over Catherine's itinerary, quickly finding her name last on the list of the presentations. "THINK POSITIVE" was printed at the end of the page. It would be a long day.

He'd heard on the news that a small burst of rain had let loose on Moraviantown, just as the ceremonies at dawn were finishing up. Social media message boards had lit up, and a virtual war between the Christians and natives broke out over who was spiritually responsible. Then Frank Dolsen pointed out that the brief rain had cleared the thick clouds of last night, and he thanked them both for contributing the hot air.

County residents driving into Chatham reported one dodgy black cloud in the north. It hadn't moved in hours. One person said it seemed ominous, but that thread was buried in messages about where to meet, who was bringing what, who still needed a ride.

Everyone but Hiram was attending the sinking of the boats and the blowing of the bridge. Thomas checked his leather rucksack. Before going to bed last night, Hiram had given him some plastic-based explosives.

"Not exactly legal," he'd said, "but in case the experiment fails. I don't want your efforts to be in vain."

Thomas had thanked him, not mentioning that the explosives man he had hired had procured some legally. He just said, "Either way, the bridge will blow. Scuttling the boats is another matter. More than half the town would rather they didn't sink. We could easily raise thousands of dollars with raffle tickets if they did stay afloat."

"You have some printed?"

Thomas nodded. Hiram actually cracked a smile.

"Still," he said, "Catherine is counting on you to start the day with a bang." Hiram coughed softly. "Have you given any thought about your plans after today?"

"I'll get those kids home first, then come back and pick Catherine up. Do you think you and Clementyne could stay and make sure she's ready?"

"Clem has already started that task." Hiram looked around him, coughed again.

"What is it?"

"My parents taught me that one must be ready to jettison, that things can be replaced."

Thomas had cocked his head to one side.

"In this case, important lessons in the physics of drowning must trump the value of the arts and culture. Please watch out for Clem this morning. Keep her away from the river."

"I'll keep both our ladies safe."

The lad had not had to ask, thought Thomas.

Catherine called him back to the present.

"You've been quiet." She was calmer and more relaxed than he'd seen her in weeks. The edge of continuous battle had been replaced by the serenity of acceptance. She was only in her shift with a corset hanging loosely over it. She had spent the last half hour painstakingly curling her hair into a Regency look. "I need your help with the laces now."

He took pleasure in fingering her curls until she protested. He ran his fingers along the bottom edge of the corset from front to back where the laces started. He looped the laces in a spiral over the hooks, expertly picking his way up the slack, pulling Catherine's body close against his. He tightened the garment up to her waist, her ribs, below her breasts. "Tight enough?"

"Perfect. Now hand me the *busque* and get your handsome face out of my curls before they go totally limp."

He watched her slip the stiff strip of ash wood into a pocket that ran down the front of her corset. It would keep her silhouette erect, her skirts smooth, her shoulders proudly set back. She motioned towards the wardrobe. A lady couldn't dress alone. He took the gown from its hanger, and she held her arms out to him. He slipped the layers of silk organza over her head, her shoulders. In a fluid motion, the organza settled over her predefined curves, and Thomas thought, this will be the last time we dress like this. We only do it here. Catherine inspected herself in the mirror and smiled at him. He caught his own look of longing, and quickly looked away. She was like a jewel in the sky blue gown. Her upper breasts were tantalizingly bare.

Catherine had caught his gaze. She shook her finger at him and pulled a gossamer shawl over her shoulders, crossed the ends and tucked them in, one under each breast. Then she pulled a heavy woollen shawl across her shoulders. It wasn't warm enough, even with central heating, to wear such a gown without it. The gown was meant for dancing. Before they left, he would help Catherine with yet another layer, a long nut-brown wool cape.

Thomas checked that his breeches were buttoned, his leggings fastened. His cravat hung loosely about his neck. Catherine would tie it. His jacket was on a well padded hanger in the sitting room downstairs in front of an electric heater, where he hoped it would dry out. He had refused the idea of wearing a powdered wig. "Maybe if the Governor was coming." Instead, he let his sideburns creep across his cheeks like the locals wore theirs, and he'd let his hair grow longer. He offered his arm to Catherine.

"This is it, my love and lady. It's time to go."

~ 17 ~

CLEM WAS SENT UPSTAIRS to see what was keeping the guests. She heard muffled voices in the girls' room, an argument, so she went into the bathroom next door and opened the medicine cabinet, knowing she could hear them more clearly through the thin part of the wall. They were arguing about where to leave the bones while they were at the docks. The dispute seemed to centre on the girls insisting the bones come along.

"He's got to see that it's the end," said Rebecca.

"He's got to hear the noise and see the fighting."

"It's a pile of bones," Miles argued. "Carrying that bundle will make everyone curious and mark Rebecca out. They'll start guessing, just like Mrs. Blackwood, and they'll want to see what's inside the bundle. It's the biggest mystery around here and their last chance to solve it."

"Let them guess," said Rebecca. "I won't give the truth away."

"Others might." Miles looked at Leticia. "We could be lynched."

"Really."

"They'll pester us and it'll take away from the day. We've got to leave them here."

"I don't trust her."

Clem knew that Rebecca was talking about her mother. She had to intervene before they made a decision. She closed the medicine cabinet door quietly and went back to hallway, calling out loudly, "Are you guys ready yet?" Then she knocked on the door and opened it. The guests were dressed and ready. She moved into the room, saying, "This was my room when I came here for summer holidays. I'm glad you girls got it." She noticed the bundle sitting upright on a low chair. She knelt down in front of it, reaching out to touch it, a bit nervously. "It looks well-loved. I'd hate to part with it if I was you."

"It's time." Rebecca's voice was tight.

"Something this valuable should be kept in a safe place today. Who knows who might wander in?" She looked sideways at Rebecca. "When I was a kid, I knew all the safe places in this house. When my grandfather died, I kept a picture of him on his deathbed in one of those places. After today, I think we'll be leaving for good, so I'm not worried about showing you that place. It can be yours."

Rebecca wouldn't be wooed so easily.

"I think your mother grew up in this house as well. I would count on the fact that she knows every hiding place, and maybe more."

"It's in the room where TinTin is working on the computers. As long as he's set up, she wouldn't set a foot in there. The machines scare her." Perhaps Rebecca shared the phobia. She was nodding vigorously. Miles smiled encouragingly at her. He was in love. He wanted to protect her. Clem pressed her advantage. "Come now, while they're in the kitchen, and I can show you what I'm thinking."

"Thank you."

Rebecca motioned for Leticia to bring the bundle. Miles brought up the rear.

The computers hummed in the parlour. Aerials of various heights circled the room. Clem motioned for Rebecca to follow, but the girl pushed Leticia towards the tangle, and pulled the parlour door shut. She would wait outside with Miles. Clem shrugged at the girl's fear. Quickly, she lifted the carpet, rolling cables aside, and tapped along a floor board until she came to the point where it lifted. There was plenty of room below. A yellowed sketch book page with her grandfather's likeness stared sightlessly up at her. He'd be okay with the bones.

"I'll be putting this in memorial too. Mom knows. It'll make it easy to get the bundle out later. Right before the ceremony would be best."

Leticia, she noticed, wasn't as intimidated by all the equipment. She came right over. The hole had to be inspected for water. She said she could not bear to think of the bundle being damaged. Clem noticed her hesitation. "It was a hiding place for former slaves when the bounty hunters came looking."

"Our family never agreed with the slave trade either."

Voices were coming from outside the door. Thomas' deep voice invited Rebecca and Miles into the kitchen for breakfast. Miles said the others would be downstairs soon. "Leticia needs to know all about that cradleboard that your daughter used to play with. You know Leticia, always curious." He said it quite loudly. Clem heard the suggestion to hurry up. Leticia did too, and she thrust the bundle in. She stood to one side while Clem covered the opening. The carpet was returned and even TinTin wouldn't know about the warrior at his feet. She thought Leticia looked satisfied.

As she pulled the parlour door shut behind them, Clem held onto Leticia's arm for a moment. "You're doing the right thing," she whispered in the girl's ear. "I promise to help however I can."

~ 18 ~

LETICIA WISHED HER MOTHER WAS HERE to see the transformation of everyone, that historical dress-up wasn't something that only happened in the backwaters of Greene County. Mr. Blackwood wore breeches and the jacket of a well-off business man. Clementyne wore the same high-waisted gown she had to the party. But Mrs. Blackwood's dress was new and stunning. She would be a success no matter what time she chose to live in. How would her mother dress, she wondered, if she were forced to time-travel back two hundred years? The Blackwoods looked every bit like prosperous settlers. The rustle of skirts, the facial hair on Mr. Blackwood, her brother's long hair, gave the whole scene a feel of authenticity. The smell of bread and eggs was just as timeless.

She clapped her hands together. "This is perfect, so cozy and real. I have to get my camera."

"Leticia, stop fooling around and eat."

"There's time," said Thomas.

Catherine nodded in agreement, then added, "You must hurry. We need to leave soon."

"I'll just be a minute," said Leticia. She waited a moment in the kitchen doorway, counting heads and making sure that everyone was sitting at the table, passing racks of toast and pots of jam. Hiram's plate was still full. Miles caught her eye, about to question her.

She rushed out, leaving behind the sounds of dishes, the voices of her hosts and the radio playing over them. They wouldn't hear her go into the good parlour. Efficiently, she pulled back the carpet and hauled the bundle from under the floorboards. She ran upstairs, happy to be wearing a short skirt and soft soled moccasins. Not that anyone was likely to pay any attention to her. Hiram had remembered to send an email with the link to his department, but that was all. Plain, boring Leticia. None of them knew that today she would be "Leticia, Indian Princess, Caretaker of the Sacred." She would honour the blood in her veins, the past grafted so visibly onto her face, her skin, her build and genes.

The cradleboard was still in the bottom of the large wardrobe. She'd asked if it had to be packed up yet. Perhaps they could keep it in the room? Mrs. Blackwood had looked at her and nodded as though she understood. But she had it wrong. Even then, Leticia thought the cradleboard might hold the bundle that had rested at Rebecca's feet in the canoe, the one Leticia had stared at all the way across the Canadian waters of Lake Erie. She unlaced the board and pulled the rags out, fingers nimble. A minute later, she had bundled the man inside, skull at the top so it would fit. It gave the impression of a baby's head. Wherever there was extra room along the sides and top, she stuffed in more rags. It mustn't clatter.

In the big mirror, Leticia posed to see how it looked with her outfit. Perfect. She'd become an Indian teen mom. Her camera was on the dresser where she left it. She took a photo of herself. Quickly, she slipped back downstairs, leaving the board in the hall by the front door. She apologized for taking so long. As she filled her plate with eggs and peameal bacon and buttered her toast, she mentioned the cradleboard. "It's amazing how well it goes with this garb."

"I'm sure it would," said Miles, playing along. He'd mentioned the cradleboard earlier in the hallway. She passed the camera to him.

"Wouldn't this photo give Dad grey hair?"

He almost choked on his toast. Then everyone wanted to see it. They liked it.

"Do you think I could bring the cradleboard?"

"Of course." Mrs. Blackwood and Clementyne spoke at the same time.

Leticia thanked them and wolfed down her breakfast. As the others tidied up, she snapped pictures. Mr. B. looked odd, talking on the telephone in his bygone gear. He nodded as he listened to the person at the other end go on and on. With his hand over the receiver, he said to her, "I could pack some extra batteries for the camera in the top of the cradleboard, if you want."

"One step ahead of you, Mr. B., already done. Now smile."

Miles wanted a picture with Rebecca. A bit of domesticity. Leticia suddenly had had enough. In the land of couples, it might be best if she waited by the door with *her* partner. The door to Hiram's lab was shut tight. He obviously hadn't noticed that she'd been in there. He was likely focussed on whatever Frankenstein project he was up to, happy to be on his own. For her part, she was happy to have the cradleboard with her, to comfort herself with the bones of another outsider.

~ 19 ~

THE BONES ARE MOVING AGAIN, to where the bipeds gather downstream, to where life is meant to gather, to where all the life forms are meant to live—easily feeding and breeding.

Near water, where they are easy to harvest.

More calcium and phosphorous for the garden.

~ 20 ~

THOMAS CHECKED HIS WATCH. The defence of the Thames was starting on schedule. On the far side of the river, American soldiers fired their rifles into the air to create the effect of war, the shock waves of sound carrying quite clearly. Hushed voices mingled, suddenly loud, then fading. One could tell it wasn't the main party of invaders, just a small group of scouts. Several British infantrymen lined up along the edge of the docks, their rifles ready to reply to the fire. Historically, there would have been a thick forest between the sides, offering cover. Now it was the breadth of the river. Sound, more than sight, brought a sense of urgency.

British soldiers ran along the dock, crying "Hurry! Hurry!" in low voices. The bateaux were weighted down with fake supplies, almost up to their gunnels. A young officer stood by, scanning the other side of the river with a spy glass, his other hand on his pistol. Frank Dolsen, a sergeant in the King's Infantry by the looks of his jacket, barked out orders at a ragged group of soldiers, needlessly berating them, much to the amusement of the crowd. A younger soldier barely paused in his work, and shot such a look of longing to drown the sergeant that the crowd roared. Then everyone took up the shout, "Hurry! Hurry! They're coming!"

Thomas worked his way through the crowd, away from the action, turning occasionally to watch the British soldiers heave more rocks into the bateaux. The events committee said the beautiful boats must be sunk, but perhaps someone could salvage them later. Thomas had no intentions of staying that long.

His explosives man, Lopsang Rampa, was waiting for him, well back on dry land, sipping tea from a flask. Rampa had set a series of both plastic and gunpowder charges on the bridge two hours ago, complaining that he was used to packing powder charges into crevices in the Himalayas, that his specialty was moving rock. Generations of men in his family had worked with gunpowder, risking their lives for whatever the current emperors and governors needed. In times of prosperity, they wanted roads or mines; in times of war, they needed better weapons. In times of peace, they celebrated prosperity with fireworks. Tonight, Rampa would fly up to Sudbury and bore holes into the Canadian Shield, back-fill old mines and create new ones. There would be work for years, as international corporations searched out valuable ores made more accessible with climate change. Tomorrow, he would talk to his employer about getting the necessary papers for his family. By next year, they would join him, and they'd move to Yellowknife where the muskeg was drying out and the air was thinner.

Near the rise, close to where Rampa stood, Thomas spotted Clementyne and Leticia. Apparently, they'd both declined to join Catherine's party on the viewing platform. He could report to Hiram that Clementyne stood well-back from the river. As an extra good measure, he'd be sure to say that Leticia was by her side. That girl had a good head on her shoulders.

He glanced up at what was called, "The Tower," the raised platform from which the dignitaries and guests watched. Given the crowd packed up there, he was rather pleased he had to stay below to run the explosives.

Catherine leaned across the high railing when she saw him and waved, beaming like the sun. The centre of his world. He bowed to her, and she blew a kiss. Minutes before the action had started, she had texted him to say that the Minister of Culture and Heritage told her there was a contract waiting for her in Ottawa. Her instincts had paid off. His partners in

Toronto would be impressed too, and his taking so much time off might be forgiven with Catherine's new connections to the federal government.

Rampa greeted him with a nod towards the river. The crowd had become silent as two seasoned, yet agile, infantrymen leapt on top of the rocks piled high in the bateaux. Each had his head bent to the task of drilling holes into the thick wood. Thomas knew the holes had been pre-drilled and corked to make the task easier. The men worked quickly, calling out numbers as they moved about the boats. For their own safety, the vessels had to sink at the same time. The tension in the crowd was real. Both of the bateaux lurched deeper into the river, and with a synchronization worthy of a ballet, the men launched themselves back onto the dock. The crowd cheered.

Thomas and Rampa let out their breaths. The idiots hadn't been wearing safety harnesses. In character, they ignored the shouts of the audience, and grimly watched the river suck the bateaux into its murky, greedy waters.

~ 21 ~

Tintin watched a video feed from the site. Clem and her father had set her camera up in the rafters of a viewing platform. On another monitor, he tracked the progress of the Sprinkler System. It was engaged for desiccation, and building over the dockside and the surface of the bridge. Out in Manitoba, a cluster of forest fires was targeted to receive the rain. The plentiful, local microwaves slowly gathered the G-waves into the fish pattern. When they first worked on it, TinTin had likened it to a wrangler trying to get the whole herd through one chute.

"As though you know anything about cattle," Pi had said. "It's more like pulling vocals and instruments from different microphones to mix the perfect sound track."

TinTin bowed to Pi's superior analogy.

While he waited for the waves to coalesce into the Sprinkler formation, TinTin hummed and tapped his foot in time to the music that Simple Pi had organized for the event. Then he stopped tapping. Clem had hidden the bundle under the floorboards. How would the old warrior feel, hidden where the slaves had, and him dancing overhead? Poor bugger.

DO IT NOW flashed across the monitors.

He forgot about everything, but the task at hand. He hooked up the Sprinkler in sequence to relay towers, stopping at the target area on the western edge of the Ontario-Manitoba border. The end destination slipped a little too far along the relay system. He dialled back the impulse, and when it stabilized, he went back to monitoring the humidity of the target area. Timing was everything. Thomas' explosives man was waiting for his signal.

Through the camera feed from the docks, he watched the re-enactment. A foot soldier from the 41st Regiment, commanded by General Proctor, was waiting to climb onto the bridge with a half-barrel cask of gunpowder, set it on end at the marked spot, and back out, unspooling the fuse as he retreated. As the Sprinkler lowered the humidity, the chances of the powder igniting increased. Anything that might cause a spark and set off the barrel prematurely had been removed from the soldier's person—no jacket, no silver coins in his pants pocket, no chain or buckles, sword or pistol. When the soldier made it back to dry land, another soldier would be ready to light the fuse.

The fuse had been soaked with gunpowder, and some phosphorous added for show. The cask on the bridge was filled with fireworks, the copper hoops specially weakened so as not to fly off into the crowd. The fireworks were a distraction. The bridge should collapse on itself, rather than explode. That was the plan Thomas and his man had devised. The plastics would go off only if the gunpowder failed. The cell phone signal for setting them off was quite secure. What could go wrong?

TinTin's monitors showed the wave pattern had achieved cohesion. The uptake of water had started in earnest.

An old Lightfoot tune played, singing about a girl swimming upstream in the world. Simple Pi's sense of the process was reassuring. It still was an effort for the humidity to congregate into the prescribed Sprinkler pattern. The next tune, *A Rainy Night in Georgia*, was a cue to relax. "Be mellow," Pi was telling him. There was nothing he could do to hurry things. He texted Thomas to ask how the speeches were going. Thomas replied, and sent a photo of Clem with a view of the re-enactment crowd spread out below. The last syrupy cords of Benton's hit song died out. The water molecules were holding along the trough. *It's Raining Men* belted out from the sound system. TinTin laughed out loud like he hadn't laughed in months, and he sang along with the Weather Girls.

"Cheers, Man!" he called out as though Pi were in the room.

He focused again on the data relay. His satellite scans didn't show any precipitation in the west yet. He sang louder, fist-pumping as though it would help. The western air mass was sucking up the humidity from the dispersal end like it was nothing. It was too dry in the west to rain. TinTin watched the dockside monitors for the humidity. Time to send the infantry man out. Just another ten percent reduction before the go-ahead for the blast.

Silence. The music had stopped. A pulse caught his eye on the western monitor. TinTin watched and listened in awe as the first riff of a song mimicked rainfall, then Roger Daltrey sang, *Only love can make it rain.* Virtual bellows were siphoning the Chatham humidity to the west, and into the heart of a flaming forest. Daltry belted out, *Love, reign o'er me!*

"The fucking beauty of it," he whispered. He kept his eyes on the hydrometer, breathing slowly in and out to stop himself from hyperventilating. The pressure kept steady. He gave the signal. It was time to light the fuse.

~ 22 ~

LETICIA SLUNG THE CRADLEBOARD onto her other shoulder as she waited for the bridge to blow up. The boats had sunk, rather quickly, and there were a lot of speeches to fill the time until the bridge went up. Mr. Blackwood stood off to one side with the Tibetan alien, who looked good in his homespun outfit, if you could look past his bags of equipment. She only knew he was Tibetan because earlier she'd asked him what tribe he was from, thinking he was Indian.

"Not with a name like Lobsang."

He asked about her baby, why its head was covered.

"I'm too young for a baby. This is just for show."

"But you want babies one day?"

"Let her graduate from high school, first." Clementyne had pulled her away.

At one point during the speeches, Clementyne held out her hands as though to give a silent and invisible offering to an equally invisible Host. What a strange woman. Leticia wondered if she might become as odd, if that happened when you hooked up with a guy like TinTin and his brilliant science. The bundle on her back grew heavy, and she shifted its weight onto her other shoulder.

On the way to the event, the cradleboard had rested across their laps in the back of Mrs. Blackwood's car. Rebecca and Miles hadn't questioned the weight. She suspected they didn't complain about the cradleboard because they were using it to hide their hand-holding. The two of them acted like they were on a date, eyes only for each other. Tecumseh was hers by default and he, at least, gave her a sense of purpose in this strange place, in what could become their watery graves.

Dr. Frankenstein had not come along. He'd burrowed back into the good parlour, perhaps more comfortable with his web of equipment than with the local people. If she were honest, if it weren't for the bones, she might have begged a way to stay with him and see what he was up to.

But some weird Native pride had snuck up on her. It was good to be an Indian here, safe to come out, to be openly brown-skinned. At least for this occasion. If only the other natives knew what her cradleboard held. Not a baby, but everyone's hero.

Suddenly the crowd hushed. Leticia turned with the others to watch a man dressed in buckskins lead a group of warriors and some rag-tag militia through the crowd. He greeted a young farm boy warmly, bowing to the boy's mother, and made his way towards the river. Unlike the military, the warriors came quietly, no whoops or swords jangling, their moccasins stealth against the wooden docks. Their leader was the funny-looking man she'd met at the banquet on the night they arrived, not at all like one imagined Tecumseh. She found out he had a mixed bag of genes. But here on the docks, the man carried an aura of authority. A young British officer by the bridge looked relieved to see him, and smartly saluted. The man playing Tecumseh grasped him, and an old sergeant, by the arms in greeting. Tecumseh gestured towards the other side of the river.

"Longknives."

He gestured towards the bridge.

"They will not like getting wet."

The crowd cheered, and the re-enactors were good enough not to break character. Tecumseh, sadly, wasn't to be of few words. Not the silent type. Spurred on by the approach of an elderly man dressed in British redcoat finery, he launched into a passionate speech. His first words were an attention grabber.

"FATHER!"

"He means the old guy, General Proctor," whispered Clementyne.

Leticia knew who Tecumseh was addressing. She knew the speech from public school days. Proctor didn't want to fight, and Tecumseh did. For authenticity's sake, the general appeared quite nervous and looked as though he'd rather move on. Shots rang out in the not too far distance to add to the sense of danger. The British riflemen loaded and shot at the imaginary foe across the river. She felt concern ripple through the crowd. Mostly local people dressed as settlers, they didn't want a fight on their hands. They didn't want their farms destroyed, to leave the bit of land they'd taken up. A group of Indian followers surged around Tecumseh, but not so they blocked the view.

At this point, the cradleboard started to vibrate. It was just a light buzz but the bones seemed to want to move forward. Leticia took a few steps, then stopped. Clementyne had put a hand on her shoulder. "Stay with me. Okay? You won't see as well if you get too close."

What did she know? Leticia wondered. Mr. Blackwood, his daughter, the Tibetan. They were removed from the crowd. She pulled the cradleboard off her shoulder and held the bundle in front of her, her arms crossed over it so that it faced out. The vibration seemed to settle. He'd just wanted to see. Maybe the words had stirred him up. If they ever were his words in the first place.

"*FATHER!*" the actor shouted for what seemed like the tenth time. "*You have the arms and ammunition which our great father sent for his red children. If you have any idea of going away, give them to us and you may go and welcome. For us, our lives are in the hands of the Great Spirit; we are determined to defend our lands; and if it is his will we wish to leave our bones upon them.*"

The crowd cheered like crazy. A whiskered fellow in shirt-sleeves ran onto the bridge rolling a cask of gunpowder, a spool of fuse slung over his shoulder. Risking life and limb on the bridge to nowhere, he set the barrel over a predetermined spot, poured dark powder from a horn around the base, then pulled a plug and stuffed the end of the fuse in.

More shots were fired from the other side.

The soldier ran backwards to the dock in a crouch, the fuse spooling out behind him. Then he slipped and flew sideways. There were no railings to catch him, only the river. The crowd groaned. Thank God there was a safety line attached to him. His fellows on shore held the line taut, suspending him for a nasty moment over the water. Then he had the wits to pull himself back, regain his balance, and keep running with the fuse. He'd kept it dry.

He leapt across the space between the bridge and the dock. Another soldier cut the fuse from the spool with a knife, and taking up a lit torch, looked up through the crowd towards someone behind her. Mr. B. and his expert. The soldier waited for the signal to light the fuse.

Please, prayed Leticia, let there be no more speeches.

The soldier lit the fuse.

Clementyne was chanting, "It will work. It will." She tapped the tips of her fingers together.

A glow, brighter than a normal fuse, traveled up the line towards the miracle Clementyne was praying for. All eyes were on the bridge. Despite the damp, the fire traveled up the line with amazing speed.

She shifted the cradleboard higher so he could see, and rested her cheek against it.

The bones rose and fell with her breath.

~ 23 ~

RAIN BARELY TRICKLES ONTO THE BLOOM of bipeds, easily
infiltrating the thin cluster of animal matter as it bobs along
the edges of the flood plain. They float because of the artifice
of human constructions.

Two skeletons embrace as one. One respires a mix of
water, carbon and oxygen. A whiff of old calcium gives him
away.

He is found.

From the bottom of her exhale, from her very core, Earth
reaches towards the bones. A dry bubble forms around her
pleasure, the momentum receding when it should be peaking.
How has the rain forsaken her?

Rain pauses above the bones, then like a thread, is drawn
towards sere forests far to the west. The dry air suckles
hungrily on the liquid ease, siphoning off the energy of Earth's
great exhale.

The subtle shift in the air is familiar—a manipulation by
that interfering one. Rain finds this experience exponentially
more unpleasant than the previous one. Now the biped's
purpose is clear—to separate the rain from the bones.

Was it not warning enough to remove his colleague?

~ 24 ~

THE HUMIDITY ON THE DOCKS DROPPED TOO RAPIDLY. Every bit of moisture was being drawn out of the air. Too fast, too much. TinTin swung his head from monitor to monitor. He couldn't believe the satellite images in the West. The end of the Sprinkler had exploded from the pressure. What they call the *exuberance effect*. Rain fanned out far beyond the forests and fell onto the dry prairie with the power of a fire hose, chunneling into the soil, undermining crops.

"Holy shit!" He gestured as though Pi was beside him. "What's going on, Man?"

A warning popped up. The microphone in the parlor was picking up a high-pitched whine. It wasn't part of Handel's *Water Music*. If he were a dog, he'd be howling. If the monitors could be trusted, a new fish wave was building independently of his intended wave, just north of the farm over the battleground. Outside, the sky was black. The monitors glowed.

"Those fucking bones!" TinTin fumbled with wires and cords, and flipped back the carpet. "Where did she hide you?"

He banged on the floorboards, listening for the hollow sound. When he finally flipped the right board back, the drawing of an old man, Clem's grandfather, stared out, sightless. The high-pitched whine dropped in frequency to become audible and strangely bearable. That the house started rocking, as though it were a boat, disturbed him more. He threw up on Catherine's family's antique carpet.

TinTin was shaking, crouched on all fours, trying to get out of the room as it tipped and slid sideways like one of those bulls in the rodeo bars. Water surged in from the west, a line spouting through the floorboards, moving towards him. His puke washed to the closed door before he could make it there.

He was ready to drown, for his lungs to fill with water, but he could breathe. It was his heart, like the china had before, that burst into a million pieces. Oddly painless. Odd to be conscious of the fact at all. He followed the shiny trail of his blood, each cell, as it spiralled from him into that microwave conduit he hadn't created.

~ 25 ~

EARTH GROWLS. HER BODY SHIVERS.

Half inside, half outside the manufactured bubble, rain pauses.

Having held back from the west for so long, rain springs into action and gleefully sprays far beyond the conduit provided. Let the forests burn and the plains take the water.

At the same time, rain gathers from the south and east, gathers what it needs to fulfill the Earth's desire, and marshals blackened skies into a massive thunderhead.

It is time to harvest the bones.

~ 26 ~

THE SKY ABOVE DARKENED AND WAS STREAKED with a ribbon the colour of old blood. Clem felt a flutter of cold air around her, the change from wet to dry that TinTin told her to expect. The fine hairs on her arms stood on end. The skin on her chest felt like it was crawling with bugs, picking it clean. The fire on the fuse was lit, and burned cleanly, and should reach the powder in the next minute. Clem touched her running nose with a hanky. Blood. The air was too dry. She shivered from cold, and fear. TinTin had warned her the rain couldn't be trusted

Beside her, Leticia also shivered, but more violently, like she was having a seizure. No, Clem realized, the tremors came from the cradleboard the girl held throughout the morning. Of course! Her fingers reached for the binding. Fumbled. Leticia swatted her away. Clem took Leticia's chin in her shaking fingers. Blood ran from the girl's mouth. "I bit my tongue."

"You brought the bones."

"I'm scared," whispered Leticia.

"Just drop them." Clem ran her hands over Leticia's arms and Leticia shuddered. "You can drop them now." Leticia breathed in like it might be her last breath and nodded, but didn't move.

Clem tipped her head back to the sky and swallowed the blood running down the back of her throat. There was shouting around them, but all she saw was the sky, thunderheads a thousand feet high, maybe more. Maybe the clouds heaved all the way to the limits of the world, pressed to bursting. The red ribbon brightened, spiralled through the masses of cumulous above in the same fish-scale pattern the boys used to build the Sprinkler System. She breathed deeply, willing that signature wave to come to her, to take the bones away.

"You want them, I know you do. I think you brought them here." She nudged Leticia. "Give them up."

A tiny voice from far away called for help. Was it her mother? The crowd on the platform was still waiting for the powder to ignite, fixed in a tableau, like in a scene from a Steam Punk illustration. Fire spiralling along a cord of red on the bridge below. Gowns of yore and men in wigs, men with whiskers and bushy beards, and the air machines of clouds brought by the rain. A lightning strike cracked the bridge in half, and boiled the river into steam. Boards from the bridge flew into the air in slow motion, splintering to pieces. Skewers of wood shot out in all directions, building themselves into darting, beautiful snowflake structures.

"Help."

Her father ran past her, shouting, and Clem knew he was calling her mother's name. That was love. That was her love for TinTin. She tipped her head back again, and breathed in, thinking, *I am one with you.* At the apex of her breath, she could clearly see through all the confusion. Leticia, just in front of her, needed help to open her arms. If the girl let the bundle drop, they could run, and if they clung to each other, they would find the right current in the roiling river and be swept downstream. All she had to do was breathe out.

Still, she waited in the moment between in and out, thought and action; Clem focussed on that unnatural ribbon of red, the spiral-wave in the thick sky. She thought she could rise like dust—that is, if she let the rest of the moisture in her body seep away when she breathed out. Breathed her last breath. She could grasp that cord, and no matter how it whipped her through the thunderheads, she would cling to it and it would bring her to TinTin. For she recognized his fading raspberry kisses in that coloured ribbon.

And there, in the last bit of space between breathing in and out, she felt the earth in her after so long of feeling just the rain. She felt her bones and sinews resonate with a huge gyre of energy. Her bones, his bones. The air was dry. Her head was burning, her hair was on fire.

Clem breathed out, and fed the flames.

~ 27 ~

BONES ROLL LIKE BEADS in the place where rock glides across rock, greased by oil and water. Hard edges are ground and powdered. Epochs fold upon themselves—Pleistocene, Pliocene, Miocene, Oligocene, Eocene, Palaeocene, Cretaceous, Jurassic, Triassic, Permian. The latest sediments crumble like soft cheese.

Earth is filled with joy, sucking hard to pull the fresh bones to her, channelling the marrow and phosphorous-rich sluice through cold aquifers into a trough of hot, circulating lava. The slurry crackles at the contact with her heat. She heaves again, again, until the sluice hardens into chalk. Earth cries with pleasure. She shoves the collective bones up against the hard wall of the Niagara Escarpment. Convulsions ripple through her vast belly, changing her form.

New material for rain to touch and explore.

On the shock waves, the rain rides westward, a riptide called back. Wash and flow. Spray, heat, the steaming clouds. Wash and flow.

Rain dances on tiptoes onto a plain of virgin Earth, tentative with the wonder of discovering her. Each drop falls in a perfectly round imprint, pocking the surface. Then more, until the drops join together, until all the circles melt into a glorious tapestry of mud. Mud with an infinite potential for life, a mix that tastes of Earth and rain, and all the rich stuff that feeds the garden they live to grow.

One Last Fight

This is what Tecumseh wished for in Amherstburg in 1813, when he urged the British General Proctor to stand and fight the Americans. One year before, Tecumseh and General Isaac Brock had run very successful campaigns against the Americans. Both men were relatively young, and impassioned. Despite fewer numbers and resources, they stayed the American aggression and kept both British and Indian Territories intact. Unfortunately, Brock died in the fall of 1812 at Queenston Heights near Niagara Falls.

He was replaced by General Proctor, an end-of-career man who had his wife and family with him. In partnership with Tecumseh's alliances, he led incursions into Ohio to gain the strategic Fort Meigs, but was unsuccessful. By September 1813, the Americans had gained supremacy over the Ohio territory and also the Great Lakes. Proctor prepared to retreat up the Thames to a safe settlement inland. The area was sparsely populated, mostly with Loyalist (to the British Crown) farmers and millers. He burned Fort Malden to the ground. There would be no going back. He agreed to fight the Americans at Chatham only because Tecumseh negotiated it, but when they reached it, Proctor was unprepared. With Colonel Harrison and fierce Kentucky militia on their heels, Tecumseh stood to fight just kilometres from Moraviantown—a mix of natives and German missionaries—the largest settlement in the area.

The Battle of the Thames on October 5, 1813 was short, and ended when Tecumseh was thought to have died on the field. General Proctor, meantime, had fled.

The war continued another year until Great Britain made peace with the United States in 1814 under the Treaty of

Ghent. Borders remained the same as prior to the war, and Indian territories were also reset to 1811. In effect, Great Britain abandoned its allies and Tecumseh's native confederacy. There would be no protection for First Nations from European settlement anywhere in North America.

In Southwestern Ontario, Tecumseh is remembered through the names of towns, parks, streets and schools. Stories abound of the way he rode up to farms and mills to warn the settlers to flee from the American militia. Not one civilian life was lost. As the 1800s progressed, Tecumseh became a character of heroic proportions and his name became popular for settlers of the next generation. In the United States, General William Tecumseh Sherman was perhaps the most famous. In Canada, the town of Chatham had Dr. Tecumseh Kingsley Holmes, who rose to local prominence.

The American troops dug a mass grave for the native militia on the battle site, yet Tecumseh was not identified among the bodies. No one knows where, or if, he was buried.

Acknowledgements

Historic and current sources mention Rebecca Galloway as a young woman of "romantic" interest to Tecumseh. Her family settled in Shawnee territory in present-day Ohio. It can be disputed whether Rebecca and Tecumseh were ever known to each other. Rebecca did leave the area to live in relative safety with family further east during the War of 1812 and married a cousin, George Galloway; it is purely speculation to say she had any impact on Tecumseh. The Galloway homestead still exists as I describe it in Xenia, Ohio.

While planning this novel, I read much about the eastern part of North America during Tecumseh's time. By no means has there been a definitive history on the War of 1812, but the consensus of opinion rallies around the fact the First Nations were the big losers. I look forward to reading and hearing the points of view of indigenous peoples on the subject. I have much to learn.

I've done some delving into science as well, and muddled up fact with fiction to create a sense of possibilities—which will likely make those in the science world cringe. However, I stand by the picture of rain I've created and the speculation on weather. The relationship between rain and earth is my own invention. The environmentalist in me enjoyed the opportunity to explore various philosophies about climate change and the place of humans in it. Thanks to Thames Regional Ecological Association in London for hosting so many great talks and conferences over the decades.

Of course, the County of Chatham is fictitious, and I've borrowed old family names from the history books. None of the characters are based on the living, but I would like to thank Nancy Hicks and her mother, Mary, of the TK Holmes family in Chatham for sharing their history in person, pictures and books. Guy St-Denis, a noted author raised in the Chatham area, has written a wonderful book called *Tecumseh's Bones*. He does not bear any responsibility for my literary version of the legend.

The support of my family, friends and colleagues while writing this novel is greatly appreciated. This book has been around for a long time. Thanks to Charlotte, Mark and Wendy; to Ruth Taylor for many interesting exchanges in Poacher's Arms; and Ernie Briginshaw for his publishing advice. The London Writers Society and its critique groups have provided feedback and friendship. Nancy Pazner and Sue Brown have been readers for the final version of the book. Charlotte Fleming has lent her considerable design talents and bulldog attitude. Sue Brown has given support above and beyond to get the novel out, believing in it and me from the first read. Finally, thanks to Steve for keeping me and the project going.

ଶେଷ

78003251R00228

Made in the USA
Columbia, SC
08 October 2017